A Shell Guide

Warwickshire

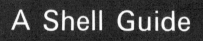

A Shell Guide

Warwickshire

by Douglas Hickman

Faber & Faber   3 Queen Square   London

First published in 1979
by Faber and Faber Limited
3 Queen Square London WC1
Printed in Great Britain by
Butler & Tanner Ltd, Frome and London
All rights reserved

Peto busts, **Chesterton**

British Library Cataloguing in Publication Data

Hickman, Douglas
    Warwickshire. – (A Shell guide).
    1. Warwickshire, Eng. – Description and travel
    – Guide-books
    I. Title II. Series
    914.24′8′04857   DA670.W3

ISBN 0–571–10831–8

Acknowledgements

In the preparation of this book, my thanks are due to all those I have met on my travels around Warwickshire who have contributed to the information collected in this volume, often by kindly showing me around their houses.

I owe a debt also to the works of a number of historians from Dugdale to Pevsner. I am especially grateful to John Piper, editor of this series, for his constant patience and sound advice and to Edward Piper for his sympathetic design and presentation.

If I am allowed a dedication, it is to my wife Jill, who has typed many of the early drafts, and to my daughters Sibella and Celia whose enthusiasm and refreshments have sustained me on my expeditions.

Douglas Hickman
Harborne
Birmingham

Note: As the map at the end of this book shows, this guide is concerned with the old county of Warwickshire, which has a distinct, though varied character of its own. Birmingham, Coventry and Solihull, now in the Metropolitan County of West Midlands, have therefore been included but not those parts of the Metropolitan County formerly in Staffordshire and Worcestershire.

Sanctuary floor, **Ratley**

List of Illustrations

Note: Captions to the photographs include place names in **bold type**. These refer to entries in the gazetteer, pages 20-189.

Front endpaper
Birmingham
John Whybrow

Title page
Kenilworth Castle
Edward Piper

Page
4 Peto busts, Chesterton
John Piper

5 Ratley
Neville Hickman

8 Maxstoke
Edward Piper

9 Hampton-in-Arden
Edward Piper

Barcheston
Christopher Dalton

Shustoke
Peter Burton

10 Great Packington
Edward Piper

11 Napton-on-the-Hill
Christopher Dalton

12 Fenny Compton
Christopher Dalton
Sherbourne
Edward Piper

13 Winderton
Christopher Dalton
Brailes
Edward Piper

14 Lord Leycester's
Hospital, Warwick
A. F. Kersting

16 Stratford-upon-Avon
Edward Piper

17 Leamington Spa
Peter Burton

19 Birmingham Town
Hall
Edward Piper

20 Alcester
Edward Piper

21 Farmhouses near
Astley (2)
Edward Piper

22 Ansley carving
Edward Piper
Ansley church
Peter Burton

24/25 Arbury Hall (2)
Edwin Smith

26 Arbury Hall (2)
Edwin Smith

27 Arbury Hall
Edwin Smith

28 Ragley Hall
A. F. Kersting

29 Ragley Hall
Peter Burton

30 Astley church
Peter Burton

31 Astley stalls
Peter Burton

33 Astley (2)
Edward Piper

34 Aston Cantlow school
Christopher Dalton

35 Aston Cantlow
aqueduct
Edward Piper

36 Berkswell (2)
Peter Burton

39 Billesley
Christopher Dalton

41 Birmingham
manufactories (4)
Peter Burton

42 St. Paul's and Holy
Trinity, Birmingham
A. F. Kersting

43 Birmingham Cathedral
and
St. James', Edgbaston
Peter Burton

44 Birmingham Cathedral
Edwin Smith

45 St. Paul's, Birmingham
A. F. Kersting

46 R. C. Cathedral,
Birmingham
Edward Piper

47 Burne-Jones glass,
Birmingham
Edward Piper

48 St. Agatha's,
Small Heath
St Paul's Square,
Birmingham
Peter Burton

51 Aston Hall
Peter Burton

52 Winterbourne,
Edgbaston
Peter Burton

53 Bournville (3)
Edwin Smith

53 (*top right*) Bournville
Douglas Hickman

54 Edgbaston (3)
Peter Burton

54 Edgbaston (*bottom right*)
John Moffatt

56 Edgbaston towers (2)
Peter Burton

57 Botanical Gardens
Edward Piper

59 Neville House,
Edgbaston
John Moffatt

62 Birmingham Canals (2)
Douglas Hickman

66/67 Birmingham (3)
Peter Burton

68 Brailes (*top*)
Peter Burton
Brailes (*bottom*)
Edward Piper

73 Burton Dassett (2)
Christopher Dalton

74 Charlecote
Edward Piper
Sir Thomas Lucy
Edwin Smith

75 Charlecote
Edward Piper

76/77 Chesterton windmill
(2)
Edward Piper

79 Coleshill font
Edward Piper

80 Compton Verney
Edward Piper

83 Compton Wynyates (2)
John Piper

84 Compton Wynyates
chapel
Peter Burton
Compton Wynyates
beacon
Edward Piper

85 Coughton court (2)
Peter Burton

87 Coventry Cathedral
Edwin Smith

89 Ford's Hospital,
Coventry
Peter Burton

90 Little Park Street,
Coventry
A. F. Kersting

97 Ettington Park (2)
John Piper

98/99 Farnborough Park
(2)
Peter Burton

100 Farnborough Park
Christopher Dalton

101 Fillongley
Peter Burton

103 Packington Hall
Christopher Dalton

104 Great Packington
church (2)
Edward Piper

106/107 Guy's Cliffe (2)
Peter Burton

108 Hampton-in-Arden
Edward Piper

110 Hampton Lucy
Edward Piper

111 Hampton Lucy
Peter Burton

113 Haseley brass
Edward Piper

114 Honiley
John Piper

115 Honington church
Edward Piper

116/117 Honington Hall
(2)
Edwin Smith

118/119 (*top*) Kenilworth
Castle (2)
Peter Burton
(*bottom*) Kenilworth
Castle
Edward Piper

120 Kineton
Edward Piper

121 Kinwarton dovecote
(2)
A. F. Kersting

125 Lower Shuckburgh
Christopher Dalton

127 Maxstoke Castle
Edward Piper

128/129 Maxstoke Priory
(2)
Edward Piper

132 Moreton Morrell
Edward Piper

133 Nether Whitacre
Peter Burton

134 Newbold Pacey
Christopher Dalton

136/137 Over Whitacre
church (2)
Edward Piper

138 Oxhill
Christopher Dalton

139 Packwood House
Edward Piper

143 Edge Hill Tower
Peter Burton

144 Leamington Spa (3)
(*top left*) *Edward Piper*
(*top right*) *Peter Burton*
(*bottom*) *Christopher Dalton*

145 Leamington Spa (3)
(*top and bottom right*)
Peter Burton
(*bottom left*) *Christopher Dalton*

St Philip's Church, **Birmingham**, 1715, by Thomas Archer

148 Rugby chapel
Edward Piper

149 Rugby church
Peter Burton

150 Sherbourne church
Edward Piper

153 Shipston-on-Stour
Edward Piper

154 Solihull
Edward Piper

156 Southam churchyard(2)
Christopher Dalton

159 Stoneleigh Abbey
Peter Burton

160 Stratford-upon-Avon
Edward Piper

161 William Shakespeare
(2)
Edwin Smith

162 Stratford-upon-Avon
Church Street
Edward Piper
Mason's Court
Edwin Smith

163 Stratford-upon-Avon
Town Hall
Edwin Smith
Clopton Bridge
Edward Piper

166 Tanworth-in-Arden
Douglas Hickman

169 Upton House
A. F. Kersting

172 Warwick Castle
Edward Piper

173 St. Mary's, Warwick
Edward Piper

175 St. Mary's, Warwick
Peter Burton

176 Beauchamp Chapel
(*top*) *Edward Piper*
(*bottom*) *Peter Burton*

177 Beauchamp Chapel
Edwin Smith

178 Lord Leycester's
Hospital, Warwick (2)
(*left*) *Peter Burton*
(*right*) *Edward Piper*

179 Warwick (2)
Edward Piper

183 Mary Arden's House
Edwin Smith

184 Winderton (2)
Christopher Dalton

186 Wootton Hall
Edwin Smith

187 Wootton Wawen
church
Christopher Dalton

188 Manor Farm,
Wootton Wawen
Edward Piper

Back Endpaper
Anne Hathaway's
Cottage (2)
Peter Burton

p8 Weathered sandstone,
Maxstoke ▷

p9 Near **Hampton-in-Arden**
Barcheston
Shustoke and Hams Hall Power
Station

Introduction

The changing landscape

Strangers think of Warwickshire as a densely populated county with some historic sites—Stratford-upon-Avon, Warwick and Kenilworth—but with the vast industrial city of Birmingham and its satellites and a great complex of roads, railways, canals, blast furnaces, viaducts, cooling towers and power lines dominating all. In fact it is still a county of contrasts. Half a million acres are still farmed, and a walker in the Edge Hills can feel as remote here as anywhere else in England. There is market gardening as well as prosperous farming, and much of the county is made up of rich, green fields between isolated villages and parks where mature trees stand in neatly layered hedgerows. These

◁ **Great Packington**

Napton-on-the-Hill

p12 **Fenny Compton** ▷
Sherbourne
p13 **Winderton**
Brailes

give it the decidedly Midland character. Everything looks a little bit neater than usual, a little bit nearer an urban influence. Early in this century Henry James, looking out of a window across a Warwickshire park, said this was 'mid-most England, unmitigated England'.

The Avon divided the Feldon, or open field country, to the south from the Arden, or woodland, to the north which, though exploited for its timber in mediæval times, still existed in the days of Shakespeare, who made it the setting for *As You Like It*; and it was a striking natural feature into the 18th century, when trees began to be cut for iron smelting. To-day the loam of the one-time woodland softens the low hills into an undulating landscape of great beauty, especially around Alcester, Henley-in-Arden and Knowle.

Noticeably less treed, the patchwork fields of the Feldon belie its heavy, ill-drained soils and stretch south-east to the steep escarpment of Edge Hills, shrouded in woods.

Though the Romans built Watling Street, the Fosse Way and Icknield Street, the dense woodland had little attraction for them and their settlements were generally confined to the roads.

Many of the more compact villages, now in open country, began in Forest clearings and grouped clearings resulted in open-textured villages with more than one centre. The sites of many of the deserted mediaeval villages often show the 'ridge and furrow' of the peasant farmer's strips, which in the 15th and 16th centuries were converted to pasture by landowners for the more profitable wool-producing sheep. Driven out, the inhabitants

had difficulty in finding a livelihood elsewhere, as there was, and is, much less common and unenclosed land than in other counties.

Of the 17th-century gardens and parks the most complete is John Fetherston's monumental yew garden at Packwood symbolising the Sermon on the Mount. At Great Packington, Ragley and Compton Verney the statues, canals and 'vistos' vanished beneath Capability Brown's mirrors of still water, expanses of grass and belts of encircling woodland.

In the 18th century the pioneer Gothic Revival architect Sanderson Miller enhanced his own grounds against the Edge Hills by crowning them with a tower modelled on Warwick, and possibly created the superb landscape of Farnborough with its spectacular terrace walk, simple Ionic temple and oval pavilion. At Stoneleigh, Humphry Repton improved the view by widening the Avon, which contributes much to two of the most romantic buildings in the county, Warwick Castle and Guy's Cliffe.

Coal mining began as early as the 14th century along the north-east edge of the Kenilworth–Tamworth plateau, and as it developed brought prosperity to the local landowners, who built big houses. Eventually these were to be deserted as the slag heaps advanced, leaving a derelict shell, as at Ansley, or a neglected park, as at Baxterley, where the valley is now being filled with mining spoil.

The first canals were the Coventry Canal, 1769, and the Birmingham Canal, 1770–2, both engineered by James Brindley. At Hawkesbury, where the Coventry Canal is joined by his later Oxford Canal, the landscape is almost entirely 19th century and Birmingham's extensive network, spanned by brick and cast-iron bridges, has been only slightly curtailed. There are also the great feats of Midlands railway engineering, including a majestic, elliptically arched viaduct just north of Rugby which carries the London and Birmingham Railway from the site of Philip Hardwick's Euston Arch to its magnificent Ionic counterpart. The most dominant industrial structure is Hams Hall Power Station at Lea Marston, with thirteen concave-sided cooling towers.

The building materials and styles

With so much forest, timber was the first building material, but grander buildings were soon of stone and are the earliest to have survived. North of Warwick there is red sandstone which has a heavy quality, emphasised by its easily eroded edges, and equally soft is the cream-to-bluish, chalky lias found west of Stratford-upon-Avon. Dark-ochre Hornton stone graces buildings in the Vale of the Red Horse, and in the Edge Hills and in the south-west the golden oolite of the Cotswolds takes over. Used here in the local tradition, it helps to create some very attractive villages.

Villas at **Stratford-upon-Avon** ...

The buildings of the great monastic foundations have mostly disappeared, though Maxstoke Priory is still a towering ruin; but the castles at Warwick, Kenilworth and, on a small scale, Maxstoke are all most impressive.

There is little Anglo-Saxon work in the county. The best is the central tower at Wootton Wawen church with a dark space surrounded by primitive arches. Norman churches show the conservative nature of the Midlands by the persistence of herringbone masonry, as at Wootton Wawen and Whitchurch, well into the 12th century. They include Corley, Stoneleigh and Wyken, as well as Berkswell, with a wide nave and a remarkable rib-vaulted crypt. Polesworth has an impressive arcade, and Norman doorways and fonts are plentiful.

The Early English style offers the short, wide nave of Merevale, casually furnished with effigies, an unspoilt chancel at Northfield, with grouped lancet windows, and Temple Balsall, with intricate geometric tracery. The relative prosperity of the late 13th and early 14th centuries resulted in extensive building activity, though Decorated was not allowed free rein and rarely became exuberant. Perhaps the frivolity of excess ornamentation was contrary to the methodical Midland mind, which accepted relatively early the more 'reasonable' Perpendicular.

The first examples were ambitious—St. Michael's, Coventry, with its splendid sandstone steeple, and the nearby Holy Trinity, its blue roof ablaze with gold stars. The chancel of St. Mary's, Warwick, has a flying-rib vault, and the Beauchamp Chapel is one of the grandest ecclesiastical interiors of its date in England. Of the village churches of the period Lapworth is one of the most memorable, and many Perpendicular clerestories were added to existing buildings to dispel the early mediæval gloom.

At Castle Bromwich a 15th-century timber-framed church is encased in Early Georgian brick and plaster. Both 15th- and 16th-century manor houses and farmhouses are also often timber-framed, with close studding at ground-floor level, a diagonally braced first floor and decorative struts in the gables, as at Grimshaw Hall, Knowle, Blakesley Hall, Yardley and Stratford House, Bordesley. Much of Stratford-upon-Avon has genuine timber framing discovered behind 18th-century brick and stucco.

Orange brick, perhaps the most characteristic of all Warwickshire building materials, came into fashion in the early 16th century, and Compton Wynyates, built of pale-rose to umber-black bricks, burnt on site, is surely the most English of all country houses. Also of brick, Charlecote, built in the very year of Queen Elizabeth's accession, has a Renaissance porch, and Jacobean Aston Hall a romantic silhouette and rich strapwork ceilings.

Smaller 17th-century houses are usually of stone, as in Sheep Street, Shipston-on-Stour, but there are exceptions, such as the cosy classical Wharley Hall and Eastcote House near Barston, 1669. During the 18th century brick took precedence, especially in the

... and **Leamington Spa**

north of the county where clay from mineworkings was fired by local coal, and a pink brick with dark ends, used to form a chequer, and a plum-coloured brindle also occur. 18th-century Birmingham was an ordered network of red-brick terraces and squares more extensive than Bath. The less ambitious churches of the period are also of brick which, at the end of the century, was used by Bonomi for his remarkably advanced Great Packington, probably as a result of his patron's admiration for Roman ruins, and by Soane for his impressive 'barn à la Paestum' against the Solihull–Warwick road.

The best Baroque is Thomas Archer's

17

cathedral at Birmingham, but the style is mainly associated with William and Francis Smith, who built the massive west range of Stoneleigh Abbey. Their Court House at Warwick was constructed after a fire, in 1692, which resulted in the rebuilding of most of the town in a restrained classical style.

The gutted western parts of the church, rebuilt in Gothic presumably to match the surviving chancel and Beauchamp Chapel, are the first major revival of the style later made fashionable by Sanderson Miller, squire-architect of Radway Grange. Besides designing classical buildings such as the Shire Hall, Miller was probably responsible for some of the Gothicising of Arbury Hall which left it one of the finest early Gothic Revival houses in the country. Though the library ceiling has Etruscan motifs, the largest and finest Pompeian scheme in England is at Great Packington inspired by the Fourth Earl of Aylesford's collection of Etruscan vases.

Stucco-faced Edgbaston is still ideal, and Leamington Spa, with its classical villas, is a most attractive Regency town. Gothic seemed so appropriate near mediæval Warwick and Kenilworth that Palladian Guy's Cliffe became a towering fortress above the Avon, and Elizabethan and Shakespearian associations were so eagerly appreciated that Charlecote, where Elizabeth spent two nights, was vigorously extended in the Elizabethan style. Jacobean mansions, such as Merevale and Welcombe, and numerous estate cottages spread across the county with the more serious works of the Gothic Revivalists. Pugin's brick Bilton Grange is disappointing compared with Prichard's sumptuous stone Ettington Park, while Scott's brick Brownsover Hall is a most successful composition.

At Bishops Itchington, Voysey, commissioned by the owner of the local cement quarries, built his first house, appropriately finished with his characteristic roughcast. Bournville, begun in 1900, has a cosy, rural character, enhanced by a central green, and the Harborne Tenants' Estate is quite arcadian. The few modern houses are best represented by Chermayeff at Rugby, Yorke at Stratford, Wormersley and Guest at Alveston and Rowbotham at Snitterfield, and the only modern country house is Pollen's flat-roofed Grove House, at Hampton-on-the-Hill, emphasised by pyramid-roofed corner pavilions.

19th-century churches are many and varied, though mostly of stone, and range from Francis Goodwin's picturesque Trinity Chapel, Bordesley, with its cast-iron tracery and plaster vaulting, to Butterfield's assured St. Andrew's, Rugby. Rickman and Hutchinson's majestic Hampton Lucy is enhanced by a sympathetic Scott chancel, and Pugin's brick-and-slate R.C. cathedral at Birmingham has a soaring east end influenced by St. Elizabeth's, Marburg. Scott's best Warwickshire church is certainly Sherbourne, and Pearson is represented by Newbold Pacey and St. Alban's, Bordesley, the latter of brick but fully vaulted in stone. Early 20th-century churches are mostly of brick; the finest, St. Agatha's, Sparkbrook, by W. H. Bidlake, is such an advanced interpretation of Gothic that other Birmingham architects turned to the Romanesque style. The most important ecclesiastical building of the 1950s and 1960s is Coventry Cathedral by Sir Basil Spence, and it is interesting to compare this with his economical churches at Willenhall, Tile Hill and Bell Green.

Birmingham Town Hall ▷

18

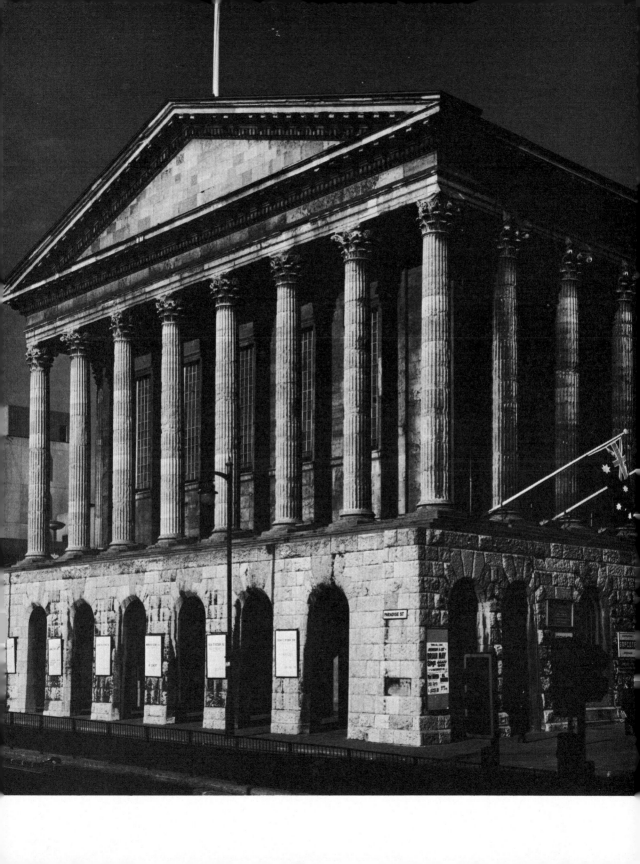

Gazetteer

The number in brackets following the place name refers to the square on the map at the back of the book where the place is to be found.

Acocks Green & Hay Mills *see* Birmingham

Admington [13] Once belonged to the Abbey of Winchcomb. *Admington Hall*, a 16th-century Cotswold house with a geometric ceiling, is behind a formal garden of yews. In 1801 it was squared up by the addition of a full-height staircase and given a classical south front facing another garden, which has specimen trees. Approach was then from the south through wrought-iron entrance gates, but is now from the north past a gabled dovecote. Pale stucco-faced stables have a Soane-ish deep segmental arch.

Alcester [10] On the site of a small Roman market centre served by at least two Roman roads, though the present town plan is mediaeval. The Roman houses which have been discovered are sited along Swan Street and Stratford Road and along a road running northeast, possibly to Mancetter. Beyond the disused railway station are the sites of the 12th-century Alcester Abbey and of the manor house, *Beauchamp Court*, marked by a moat, a mile distant along Priory Road. The rivers Arrow and Alne water the town. At the beginning of the 19th century over 500 people were employed in scouring, eyeing and filing needles in their outhouses, many of which still stand. Creamstone *church* (St. Nicholas) has a 14th-century tower, crowned by a cluster of pinnacles and pierced battlements; but the body dates from 1729–30, following a fire, and 1871, when the east end was rebuilt. The architect after the fire was Thomas Woodward of Chipping Campden, who provided a Gothic exterior in keeping with the tower and a bold classical interior with massive cream Tuscan columns, supporting a coved plaster ceiling. Dark chancel opens through triple-arched arcades into even darker side chapels. Impressive white-marble figure of First Marquess of Hertford, 1828, by Chantrey, reclining on a Grecian couch against a Gothic panelled background. Alabaster recumbent Sir Fulke Greville, d.1559, and his wife. Victorian font strikingly geometric. Southern end of the gently curved High Street was 'The Bull

Malt Mill Lane, Alcester

Ring' before the block of houses against Stratford Road was built, and the part nearer the church was known as 'The Shambles'. Both have many Georgian red-brick fronts hiding timber-framed houses which can be seen from the rights-of-way between the shops, once known as 'tuers' or 'Tueries'. *Savory and Moore* have an elegant black-painted bow, and inside is a fine exhibition of medicinal jars and implements from the Bronze Age to the 19th century. Nearly every building on the east side was at some time an alehouse; *The Bear*, as the arch indicates, was a coaching inn. Butter Street has a row of cottages, all that is left of a ring of houses which enclosed the churchyard, and opposite is the Georgian *rectory*. Sumptuous but small-scale *Churchill House*, 1688, with a rich cornice and balcony, has early 17th-century timber framing, and the part-plastered *Town Hall*, 1618, no longer stands on open stone arches. Each October the Manor Court (Court Leet) is held here; the High Bailiff is elected, together with his officials, with such titles as Ale Tasters, Bread Weighers, etc. Timber-framed *21–31, Henley Street*, once the Greyhound's Head Inn, have rich scroll brackets; across Gunnings Bridge, stone *Oversley House*, 1837, was originally the workhouse. Former *Baptist Meeting House*, 1735–6, is round-arched with Gothic timber tracery, and the *Baptist church*, 1859, is Italianate. Church Street, which wraps around the parish church to join High Street, has gabled, timber-framed houses and Grecian *Arrow House* with two-storey Ionic pilasters. Descending from the churchyard to the river, the narrow, curved *Malt Mill Lane*, is lined with timber-framed and brick houses, renovated in 1975 by Associated Architects.

Farmhouses between Over Whitacre and Astley

Alderminster [14] In the patchwork valley of the River Stour, the impressive lanceted 13th-century central tower of the *church* (St. Mary and Holy Cross) catches the eye from the busy Stratford–Oxford road. After the greater part of the south wall had fallen outwards, the Norman nave was restored, in 1884–5, by F. Preedy, who added an unconvincing Norman-style south doorway. North doorway is real Norman. Unpainted, plastered interior is lit by clear-glazed lancets, and the tall, bulky Victorian font has intricately carved scenes. Through a white gate beneath a dark cut-yew arch is the white-painted *Alderminster Lodge*; a Tudor-style early 19th-century building with an ogee-arched porch. Stucco Georgian *Bell Inn* faces speckled-brick *High Meadow*, and nearer Stratford are pale-brick estate cottages, 1858–9, as at Preston-on-Stour.

Allesley *see* Coventry

Alveston [11] Desirable residences. The present centre is around a long green, enclosed by chequered-brick and stucco Georgian and early 19th-century houses in both classic and Gothic dress; closing one end, against a river walk, is the nautical *Ferry Inn*. The old centre is further to the north-west, where all that survives of the old church is an 18th-century whitewashed brick chancel with a plastered interior. Delicate white-marble wall monuments, gilded royal arms, a chunky Norman tympanum and a sober effigy of Nicholas Lane, d.1595. Overgrown churchyard has a three-sided obelisk to George Glover Hurst, d.1838. 16th-century *Old Vicarage* is close-studded and straight-roofed. Early Victorian

Ansley: *above* Norman carving on the chancel arch, and *below* the Georgian sanctuary

Gothic front to *Alveston Lodge*, the refacing of an earlier building, looks like the work of Gibson, who built the second vicarage in 1859; and the gates opposite lead to the late 17th-century *Alveston House* with dark cut-yews above the River Avon. Against the fields to the south is the new *church* (St. James), 1839, by W. Walker, with an uneasy single-span roof modelled on that of Westminster Hall. Arts and Crafts screen and painting, an attempt to improve a rather stark interior, are presumably by Temple Moore, who designed the *vicarage*, c. 1908, a roughcast building with an ample hall and surprisingly modern stone fireplaces incorporating Delft tiles. White-painted *Kissing Tree House* has a stone south front, and *The Lodge*, c. 1840, Gothic tracery and dummy arrow slits. Modern houses are *Cedar Leys*, 1964, by Peter Wormersley, and *The White House*, 1962, by Patrick Guest.

Ansley [5] Brick farm buildings and cottages and many inter-war terraces and semis. *Providence chapel*, 1822, is lean Gothic with the chapel house under the balcony at one end. Outside the village, at Church End, the *church* (St. Lawrence) has a tall, pinnacled, orange-brown tower, a Norman nave with later windows and clerestory, a Norman chancel, rendered and weathered to a silver grey, and a pedimented 1760 sanctuary. A wide Norman arch frames the dim old chancel furnished with box pews; and, by the jambs of a further round arch, two large urns are silhouetted against the Georgian sanctuary, of drawing-room proportions and brightly lit by a Gothic window containing fragments of mediaeval glass. Beneath the raised floor is the Ludford-Astley vault; and on the walls are memorials by Hollins. Churchyard: base of the old cross, slate headstones, and a pink-marble sarcophagus to William Carside Phillips, d.1929, owner of

the local mine. *Ansley Hall*, now empty and very picturesque, is part rendered Elizabethan and part brick Georgian with Gothic sash windows. An 18th-century orangery has large architectural details from elsewhere, and on the other side of the A47 is a walled garden with a two-storey tower and the round-arched *Ansley Hall Coal and Iron Co.*, 1924, with cast-iron windows.

Ansty [8] The *church* (St. James), mainly 1856, by Scott, has a mock-mediaeval steeple. Dark nave with a 14th-century north arcade, and small 13th-century chancel with stencilled walls framing rich Victorian glass. Grecian monument, which has a woman mourning the death of Simon Adams, in 1801, is by Cooke and, above the road, pedimented *Ansty Hall*, was built for Richard Taylor, a Roundhead leader.

Arbury [5] *Arbury Hall* is the most complete surviving example of 18th-century Gothic Revival in the country. In Henry II's reign an Augustinian priory was founded here which, in the time of Elizabeth I, was totally demolished to make way for 'a very fair structure in a quadrangular form', only parts of which survive, principally the long gallery. As soon as Richard Newdigate inherited the property, in about 1670, he started building the brick *Stables*, probably by Sir William Wilson, with stone-cross windows, shaped gables and a central doorway, said to be a design by Sir Christopher Wren. *Chapel* followed in 1678, formed in the north-east corner of the house, with intricate stucco ceiling of flowers and fruit by Edward Martin, carved wainscot and chequer-board floor. Elaborate lock to the door by John Wilkes of Birmingham. The rest of Arbury Hall is due to Sir Roger Newdigate, fifth baronet, founder of the verse prize at Oxford. In 1750 he started

Arbury Hall   ▷

Arbury: Saloon ceiling

Gothicising the *Library*, the bow window of which is probably by Sanderson Miller of Radway Grange, with William Hiorn as mason-architect. Interior has ogee-gabled bookcases, Gothic panelling and segmental ceiling with classical painting and Etruscan motifs. *Drawing Room*, with matching bow, 1762–3, by Henry Keene, Surveyor to Westminster Abbey, has panelled four-centred tunnel-vault ceiling, panelled walls and a chimneypiece with coloured marble inserts by Richard Hayward of Bulkington, inspired by the canopy of the monument to Aymer de Vallance in Westminster Abbey. In centre of south front, *Dining Room*, 1771–91, also by Henry Keene, occupies the site of the Elizabethan Hall—hence its great height, which allows space for a fine fan vault. Chimneypiece here suitably large-scale, with many small niches; plain walls are relieved by Gothic niches with elaborate canopies, containing casts of antique classical statues, which seem inappropriate today. *Cloisters*, 1785, and *Saloon*, 1786, both by Henry Couchman, the latter possibly from Keene's designs; Couchman was, however, paid for 'Sundry Skitches from Westminster Abbey'. Ceiling, derived from Henry VII's Chapel, is more elaborate and less correct than the fan vault in the dining room; and the large bow window, 1793, has rococo-Gothic glazing, scagliola shafts and small pendants. *School Room*, 1788, and *Little Sitting Room* also have fan vaults. After this splendid riot of fine plasterwork, the exterior seems sober, if not austere, though it is surprisingly well proportioned, considering it is a new face to an Elizabethan structure. Gardens, like the house, are due largely to Sir Roger Newdigate and a good example of the informal picturesque manner prevalent

23

in the second half of the 18th century. Lake may be a survival from the days when Arbury was a monastery. Against the stable forecourt wall, two mullioned bay windows and a four-centred doorhead from the old house. Amid the trees, beyond the lawn, is an *ice house*; and a few of the Forest of Arden oaks can still be seen among the woods and plantations of the last century. *South Farm* was the birthplace of Mary Ann Evans, b.1819—George Eliot the novelist. Cheveral Manor, which figures prominently in her 'Scenes of Clerical Life', 1857, is Arbury Hall and Sir Roger Newdigate her Sir Christopher Cheveral. *Arbury Mill* was the mill George Eliot knew best, but the *Mill House* has been considerably altered since her childhood. Stone stairs, on which she is said to have sat to read and write, are as she knew them; and perhaps then as now, the front door at the top of the house led on to a lawn which covers what was the old mill race. *Tower Farm*, *Round Towers*, *South Lodge* and *Astley Lodge* all have red-sandstone towers.

Arley [5] A mining parish with a pit shaft actually in the village; but the colliery was closed in 1968. Miners' red-brick terraces with wide, arched windows, and detached bungalows of all shapes and materials. Nave of the *church* (St. Wilfred) is light and intimate, with a white-painted boarded ceiling, but the chancel is dark, with fragments of old glass glowing in a north window. *School* has a frantic polychromatic brick gable, and next to this is a black-and-white cottage. *New Arley* is Edwardian and in the Arts and Crafts tradition, as is the *church* (St. Michael), 1927, with brick walls, stained hardwood window frames and a sweeping roof, but a stone-dressed classical porch.

Arbury Hall:
above centre of south front
below the Drawing Room

Arbury Hall: terms

Armscote [14] Attractively grouped, and at the north end of a chain of similar villages to the west of the Roman Fosse Way. Houses and cottages are of stone or brick, thatched or tiled, and one thatched *terrace* is of this century, with Lethaby-influenced flush mullioned windows. Behind a rose-clad high wall is the gabled 17th-century *manor house*, which has a priest's hole beneath the roof. Domestic-looking *Friends' Meeting House*, 1705, retains its original seating.

Arrow & Ragley [10] Black-and-white and pale-brick cottages against Ragley Park. By the winding River Arrow and the disused Roman Icknield Street, the *church* (St. James) is sheltered by tall, wind-swept cedars, which almost hide its spiky Gothick tower covered in pink roughcast. By contrast the wilful north aisle, 1865, is of grey lias with robust yellow-stone tracery. Interior has stumpy columns, vigorously carved capitals and monuments to the Seymour-Conway family,

interred below the chancel. Against the road, the angular orange-brick *estate office* has a dovecote in the chimney; and on the corner of the road to Inkberrow is a pretty stucco *cottage. Arrow Mill*, mentioned in Domesday, was grinding corn up to the 1960s, when it was carefully converted into a restaurant. *Ragley Hall* is guarded by a pair of pyramid-roofed lias lodges. Monumental east front, 1680–90, by Robert Hooke, has a fine Ionic portico by James Wyatt, behind which is the large, full-height *Great Hall*, decorated by Gibbs and mocked at by Horace Walpole. Ceiling shows Britannia in a lion-drawn chariot, by Vassali, and around the walls are busts and urns on brackets above figures of War and Peace over the fireplaces. *Study*, also by Gibbs, has a painting of the Earl of Conway who began the building of Ragley to replace the mediaeval embattled castle, and *Library*, originally chapel, has carving by Grinling Gibbons and a view over the lake to the Cotswold hills. In

Billiard Room by Gibbs, putti carry a cornucopia across the ceiling and from the windows can be seen a small hill, on which in the early 1800s was built *Oversley Castle*, following a suggestion by the Prince Regent. *Small Dining Room* has an overmantel by Kendall of Warwick; *Dining Room* is by Wyatt, as is *Red Saloon* with Cornelis van Haarlem's great painting *The Raising of Lazarus*. *Blue Drawing Room* has ceiling by Wyatt, and *Prince Regent's Bedroom* an oriental-style bed. Garden was destroyed in the 1750s by Capability Brown, who replaced many formal avenues by clumps of trees and a greatly improved lake.

Ashborne [11] A kink in the road allows a good view of a row of thatched black-and-white cottages; and where the marl ends there is a long grey-stone terrace. Behind a forecourt a Nonconformist *chapel*, 1843, has corner piers topped with pineapples; and the characterful red-and-yellow-brick

school carries an unusual combined bell and clock tower.

Ashow [8] In a coomb against the River Avon and approached along a tree-covered drive, leading through the village to the church against the babbling river. Unsympathetic private houses convinced Lord Leigh that tighter control was necessary, and the latest houses, to his specification, have considerably improved the scene. Timber-framed terrace has been completely reconstructed, and some Austrian-style Victorian cottages are busy with tacked-on timbers. Raised footpath leads, past some real timber-framed houses, to the roughly coursed orange-brown-stone *church* (Assumption of Our Lady), which has three Norman windows and the remains of a Norman doorway. Pink west tower is Perpendicular and the south side of the nave, c. 1800, is of contrasting light-grey ashlar, with simply traceried Gothic windows. Tall, whitewashed interior has a fine open-timber roof, revealed by the removal in the 1960s of a match-boarded ceiling and a part-lath-and-plaster chancel arch. Box pews, late 18th-century pulpit, blackboard with the Lord's Prayer, Ten Commandments and Creed in Gothic letters, and painted George III arms, in a marbled, moulded frame.

Astley [5] Tucked away behind a Tudor-style school, built, in 1871, for Charles Newdigate Newdegate, and a row of rough-rendered cottages, the *church* (St. Mary) has a soaring, silver-rendered nave, originally the chancel of a collegiate church built, in 1343, by Thomas Astley. In 1608 Richard Chamberlain added the present red-sandstone tower and the lighter-stone chancel to make a very handsome parish church. Light nave has a set of stalls, c. 1400, with paintings of the Apostles and Prophets, and misericord seats; and on the walls are painted inscriptions in strapwork surrounds. Chancel arch is cut through the enormous Perpendicular east window of the collegiate church, infilled with plaster between the tracery; chancel, though humble by comparison, has very convincing Perpendicular windows for its date, Gothick plaster ceiling, chequerboard floor and wrought-iron communion rail, c. 1700. Three alabaster effigies are of the Grey family who lived at nearby *Astley Castle*. Lady Jane Grey's father, Henry, Duke of Suffolk, fled to Astley Park when Sir Thomas Wyatt's rebellion failed, and hid in a great oak for three days and nights, until he was betrayed by his keeper and executed on Tower Hill in 1554. Stone *monument* on Duke's Farm records the event, and the chair and table he used in the oak are at Arbury Hall. Castle, a rebuilding of 1555, is an embattled red-sandstone rectangle. Stables are late 18th-century Gothick. Astley was the 'Knebley' of George Eliot, whose father's first wife has a memorial in the church and whose aunt, Mrs. Ann Garner, one of the Dodson sisters in 'The Mill on the Floss', lived at *Sole End Farm*.

Ragley Hall, Arrow
opposite the Great Hall and
right the west front

Astley

Aston *see* Birmingham

Aston Cantlow [10] Red-brick terraces, black-and-white cottages and, opposite the long, timber-framed *King's Head*, the early 16th-century close-studded *Guild House* with a jettied upper floor. In the 18th century the village was known for paper making, and later needle scouring. Blue-and-yellow-lias *church* (St. John Baptist) has a most handsome tower with twin Perpendicular bell openings. Cavernous geometric porch by Butterfield, 1850, leads to a lofty, whitewashed interior, not spoilt by his restoration for The Society for the Maintenance of the Faith. Mary Arden,

Shakespeare's mother, was possibly christened here. Both the stone screen and communion rail are early examples of Butterfield's inventive genius; east window has a Crucifixion by Kempe. Churchyard is bounded by long red-brick barn, whitewashed cottages, elegant classical *vicarage* and lias *school and master's house*, by Butterfield, c. 1843, which has a series of descending roofs. *Aqueduct*, with thirteen tall, tapering brick piers, 1813, carries the Stratford-on-Avon Canal.

Atherstone [5] An old market town around the Roman Watling Street, above where it plunges downhill to

cross the River Anker. Coal mining, quarrying and hat making were the industries here. Most of the centre is Georgian, but the market place was created recently. *Church* (St. Mary) has hard, un-coursed-stone nave and aisles, 1840, by T. H. Wyatt and Branden, octagonal 14th-century central tower, the upper stage with pretty rose windows of c. 1800, and orange-pink sandstone Perpendicular chancel, once an independent chapel taken over by the Austin Friars c. 1375. To the north, Norman doorway has zigzag ornamentation. Tall, narrow arches beneath tower divide dark, dull nave from light chancel, which has a large Perpendicular east window. Side windows have glass by Kempe, 1890 and 1899. To the east of the church, Friar's Gate has 18th-century houses which continue over an elliptical archway into Market Street, where *19* is complete with pedimented stone doorcase and iron railings. *15* and *17* are timber-framed beneath the pebbledash and have a massive brick chimney-stack. *Long Street*, the Roman Watling Street, has Georgian houses; but in the last ten years many of these have been demolished, leaving ugly gaps. Each year the shops are boarded up for a ball game which dates from the 12th century. Jolly red-brick *Albert Hall*, 1876, has a triple-arched window and at the bottom of the hill are the ponderous late 17th-century *Conservative Club* and the timber-framed *Old Swan*. *Independent chapel*, North Street, and *Wesley chapel*, Coleshill Road, are both early 19th-century brick preaching boxes, one Ionic, the other Gothic. Picturesque Tudor-style *railway station* is now derelict; between the railway and the Coventry Canal are a pair of houses in the same style, an attractive terrace of Georgian houses and a lockkeeper's cottage. Set against a backcloth of dark trees on the Merevale Estate, *Beehive Cottage*, Coleshill Road, dates from c. 1800.

Astley: painted stalls

Atherstone-on-Stour [10] (near Preston-on-Stour) Virtually untouched since 1876, when the humble, barn-like *church* was rebuilt by John Cotton, in the Decorated style in light-grey stone. Owing to its unsound site there are cracks in the tower and distorted tracery in the west window. Crucifixion by Kempe. Font is tub-shaped and, clamped to the exterior of the east wall, classical monuments carry flaming obelisks. An aisled barn, braced with telegraph poles in 1914, served as the church during the rebuilding. Georgian *Home Farm* and *rectory*. Just east of the Stour are the remains of the horse tramway to Shipston-on-Stour, built by Telford in 1820.

Attleborough [5] Early Victorian red-brick *church* (Holy Trinity) by T. L. Walker, architect of the Chamberlain Almshouses, Bedworth, in Commissioner's Early English, with regularly spaced lancet windows, low-pitched classical roof and south-west steeple. Busy Attleborough Road has some *weavers' cottages*, which have lost a storey, and, at their rear, a large brick *mill* has a solid staircase bastion. Against the River Anker an even larger brick fortress, *Anker Mill*, with seventeen bays of timber-framed windows and tall octagonal chimneys is occupied by Fielding and Johnson, established 1818, who built the original *Bond Street Mills*.

Austrey [2] A few timber-framed cottages, some Georgian terraces and farms and many post-war houses. *Church* (St. Nicholas) has an Early English tower and an early 14th-century nave with slender arcades. 18th-century *vicarage* with elegant Regency porch; mediaeval *village cross* outside the pub. Elevated austere *Baptist chapel*, 1808, behind fine engraved slate headstones by Proudman of Measham, and to one side of a long brick barn, the gateway to *Elms Farm* leads up steps into a walled front garden.

Avon Dassett [14] Tumbling down a steep hill towards a tributary of the River Cherwell and the Warwick–Banbury road. Splendid clear-cut steeple of the *church* (St. John Baptist) 1868, soars out of the hillside, leaving the folded roof of the nave and aisles, which are cut into the ground, to blend with the natural contours. Approached from the south, up steep, winding steps between stone walls overhung by tall trees, this superb Victorian piece is obviously by one of the masters of the Gothic Revival. Tower has rounded staircase projection, and spire is accompanied by four square spirelets which follow its outline. Early 13th-century figure, fragments of old glass and 18th-century headstones. Mullioned, Hornton-stone *rectory* has a 13th-century wing; in the garden is a pyramid-roofed dovecote. At Arlescote, against Edge Hill, the creeper-clad brown-stone *manor house* is framed by tall gate piers and ogival-roofed pavilions.

Baddesley Clinton [8] (near Wroxall) Opposite an estate of modern houses, a Victorian R.C. *church*, with lancet windows and an octagonal bell turret, stands in front of a slate-roofed convent. In a ring of trees down a long lane, domestic-looking Perpendicular parish *church* (St. Michael) is betrayed by its handsome white-stone tower. Massive masonry walls are plastered to blend with the smooth white-stone clerestory, below which hang dark hatchments. Quaint strapwork screen for Edward Ferrers. Twelve generations of Ferrers lie under the floor, including Henry Ferrers the antiquarian, d. 1633. East window, with members of the Ferrers family and their shields, one with thirty-two quarterings, has clearly defined colours. Elegant chamber organ of 1797. Secluded *Hall*, a perfect late mediaeval manor house, has a wide moat spanned by a creeper-clad Queen Anne bridge. Entrance

front is the work of John Brome and his son, but the great window, in the entrance tower, is Elizabethan, an alteration for Henry Ferrers. Many hiding places, one, by the expert hide builder Nicholas Owen, below the level of the moat. Panelled interior with moulded beams, Elizabethan stone fireplaces, heraldic glass and tapestries. 17th-century stables, and pools covered with water lilies.

Baddesley Ensor [5] A compact mixture of terrace and semi-detached houses, from the 19th century to the present day, between Watling Street and Baddesley Mine, where many inhabitants are employed. Name is derived from 'bede ley' (a priest's clearing in a forest) and Thomas d'Ednesoure, who gave the ground for the original Norman church (St. Nicholas) by the manor house, outside the present village. This church was so inconveniently placed that, during the early 19th century, it was deliberately allowed to fall into ruins and the stones were used by the local inhabitants as building material. Red-sandstone *Church House* has three Gothic arches, presumably from the old church; and the demolished Church House Inn incorporated a Norman arch, with zigzag ornamentation, now in the churchyard. New *church* (St. Nicholas), built, in 1845, between the village and Grendon Common, on land given by the Dugdale family, was designed by architect of Merevale Hall, Henry Clutton. Vigorous exterior with small windows and sturdy tower and spire; but south porch, vaulted with golden stone, leads to dark, disappointing interior, not improved by modern glass. Pulpit, of the refectory type corbelled from the wall, probably inspired by the one at Merevale; sanctuary wall arcading is a memorial to William Stratford Dugdale, who died from injuries received in an explosion in the Baxterley Pit. Modern *church*

cel arches, supporting an octagonal bell turret, and lancet windows. Two fine early 15th-century brasses commemorate Sir William Bagot and his wife, who owned Baginton Castle, of which only the basement remains, to the east of the church. Tablet to Mrs. Campion, d.1632, with Mannerist statuettes of Faith, Hope and Charity, is the earliest known purely classical work in the county. Bromley family vault has Jacobean-style screen, dated 1677, and monument by Flaxman. Most of the church furnishings, including the pews, are 18th-century. *The Old Mill*, once used to grind clay for pottery, instead of corn, has an eighteen-foot-diameter mill wheel in working order.

Barcheston [14] (near Shipston-on-Stour) Reduced by the enclosures to little more than the church, rectory and manor house, the latter now mainly 17th century. Here, in the late 16th century, Richard Hicks established his famous manufacture of arras, after being sent by William Sheldon to the Netherlands, to learn the art. Grey, lichen-covered *church* (St. Martin) has a leaning 14th-century tower, supported by a massive buttress crashing into a window, and which contains two 15th-century priest's chambers connected by a spiral staircase. Sloping 12th-century north arcade ends on a carved hand on the tower, and supports a tall, rough-stone wall lit by a single-sided clerestory. Chancel arch is off-centre, and all that remains of a Georgian painted-glass window are two winged cherubs against clouds. Calm alabaster effigies of William Willington, 1555, and his wife and, in memory of the master weavers, a colourful Arts and Crafts tablet, with cornflowers, primroses and strawberries.

hall is a good, simple shape; and, set against a group of trees on the road to Wood End, the mellow-brick *Baddesley Farm*, part 1789, is framed by a solitary Scots pine.

Baginton [8] Once a Bronze Age and Roman settlement on a hilltop plateau above the River Sowe. Many military buildings, three granaries and a gateway have been discovered at *The Lunt (Roman fort)*; another exciting find is the famous Baginton hanging bowl. Red-sandstone *church* (St. John Baptist) has Norman chancel, two triple chan-

Astley castle

Old School, **Aston Cantlow**

Barford [11] Old terraced and new detached houses where the busy Warwick–Oxford road crosses the River Avon. Behind a wall, Regency *Barford House* has giant Ionic pilasters, a garlanded urn and a central dome. Street leading to the church has both timber-framed and Georgian houses, and is closed by the creeper-clad Perpendicular tower of the *church* (St. Peter) hiding a body rebuilt, in 1884, by R. C. Hussey. Interior is large and light with creamwashed plaster walls, clear glazed windows and elegant arcades framing serried ranks of box pews with poppy heads. East window, by Holland of Warwick, is of St. Peter and the four Evangelists beneath splendid Gothic canopies. Set into Gothic niches are large urns to the Mills family, one, 1820, by Henry Westmacott.

Barston [8] (near Knowle) On a broad hill encircled on three sides by the River Blythe. *Church* (St. Swithin), 1721, is of a most attractive light-red brick and is sheltered by a tiled roof. Naïve round-arched windows survive in the part-ivy-clad tower walls; the nave windows have been Gothicised by the Victorians, who added a porch and a vestry. Cream-washed tower vestry has flamboyant hatchments and the body, though still plastered, has open-timbered roofs and a High Victorian chancel arch. Churchyard is enclosed by tall trees which shelter an 18th-century *vicarage*, once the glebe house. Downhill, terraces of timber-framed and brick cottages. Uphill, the sash-windowed *Bull's Head*, a timber-framed *malt barn* with a Gothic front from the days when it was the village hall, and the massive Georgian *The*

Firs with ball-topped gate piers. Brick *Wharley Hall*, dated 1669, has large timber-framed barns; and *Eastcote House* is similar, with brick-pedimented windows. Black-and-white *Eastcote Manor*, originally built *c.* 1560 as Wharley Hall, has a large Victorian addition. Timbered *Eastcote Hall*, approached along a deep gravel drive spanning a moat, is framed by a taller, weather-vaned bellcote, c. 1900, and Scots pines. 15th-century hall survives, divided into two storeys. Fed from five springs, the moat drains into the River Blythe through a pool, overhung by trees, in gardens made natural by Percy Cane.

Barton-on-the-Heath [14] On a hill with the *church* (St. Lawrence) probably founded in Anglo-Danish times, ringed by trees. Body is Nor-

Aqueduct on the Stratford-on-Avon Canal, **Aston Cantlow**

man; west window is blocked by a thin, tapering tower with a saddleback roof. Creamwashed interior is lit by a big Perpendicular window in the north wall, which has delicate yellow-glass falcons, overpowered by poor Victorian glass. Small Norman chancel arch and deeply splayed chancel windows with lively arrangement of old glass. High-roofed south chapel contributes much to the exterior, enriched by wall monuments.

Churchyard bounded by walls and the long, stone-roofed *Old Rectory*, its country-classical brick front facing across a valley to Barton Hill. On the village green, a domed wellhouse has classical columns; and, behind a high stone wall, the Cotswold-tradition *Barton House* is said to have been built in 1612 by Inigo Jones.

Baxterley [5] A mining village, but rural in character, as it came before

the mine. In the fields, the *church* has a west front and bell turret built by Hugh Glover, son of Robert, burnt as a heretic at Coventry in 1555. Exterior is of red sandstone, with the exception of the 19th-century additions including the north aisle, added by Paul and Bickerdike in 1873. Small Norman chancel arch is curiously off-centre, possibly as a result of the removal of a south arcade. Chancel, c. 1200, has a primitive priest's doorway

SACRED TO THE MEMORY OF
ELIZABETH EMMA,
WIFE OF JOHN EARDLEY EARDLEY-WILMOT, ESQᴿᴱ OF BERKSWELL HALL, IN THIS PARISH,
AND DAUGHTER OF C.H. PARRY, M.D.
OF THE CITY OF BATH

Berkswell: church
and detail of
Westmacott
monument

and two slit windows with deeply splayed reveals; the three lancets over the altar, 1871, replace a square-headed window of three lights, built into the Victorian vestry. Rare crozier head, c. 1200, found in a wall in 1958, is the oldest piece of church equipment in wood in the county. In the churchyard is a neat rendered-brick schoolroom, 1839, inscribed 'Feed my Lambs'. Sandstone *Baxterley Old Hall* was burnt down and replaced by a brick farmhouse but parts of the moat can be seen and, against the cross-roads, an arch in a wall. Stone cottages opposite are the original outbuildings. Next to the council estate, the 18th-century brick out-buildings of *Baxterley Hall* enclose three sides of a court. Main eleva-tion, with rusticated window sur-rounds and a pediment, faces across a green valley, gradually being filled with spoil from Baddesley Colliery. Well clear in a clump of trees, two intriguing *follies* have sandstone elevations built into the living rock and Piranesi-inspired interiors with wide brick wall arches supporting brick barrel vaults. Baddesley Colliery Bowling Club has an 18th-century sand-stone *lodge*, trying to look 16th-cen-tury, and further east a pretty pair of early 19th-century stone *cottages* has a simple plastered quatrefoil. Well sited in the valley, and distin-guished by a tall circular chimney, Baddesley Mine is where, in 1882, many men perished, including William Stratford Dugdale.

Bearley [10] Many council houses and bungalows to the west of the old centre, where the *church* (St. Mary) was sensitively reconstructed by Neville Hawkes in 1961–2. Tower, of mellow reused bricks, has timber louvred gables; stone body in-corporates a Norman doorway and small Gothic Revival windows. Interior is round-arched with not-too-smooth plaster walls and light-toned oak fittings. Beyond some black-and-white cottages, the in-formal *manor* has a Greek Doric porch and Gothic *stables*. Charles II passed by Bearley Cross, with Mis-tress Lane on the pillion, when he was fleeing from Worcester, and just avoided a troop of horse.

Beaudesert [10] Timber-framed cottages in the fields to the east of Henley-in-Arden, barely a stone's throw across the River Alne. An oblong hill was possibly fortified by an early British tribe, since the adjacent ancient hill track, known as Edge Lane, would have enabled travel on high ground, to avoid the perils of the Forest of Arden valleys. In the 12th century the Norman Thurstan de Montfort built a motte-and-bailey castle; an old road winds up to the inner court-yard, once surrounded by a pali-sade inside a deep ditch. Further west was an outer courtyard simi-larly defended. *Church* (St. Nicholas) is impressively Norman with an embattled 15th-century tower. Majestic chancel arch is off-centre, as the north wall has been rebuilt. Glass by Morris and Co., 1864–5, except in the shafted east window, where it is by Holland. Norman chancel, apart from the stone rib vaulting, added by Thomas Garner, in 1865, to origi-nal wall piers and corbels. Outside on the east wall, monument to the Revd. Richard Jago, d.1741, a former rector and father of the poet.

Bedworth [5] A dreary mining town, with Edwardian and inter-war houses, which was firmly estab-lished as a coal mining centre by the end of the 17th century, with numerous 'spoil banks' indicating shallow workings. French Protes-tants, fleeing from persecution, sought refuge here and set up their hand looms in their homes to weave silk ribbons. Old centre, around the High Street, has some run-down Georgian houses; many of the 19th-century terraces are of patterned red-and-yellow brick. Red-sand-stone *church* (All Saints) 1888–90, by Bodley and Garner, but not one of their best, has a Perpendicular west tower, from the previous church, with a clock, 1817, in a Gothic panelled frame. Large, dark interior has brown-glass Cruci-fixion, with figures standing on the branches of the Calvary tree, 1890; St. Peter and St. Paul, in vivid colours against a grey-brown background, 1929; and an almost abstract St. Luke, in clear, bright colours, R.F. 1965. Cloistered *Chamberlain Almshouses*, founded by the Revd. Nicholas Chamberlain, in 1715, were rebuilt, in 1840, by Thomas Larkins T. Walker, with a pretty ogival clock tower, and a stone-roofed pump house. *Zion Baptist chapel*, 1798, has round-headed windows, with Gothic tra-cery and cut ruby-flashed glass; *Old Meeting United Reformed church*, 1726, the parent of Independency in the district, has similar windows in two storeys. King Street retains some chequered blue-and-yellow-brick houses, and High Street boasts the timber-and-bronze-glass *Civic Hall*.

Bell Green *see* Coventry

Bentley [5] On high ground and well wooded, with the sandstone east wall of the mediaeval church, pierced by a Perpendicular win-dow, standing in a field. Early Vic-torian church has gone, leaving a walled graveyard and the *Horse and Jockey* as the only recognisable centre. Cottage is longing to be re-thatched, and the pediments of two tall 18th-century farmhouses have a plastered lunette and a Gothic window.

Berkswell [8] Secluded and peace-ful, though near to Coventry. Many cottages and farmsteads around a tidy green with stocks. Brick mak-ing and, around 1700, flax growing. Name is derived from the Anglo-Saxon Bercol who owned the well, in the Forest of Arden, where monks from Lichfield set up camp and later baptised the King of the Mercians. The King built a little church with a large crypt; the present *church* (St. John Baptist) is mainly the 12th-century rebuilding by the Normans, who provided a new crypt and reconstructed the old one, both lit by small windows immediately under a low rib vault. Smooth red-sandstone chancel, a complete Norman piece, has shafted windows and above the chancel arch, which has scalloped capitals, are inscriptions in ogee Gothic frames, possibly from the 18th-century reredos. South gallery and box pews. Monument, by Westmacott, to Mrs. Eardley Eardley Wilmot, who died at 29, is decorated by symbolic roses and sickles. Norman south doorway is covered by a timber-framed 16th-century porch, an upper room of which has an 18th-century hunting parson's hobby horse, used during sermons as its owner only became eloquent on horseback. *Berks Well* is sixteen feet square, for immersion baptisms. 17th-century *Old Rectory* has two large shaped gables. *Almshouses*, 1853, and a solitary shop with fine bow windows. *Bear Inn* and *Nailcote Hall* are timber-framed; the stone *Ram Hall*, c. 1600, has its original staircase. Plain *Berkswell Hall*, c. 1820, has a confused Italianate entrance; and the decaying *Blind Hall* is said to be haunted.

Bickenhill [7] Warm brick Georgian and early Victorian farms and houses. Some fields have mediaeval ridge and furrow. In the churchyard, a massive sarcophagus to the Thornleys of Marston Hall and Gilbertstone House. *Church* (St. Peter) has a cream-coloured Perpendicular steeple, decorated with a gilded sundial and a one-handed clock, and the red-sandstone body, roofed with rich red tiles, has many square-headed windows. Sturdy Norman north arcade has scalloped capitals; early 14th-century chancel has a Perpendicular arch to the

north chapel, decorated with monsters. Perpendicular screen, at the east end of the north aisle, was probably originally behind the altar, giving access to an east vestry, and the east window is now filled with Hardman-style glass. Two new bungalows replace the school, and *Yew Tree Farm* retains its cross windows. *Church Farm*, with a Victorian Tudor-style front, has a large, pale-brick barn; and, against a mediaeval way, Regency *Church Garth* was the vicarage. Clock Lane has a pretty pair of Victorian Tudor-style *cottages*; and, next to a timber-framed barn, the gabled *Grange Farm* looks Tudor. *Hurdle Hall*, by Birmingham Airport, is now in ruins. Across the railway, the vast National Exhibition Centre has a cluster of dark, flat-roofed *halls*, and a large lake enlivened by a tall fountain laps against the terrace of the 1,000-bed *Birmingham Metropole Hotel*. Approach to the site is Scandinavian in character, as the halls are screened from the hotel by a lavish plantation of trees, which skirts the lake and also occupies a small island.

Bidford-on-Avon [10] Where the Roman Icknield Street crosses the River Avon and the now very busy Stratford–Evesham road. 15th-century *Bidford Bridge*, so narrow that it will only take single file traffic, was partly destroyed during the Civil Wars but retains some of its mediaeval cutwaters. In a large churchyard sloping down to the river, the *church* (St. Laurence) has a tower which resembles a fortress and, considering its position near the bridge, may have been used as such. Dark chancel may be mediaeval, but was so heavily 'restored' in 1886–9 that little of the original stonework remains. Nave and aisles, covered by a single low-pitched roof, were built in 1835, by Joseph Lattimore of Stratford, in an unusual round-arched style, and are well lit by square-headed windows with decaying stucco hood

moulds. Monument to Dorothy Skipworth, d.1655, has a very fine Florentine-style bust in a circular niche surrounded by a garland; three early 19th-century monuments, each with a sarcophagus, are by Davis of Bidford. Rock-faced Victorian *vicarage* with pierced bargeboards. Stone-gabled *Falcon Inn* is where Shakespeare and his friends are reputed to have become so drunk that they slept the night under a nearby tree. *1 The Bank* is smaller, and with brick gables. Barton has both timber-framed and stone houses, including a stone *manor house*, 1663, built for John Payton.

Billesley [10] (near Wilmcote) A hamlet in beautiful undulating country with the lines of houses, deserted by the 15th century, still traceable to the south of the church. Massive, straight-roofed early 17th-century *Billesley Hall* has warm lias walls and brown-stone windows, and nearby is the small *church* (All Saints), shrouded in trees. An ogival bell turret terminates a short tree-lined walk, and thick 12th-century walls surround both nave and apse. Creamwashed interior, with west gallery, box pews and, behind a curtained arch, a large family pew, complete with fireplace. Here lies buried Mr. Knottesford, who ministered till 1859. Living at Alveston, he came across country by family coach, and after morning service ate a cold meal in front of the fire. A rest was followed by evening prayers, at which he delivered a sermon, and then he was taken home. Painted royal arms and white-marble monuments, with draped urns, to the Mills family, who lived at the Hall—the later ones by Hollins.

Bilton [9] On a hillside. Decorated red-sandstone *church* (St. Mark), which has a spire, was restored by Bodley in 1873, when he added the Perpendicular-style north aisle, with fragments of old glass in the

east window, lavishly stencilled the chancel walls and richly painted the chancel roof. Octagonal mediaeval font, on a later base, is well framed by the smooth tower arch, and, in the chancel are a large ogee-arched Easter sepulchre and more fragments of old glass, including a number of heads, a Crucifixion, and a man killing a boar. Late 17th-century communion rail is from Great St. Mary, Cambridge, and the early 17th century organ case from the old chapel of St. John's College, Cambridge, which was rebuilt by George Gilbert Scott in 1863. Nearby is a black-and-white cottage; the green has pieces of an ancient stone cross. Against terraced lawns and yew hedges, brick *Bilton Hill*, built in the early 17th century by Edward Boughton of Lawford, has a full-height entrance staircase. Addison bought the estate in 1711.

Binley *see* Coventry.

Binton [10] On a hill above the treed Avon valley, with the road cut into the ground to give an even gradient. *Church* (St. Peter) was rebuilt, 1875–6, by F. Preedy, as the partly Norman building was in disrepair and had a leaning tower. Blue-lias walls with Cotswold-stone dressings, a well burnt Broseley-tile roof and distinctive blue-enamel clock faces. Foundation stone was laid by Emily Mary, Marchioness of Hertford, to whose estate the village had belonged since about 1700. West window, obviously based on photographs and—unbelievably—by Kempe, is dedicated to Scott of the Antarctic, who married the rector's daughter in 1908. Below the church, *Binton Grange* (formerly the rectory), is 18th century with a 16th-century timber-framed barn; and *The Thatched House*, probably 15th century, is of cruck construction with well weathered wattle-and-daub

Billesley

infill. *Gothic village hall* (formerly the school), 1872, and round-arched *Congregational church*, 1886.

Birdingbury [9] Georgian and modern houses against the road and by the River Leam. *Church* (St. Leonard), a putty-coloured Doric temple, is made less pagan by Victorian Gothic windows, a polygonal sanctuary and a steeply pitched roof. Original box pews, pulpit and west gallery front, complete with royal arms. Sanctuary has an encaustic-tile floor, shafted walls, a painted and gilded vault and rich glass, illustrating the life of Christ. South chancel window, in memory of the Revd. Richard Hickman, M.A., 1901, has red and yellow apples in blue-green trees against a deep-red sky. Churchyard has a severe black-slate table tomb to Sir Theophilus Biddulph, Sixth Baronet, d.1854, whose family lived at the nearby Jacobean-style *Birdingbury Hall.* Elegant stucco-faced *Old Rectory. Railway bridge*, with wide elliptical arches in blue brick, and picturesque disused *station.*

Birmingham* [4] Originally deep in the forest, and possibly settled by people moving up the valleys of the Trent and Tame during the 6th and 7th centuries. The old village centre around the church of St. Martin is on the southern slope of a red-sandstone ridge above the River Rea—stone found useful for the more important buildings. The majority of houses were framed in timber, of which there was a plentiful supply, and stood around the village green on the site of the present Bull Ring, named after a ring in the ground for tethering cattle, and along the road to the river crossing now known as Digbeth. The manor house occupied a

* *The named districts of greater Birmingham are to be found in alphabetical order immediately following this entry on central Birmingham (page 49)*

moated site near the river, the moat linked to that of the parsonage further west at the junction of Edgbaston and Pershore Streets. 14th-century Birmingham, though larger than its neighbours, was still agricultural, but by the 16th century the town was 'echoing with forges' and boasted some 'handsome buildings'. By the 18th century the family estates on the high ground to the north-west were opened up for building, starting with the district around Old Square, and between 1711 and 1725 Thomas Archer's ambitious Baroque church of St. Philip was built on land given by Robert Phillips, to whose name the dedication alludes. The new developments catered for small craftsmen, many moving from 'foul-smelling buildings' in the more congested parts of the town. In 1770, James Brindley's Birmingham Canal was completed, linking the town to the coalfields of the Black Country, almost halving the price of coal and greatly increasing trade. The town continued to grow, and in 1778 the open fields to the north-west of the canal were laid out, to the fashionable gridiron pattern of the time, around Roger Eyken's new chapel of St. Paul. Plots of land were leased to craftsmen speculators, who built attractive three-storey brick terrace houses, some of which survive. At the beginning of the 19th century several dignified classical public buildings were erected in the centre of town, mainly by local architects, and the town was linked by rail to Liverpool in 1837 and to London in 1838, Philip Hardwick's Ionic 'arch' at Curzon Street being the terminus for both lines which arrived by the Rea valley. The introduction of the railways into the heart of the town during the second half of the 19th century necessitated widespread demolition, and the new Italianate railway hotels set a new scale for subsequent redevelopment, especially the rebuilding between 1863

and 1873 of the whole of the north side of Colmore Row to a set cornice height. Two years later Joseph Chamberlain launched his Improvement Scheme which proposed a new street 'as broad as a Parisian boulevard', across the Georgian street pattern, from New Street to the Aston Road but, though it cleared away many rundown properties behind the main street frontages, it also resulted in the demolition of a number of fine Georgian houses including those in Old Square. By 1943 the congestion of traffic in the city centre required major improvements, which resulted in 1971 in a ring road enclosing the central shopping area but not the mother *church* (St. Martin) surrounded by markets at the bottom of the hill. First church about which anything is known was, in the opinion of Rickman, late 13th-century. This was enlarged and in late mediaeval times consisted of a lofty nave and chancel, north and south aisles and a north-west tower and spire. In 1690 the churchwardens 'dressed the church in brick', and in 1781 the spire was partly rebuilt by John Cheshire. In 1853 the brick casing was removed from the tower by P. C. Hardwick, who added the open-air pulpit. Body of the church was entirely rebuilt in 1873–5 by J. A. Chatwin, in the Decorated style with pinnacled exterior and a dark sandstone interior, covered by an open-timber roof similar to that of Westminster Hall. Chatwin was a pupil of Barry and helped him to detail his Palace of Westminster. Three recumbent effigies of the Birmingham family and a fine stained-glass window, 1875–80, by Burne-Jones and William Morris. *Birmingham Gun-Barrel Proof House*, Banbury Street, 1813, by John Horton,

Birmingham manufactories ▷
above left Fawcett Bros.
right Newhall Hill, **Winson Green**
below left and right Argent Works, **Winson Green**

Birmingham churches: St. Paul's and Holy Trinity, **Bordesley**

is a long brick building in the local classical tradition, with a striking centrepiece containing a group of splendid trophies by William Hollins. Smoky, smooth-stone *Curzon Street Goods Station*, 1838, by Philip Hardwick, the original terminus of the London–Birmingham Railway and the Ionic counterpart of the demolished Doric Euston Arch, has massive, unfluted columns fronting a compact booking hall, adjoining a stucco-faced extension, originally the Queen's Hotel. Half hidden by the inner ring road, the R.C. *Church of St. Michael*, New Meeting Street, was first built on this site, as a Unitarian chapel, in 1727. Gutted by fire in the 'Church and King' riots of 1791, it was rebuilt in 1802, with paired Ionic pilasters. High Street,

originally lined with half-timbered houses and used as a cattle market, was the starting place for the London stagecoach. Today the most outstanding buildings are the streamlined *Co-operative* and *Times Furnishing Co. Ltd.*, both built during the 1930s, and the *Rotunda*, a circular office tower by J. A. Roberts. New Street dates from the early 14th century, but all the buildings are post-1800. *Midland Bank*, 1867–9, built, by Edward Holmes, as the head office of the Birmingham and Midland Bank, is a classical palazzo with Greek details; and the *Birmingham Daily Post*, by H. R. Yeoville Thomason, the architect of the Council House, is in his favourite round-arched style. Buff-terracotta 1890s *Newton*

Chambers, a lively design by Essex Goodman and Nicol, retains remnants of a delightful Arts and Crafts coffee house. Temple Street takes its name from an old summer arbour; the Regency *Temple Buildings*, built, by Charles Edge, as a fire station, are an interesting study in recessed planes. Also by Edge, *The Trocadero*, originally built for The Norwich Union Fire Office, has a yellow-glazed Art Nouveau front, the best example of its type in the city. Brick Italian palazzo, 1853, by S. Hemming, was *The Unity Fire Building. 97 New Street*, was built in 1865, by H. R. Yeoville Thomason, as the Masonic Hall, originally with a slate-hung obelisk on the corner, and, closing the vista, the *Town Hall* is modelled on the

The Cathedral and St. James', **Edgbaston**

Temple of Castor and Pollux in the Roman Forum. Architects were J. A. Hansom and E. Welch, who had to stand surety for the building and, in 1834, were declared bankrupt. Interior is of the Georgian assembly-room type with a towering, subtly coloured and gilded organ by Hill. Mendelssohn's 'Elijah' and Elgar's 'Dream of Gerontius' were first performed here. Gothic buff-terracotta *Queen's College Chambers*, Paradise Street, a 1904 refronting by Mansell and Mansell, is now grafted onto an office block. Queen's College, which grew out of a school of medicine and surgery, founded in 1825, was incorporated by royal charter in 1843, and the medical and scientific departments, transferred to

Mason College, developed into Birmingham University. Bold classical *Council House and Art Gallery*, 1874–9 and 1884–5 by H. R. Yeoville Thomason, has a mosaic by Salviati and sculpture portraying Britannia rewarding Birmingham manufacturers. Clock tower, known as 'Big Brum', consciously asserts the strength of local government against its Westminster counterpart. Interior has a grand staircase, beneath a vaguely Moorish dome, leading to an airy suite of reception rooms overlooking a statue of Queen Victoria, by Thomas Brock, unveiled in 1901. *Central Libraries*, 1971, by The John Madin Design Group, are the main group of a civic and cultural centre planned to link the Victorian

Council House to the partly built 1930s Baskerville House. A hollow inverted ziggurat raised on columns, the Reference Library contrasts well with the vertical lines of the Town Hall and frames new views of the surrounding older buildings, including the white-domed *Hall of Memory*. *Chamberlain Memorial* was built by J. H. Chamberlain in 1880, when Joseph Chamberlain was only forty-four. A Portland-stone steeple acting as a fountain, it has a portrait medallion by Woolner. Colmore Row was finally infilled, in the 1820s, with fashionable stucco; *102–6 and 112 Colmore Row*, with *1–6 Bennett's Hill*, are most probably by Charles Edge. Waterloo Street has more examples: *37*, with Temple of the

43

Winds capitals, probably by Rickman and Hutchinson. Corinthian *Midland Bank*, built in 1830, by Rickman and Hutchinson, for the Birmingham Banking Company, has a rounded corner by H. R. Yeoville Thomason; and the round-arched *National Westminster Bank*, the 1869 rebuilding, by John Gibson, of Cockerill's 1833 branch Bank of England, has a cavernous corner entrance and a Greek Doric interior. Samuel Lines, the painter, lived at *3 Temple Row West* and is buried beneath the Egyptian-style pylon in the churchyard opposite. *Lloyds Bank*, Temple Row West, was built, as early as 1862–4, by J. A. Chatwin for *The Birmingham Joint Stock Bank*; in Colmore Row his unbelievably French *Grand Hotel*, 1875, stands at the end of the city's most impressive sequence of Italian palazzi, including *Barclays Bank*, built, in 1867–9, as the head office of the Birmingham and District Bank, and the *Union Club*, 1869, both by H. R. Yeoville Thomason. *Birmingham Cathedral*, consecrated in 1715 as the parish church of St. Philip, is certainly one of the most distinguished buildings of its kind in the country. The first church to be designed by Thomas Archer, a Warwickshire man of Umberslade, who travelled abroad and studied the work of Bernini and Borromini, it is 'a most subtle example of the elusive English Baroque'. West doorway surrounds, with polygonal jambs, show the influence of Borromini, and the west tower, completed in 1725 with the aid of a gift from George I, is a brilliant combination of concave and convex shapes terminating in a dome, topped by a galleried open lantern. Round-arched arcades and panelled balconies. Shallow apse was replaced, in 1883–4, by a magnificent chancel, by J. A. Chatwin, which has giant Corinthian columns; and the fine organ case, originally at the west end, is by Thomas Schwarbrick. Chancel rail is by Jean Tijou

St. Paul's, **Birmingham**

or Robert Bakewell, but the chief ornament of the plain, plastered interior is certainly the splendid series of stained-glass windows around the apse and beneath the tower, designed by Sir Edward Burne-Jones and made by Morris and Co., 1884–97. Burne-Jones, who was born in Bennett's Hill and baptised here on 1 January 1834, filled the large, round-arched windows with vibrant, swirling scenes which complement the classical style he came to admire. Art Nouveau *Scottish Union and National*

Insurance Company, Colmore Row, 1902, by Henman and Cooper, is appropriately of grey granite and the *Eagle Insurance*, 1900, by Lethaby and Ball, has a post-and-beam expression and an originality of detail which are at once both primitive and forward-looking. Though this is the most outstanding building of its period in the city, most of the work of the Arts and Crafts movement is on the Colmore Estate, between Colmore Row and St. Paul's Square, parts of which look like Amsterdam, without the

◁ **Birmingham** Cathedral

Roman Catholic Cathedral, **Birmingham**

also designed the playful *134 Edmund Street*, 1897, the Norman Shaw-influenced *123–31*, originally with elaborate plaster spandrels, and the intriguing *St. Philip's Chambers*, 41–3 Church Street. Virtually styleless *44–5 Great Charles Street*, built in 1895, by A. S. Dixon, for the Guild of Handicrafts, is in the Webb-Lethaby manner of domestic architecture. Alongside the *Birmingham and Fazeley Canal*, 1790, the red-brick *56 Water Street* is a grand manufactory on a round-arched base; Ludgate Hill, leading up to St. Paul's Square, is obviously named after its London counterpart. Blackened stone *Church of St. Paul* has a very fine neo-classical steeple, by Francis Goodwin, and a body built, in 1777–9, by Roger Eykyns. This was the church of Matthew Boulton (whose pew was No. 23), James Watt (who didn't go to church much but held the freehold of pew No. 100), Ralph Heaton, Edward Thomason and many other early manufacturers and merchants who made Birmingham famous. Galleried interior is a revelation. Ionic columns support the smoothest of elliptical ceilings and the altarpiece; a pedimented Venetian window, probably by Samuel Wyatt, has rich painted glass by Francis Egington, depicting 'The Conversion of St. Paul', from the painting by Benjamin West. Francis Egington was originally employed by Matthew Boulton and this window, his best and most renowned work, was universally admired at the time. Monuments include a bust of William Hollins, d.1843, Birmingham's first architect and sculptor of note, by his son Peter. Square retains some of the original brick houses of the 1770s and 80s which, with their columned and pedimented doorways, hint at the world of Mozart and the brothers Adam. Constitution Hill has an interesting collection of 19th-century façades starting at the ogival terracotta tower of *H. B. Sale*, 1896, and progressing past the

canals. From the 1880s, the 18th-century brick terraces gave way to brick chambers, with either terracotta or stone dressings. Frederick Martin's pink *19 Newhall Street*, built, in 1896, for the Bell Edison Company, is the best home-produced terracotta building in the city. Venetian Gothic *98 Edmund Street*, built, by Martin and Chamberlain, for the school board, predates their best essay in the style,

the *College of Arts and Crafts*, Margaret Street, 1881–5, which has even more naturalistic stone carving and a twelve-foot-diameter buff-terracotta panel representing lilies on a lattice. J. H. Chamberlain, chosen by Ruskin as a trustee of St. George's Guild, was a devoted exponent of Ruskin's ideas. Elegant *95 Cornwall Street*, 1901, and the more robust *93*, are both by T. W. F. Newton and Cheatle, who

Birmingham Cathedral: detail of the west window ▷

Birmingham: St. Agatha's, **Small Heath** and St. Paul's Square

round-arched *Hen and Chickens* to a splendid though decaying row of Venetian Gothic *shops*, built in 1881, by J. S. Davis. Brick-and-slate R.C. *Cathedral of St. Chad*, built in 1839–41, by A. W. N. Pugin, originally soared out of the brick-and-slate houses of the gun makers' quarter. Unquestionably one of the major works of one of the most important architects of 19th-century Europe, its style is that of Baltic Germany in the 14th century, but treated starkly, with broad, clear-cut masses. Entrance front has twin steeples, and the ground falls sharply towards the towering apse, influenced by St. Elizabeth's, Marburg. Interior is also Germanic, almost of the hall-church variety, and the effect is of soaring height enhanced by plain,

white walls, slender stone arcades and a richly stencilled roof. Rood screen was removed, in 1967, and many of the original furnishings, which Eastlake praised so highly, have either been broken up or dispersed. Intricately carved dark-wood pulpit, c. 1520, is probably from the abbey of St. Gertrude, Louvain; the lavishly gilded reredos, in the form of a Decorated tomb chest, has a luxuriously cusped arched canopy. Chancel and north chapel windows are by W. Warrington, to Pugin's designs, and the excellent transept window was made by Hardman and Co. in 1868. Marble-and-stainless-steel *Birmingham Post and Mail House*, Colmore Circus, by J. H. D. Madin and Partners, is a remarkable achievement for the mid-1960s,

when the majority of commercial building in the city gave little thought to appearance; but the red-terracotta *General Hospital*, Steelhouse Lane, 1894–7, by William Henman, probably assisted by Thomas Cooper, is now mutilated beyond belief. Cooper was chief assistant to Alfred Waterhouse during the construction of the Natural History Museum, South Kensington, and both buildings, which are in round-arched styles, are dominated by polygonal towers with high-pitched roofs. Joseph Chamberlain's *Corporation Street* emerged piecemeal in a variety of styles. *Victoria Buildings* is French Renaissance with voluptuous bay windows; *Central Chambers*, 1881, by W. H. Ward, has a main gable inspired by the Château de Chambord; and the *New Victoria Hotel*, 1887, by Dempster and Heaton, has giant pilasters. Red-brick-and-buff-terracotta *City Arcade*, c. 1900, by T. W. F. Newton and Cheatle, with details modelled by W. J. Neatby, is a jolly Art Nouveau design with rich, green-glazed shopfronts; and *10 Cherry Street*, 1881–2, by J. L. Ball, is one of Birmingham's first Arts and Crafts buildings, following the work of Philip Webb, who had found a new expression in the English brick versions of classical architecture of the 17th and early 18th centuries. Its primitive, stumpy pilasters and steep triangular pediments predate, by eighteen years, the revolutionary *Eagle Insurance* which he designed with Lethaby and which became a European landmark in the break from Revivalism. Warm-stone *Corporation Square*, by Frederick Gibberd and Partners, has long, low elevations with groups of slit windows; and beyond Old Square, now a traffic island, 1890s *County Buildings*, by Crouch and Butler, has buff-terracotta balcony fronts showing house furnishers and vegetarians, for whom it was originally built. The late but dignified classical *County Court* enhances the ornate, hot-red-terracotta *Victoria Law Courts*, won in competition by Sir Aston Webb and Ingress Bell. Built in 1887–91, in the French style of François I, the principal features create the lively silhouette of a Continental town hall, and the vast entrance, lined with buff terracotta, has large stained-glass windows depicting Warwickshire worthies and Birmingham trades. *Methodist Central Hall* built, in 1903–4, by the local architects, E. and J. A. Harper, is also of red terracotta, but with a tall, stern tower.

Acocks Green & Hay Mills—Birmingham

On the busy Warwick Road, dominated by the Ruskinian pink-and-cream *church* (St. Mary The Virgin), 1866, by J. G. Bland, who designed many Kidderminster carpet factories. Chancel, 1894, by J. A. Chatwin, has an east window of the Crucifixion by Burne-Jones. *Acocks Green County Primary School*, 1908, revelling in open pediments and swags of fruit. *Methodist church*, 1882. *Regency Hay Hall* (Reynolds Tube Co.), Redfern Road, was the home of the Hay family, who had built a 15th-century open hall. A massive roof truss remains, also a timber-framed porch and a solar wing, with 16th-century stone-mullioned windows, and a wall painting. The industrial development of Hay Mills followed the *Warwick and Birmingham Canal*, cut straight and deep in 1799. Brawny *Bulls Head* pub has a clock tower. By the River Cole, the red-brick *Church of St. Cyprian*, 1873–4, was built by Martin and Chamberlain for James Horsfall, against his wire-and cable-making factory.

Aston—Birmingham

The Holte family, here from the 14th to the 19th centuries, built Aston Hall: favourite subject of early 19th-century topographers, but by 1850 its park was already reduced by the railway and by building plots. District of Lozells was laid out and, by 1880, park was hemmed in on all sides by slate-roofed terraces. Recently scene changed again as handsome Georgian vicarage and many terraces made way for curved elevated road hard against the park. Parish was once very large, and the smoky-red-sandstone *church* (St. Peter and St. Paul), on the southern bank of the River Tame, has powerful 15th-century tower with narrow bell openings and spire. Body was rebuilt, 1879–90, by J. A. Chatwin, and is his most magnificent interior. The aim of the donor, John Feeney, proprietor of the 'Birmingham Post', who also gave art galleries to the city, was 'to erect a much larger and more imposing structure, which should preserve the architectural features of the ancient church'. Windows of south chantry are copies of those in the old chancel, but nave arcades are in the architect's favourite 14th-century style, developed with great elaboration in the choir. Absence of a rood screen gives a sense of space and a clear view of the polygonal sanctuary, which has a hammerbeam roof. 14th- and 15th-century effigies: two probably from Maxstoke Priory, and one of Sir Thomas Erdington, whose son built a chantry chapel. Monuments to Holte family include one to Sir Thomas, who built the hall, and another by Westmacott. Monument to Sir John Bridgman, 1726, is by James Gibbs; and Arts and Crafts plaque, 1902, to John Feeney, with little hearts hung on trees, by Sir George Frampton. Facing the church, *Aston Hall*, of mellow red brick, has shaped gables, domed towers and side wings linked by walls to two-storey lodges. Built in 1618–35, probably by Thorpe, who designed Kirby, Wollaton and Longleat and included a plan of Aston in his famous book of drawings, now in the Soane Museum. Classical influence shows especially in spacious, stone-flagged *Entrance Hall*, though this was remodelled in the early 19th century by R. H. Bridgens for James Watt jnr., whose elephant crest is prominent in the frieze. *Small Dining Room* has panelling from house in Old Square which belonged to Dr. Hector, a close friend of Samuel Johnson. Principal rooms are on the first floor, gained by a full-height cantilevered staircase, with pierced strapwork balustrade between the newels (damaged during the Civil War). *Great Dining Room* and *King Charles's Room* are enriched by strapwork ceilings surrounded by high-relief friezes; the former room has a freestone-and-black-touch chimneypiece. Panelled *Long Gallery* has an elaborate ceiling, and the adjoining *bedroom*, furniture used by Victoria and Albert, when they visited Stoneleigh Abbey in 1858 prior to a visit to Aston. The Queen declared 'the hall and park to be now opened as a place of recreation for the people of Birmingham' to find out later that they had not yet been fully purchased. On axis of east front, a metal copy of the *Warwick Vase* by Sir Edward Thomason. Bright-red-brick *Aston Villa Football Ground* sports some shaped gables; originally classical *Holte Hotel* was made Jacobean in 1897, by addition of shaped gable and tower. The best pubs, however, are along the Lich-field Road, where Mitchells and Butlers vie with Ansells on their home ground. Hard red-brick and buff-terracotta *Church Tavern*, with slate spire, retains most of its original interior, as does the bold *Britannia* which overcomes the disadvantages of not being on a corner by having a large full-height bay window to catch the eye. Earlier classical *The Vine* is strikingly painted in two shades of brown; *Golden Cross* is decorated with barley ears and hops. Aston Cross, marked by a classical *cast-iron clock*, 1891, by Arthur Edwards, is dominated by cream-faïence *Ansells Brewery*, very different from the earlier, arched, brick *Fredk. Smith's Maltings*, Lichfield Road, and *Midlands Vinegar Brewery*, Upper Thomas Street. *Aston Manor Post Office*, 1800, is Queen Anne Revival in hot-red brick and terracotta; and *Aston Unionist and Labour Club*, 1907, by A. Gilby Latham, freely classical with octagonal cupola and neglected sign: 'BILLIARDS 16 TABLES'. On the High Street, impressive Jacobean *Bartons Arms* has perhaps the best Victorian pub interior in the city, rich with mahogany fittings, glazed tiling and stained glass. Here stayed many well-known entertainers from the nearby *Aston Hippodrome*, c. 1907, including Charlie Chaplin, who clipped his cane in with the billiards cues. From the *Aston Local Board Offices*, 1880–1, John Bright viewed a mile-long procession and fireworks in his honour. Of the churches *St. Joseph's* (R.C.), is part A. W. Pugin, the *Sacred Heart and St. Margaret Mary's* (R.C.), 1922, by Harrison and Cox, rich Romanesque, and *Christ Church* (Methodist), 1864–5, by James Cranston of Oxford, vigorous Venetian Gothic with a steeple.

Bordesley—Birmingham Originally mediaeval, but now with much industry against the River Rea and the roads to Coventry and Stratford. Of the timber-framed buildings, the remarkably symmetrical *Old Crown*, originally a mansion but now a pub, is reputed to date from 1360, though it is mainly 16th century. The building of the Warwick and Birmingham Canal, in 1799, encouraged workshops, warehouses and brickworks, and by 1810 building had reached as far as Highgate Park. David Cox, the landscape painter, was born in Heath Mill Lane in 1793, the son of a whitesmith and worker in small iron-wares. At the entrance from Deritend is a handsome orange-brick building in the Gothic style, built by J. A. Chatwin, for *Lloyd's Bank*. Round-arched *Church of St. John and St. Basil*, built in 1910, by Arthur Stansfeld Dixon, has a white interior with monolithic columns and a rich apse. In the back streets, Martin and Chamberlain's apsidal *Allcock Street Board School*, 1875, stands against a vast incomplete viaduct; the weathered sandstone *Church of St. Andrew*, built in 1844–6, by R. C. Carpenter, is in the 'Middle Pointed' style favoured by the Ecclesiologists. Notable for its asymmetrical massing, its tower has lost a Rutlandshire spire and the east-window tracery is no longer reticulated. Nearby is the Birmingham City football ground. Well sited on Camp Hill, the pinnacled, golden Bath-stone Trinity Chapel, built in 1820–2, by Francis Goodwin, is an excellent example of Georgian Perpendicular Gothic. Loosely modelled on King's College Chapel, Cambridge, it has a cavernous arched front, which owes much to Peterborough Cathedral, and intricately traceried cast-iron windows. *179 Bradford Street* is a typical 18th-century Birmingham house, though Tuscan doorways were more usual than Ionic. Jacobean-style *Lench's Trust Almshouses*, Ravenhurst Street, built in 1849, by Hornblower and Haylock, now face much waste land. Venetian Gothic *Bordesley Teachers' Training College*, originally built in 1883, by Martin and Chamberlain, as King Edward VI Camp Hill Grammar School for Boys, has been spoilt by later additions; the timber-framed *Stratford House*, built in 1601, for Ambrose Rotton and his wife Bridget, is a typical Warwickshire suburban mansion. Moseley Road has elegant stucco houses, one with an unusually generous round bay; Highgate Place has an Egyptian-style railway bridge with tapering pylons. Highgate Park shelters a bronze *statue of Edward VII* by Albert Toft, exiled from Victoria Square, and, well sited on a ridge, stand the massive *Highgate Hotel*, 1903, the first of the 'Poor Men's Hotels', and Pearson's soaring *Church of St. Alban the Martyr*, 1879–81, its stone-vaulted interior enriched by filigree screens. Adjoining comfortable Queen Anne Revival *Lench's Trust Almshouses*, built in 1879, by J. A. Chatwin, are the earliest known examples of the style in Birmingham.

Bournville—Birmingham In 1878 Richard and George Cadbury decided to move the family chocolate business from the cramped, smoky Bridge Street premises to open country, to the south of Birmingham in the valley of Bournbrook, with the advantages of fresh air and good canal and rail communications. The name Bournville was deliberately coined, as French chocolate enjoyed the highest reputation, and of the first houses, built for key

Aston Hall

Winterbourne, **Edgbaston**

workers, only one remains, in Bournville Lane, superficially resembling the tunnel-back design. In 1895 George Cadbury bought 120 acres adjoining the factory and, after appointing W. Alexander Harvey as his architect, began to develop the Bournville Estate. He wished to improve the living accommodation of factory workers everywhere, but from the outset wanted a mixed community and the proportion of Cadbury employees has remained at less than half. Bournville soon became a magnet for housing reformers, including the Garden City Association, when they were preparing plans for their first new town at Letchworth. *The Green*, a conscious

reconstruction of a traditional village centre, with the public buildings, but no public house, grouped informally around its edges and a copy of a late 16th-century yarn market at its centre, is at its most alluring when carpeted with spring flowers. *Holly Grove and Beech, Elm, Laburnum, Sycamore and Thorn Roads* have compact cottage-style houses, which avoid monotony by the varied use of simple elements such as bay windows and porches, and the well proportioned *church* (St. Francis of Assisi), 1925, is simply Romanesque with good brickwork. Also by Harvey, the *Friends' Meeting House*, 1905, has roof trusses which spring from the floor like mediaeval crucks and the Tudor style *Junior*

Schools, 1902–5, George and Elizabeth Cadbury's gift to the village, with classrooms designed to enforce a maximum of forty-five pupils per class, are dominated by a massive entrance tower supporting a green copper lantern housing a carillon of forty-eight bells. *Ruskin Hall*, 1905, is similar; the *Day-Continuation Schools*, 1925, by S. A. Wilmot, show Lutyens' influence. 15th-century timber-framed *Selly Manor House*, originally about a mile nearer Selly Oak, and the cruck-construction *Minworth Greaves Manor*, originally on the Kingsbury Road, were moved to help the village character, as the half-timbered *shops*, *pavilion* and early *factory* are far from mediaeval in character.

Bournville details

Edgbaston details

Edgbaston—Birmingham   A fashionable inner suburb world-famous for its County Cricket Ground. Elegant stucco houses, office towers along the Hagley Road, and the University and Queen Elizabeth Hospital to the south. There does not seem to have been a rural village as such, but a scattering of red-brick farms and cottages, most thickly grouped around the Harborne Road crossing of Chad Brook, and though Edgbaston is less than three-quarters of a mile from the city centre it remained quite rural till early in the 19th century. Parish was originally part of the chapelry of Harborne, from which it is divided by Chad Brook. On high ground against the manor house, to which it presumably owes its foundation, the red-sandstone *church* (St. Bartholomew), retains its modest character, though the only mediaeval pieces are parts of the north and west walls and the lower courses of the tower. Reconstructed after Civil War damage and in 1810, when the north arcade was removed and the body covered by a single-span roof. South aisle, added in 1850, by F. W. Fiddian, has a dainty Perpendicular arcade, copied, though not exactly, by J. A. Chatwin, when he rebuilt the north arcade in 1885. At the same time he built the chancel and chapels and in 1889, the outer south aisle. The main east window is a combination of the pre-1885 ones, to avoid altering the 1850 glass, and the one in the north chancel aisle, glazed with an Ascension, was originally inserted by F. W. Fiddian high above the altar. Finely jointed pink-sandstone walls display impressive 18th- and early 19th-century marble monuments, including an architectural one to Sir Richard Gough, d.1727, one to Lord Calthorpe, d.1798, by King and Sons of Bath, a Grecian one to Frances, daughter of Gen. Carpenter, d.1827, showing the influence of Soane, and three by William Hollins, one with a bust

and one with a weeping tree in an urn. The other with a lifelike snake twined around a stick and a sprig of foxglove, is in memory of William Withering, a member of the celebrated Lunar Society, who lived at nearby Edgbaston Hall and is best known for his 'Account of the Foxglove', 1785. A classic of medical literature, it gave a full account of his measured use of digitalis in the treatment of heart disease. Brick *Edgbaston Hall*, rebuilt in 1717, for Sir Richard Gough, stands in extensive grounds descending to a pool, probably formed in the 15th century for Friday fish, and the estate of 1,500 acres covers most of Edgbaston. When, in 1815, the Worcester and Birmingham Canal was cut, Sir Henry Gough did not allow industry along its banks and, as his estate became a retreat for rich manufacturers, his leases precluded any commercial or dense residential development. Many of the early houses were of brick. By 1824 building had spread from Islington and Five Ways to *97–107 Hagley Road*, the best surviving stucco façade in Birmingham, and along the eastern side of Calthorpe Road. In Vicarage Road there was just the existing former *vicarage* and, though Carpenter Road did not have a single house, Wellington Road, cut straight and wide from the church to the Bristol Road had tall semis at its busy end. More ambitious structures followed, mostly of stucco, which continued well into the 1870s; houses often stood in extensive grounds. *Botanical Gardens*, planned by J. C. Loudon, whose wife was a native of Birmingham, has humid glasshouses including a lily house, built in 1854, to accommodate the giant Amazon water lily given by Sir Joseph Paxton. A miniature Crystal Palace, the group faces south over a cast-iron bandstand and a most convincing rock garden. *Ash Grove*, 12 Vicarage Road, has a superb cast-iron pergola; *Camden Lodge*, 107

Harborne Road, is in the severe, linear Greek Doric style of Charles Edge, who lived at Gothic Cottage on the other side of Vicarage Road. High Victorian Gothic *Ferndale*, 1868, shows the influence of Butterfield, especially in the dormers; and the Jacobethan *Stafford House*, built for Branson and Gwyther, the large railway contractors, has elaborate strapwork crestings and a quaint entrance screen. *Highfield Gate*, 81 Harborne Road, is delicately Italianate, with a chimney on each corner, showing the influence of Barry; *21 Highfield Road*, built in 1961, by Norrish and Stainton as their own offices, has a neatly glazed upper floor. *Church of St. George*, built in 1836–8, by J. J. Scholes, was originally a simple, symmetrical structure, in the economical Early English style and with four tall pinnacles. Interior had galleries behind the most slender arcades, one of which survives, and there is a panelled plaster ceiling. Chancel, 1856, by Charles Edge. In 1884–5 a new church, of almost cathedral scale, was added by J. A. Chatwin in a more substantial version of the same style. *35 Calthorpe Road*, c. 1828, is an unusual Greek design with the upper storey expressed as an attic; and the impressive *Ashley House*, next door, has Graeco-Egyptian touches. Venetian Gothic *Hampden Villa*, 19 Greenfield Crescent, built, c. 1875, by J. H. Chamberlain for Jonathan Pratt, Secretary of the Royal Birmingham Society of Artists, has rich naturalistic stone carving and unusually bracketed gables. Stucco Italianate *Needwood* and *Beechwood*, 38 and 39 Frederick Road, were built in 1850, by J. A. Chatwin before he entered Barry's office. *The Round House*, 16 St. James' Road, originally thatched and considerably extended, was built for Joseph Luckcocks, the brother of James, a rich button manufacturer interested in the picturesque; and *West House*, superbly sited on a hillside,

is picturesque Regency with shades of early Nash. Pink-sandstone *Church of St. James* was built in 1852, by S. S. Teulon, for the Gough Calthorpe family, for whom he also designed the exciting Elvetham Hall, Hants, and has a large, patterned tile roof echoing the slope of the site. Splendid portico to *The Cedars*, 74 Wellington Road, has coupled Tuscan columns supporting a triglyph frieze, with trophies and ox skulls; *Woodfield*, next door, has a similar though simpler portico and a steeply roofed, polychromatic coachhouse. The first house in the district, it was built on an extensive piece of ground leased to Josiah Richards, patentee of oriental amulets, jeweller, glass cutter, toy maker and dealer in corals, cornelian beads etc. Handsome *Field Gate*, 61 Wellington Road, c. 1828, has full-height pilasters with palmetto capitals; *Lansdowne*, next door, stands on an undercroft over the carriageway. Original building was considerably extended in the 1870s for J. H. Shorthouse, author of 'John Inglesant'. *The Woodlands*, c. 1828, with a fine pediment supported by rich consoles, is followed by new houses on the site of J. A. Chatwin's house, and opposite is the impressive *Beech Mount*, c. 1847, a grand Corinthian palazzo. *Convent of the Holy Child Jesus* (originally Hallfield) was built, c. 1861, most likely by H. R. Yeoville Thomason, for Samuel Messenger, chandler and lamp manufacturer. Though Thomason admired Wren, there are Greek touches, evidence of his training with Charles Edge. Oval staircase enclosure and first-floor gallery with sculptured lunettes. Ampton Road has a picturesque group of *estate cottages* and the

Edgbaston:
far left the Waterworks
left the Monument
opposite the Botanical Gardens

robust *Fairlight*, 8 Ampton Road, is surely by Thomason, who lived nearby. Tudor-style *church schools* and later master's house. Delicately detailed Venetian Gothic *Shenstone House*, 12 Ampton Road, built in 1858, by J. H. Chamberlain, shuns sham stucco to follow Ruskin's 'Lamp of Truth'. Chosen by Ruskin himself as trustee of St. George's Guild, Chamberlain was to design Birmingham School of Art, many Board schools and a number of Edgbaston's largest houses. Simple *4* and *6 Carpenter Road*, the best example of the Regency style in the city, have delicate Oriental porches and the earlier, sandstone-faced *Royal School for Deaf Children* has an impressive portico and fine plaster ceilings. University halls of residence are well grouped around an artificial lake to the north of Edgbaston Park Road. Two superb Arts and Crafts houses are the roughcast *Garth House*, 1901, by W. H. Bidlake, with colourful rose gardens, and the mellow brick *Winterbourne*, 1903, by J. L. Ball, with simple triangular gables. *King Edward VI Grammar School* was built in 1940, when the school moved from Barry's building in New Street with the vaulted upper corridor, now a war memorial *chapel*. Domed Byzantine-style University buildings, which radiate around the tall Siena-inspired campanile, known as *Chamberlain Tower*, were built in the early 1900s, by Sir Aston Webb and Ingress Bell, and have scenes by Anning Bell. Ponderous redbrick quad is enlivened by the *Staff House*, built 1961–2, by Casson Conder and Partners, with elegant, boldly outlined windows. Manorhouse *Union* by H. W. Hobbiss faces Robert Atkinson's bulky *Barber Institute*, housing the University art collection, and an equestrian statue of George I, attributed to J. van Ost the elder, is from Grattan Bridge, Dublin. Post-war buildings, in all the modern idioms, include the organic *Faculty of Commerce and*

Social Science, 1965, by Howell, Killick, Partridge and Amis; the elegant *Department of Education*, 1968, by Casson Conder and Partners; and Arup Associates' industrial *Mining Minerals and Metallurgy*, 1966. Across the narrow hump-backed canal and railway bridge, the buff-brick 1930s *Queen Elizabeth Hospital*, by Lanchester and Lodge, has a Cubist clock tower. To the south, all that can be seen of the timber *Metchley Roman Camps*, c. A.D. 50–60, is a reconstructed corner severely damaged by vandals. Georgian *Mass House*, Pritchetts Road, has good plum coloured brickwork and Farquhar Road has some impressive Arts and Crafts houses, notably the roughcast *17* by the younger Martin, of Harborne Tenants' Estate fame, for himself. Yateley Road has steeply gabled Arts and Crafts houses by Herbert T. Buckland, and the Gothic *Berrow Court*, by Martin and Chamberlain, has panelled entrance and staircase halls, with fine naturalistic carving and marquetry. Many-gabled *White Swan* is well known for its skittle alley and its ghost! In Regency times John Wentworth, a man of property, shot himself and his dog here, driven mad with grief, for his mistress had just died in his arms after an accident on Harborne Hill. Queen Anne Revival *20 Woodbourne Road*, for John Barnsley the builder, owes much to Norman Shaw. Unassuming *17* and *19 Rotton Park Road* by J. L. Ball, No. 17 for himself, have cottage casements. J. A. Chatwin's hard Gothic *Church of St. Augustine*, 1868, has a tall steeple, 1876, and a richly gilded apse and the Romanesque brick and tile *Church of St. Germain*, City Road, by E. F. Reynolds, claims to be the only church in the country to have been built during the First World War. *Church of the Birmingham Oratory*, Hagley Road, originally built, c. 1852, for Cardinal Newman and his congregation, was enlarged in 1858 and 1861 in the Romanesque style by John

Hungerford Pollen; and the existing Chapel of St. Philip, with its rounded apse and paintings by the architect, dates from this time. Church, rebuilt, in 1903 by E. Dorian Webb with a copper dome, has much marble and mosaic. Brick *Oratory House*, a dignified palazzo, built in 1852, by Terence Flanagan, contains a remarkable Grecian refectory; and, against the pavement, Clutton's former *Oratory School* has a solid ground floor pierced only by the entrance to the church, through a quiet cloister. Beyond white office towers the classic dark-glazed *Neville House*, 1976, by D. Hickman of The John Madin Design Group, stands on a rough granite terrace; and at Five Ways the same architects' slightly earlier *Metropolitan House* tower is all faceted brick and reflective glass.

Erdington—Birmingham

A red-brick suburb on the red-sandstone cliffs of Gravelly Hill above the River Tame, now dominated by cooling towers and the largest interchange in Europe, 'Spaghetti Junction', connecting Birmingham to the M6. In Anglo-Saxon times it was held by Edwin, grandson of Leofric, and the fortified manor house, which stood above the river by Bromford Bridge, was owned, from 1647, by the Holtes of Aston. A hamlet grew up around the Sutton Coldfield road, with stucco-faced houses on Gravelly Hill, and expanded rapidly, following the railway of 1862. Disappointing High Street, by-passed in the 1930s, has Rickman's Gothic *church* (St. Barnabas), built in 1824, two years later than St. George's, with identical cast-iron window and door tracery. Cosy brick *Almshouses*, 1930, replace those provided by Sir Thomas Holte, in 1655–6, and the *Free Library*, 1906–7, by J. P. Osborne, is free Queen Anne. Pretty stucco *United Reformed Church* has three stepped lancets closing an avenue of tall trees and the ambitious red-sandstone R.C. *Church of St. Thomas and St. Edmund* was built in 1848–50, by Charles Hansom, the designer of the cab and Birmingham's classical Town Hall. Josiah Mason's Orphanage, 1863, is commemorated by a bronze bust of the pen manufacturer on a traffic island; and the *Taylor Memorial House*, formerly The Grange, was, from 1877, the home of Sir Benjamin Stone, photographer, politician and manufacturer. Long hall was once decorated with 'curios from all climes', and the wings of a huge albatross hung over the staircase. Superbly sited in a rolling park, the many-gabled *Pype Hayes Hall* is timber-framed behind stucco. The Birmingham and Fazeley Canal, 1790, which brought goods from Liverpool and Manchester and grain from Oxfordshire, has a pretty Gothic house. Late 1960s *Castle Vale* estate, housing 20,000 people, on the old Castle Bromwich Aerodrome, is flat and treeless; and the *Tyburn Road* has inter-war ribbon development with large factories, such as Fort Dunlop, built on the flood plain of the River Tame. White-painted *Rookery*, 1794, has the earliest plate glass in the Midlands, c. 1820, and the imposing *Highcroft Hall Mental Hospital*, built in 1869, a large, foreign Gothic steeple. Homely Queen Anne-style *Aston Union Cottage Homes*, built in 1900, by Franklin Cross and Nichols, cluster around a green with a clock tower; and the 1860s *Witton Cemetery* has sandstone chapels with steeples. Amid trees, 1830s Tudor-style *St. Mary's College*, mainly by Joseph Potter, has a chapel, extended and decorated in 1837, by A. W. Pugin, who incorporated 15th-century Flemish work in the reredos and a 17th-century communion rail from Louvain. Pugin, introduced to the College by the Earl of Shrewsbury, became Professor of Ecclesiastical Antiquities and created the theological library and mediaeval museum. Early furniture by Pugin,

Neville House, **Edgbaston**

who also designed the canopy on the terrace and the gatehouses.

Hall Green—Birmingham Inter-war houses around the River Cole and the Stratford Road with the white-painted 1930s *Petersfield Court* risking rounded corner windows and a flat roof. The Hall Green was opposite the hall occupied by Job Marston, who, when he died in 1701, left both the green and money for the erection of a chapel-at-ease to Yardley, as he considered the cross-country journey too great. Originally known as Job Marston's Chapel, the brick *church* (The Ascension) was built in 1704, possibly by William Wilson. The most distinctive Queen Anne church in the county, its body is divided by stone pilasters and its octagonal belfry crowned by a dome. Light, clear-glazed nave and sympathetic 1860 transepts and chancel. Gallery, box pews, large hatchment and early 19th-century royal arms.

Handsworth—Birmingham Originally scattered across a valley between woodland, above the River Tame, and a windswept heath. Later Matthew Boulton transformed the heath into a landscape garden around his famous Soho Manufactory, built in 1761–4, against Hockley Brook. Designs for Soho silver were supplied by some of the most famous names of the day, including the Adam brothers, Chambers and Flaxman; and in 1776 Boulton and James Watt set up the first steam engine in the Midlands. Though the famous workshop has gone, Boulton's house survives, with the many elegant terraces which formed the first recognisable village. Part of the valley became a park, which has an artificial lake reflecting the church, and Handsworth Wood shelters spacious Arts and Crafts houses converted into flats. First stone *church* (St. Mary) was built about 1160 with a tower at the east end,

59

the lower stage of which remains. In the 14th century this building was extended northwards, and in the 15th century the tower was built up in golden limestone. Increase in population, following the establishment of the Soho Manufactory, resulted in 1820 in the addition, by William Hollins, of the broad Gothic transept, once filled with galleries and pews. Watt Chapel, built five years later, balances the 15th-century Wyrly Chapel on the other side of the chancel. The architect first selected was William Bridgens, employed by James Watt jnr. to restore Aston Hall, but the work was executed by William and Peter Hollins under the direction of Thomas Rickman. An elegant stone-vaulted shrine to protect the white-marble sculpture of Watt by Sir Francis Chantrey; the lighting was arranged to enhance the mood of the seated figure engrossed in a design. Dark nave and aisles built in 1876–8, by J. A. Chatwin. Lighter chancel with fine mural monuments to Matthew Boulton, 1809, by Flaxman, William Murdock, 1839, by Chantrey, and others by William and Peter Hollins and E. H. Baily. Francis Eginton, the glass painter, and William Booth, the notorious forger, are buried in the churchyard. Picturesque *verger's house*, by Edge. *84*, *133* and *135 Handsworth Wood Road* are consciously Arts and Crafts, and *The Anchorage*, 1888, by Joseph Crouch and Edmund Butler has a superb central hall. *60* is a winning neo-Georgian piece, *97* and *99* are Venetian Gothic and the originally thatched *Browne's Green Lodge*, c. 1810, is a simple cottage orné. Late 18th-century *Hawthorn House* has an Ionic entrance hall with classical reliefs and a colourful painted-glass window, 1862, with figures of trade, commerce and wealth. Cruck *Old Town Hall*, and Bidlake's serene *Church of St. Andrew*, 1907, create a village centre and, on high ground against Sandwell Park, Bidlake's dainty

cemetery chapel is stone vaulted. *New Inns* has a luxurious ballroom, opened by Edward VII, and the imposing terracotta *Red Lion*, Soho Road, has a superb bar back. Georgian *Union Row* ends against a late 18th-century chapel with an awkward Victorian façade; and, standing high above Hockley Brook, the crumbling sandstone *Church of St. Michael*, 1852–5, by W. Bourne, carries a fine steeple. Slate-faced *Soho House*, the home of Matthew Boulton, and almost certainly by James Wyatt, has giant Ionic pilasters and elegant interiors. Early 1920s *Supreme Works*, by H. W. Hobbiss, is decorated with William Bloye's version of the Mycenae lions and column for the goldsmith J. H. Wynn. Georgian *20–46 Hamstead Road* has been ravaged by Charleville Road and ugly bay windows. J. L. Ball's bold brick *Carnegie Infant Welfare Institute* rides on round arches into Hunter's Hill, crowned by Pugin's modest *Convent of Our Lady of Mercy*. Built in 1840–5, it has windows by John Hardman, the founder, whose daughter was superioress. *Hardman's house*, opposite, though altered and extended by Pugin, is still recognisably Regency. *The Limes* has intriguing Doric porches with exaggerated perspective. Decaying *Barker Street*, the only surviving Regency terraced street in the city, is being insensitively 'improved'.

Harborne—Birmingham

Brick, and on high ground separated from the city by the Chad Brook valley and bosky 19th-century Edgbaston, which protected it from commercial development. Against large trees and a variety of memorials the 15th-century redsandstone tower of the *church* (St. Peter) is the only part to have survived the 1867 rebuilding, by H. R. Yeoville Thomason, in an angular Gothic style. Light nave has vigorous capitals; apsidal chancel with glass in memory of David Cox,

the landscape painter, who lived from 1841 to 1859 at *Greenfield House*, and is buried in the churchyard. Regency *Harborne Hall*, now a convent, is overpowered by Gothic extensions by John Henry Chamberlain for Joseph Chamberlain's daughter, including a gaunt gabled tower and a spired billiard room with naturalistic decoration. Vast central hall with galleries incorporating cast-iron sunflowers. 18th-century *Bishop's Croft*, the residence of the Lord Bishop of Birmingham, has Arts and Crafts plasterwork, panelling and metalwork by A. S. Dixon, who also designed the free-standing classical chapel, 1923. Elliptically arched brick *Church House*, 1965, carries a diocesan arms by D. Hickman. Albert Road has elegant Regency houses built before the road, and an Italianate pair has towers, like Osborne, I. O. W. Greenfield and Vivian Roads are classical and Gothic; Regency *St. Mary's Retreat*, built for the Master of the Birmingham Mint, has a prettily pinnacled cast-iron vinery. Stucco Gothic *Metchley Abbey* and brick 1930 *Bluecoat School*. Brick Gothic *Board School*, 1880–1, has a French steeple and *South Street* (originally Josiah Street), *Bull Street* and *York Street*, built during the 1850s, by Josiah Bull York of Coleshill, have modest classical terraces. Decisive *Methodist chapel*, beneath a sharp slatehung spire, has a cosy Arts and Crafts extension by A. Harrison. Closing the vista along High Street, *The Junction*, 1903, is a robust gin palace with acid-etched windows and the orange-brick *Lloyds Bank*, 1906, is Queen Anne Revival. *Library*, originally the Masonic Hall, 1890, is probably by A. B. Phipson, who lived in Metchley Lane. *Police station*, originally the free charity school, was partly rebuilt in 1821, and the *Original Police Station* near the corner of Serpentine Road has a round archway leading to cells. *Vine Terrace* was originally occupied by nailmakers, and the *Institute*, Station Road, has a foundation stone laid by Henry Irving in 1879. Pioneer *Harborne Tenants' Estate*, of pebble dashed and brick houses built, c. 1908, by Frederick Martin, is quite arcadian.

King's Heath—Birmingham Built up around the Alcester Road, following the opening, as early as 1840, of the Birmingham–Gloucester Railway, and now surrounded by 20th-century semis. A hint of what the countryside was like lingers around Cock Moors Woods, Chinn Brook and the Stratford-on-Avon Canal, 1796, which just south of Brandwood End Cemetery enters a long tunnel. Brickworks existed at both Mill Pool Hill and Dawberry Fields, and presumably a limekiln in Limekiln Lane. Set in a churchyard in the busy shopping street, the long sandstone *church* (All Saints), built in 1859, by F. Preedy, has a decisive steeple with deep belfry openings. Clear-glazed, stone-paved interior is severely Anglican. Parcel-gilt iron-filigree screen. Chancel arcade has splendid carved birds, pomegranates and grapes, and the intricately carved reredos frames a hard mosaic of the Deposition. By contrast, the R.C. *Church of St. Dunstan*, built in 1972, by Laurence Williams, is appropriately Continental. An ascending spiral of buff brickwork culminates in a slender tower, on which a large figure of Christ, by John Poole, is lit from above. Exquisite chunky-glass stations of the Cross glow beneath the gallery. Impressive stone-fronted *Red Lion*, Vicarage Road, built in 1903–4, by C. E. Bateman, is reminiscent of the 17th-century Dolphin Inn, Norwich. *Cartland Road*, flanked by stone-mullioned brick houses by Bateman, has another house possibly by the same architect. Part-half-timbered *247* and *249 Vicarage Road* and the Early-Georgian-style *310* may also be his work. Cream-painted, Georgian-

tradition *Horseshoe* probably dates from the early years of the adjacent canal, when the main road was just a country lane, and *Bells Farm*, Bells Lane, refronted in brick in 1661, is basically timber-framed.

King's Norton—Birmingham On a wooded hill above the green Rea valley, a soaring sandstone steeple rises out of trees. Worcester–Birmingham Canal, opened in 1815, brought a ring of manufactories, including Nettlefold and Chamberlain, who made screws, and Heaton, who minted coins, notably the 1874–82 pennies, with an 'H' under the date, which are now collector's pieces. Facing the village green, the timber-framed *Saracen's Head Inn* is where Henrietta Maria slept on her way to meet Charles I at Edge Hill. Beyond a fine Corinthian monument to the Middlemore family, the *church* (St. Nicholas) has an exceptional 15th-century steeple, only bettered, in Warwickshire, by that of St. Michael's, Coventry. Of the Norman church one window survives, reset in the north wall of the 13th- and 14th-century chancel, which has large ballflower decoration around the arch and a group of five lancets above the altar, glazed with an impressive Crucifixion, in the style of Kempe. 13th- and 14th-century nave arcades, 17th-century clerestory and Victorian hammerbeam roof. Transverse south aisle roofs are 17th century. Tall tower arch opens into an even taller tower space, lit by a high clear-glazed window and furnished with a pink-and-white-alabaster slab incised with the figures of Humfrie and Martha Littleton, of Groveley, 1588, recumbent effigies of Sir Richard Grevis, 1632, and his wife, of Moseley Hall, and several hatchments. Timber-framed early 15th-century *Old Grammar School*, originally the priest's house, is where John Baskerville developed his love for calligraphy and taught writing, after doing duty as a foot-

man at the rectory. Gothic *Kings Norton County Primary School*, 1878, has a Flemish extension with hot-red-terracotta gables. Lifford Lane crosses the Worcester and Birmingham Canal, the River Rea and the Stratford-upon-Avon Canal, all within the space of a quarter of a mile; where the canals meet, there is an unusual guillotine lock. River flows through the grounds of 17th-century *Lifford Hall*, and beyond is a reservoir and a tree-lined river walk. *Primrose Hill Farm* is partly timber-framed. Where the Worcester and Birmingham Canal passes through the one-and-a-half-mile *Wasthill Tunnel*, the only reminder that Hawkesley Hall once crowned the hill, is an avenue of elms, now dead.

Ladywood—Birmingham Originally with elegant stucco-faced houses, as in adjacent Edgbaston, some of which survive. Victorian brick terraces, which engulfed the area, were swept away by the comprehensive redevelopment of the 1950s, leaving a mixture of tall flats and long terraces. Red-sandstone *church* (St. John the Evangelist), built in 1854, by S. S. Teulon, has uninspired 1881 extensions by J. A. Chatwin. Simple, well-proportioned tower provides a valuable focal point from both Ladywood Middleway and Monument Road, the latter on the line of the Roman Icknield Street. *Monument*, a ninety-six-foot-high battlemented brick tower, built in 1758, for John Perrot, to enable him to view his estate and entertain his friends, has a superb Rococo Gothic ceiling in the top room and *Edgbaston Pumping Station*, built c. 1870, by Martin and Chamberlain, has a slender chimney dressed as a Venetian tower. *Rotton Park Reservoir*, constructed in 1825–9, by Thomas Telford, as a water supply for the improved Birmingham Canal, is also used for sailing. 1960s *Chamberlain Gardens*, by the C.A.'s Department, is certainly the most

Birmingham canal scenes

attractive part of the new Lady-
wood. J. R. R. Tolkien, author of
'The Hobbit', lived where Beaufort
Road turned into the Hagley Road.
Jacobean-style *Lench's Trust Alms-
houses*, built in 1859, by Horn-
blower and Haylock, now face
Ladywood Middleway and the
Public Works Dept., Sheepcote
Street, occupies a functional semi-
circle of stables for canal horses,
half hidden by later lodges.

**Moseley & Balsall Heath—Bir-
mingham** Moseley, a hamlet on
the Alcester road, developed after
the opening of a railway station, in
1867, into a spacious High Victorian suburb, now occupied by

students. Western half, separated
from the village by the grounds of
Moseley Hall, acquired many fine
Arts and Crafts houses, following
the cutting of Salisbury Road at the
turn of the century, and still retains
much open space, including Highbury and Cannon Hill Parks and
the County Cricket Ground in the
valley of the River Rea. Balsall
Heath, with some elegant early Victorian houses, but mostly crammed
with undistinguished mid-Victorian terraces, occasionally picked
out in bright colours, is now the
city's Asian quarter. *Church* (St.
Mary), is mainly by J. A. and P. B.
Chatwin, but retains an early 16th-
century tower and two wall monu-

ments by William and Peter Hollins. Cast-iron churchyard gates are
possibly by Rickman, who in 1823–4
altered a structure of 1780. Moseley Road has unusual stucco-faced
houses, William Hale's instructive
Venetian Gothic *Institute*, Cossins
and Peacock's elliptically arched
Library, and a stodgy classical *School
of Art*, by W. H. Bidlake. *Church of
St. Anne*, by F. Preedy, can be seen
from across the river valley.
Bidlake's Tudor-style *Amesbury
Court* was built around a large hall,
housing an organ; and his *38 Amesbury Road* has a lush golden-stone
doorway. Severely handsome *Moseley Hall Hospital*, built in 1799, for
John Taylor, the button maker

and banker, stands on the site of a larger mansion, destroyed in the riots of 1791, and an earlier timber-framed structure. It was held from the time of the Conquest by the Grevis family, the last member of which came before Hutton in the Court of Requests, in 1786, as a poor debtor. Grounds, of which Moseley Private Park was part, are said to have been laid out by Repton; they have an 18th-century *dovecote*. Here lived J. Cadbury, who moved to newly built Jacobean *Uffculme*. Ponderous Gothic *Highbury Hall*, built in 1879–80, by J. H. Chamberlain for Joseph Chamberlain, has naturalistic stone carving, a vast hall and a richly panelled study. Newton and Cheatle's Arts and Crafts *Fighting Cocks* has blue-green-glazed bars. Collegiate *Moseley Boys' County Grammar School* was built in 1855–6 for Spring Hill Congregational College. First opened in 1830, in the house of George Storer Mansfield, the college moved to Oxford in 1885 and became Mansfield College.

Northfield & Longbridge—Birmingham

Above the River Rea and behind the Bristol Road shopping area, where Victoria Common is now a park. Longbridge sprang up around the now large-scale Austin Motor Works, opened in 1905. Dark, tranquil *church* (St. Laurence) has a superb 13th-century chancel, with triple lancet windows, a north aisle, built in 1900, by G. F. Bodley, a pulpit incorporating some 15th-century woodwork from the former screen and, over the tower arch, a painted Hanoverian arms. Cream-painted *Great Stone Inn* is named after a large glacial stone in the adjoining sandstone *pound*. Road winds its way down to the river between high retaining walls, the last of the nailers' cottages, with a pigeon loft, and *Northfield Schools*, built in 1837, with Gothic cast-iron tracery. Above a lake on Griffins Brook, the

stucco *manor house* has timber-framed bay windows, added for George Cadbury, who lived here from 1894. Elaborate Jacobean-style staircase, and a large carved fireplace inscribed 'East, West, Hame's Best'—though Cadbury called the house a barn, and left it to the city. Classical *Royal Orthopaedic Hospital* and *The Woodlands* were built as houses; the latter was converted into an open-air hospital, for the Birmingham Cripples' Union, by George Cadbury, who came here every Sunday evening, armed with bars of chocolate for all, to spend a little time with every patient. Golden-stone *Traveller's Rest* was built in 1925, by Batemans, who followed up, in 1929, with the *Black Horse*, a vast timber-framed manor house with a Cotswold-stone roof.

Perry Barr & Kingstanding

see Birmingham. Where the Romans built a bridge to carry their Icknield Street over the River Tame, on the line of an ancient British saltway. Walsall Road was constructed as a turnpike, in c. 1830; and since the 1920s the area has been rapidly built up, leaving only Perry Park and Playing Fields, and the cement quarries. Kingstanding, which has a hillock thrown up by soldiers with spades, upon which King Charles stood, during the Civil War, is the largest pre-war municipal estate in the city, with wide roads and verges. Pinnacled, smooth-red-sandstone *church* (St. John the Evangelist) was built in 1831–3, by John Gough, who is buried beneath the altar. Goughs lived at now demolished Perry Hall, built on the left bank of the river for Sir William Stanford, a Catholic judge in the reign of Queen Mary. A gabled 16th-century building, with the addition of an 1840s porch, by S. S. Teulon, carried on an arch across the moat. Goughs also built the now disused early 18th-century river bridge, known locally as the 'zig-zag' bridge because of the line of its

parapets; and the 1930s *Boar's Head* has a gilded boar's head from the Gough arms, on a pole. Brick *Church of St. Matthew*, built in 1964, by Maguire and Murray, ascends in a spiral from a cosy baptistry to a lofty top-lit sanctuary; and the *R.C. Convent of Mercy, Old Oscott*, opened as Oscott College in 1794, occupies a plain 18th-century house, where Cardinal Newman founded the English branch of the Oratorians. *Odeon Cinema*, Kingstanding, a super piece of 1930s streamlining, has ivory faïence, highlighted by crackling neon; and the typical 1930s ribbon development of the Walsall Road is punctuated by a neo-classical pub, an early crematorium and another massive cinema.

Quinton—Birmingham

Inter-war semis and, against the motorway slip road, simple yellow-sandstone *Christ Church* with lancets and a bell turret. Plastered interior has worn, richly coloured glass, 1860s and 1870s, by Alex Gibbs, and the more domestic west entrance, added in 1952, by G. H. While, has a painting, 'The Sower', by Harry S. Sands. Robust cast-iron gate piers. At the lower end of the High Street, mullioned 'The Cottage', one of the few bits of the original village.

Saltley & Ward End—Birmingham

River Rea and the railway are surrounded by goods yards and gas works. Crumbling sandstone *church* (St. Saviour), built in 1849–50, by R. C. Hussey, is in the Perpendicular style and has a tall tower which once had a spire. *Adderley Park*, Birmingham's first public park, was presented to the corporation in 1856 by Charles Bowyer Adderley, first Baron Norton, whose now demolished library and museum, built in 1855, by G. E. Street, shared with Oxford Museum the honour of being the first Gothic Revival museum in the country. Ferry's *St. Peter's College*, built in

1847–52, is modest, and has a simple round-arched chapel by J. L. Ball. Dark 1930s Romanesque *Church of Our Lady of the Rosary and St. Teresa of Lisieux*, by G. Drysdale, is enriched by a mosaic apse and good woodwork. The area around Great Lister Street, which began as a smart early 19th-century suburb, was comprehensively redeveloped during the early 1950s, and some of the earliest high blocks, by S. N. Cooke and Partners, are of brick with chunky radiating arms. Brick *Church of St. Matthew*, built in 1839–40, by William Thomas of Leamington, is a Gothic preaching box, named by the first vicar 'St. Matthew in the Wilderness'. Pink-terracotta *Public Library*, has a tower and sculpture; classical *Public Baths* have jolly, open turrets. *Anglican Convent of the Incarnation* occupies an attractive 18th-century house, originally the manor house of Alum Rock, formerly known as Little Bromwich, and the *Church of St. Margaret*, built in 1834, on the site of an early 16th-century chapel, has a Hollins bust of William Hutton, the local historian. He retired from public life after the riots of 1791 and, having repaired the damage to his residence at Bennett's Hill, Washwood Heath, lived here till his death, in 1815, at the age of ninety-two. At eighty-two he considered himself a young man and said he could walk forty miles a day. *Bromford Bridge Housing Estate*, built on Birmingham Racecourse in 1968, has a population of 6,000 in both low and tall blocks.

Selly Oak—Birmingham

Victorian terrace houses and shops, where the road to Bristol crosses the Worcester Canal, and spacious Arts and Crafts houses occupied by lecturers to the University, just across Bourn Brook. Dudley canal, constructed in 1801, leads to the blocked Lapal Tunnel near the ruins of Weoley Castle, a mediaeval fortified manor house, probably on the site of a pre-Norman settle-

ment. Built of Weoley Castle and Bath stone in 1861, the stripy *church* (St. Mary), by E. Holmes, is a treasure house of Victorian furnishings. Interior was improved in 1961, by Dykes Bower, who lavishly painted and gilded the marble-columned reredos. Beneath the steeple, the arcaded red-sandstone font, 1861, by William Butterfield, has marble columns and steep star-crowned gables, and the stained-glass Ascension, over the altar, is the gift of G. R. Elkington, the patentee of electroplate. Other windows are in memory of the family, and an impressive brass shows the Elkingtons at prayer. North transept window in memory of the architect's wife, who died at the age of thirty-one during the construction of the building. Awkward Gothic *St. Mary's C. of E. Primary School*, built of red sandstone in 1860, may also be by Holmes. Inter-denominational Selly Oak Colleges began with the opening in 1903 of Corinthian *Woodbrooke*, formerly the home of G. R. Elkington, Josiah Mason and then George Cadbury, who dammed the brook to form a lake and planted many specimen trees. *Kingsmead Close*, built in 1913, by W. Alexander Harvey, has massive brick stacks and *Fircroft College* occupies a house, built in 1902, by the same architect, for George Cadbury, jnr. Domed *Church of St. Lazar*, built in 1968, by Dragomir Tadić, for the Serbian Orthodox Church, was executed entirely by Serbian craftsmen. Colourful interior has a marble floor, a symbolic connection with the ancient monasteries of Studenitza and Sopocane, and sandstone pillars from the same quarry as the stone for the original Lazarica in Krusheratz. Rich alsecco paintings depict Christ Pantokrator surrounded by prophets and evangelists in the dome. Walnut furniture is overlaid with copper and the iconostasis has twisted columns. George Cadbury's timbered *Selly Oak Institute* looks out

of place in the Victorian part of the suburb, especially next to the *Station Inn*, all bay windows and etched glass. Martin and Chamberlain's Gothic *pumping station* stands proudly behind lodges; and, on the crest of Serpentine Hill, their *Church of St. Stephen* has a tall steeple. A small *loggia* in the garden of Highfield, Selly Park Road, originally the east end of Archer's Church of St. Philip (now Birmingham Cathedral), was reconstructed here following the addition of Chatwin's splendid chancel.

Sheldon—Birmingham

Large pre-war housing estates around Lyndon Green, and post-war at Garretts Green and Kitts Green. Engulfed 14th-century *church* (St. Giles) was sensitively restored in 1867, by Slater and Carpenter, who rebuilt the chancel and part of the north aisle. 15th-century west tower, 16th-century timber-framed porch and a most attractive reset 15th-century reredos with tall crocketed pinnacles. Red-and-blue-brick *Sheldon Hall*, a typical early 16th-century Warwickshire manor house, was bought in 1751, by John Taylor, of Taylor and Lloyd's Bank who, wishing to be called squire, bought the title of Lord of the Manor of Yardley for £9,000.

Small Heath, Sparkbrook & Sparkhill—Birmingham

Bisected by the Warwick and Birmingham Canal, 1799, and the Birmingham and Oxford Junction Railway, 1852, which attracted Factories, followed by slated brick terraces, leaving only a few small parks. Most impressive of a number of ambitious Arts and Crafts churches is undoubtedly the soaring brick *Church of St. Agatha*, 1899–1901, the masterpiece of W. H. Bidlake and one of the finest churches of its date in Europe. Spectacular tower, the result of a last-minute gift, dominates the Stratford Road, with its deeply louvred belfry windows, pierced corner pinnacles and needle spike. Cream-brick, lozenge-shaped piers slice the nave into tall, narrow bays and support brick wall arches and freely carved clumps of foliage, from which spring broad transverse arches, giving a vaulted effect. Ruskinian *Stratford Road County Primary School*, built in 1885, is a formal essay in the style of John Henry Chamberlain; on the other side of the road, the tile-hung spire of the brick *Baptist chapel*, 1878–9, perhaps the best work of William Hale, makes an excellent foil to St. Agatha's tower. By the railway bridge over the Stratford Road, *Shakespeare Inn* has elaborate Gothic fronts, in the style of William Burgess, and *Angel Inn* dates from the early 19th century, when there was a tollbar across the road. Mellow brick former *St. Agatha's Vicarage*, built in 1901, by W. H. Bidlake, is a good example of his domestic building, and 18th-century *Farm Park*, built by the banker Sampson Lloyd II, retains its original avenue of elms. 1920s Tudor-style *Antelope*, an early work by H. W. Hobbiss, has a fine bas-relief by William Bloye, in the manner of Eric Gill; 1930s Congregational *Stratford Road Chapel*, by W. H. Bidlake, is surprisingly Romanesque. On the River Cole, brick *Sarehole Mill*, built in 1773 and the last watermill of its kind in the city, stands on the site of one leased by Matthew Boulton, probably for the production of his buckles and other 'toys', and reinforced-concrete *Chrysler*, formerly Birmingham Small Arms, has large windows whose light aided the manufacture of First World War rifles.

Winson Green & Hockley—Birmingham Between the Hockley Brook and the Dudley Road, and with Brindley's 1770 canal meandering between H.M. Prison, 1845, the City Mental Hospital,

1849, Dudley Road Hospital, 1850–2, and the Infirmary, 1889. In 1824 Thomas Telford found the canal 'little better than a crooked ditch', and so reduced its length by cutting off numerous bends, and widened it all the way to Aldersley. Unassuming *Bellefield Inn*, Winson Street, has a boldly tiled smoke room, which incorporates Frith and Landseer engravings; stucco terraces at Brookfields are all that was built of an ambitious plan by Pigott Smith. Red-brick *church* (St. Peter), built in 1901–2, by F. B. Osborne, has a distinctive west tower and the steepled *Spring Hill Library*, a red-terracotta shrine to the literary arts, built in 1893, by the younger Martin, has excellent Arts and Crafts metalwork and glass. Angular, slate-hung *Florin*, 1974, by The John Madin Design Group, has an open timber roof. *The Mint*, founded, in 1794, by Ralph Heaton, who used machinery of Boulton's design, occupies an arcaded brick building of 1860. Staffordshire-blue-brick gateway leads to the *C. of E. Cemetery*, laid out in 1848 and now with many white-marble memorials against the surrounding industrial background. Chapel stood above the surviving amphitheatre of vaults cut deep into the hillside. *War Stone*, a felsite boulder deposited near here by a glacier during the Ice Age, was once used as a parish boundary mark; it was at that time known as the Hoar Stone. Below precipitous sandstone cliffs, supporting the busy house-workshops of the jewellery quarter, *Birmingham General Cemetery* is enclosed by high, spiked railings between massive sandstone piers. Laid out in 1836, by severely Greek Charles Edge, around a windowless Doric temple, the cemetery originally had a lookout, for body snatchers, stationed high on a cliff. The temple has gone, but the underground catacombs remain; overpowering sense of death in the midst of life. Here Edward Burne-

Jones and his school friend Carmell Price spent many holiday afternoons reading history and romance, and in 1914 Joseph Chamberlain's ashes were scattered. Icknield Street Board School, 1883, one of Martin and Chamberlain's most successful compositions, has many-gabled classrooms around a superb Continental spire; *Gothic Inn*, 1860, and *Great Hampton Street Works*, 1872, originally a pearl-button manufactory, show an admiration for Venice. *Time Works*, Barr Street, 1856, has large windows divided by slender cast-iron columns, to give plenty of light for watch making, and Great Hampton Row a splendid pair of *cast-iron gates*, by Thomas Rickman, to the derelict churchyard of his demolished church of St. George's-in-the-Fields. Rickman's Gothic-canopied tomb, by R. C. Hussey, survives, though mutilated. *Midland Bank*, Warstone Lane, 1892, is enriched by sculptures of a merchant, a glassworker and a metalworker; at the heart of the jewellery quarter, a cast-iron *clock tower*, made at the Soho Clock Factory in 1903, commemorates Joseph Chamberlain's visit to South Africa. The first principal of the Venetian Gothic *School of Jewellery and Silversmithing* was R. Catterson-Smith, associated with Burne-Jones and William Morris in the production of the Kelmscott Chaucer; the roads surrounding Victoria Street are lined with a rich collection of small, individually designed workshops, built throughout the 19th century and into the 20th in all the current styles, from Greek Doric to Art Nouveau. Of the larger manufactories, Grecian *Victoria Works* has a later, finely modelled portrait medallion of Queen Victoria in rich leaf carving; Lombardic, polychromatic-brick *Argent Works* was in part built as a Turkish bath. Newhall Hill has a boldly arched blue-brick building; Italianate *New Hall Works*, surmounted by a royal arms, is now

the finest manufactory of its type in the city. Soaring high above the sand pits Chatwin's bold brick *Greek Orthodox church*, 1873, was originally Catholic Apostolic.

Yardley—Birmingham Farms and fields were swallowed up in the 1920s and 30s, following the advent of the cheap city tram. *Church* (St. Edburgha), at the heart of the old village, has an austere 15th-century steeple against an extensive, mellow tile roof. Tudor rose and pomegranate over the north door record that the manor was given to Catherine of Aragon by Henry VIII, after he had married Anne Boleyn. Heavily-timbered south porch is 15th-century, and protects a simple 13th-century doorway. Nave and transepts are mainly 14th-century; west window, of the Last Supper, is by Hardman. Chancel was lengthened in 1890. 15th-century alabaster tomb chest incised with figures of Thomas Est, governor of Kenilworth Castle, and his wife, Marian de la Hay, the last of the Hay family, who lived at Hay Hall; a small black oval tablet, with cherubs' heads and weeping putto, is to Job Marston, d.1701, who gave a chapel to Hall Green. A curtained cave contains the marble statues of the Revd. Dr. Henry Greswolde, rector of Solihull, d.1700, and his wife; chancel, repaired by one of his family in 1797, has a handsome marble vase by Peter Hollins to Edmund Greswolde, d.1836. Long, timber-framed *school house*, against the churchyard, is 15th century, though there is evidence of a school as early as 1260, and of monks from Maxstoke Priory giving instruction. Row of whitewashed brick cottages has a modest corner shop with post office. Village blacksmith occupies an old farm. Victorian *school* is bricked up; excellent Arts

Birmingham:
opposite Spring Hill Library,
Winson Green *right above* in
Corporation Street and
Victoria Law Courts entrance

and Crafts *almshouses*, built in 1903, house a number of black charity boards, presumably from the church. Timber-framed *Blakesley Hall*, a 16th-century farmhouse now used as a museum, has massive corner brackets and a large chimney. Against the Coventry Road, James Roberts's elegant 1960s *Tivoli Centre* contrasts with Richard Seifert's S-shaped *Swan Office Block*; elaborate polychromatic lodge to *Yardley Cemetery and Crematorium* guards chilly marble statues and permanent granite obelisks.

Bishop's Itchington [11] Before the enclosures this was Itchington Superior, on the site of *Old Town Farm*, where remains of the church have been found, and Itchington Inferior, the present village. On undulating ground, above the River Itchen, and with views of distant hills, the loosely knit new village has many pale-brick houses built for the workers at the once thriving local cement quarries, closed in 1969. Large Decorated-style *church* (St. Michael), built in 1872 by Ewan Christian, replaces a simple chapel-of-ease. Unaffected white interior has a wide-arched north arcade, a terrible St. Michael in the east window and a rich marble, mosaic and tile reredos. Rendered-lias Georgian *vicarage* and, in the fields, the modernised *Manor House*. Victorian Gothic *school and schoolhouse* (Ewan Christian?) and Gothic speckled-pale-brick *Independent Chapel*, 1836. Fisher Road is named after the chief landlord, who tried to call the village Fisher's Itchington. *Memorial Hall* and adjacent house are of local cement blocks. On high ground, Voysey's first country house, *The Cottage*, built in 1888, for Sir Michael H. Lakin, owner of the local cement quarries, is appropriately roughcast. Large living hall and a long gallery lead to a simple staircase and, beyond a typical boarded door, the dining room has low-level windows and a fine brick fireplace.

Bishop's Tachbrook [11] Timber-framed and brick cottages on a hill. Founded in Norman times on its own rise, the *church* (St. Chad) has a stately Perpendicular tower, straight-headed windows and Gothic arcades with continuous mouldings. An aisle window, 1864, by William Morris and Philip Webb, is to John Garner, a relative of Thomas Garner, the Victorian church architect, who lived at nearby Wasperton Hill. Memorial, with a Latin inscription by Walter Savage Landor, is to his brother Robert, and there is another to himself. The Landors lived at 'Savage's House', 1558. To the north are tall trees and, to the south-east, two timber-framed houses. Across the brook, *Chapel Hill Farm* has the stone carcase of the church to Tachbrook Malory, depopulated by the enclosures in 1505.

Bishopton [10] (near Stratford) Above the Stratford-on-Avon Canal, before it climbs through ten locks to Wilmcote. Success of Royal Leamington Spa led the cautious Granville to predict that Bishopton would soon be its equal, yet little survives to commemorate the attempt. Ochre-washed *Spa Lodge* and *Bruce Lodge*, 1837, simpler *Pump House*, with wavy eaves, and a few Tudor Gothic villas. A *cottage orné* stands by a rough drive leading, past the railings of the now churchless churchyard, to a red-brick Italianate house shrouded in trees.

Blackwell [14] A ragged village by the Roman Fosse Way; the larger houses L-shaped and with mullioned windows, and the smaller ones in terraces. Red-brick council semis and brown-brick moderns.

Bournville *see* Birmingham.

Bourton-on-Dunsmore & Draycote [9] Thatched timber-framed and tiled brick houses at the foot of a steep hill, from which flow streams into Draycote Water. Gothic *Baptist Church*, 1869, has paintless pierced bargeboards; uphill, through an arched railway bridge, the *church* (St. Peter) was almost entirely rebuilt, in 1842 and 1850, by J. Potter, whose father supervised James Wyatt's alterations to Lichfield Cathedral. South arcade and clerestory are mediaeval and coloured red to match the later work. Jacobean communion rail, early 17th-century pulpit, box pews and a rich window by Kempe. North chapel has an effigy of a lady, c. 1300, and engraved slabs and painted hatchments to the Shuckburghs. Stately Georgian *Bourton Hall*, now used for storing grain, retains its impressive staircase, lit by a large oval dome, and elaborately garlanded ceilings covered with cobwebs. Pedimented *chapel*, linked to the house by a quadrant wood gallery, has a marble doorway with a delicate relief of Raphael's Sposalizio, and a dignified interior with a richly gilded ceiling and a pretty garlanded gallery. *School*, 1836, and *estate cottages*. *Village hall* is the extension of a most original building, which has radiating arms and a curved verandah and is worthy of Soane.

Brailes [14] In a wide valley by Brailes Hill and, in mediaeval times, a bustling market town with important wool trade and thriving water mill. It was probably the third-largest town in the county, after Coventry and Warwick, and aerial surveys have revealed extensive networks of roads in the fields. Main street is curved and has a few thatched dwellings, many terraced 17th- and 18th-century houses and a quaint stucco villa with elaborate bargeboards. Imposing *church* (St. George)—'the Cathedral of the Feldon'—reflects the mediaeval prosperity. Perpendicular west tower enclosed by houses, but north side of the churchyard is open to fields, from which the contrasting height of the tower and length of the nave can be fully appreciated. There was a church here in the 11th century, stones of which are built into the interior of the tower, and the foundations of the 12th-century building survive beneath the south arcade. Through a wide-arched Perpendicular porch the Decorated interior has a tower arch of cathedral proportions; and beyond the chancel arch, increased in height during the 19th century, the chancel is mainly lit by a large Perpendicular south window. Interior was modernised in 1824 and scraped in 1879. Georgian *vicarage*. Over a stream, R.C. *Church of St. Peter and St. Paul* was fitted out in 1726 in the upper part of a barn, said to be 13th century and once used as a malthouse. Victorian *school* with plate tracery and a bell turret. Upper Brailes has an Italianate *Primitive Methodist chapel*, built in 1863, and the remains of a motte-and-bailey castle, which once guarded the Fosse Way.

Brandon [8] An estate village to the north of the River Avon and against a sharp bend in the Coventry–Rugby road. Well known for the *Coventry Stadium*, which has regular motorcycle and stock-car races. Main road cuts through the village green, around which stand a thatched *cottage*, the Tudor-style *village stores*, formerly the bakery, and three polychromatic-brick *estate cottages*, 1866, in which lived the woodman, the local brewer and the groom. Timber-framed *Ivy House Farm* was built in 1640; and the school, 1888, and the *Brandon Club*, 1885, have half-timbered gables. Elegant *Brandon Hall Hotel*, formerly the seat of the Salisbury family, is Regency with a later Italianate porch.

Bretford [9] On a busy road junction where the Coventry–Rugby road does a hairpin bend to cross the River Avon. Timber-framed *Old Oaks* and some long brick terraces

face a long, part-timber-framed *farm*, formerly *The Bell Inn*, and a minute derelict *Congregational chapel*.

Brinklow [9] On a hill, which may have been an ancient burial mound and round which the Romans diverted the Fosse Way. In the time of King Stephen the Mowbray family constructed the *motte-and-bailey castle*, which is regarded as one of the best surviving examples in the country. Broad Street has many houses built with a continuous frontage, which gives the village the air of a small town. In the 19th century it was noted for its alehouses, frequented by navigators on the Oxford Canal, which brought several industries, among them boat building and candle making. Crumbly cream-stone *church* (St. John the Baptist) is mainly Perpendicular, though the rubble walls of the north aisle and chancel are part of the 13th-century building of the Austin Canons of Kenilworth. Approached through a carved timber-framed porch, the lofty interior has graceful arcades without capitals and the floor slopes upwards, almost twelve feet, from west to east. This unusual feature seems to have existed during the 13th century, though it was made steeper in the 1860s and steps have been added in the choir and chancel. High-pitched nave roof on ugly timber wall shafts, chancel arch with a Christmas salutation and aggressively cusped roof members. Two stone ambos are the remains of a heavy Victorian screen, and the sanctuary is lined with horrid, brightly coloured Minton tiling, covering a mediaeval piscina and possibly an aumbry! A lancet has a simple stained-glass Baptism of Christ with a bright blue background and, at the top, the Hand of God the Father. In memory of Richard Rouse Bloxam, rector 1793–1840, and, until 1826, also Under Master of Rugby School, it is surely by the same artist as the east window at

Harborough Magna, where his son Andrew was rector. Another son, Matthew Holbeache Bloxam, is known for his 'Gothic Ecclesiastical Architecture' and a third, John Rouse Bloxam, as 'the real originator of the ceremonial revival in the English Church'. Churchyard has many well carved memorials, including some by Thomson of Brinklow. *Congregational church* is basically Georgian, with a later front, and the grand Georgian *Dunsmore House* rises above a row of thatched timber-framed cottages. Opposite the church, *The Crescent* is formed by many Regency cottages, a stuccoed timber-framed house, and a restrained Regency house in yellow brick with plain angle pilasters. *C. of E. school*, originally built in 1826, has Gothic extensions and a turret now cloaked in ivy.

Broom [10] Modern semis and bungalows. *Broom Mills* is the most prominent feature, with its angular asbestos tower. *Church* dull. *Malt house* timber-framed, with gables and a bellcote: long and low. *Broom Hall Inn*, behind its ilex tree, 16th century.

Brownsover [9] (near Newbold) A hamlet with a simple yellow-stone *church* (St. Michael), partly 15th century but mainly by George Gilbert Scott, 1877. Plastered interior has fragments of Perpendicular and Jacobean panelling, from elsewhere, and an 18th-century Flemish pulpit. Timber-framed *house* is reputed to be the birthplace of Lawrence Sheriff, b.1515, founder of Rugby School. Patterned-red-brick *Brownsover Hall*, originally built in 1450, is also by Scott, and has a tall, asymmetrically placed tower as at Kelham. *Dining Hall* has a large stone fireplace beneath the horns of an Irish elk, probably the finest specimen in the country, and *Staircase Hall* a first-floor arcade with red-marble columns. *Inner Hall*, like an undercroft, leads to *Ballroom*, which has a large oak-shuttered bay window for the musicians. Grounds, which descend to the old arm of the Oxford Canal, have a *weeping willow*, originally at the grave of Napoleon and probably brought from St. Helena by his surgeon, Barry O'Meara who, as the third husband of Theodosia Boughton, lived at the hall. Theodosia's first husband was convicted for murdering her brother and was executed at Warwick in 1781.

Bubbenhall [8] Timber-framed houses and barns and slated pale-brick cottages against the River Avon. The lane to the church has a quiet mixture of old and new and, in a stone walled churchyard against the river, the cream-grey *church* (St. Giles) is 13th century with red-sandstone lancets. Heavily buttressed, eroded stone tower. Brick porch, 1616, has pretty cast-iron gates. Early English chancel arch and Victorian east window. Extensive landscape.

Budbrooke [11] (near Hampton-on-the-hill) *Church* (St. Michael) has a distinctive tower with flat Norman pilasters, two tiers of belfry openings and 18th-century pinnacles. Nave has a blocked Norman doorway and an Early English arcade, and must have been very dark before the arrival of the crude Perpendicular east window, Georgian plaster, and the arid Victorian transepts. *Vicarage* is a new brick box to comfort rather than inspire.

Bulkington [5] Cricket on the green but the village has expanded greatly. Amid slate headstones and table tombs, the *church* (St. James) has a fine late 14th-century west tower. Porch, 1907, incorporates two Norman fragments; 13th-century nave has a Perpendicular south clerestory and box pews. Restored in 1865, when the 14th-century chancel was given a new arch by G. T. Robinson. Font by

Richard Hayward, 1789, has a white-marble bowl, decorated with delicate classical figures, on an antique Roman column drum, of Numidian marble, brought back from the Grand Tour in 1753. Hayward was born in the parish in 1728; his statue of Lord Botetourt, 1773, at Williamsburg, Virginia, is the oldest public statue in North America. Monuments by him are in Westminster Abbey, and there is one here to his parents (a woman weeping among Gothic ruins). Also by Hayward: an altar slab and an oval tablet. Church Street has some 18th- and 19th-century cottages in the pale-red brick characteristic of the district; and *4*, said to date from 1506, is timber-framed on a brick base. Originally thatched. Interior has a large inglenook fireplace and some wattle-and-daub infill.

Burmington [14] On each side of a curved lane, followed by a part-stone, part-brick terrace, pale-speckled-brick houses and a later Italianate pair. Derelict ivy-clad stone *school*. In the Tudor style and with pretty pierced bargeboards, it looks more like work of the 1840s than of 1877, and stands against a churchyard almost devoid of headstones. Base of an old cross. Lanceted *church* (St. Barnabas and St. Nicholas) has a small pyramid-capped tower. West gallery. Ruined for four years, the mediaeval building, which had a central tower, was rebuilt in 1693. In 1849, nave extended westwards and tower and vestry added. Bright geometric glass. To the south-west a picturesque house has a twin-arched Norman window. Uphill towards Sutton, a speckled-brick house, 1730, stands behind a timber-framed granary on staddles.

Burton Dassett [11] (near Avon Dassett) Dercett is Saxon for 'abode of wild beasts' and a Saxon burial place has been found on Mount Pleasant, the hill overlooking Northend. The 13th century added

to the prosperity of the village, and a market flourished. A population, already depleted by the Black Death, suffered further from evictions and enclosures by a selfish landlord and never recovered. At one time there was a lane of houses to the south of the church, each with a toft of land, and more dwellings below the holy well. Wicked landlord, Blenknap, built the stone *beacon tower*, on top of which a cresset could be lighted in times of emergency and around which visitors to the country park now ride ponies and fly kites. *Church* (All Saints) of local iron-bearing limestone. Severe exterior with a buttressed west tower, two doorways, resited when the aisles were added, and small lancet windows. South arcade has octagonal piers with circular capitals, and the 13th-century north arcade is similar, with much amusing carving. Sloping floor to the nave and seventeen steps up to the altar. Transepts with large free-standing table tombs. There used to be a Doom over the chancel arch, probably contemporary with it. In the late 14th century the Virgin, St. John the Baptist and two censing angels were painted over the earlier work, and over these the post-Reformation royal arms, of which little remains. Whole central area has been peppered with shot, but whether this was aimed at the royal arms or at a crucifix is impossible to tell. Much post-Reformation cartouche painting of two periods. Long, light chancel, plastered and white-washed. Oak communion table, dated 1618. In 1890 J. Cossins miraculously restored the building without spoiling its character. *Holy well* has a Grecian well house, 1840, with ferns growing out of the walls; next to this, three hardened-clay cottages with thatched roofs have, within living memory, gradually returned to the land. Amid large trees, the Hornton-stone *vicarage*, dated 1696, has a tile roof and pierced bargeboards, 1847.

Burton Hastings [5] In a churchyard, with two interesting mid-19th-century Graeco-Egyptian table tombs, the *church* (St. Botolph) has a Perpendicular tower and a cheerful stone interior with a wide chancel arch. To the south, two three-storey Georgian houses stand sentinel.

Butlers Marston [11] 17th- to early 20th-century soft-grey-lias houses dressed with ochre-coloured stone and patched with red brick. Once on the salt road from Droitwich to London, the old village was to the east of the church, but was rebuilt after the Black Death across the broad river valley, as lush as a Pre-Raphaelite painting and overlooked by the ochre-stone Perpendicular tower of the *church* (St. Peter and St. Paul). Nave and south aisle are covered by a purple-tiled roof and to the west end are cramped, decaying memorial slabs. Odd details on the Victorian vestry and porch. Dark, but white-painted, interior is dominated by a chunky late Norman arcade, its massive round piers with pointed arches expressing the width of the wall above. Sensitively carved pulpit, 1632, and Georgian Lord's Prayer, Ten Commandments and Creed. Beyond a dainty 1930s screen in the Gothic Revival chancel arch, the scraped chancel is dark with Victorian glass. The outbuildings of *Monks Bridge* (formerly the vicarage) are wrapped around the churchyard, which has at the base of a mediaeval *preaching cross*. *Manor house*, once with fishponds and a dovecote, now has sash windows. Derelict ivy-clad school, 1871, by William White, and plain Gothic ochre-stone *Wesleyan chapel*, 1923.

Caldecote [5] Among dense yews, the 15th-century *church* (St. Theobald and St. Chad) has a hard, random-stone exterior and an awkward bell turret, the result of the 1857 restoration by Ewan Christian. Wide nave, with crumbling plaster walls, is mainly lit by two windows high up in the west wall. 17th-century Purefey monuments, with kneeling figures. A piece of mediaeval screen has intricate tracery, and the late 13th-century south door fine scroll hinges. Jacobean style *Caldecote Hall*, 1879–80, by the Goddards, is now flats. Pretty terrace of cottages.

Canley *see* Coventry.

Castle Bromwich [4] On high ground amid trees to the south of the M6, which encircles the mound of the castle against the River Tame. Beyond are the multi-storey blocks of flats of Birmingham's outer suburbs. Red-brick *church* (St. Mary and St. Margaret), 1726–31, by Thomas White, is unique, as it encases a 15th-century timber frame with clerestory and aisles, the exceptionally high parapets concealing the outdated high-pitched roof. Though there is no longer a clerestory, the interior is light, with large clear-glass aisle windows with a sight of the yew trees in the churchyard. Tuscan columns support segmental arches. Chancel, which probably owes its exceptional depth for the period to the form of the original building, has giant fluted pilasters, influenced by Thomas Archer's St. Philip's, Birmingham. Marble reredos originally framed the Ten Commandments on the side walls. Three-decker pulpit, box pews and baluster font, with original wooden cover, have all survived. From the churchyard, decayed wrought-iron gates, probably by Benjamin Taylor, lead to the walled gardens of the Jacobean *Castle Bromwich Hall*, facing away from the church along an avenue of trees. In the second half of the 17th century, Sir John Bridgeman added the third storey and a delightful stone porch with barley-sugar columns and allegorical figures by Sir W. Wilson. Jacobean-style tower, 1825, by Thomas Rickman; spacious staircase has late 17th-century ceiling by Gouge, with flowers and fruit; dining room, boudoir and saloon also have excellent stucco; long gallery has ceiling by Rickman. Unsurfaced Rectory Lane has three Arts and Crafts houses by C. E. Bateman. Behind a cottage garden, *Birnam* and *Millbrick*, 1897, of bricks from a mill at the bottom of the hill, are disarmingly unassuming, and Millbrick has panelling that was formerly the pew ends at Water Orton old church. Consciously Queen Anne-style *Rectory*, 1911, has a delightful barrel-vaulted oratory with a small stained-glass Crucifixion. Remainder of the village is a mixture of Georgian houses, farm buildings and 20th-century semis and flats. Behind a cobbled forecourt, the impressive *Bradford Arms*, built c. 1700, has slightly projecting wings and a fake timber interior.

Catherine-de-Barnes Heath [7] A 19th-century hamlet where the Solihull–Hampton-in-Arden road crosses the Grand Union Canal by a hump-backed bridge. Now linked to Solihull by well spaced modern houses behind wide green verges. Twin-gabled mock-timbered *Boat Inn*, a poor 1930s building by Newton and Cheatle, replaces one by the side of the canal; next to this, the obsolete *school*, built in 1879, by J. A. Chatwin, for Joseph Gillott, has a steeply roofed bellcote.

Cawston [9] (near Bilton) Here the Cistercian Order had two bread ovens which baked, each week, sixteen quarters of corn for common bread and six quarters of better quality for the monks and lay brothers. In 1307 a carelessly placed candle caused a serious fire, and it is clear from the inventory of damage that this was not just a farm but a miniature monastery. By a tributary of the River Avon, the roughcast Georgian-style Cawston House built, in 1907, by H. B. Creswell, has full-height bay windows, a cavernous civic porch and stables.

Burton Dassett church and churchyard ▷

At an angle to the road, the mellow-orange-brick *Potsford Dam Farm* is Georgian as is *Cawston Grange Farm*, c. 1730, with a pyramid-roofed extension. Timber-framed *Cawston Old Farm* has a brick wing, c. 1800, with a generous expanse of roof.

Chadshunt [11] (near Kineton) An estate hamlet with a pretty red-and-cream-brick *post office*, two quiet Victorian Tudor-style houses and some rich-red-brick barns. Approached up steps and around the massive octagonal base of the churchyard cross, the *church* (All Saints) has a long Norman nave, with a distorted south doorway, and a battlemented west tower. Blue-lias belfry contrasts with the brown stone of the rest of the building. Chancel is Early Georgian,

with finely jointed stonework, and the Venetian east window and round-arched south windows have cream-grey stone surrounds. On the north side of the nave is an early Georgian chapel, containing a raised family pew which has 16th-century Italian glass and an elliptically arched doorway, complete with foot scrapers. Opposite, beneath trees, a simple gate leads to the terraced gardens of the white-painted *Chadshunt Hall*, and nearby is a stone quarry.

Charlecote [11] An estate village, the warm brick of the early Victorian Tudor-style cottages contrasting with the cream sandstone of the *church* (St. Leonard) built, in 1851-3, by John Gibson, for Mary Elizabeth Hammond Lucy. On the

edge of Charlecote Park, its sharp open steeple is balanced by a smaller spire to the Lucy family chapel and the main entrance, below a large, round west window, leads to a dark, aisleless nave which is stone-lined and stone-vaulted. Interior retains its original fittings, most of which are of wood carved by Davis. South and west windows are by O'Connor, and those on the north side by Holland of Warwick and Kempe. Even darker chancel has a glowing east window, 1852, by Willement, with Christ and the four Evangelists in red cloaks under orange canopies, and in the Lucy Chapel a rose window, also by Willement, has the arms and badges of the Lucys. Here are three monuments to the family, the most notable, by Nicholas Stone, un-

below and opposite **Charlecote** and Sir Thomas Lucy

questionably the leading English sculptor in the early 17th century, with a semi-reclining figure of Sir Thomas, d.1640, backed by a composition of books by Homer, Horace, Virgil, Cato and Xenophon, and Winter's Ayres. Landscaped by Capability Brown, the park around the churchyard has peaceful groups of deer, and on the other side of the road the Tudor-style *vicarage*, 1836, is a perfect William IV piece with fine moulded ceilings and a Gothic white-marble fireplace, reminiscent of Wyattville's work at Windsor. *Charlecote Park*, the seat of the Lucy family, is closely associated with William Shakespeare and Queen Elizabeth I. The Virgin Queen spent two nights here in 1572 on her way to Kenilworth; but only legend relates that the young William Shakespeare was caught poaching deer by Sir Thomas Lucy. It is certainly true that, as can be seen through the house, the arms of the Lucy family include a rebus consisting of three luces—an archaic word for a fresh-

water pike. Shakespeare, in 'The Merry Wives of Windsor', gives Justice Shallow a coat of arms including a 'dozen white luces'. It has therefore been said that Shallow is a portrait of Sir Thomas Lucy, who built the original house in the very year of the Queen's accession. The first true example of Elizabethan architecture in the county, its most complete surviving part is the remarkable gatehouse with polygonal angle turrets, a large oriel and a rib-vaulted carriageway. Basic silhouette of the entrance front is that of the 1550s but, with the exception of a few patches of blue-diapered brickwork and the decidedly Renaissance porch with two tiers of coupled columns, the rest dates mostly from 1823–67. Original house, inherited by George Hammond Lucy in 1823, was considerably smaller; he added the dining room and library in the early 1830s. Lucy's first step was to improve his collection of objects and pictures by attending the 1823 sale of the Beckford collection at Fonthill Abbey, where he bought furniture, lacquer and ceramics. Restoration and building were supervised by Thomas Willement, the stained-glass designer, who started his career working for Wyatt at Fonthill and, besides designing furnishings, was a keen scholar, antiquary and collector. He restored an important set of 16th-century armorial stained-glass windows portraying the genealogy of the Lucy family, and executed a remarkable new set to bring the family up to date. All these windows extend through the Library, Dining Room and Great Hall. State rooms have been arranged as far as possible in the manner in which they were in the 1880s. Well lit *Great Hall*, with a wood-grained, arched plaster ceiling and a fireplace by Willement, has a fantastic collection of family portraits and, as a centrepiece, the superb pietra-dura table, from the Borghese Palace via Fonthill, with

a fine 16th-century slab and a remarkable base, c. 1816, bearing Beckford's crest. Small Gothic tables are also from Fonthill. *Dining Room* has the famous elaborately carved 'Charlecote Buffet', 1858, by Willcox of Warwick, and the stucco ceiling, with pendants, the gold-and-flock wallpaper and the carpet are by Willement. *Library* ceiling, wallpaper and carpet are again by Willement, who also designed the overmantel and bookcases, which were carved by Willcox. *Billiard Room* (The Ebony Room) and *Drawing Room* were decorated, in 1852–6, by John Gibson. Close to the River Avon, the west front is part c. 1850 and part by Gibson, who also remodelled the south wing, adding large octagonal turrets with ogee caps. Elizabethan *Stables* and *Brewhouse*. House is open to visitors.

Chelmsley Wood [4] (near Castle Bromwich)

From 1966 to 1973, an extensive estate of over 15,000 houses and flats was sadly built in the green belt, to house the inhabitants of Birmingham's cleared inner suburbs. River Cole has a public walkway running ten miles through south-east Birmingham and joins Kingshurst Brook in *Town Park*, where there is a lake, fringed on one side by part of the woodland from which the area takes its name.

Cherington [14]

Cotswold-tradition houses against the River Stour, surrounded by hills. 13th-century *church* (St. John Baptist) has a dignified west tower. Rough stone interior, smoothed by many coats of limewash, has a light north aisle, with 18th-century Gothic windows, and the east end of the arcade is continued by an elaborate ogee-arched monument with an effigy on a tomb chest. Large Perpendicular south window is filled with fine early 16th-century heraldic glass which, with that in the north windows, was nearly all collected by an 18th-century rector. Richly carved Jacobean altar with twin Corinthian columns, an 18th-century painting of cherubs and a gilded sunburst. Now empty, the plain classical *rectory* has a Gothick traceried sash window with fragments of the 18th-century rector's glass and, behind a gravel forecourt, the wisteria-clad *Cherington House* is entered through a pretty Gothick porch with delicate ball finials.

Chesterton [11] (near Lighthorne)

In a coomb, and one of the most inaccessible and interesting places in the county. Now dispersed, but once with a prosperous main street; considerable signs of former buildings can be found in the fields west of Chesterton Green. Domed classical *windmill*, built in 1632, stands on an open arcade, through which can be seen the surrounding country. Though often attributed to Inigo Jones, it was probably designed by Sir Edward Peyto, whose curious 17th-century house was pulled down about 1802, leaving only trees, a neglected lake and, against the churchyard, a pedimented brick *arch*. Decorated light-grey *church* (St. Giles) is long and low, without aisles. Stumpy, part-ivy-clad tower supported by large diagonal buttresses. Plastered interior with chequerboard floor, and Peyto tombs, with recumbent effigies and busts. *Roman settlement* has a roughly rectangular earthwork; at Chesterton Green a pair of timber-framed houses has corrugated iron-roofs.

Chilvers Coton [5] (near Nuneaton) Following an air raid in 1941, which left only the chancel and Perpendicular tower, the *church* (All Saints) was rebuilt by a team of German prisoners-of-war, with square piers and simple Gothic windows. The benefactor's boards were written by Henry Beighton, F.R.S., 1687–1743, Warwickshire's greatest map maker, before the Ordnance Survey, and a well-known engineer who improved the conditions of the miners; he is buried in the churchyard. Oak panelling around the chancel is made out of the old pews, and the pulpit and lectern, by Schonmeyer, incorporate original pieces. Mary Ann Evans (George Eliot), born 1819, was baptised here (Shepperton Church) by the Rev. B. G. Ebdell (Mr. Gilfil) and regularly attended services until she was over twenty-one. Under a yew tree, a memorial with an urn is to Emma Gwyther (Milly Barton), and by the churchyard cross is a table tomb to George Eliot's parents. Symmetrical *Free School*, originally founded by Lady Newdigate in 1745, and the large stone *College for the Poor* are both buildings erected by her son, Sir Roger Newdigate; the latter, constructed in 1800 by French prisoners-of-war is described in Amos Barton. 'Dreary, stone-floored dining room', in which Amos Barton preached, is now the chapel of Coton Lodge. Impressive *The Arches*, carrying the railway across the Coton Road, has recently been cleared of houses and the secluded *Griff House*, the home of Mary Ann Evans from 1820 to 1841, is part 18th century and part timber-framed.

Church Lawford [9] A cluster of timber-framed and brick cottages where the River Avon was crossed by the Roman Fosse Way. Tall Georgian house facing the green, and many modern houses. Rock-faced *church* (St. Peter) is mainly of 1872, by Slater and Carpenter, but has a 13th-century south doorway and a 14th-century north arcade. Jacobean pulpit with sea serpents, 18th-century communion rail, and a chancel window by Kempe.

Churchover [9] By the River Swift and with the *church* (Holy Trinity) on high ground; this was reconstructed in 1896, by Bassett Smith, with a mosaic of colourful stones. Powdery-white Perpendicular tower and weathered Early English doorway. Plastered nave has a south arcade of c. 1300, and a steep pitch-pine roof. Almost at the centre, a massive Norman font, with a rope moulding, is crowned by an octagonal wooden spire, 1673, carved with stylised plants. Sea-blue, purple and orange east window, 1918, by A. Rosenkrantz, and a green-and-yellow window, 1896, by Kempe. Monument to Robert Price, c. 1594, and another to Charles Dixwell of Coton Hall, 1641, have kneeling figures facing each other across prayer desks. Charles Dixwell's grandson, John, was one of the judges at the trial of Charles I and signed the death warrant. Brick *Old School*, 1841, is Georgian in character, and *School House* has segmental arched windows. Small-scale brick terrace with a moulded stone cornice and a Victorian terrace with wavy bargeboards. Village hall, 1895, and, facing the green, three cottages with blue-brick diamonds. Elegant *Coton House* is the 1787 rebuilding of a moated Elizabethan mansion, on the site of a monastic grange built by the monks of Combe Abbey. Part of the moat survives, but the village has disappeared, probably under the park. Ascribed to Samuel Wyatt, the present house contains a delightful oval room, expressed on the main front as a graceful bow capped by a shallow dome.

Claverdon [10] 'Cloverdown', and at the time of Domesday untouched by Roman roads. Not until comparatively recently, when the Arden–Warwick road was constructed, did history finally catch up with the village which, since the last war, has been spoilt by private developments. Grey-stone *church* (St. Michael and All Angels) was rebuilt twice during the 19th century, with the exception of an upright Perpendicular tower, a Decorated chancel arch and a mediaeval sanctuary. Elegant 1828–30 nave was a Tudor-style preaching box with tall, square-headed windows and the usual proliferation of galleries and box pews. Fifty years later this was rebuilt by Ewan Christian, who, in attempting to restore the church to its original form, made the nave uncomfortably high, by the introduction of a clerestory. Chancel also suffered at his hand by the introduction of a Decorated-style east window, fortunately with fine luminous glass by Kempe, and the addition of an organ chamber and a chapel. Tomb of Thomas Spencer, d.1630, has a round arch enclosing a mullioned and transomed window, most likely rescued from the demolition of the Spencer house, c.1660, and the tablets to the Galton family include one to Sir Francis Galton, F.R.S., grandson of Erasmus Darwin, F.R.S. As a scientist he was a pioneer in the study of weather, and by 1895 was already carrying out research into the laws of heredity. He discovered that fingerprints are permanent and that no two are exactly alike, and also made contributions to the study of psychology. Clock by William Wilkes of Wolverton. Timber-framed *Park Farm* adjoins a long barn, and *Park Farm Cottages*, built around a timber-framed core, have early 19th-century cast-iron windows, said to have come from

Coleshill font

the church. *Smithy* is entered
through an inverted horseshoe and
the Italianate *National Schools*,
1848, have round-arched blue-
brick window frames. Part-timber-
framed *hall* stands behind a giant
fir; the stone *tower house* is said to
have been part of Sir Thomas
Spencer's great house.

Clifford Chambers [10] Mellow
timber-framed and brick cottages
enclosing a green leading to the
wrought-iron gates of the *manor
house*, mainly rebuilt by Lutyens, in
a restful classical style. Moated
mediaeval manor, regarded as one

of the finest specimens in the
country and probably first built by
the monks, passed into the posses-
sion of the Raynsfords, one of whom
married the lady celebrated in the
sonnets of Michael Drayton. Village belonged to the manor till the
early 1950s. *Church* (St. Helen) has
a thin Perpendicular tower with
crudely cut belfry openings and a
large clock. Nave is aisleless, and
chancel was overrestored, in 1885–
6, by John Cotton, who removed
the narrow Norman chancel arch.
Jacobean pulpit and 17th-century
communion rail. *Rectory* is 16th
century and was occupied during

William Shakespeare's early years
by a John Shakespeare. Timber-
framed and of the hall type with
two gabled cross wings, it was
underbuilt in Georgian times. During the 19th century, three generations of the Annesley family, the
lords of the manor, were successive
rectors here and, as the rectory was
made into two cottages, it was
spared 19th-century alterations.
Estate cottages, 1923 and 1927, by
Lutyens, have been spoilt by the
removal of the glazing bars. *Clifford
Chambers Mill* is occupied by Tibor
Reich, whose deep-textured furnishing fabrics are well known.

Compton Verney

Clifton-upon-Dunsmore [9] Between Watling Street and Rugby, whose parish church was, as far back as the 12th century, a 'chapel-of-ease' of the mother *church* of Clifton (St. Mary); an indication of the importance of the village and of the difficult travelling conditions. Low sandstone tower was partly rebuilt in the 16th century; a few stones and a priest's doorway from the 12th-century church were incorporated in the 13th-century chancel, which has three stepped lancets above the altar. 13th-century south arcade and aisle, and Perpendicular north arcade: St. Paul and Timothy his son, by Kempe. Victorian chancel arch is possibly part of the 1894 restoration

by G. F. Bodley, when a chancel vault revealed a human heart, wrapped in tow, in a drum-shaped lead casket. Brick terrace houses follow the road round the churchyard. *Wesleyan chapel*, 1862. Brick *Clifton Manor*, c. 1710, has 1895 Queen Anne Revival extensions. Original staircase survives, but the hall has been extended into an adjacent room and panelled with the Georgian box pews from the church. Dining room has a sideboard and overmantel made out of inlaid church panelling, the overmantel with I.H.S. in an oval, possibly from the pulpit. Red-brick *Townsend Memorial Hall*, 1885, by C. C. Woodward, is not memorable.

Clopton House [11] (near Stratford-upon-Avon) Held by the Clopton family from the days of Henry III until the early 19th century. Courtyard house on mediaeval lines, with the hall in the west range and, on the east front, an entrance porch, c. 1600, with two small caryatids and a timber-framed upper floor. Symmetrical brick-and-stone south and west fronts are late 17th century. Panelled hall has an overmantel of about 1600; the other rooms, including the chapel under the roof, where the Gun-powder Plot conspirators met in 1605, have late 17th-century fittings.

Coleshill [5] A market town, on a hill above the River Cole and

80

crowned by the magnificent steeple of the parish church, one of the best examples of the work of the Warwickshire school. In the 17th and 18th centuries the village was on the main route from London to Chester and, as it was where the mail was put down for Birmingham and where the horses were changed, there were many inns, wheelwrights, blacksmiths and saddlers. In 1728 a fine of thirty shillings was imposed on anyone carrying a naked fire along any street, so the houses, which were timber-framed, would probably have still been thatched. Today the town is of Georgian red brick, though the High Street has a recently restored timber-framed *coaching inn*, 118–20, with curious geometric timbers. Before the restoration of 1859 the *church* (St. Peter and St. Paul) was hemmed in by houses, a few of which remain, commanding distant views of Hams Hall Power Station beyond the River Cole. Dark tower porch has a lofty arch to the dull-rendered nave. Lavishly glazed chancel. Many rich monuments include two cross-legged knights, three brasses and, to the Digbys, four tomb chests, with fine sculptured figures, and a big urn. Chief glory is the Norman font, c. 1150, with the Evangelists and a Crucifixion. Marketplace originally almost filled the entrance to Church Hill, but only the *pillory, whipping post and stocks* remain. Opposite the church, a Georgian house has giant Ionic pilasters, and another is Gothic. High Street plunges downhill to cross the river by a 16th-century bridge, amid pollarded willows in front of the fine 18th-century *St. Paul's House*. Adjoining St. Paul's School, a severe example of the Queen Anne Revival, is now deserted and further uphill, neo-Georgian houses mock the surviving genuine examples. Economical Early English-style *Congregational church*, c. 1830, and Greek Doric *St. Andrew's Home*, c. 1825. *Swan Hotel*,

High Street, formerly a coaching inn with a central carriageway, has a magnificent overhanging cornice. Byzantine-style R.C. *Church of the Sacred Heart*, 1938–42, intended to have mosaic, as Westminster Cathedral, has Pugin's rood from his R.C. cathedral at Birmingham. *Coleshill Hall*, 1873, originally the seat of the Digby family and now a hospital, is angular Gothic with a porte-cochère tower leading to a top lit hall with iron columns and tracery. Gilson has some picturesque timber-framed cottages and a barn, and *Montrose Cottage* and *West Lynne*, built out of bricks from the demolished Hams Hall.

Combrook [11] A cream-stone estate village in the valley of the brook draining the lakes of Compton Verney into the River Dene. Old thatched houses and, by John Gibson for the Verney family, many Victorian estate cottages, a sober school, and the *church* (St. Mary and St. Margaret), 1866. Poorly proportioned west end has an ogee-arched porch, carrying overlarge angels, a large circular window and an awkward bell turret. Dark, fussy interior is relieved by an 1831 chancel, which has a plain Gothic arch reminiscent of an early steel engraving.

Compton Verney [11] Against the Roman Fosse Way and with the Kineton–Warwick road dividing a long lake to the south of the deserted mansion of the Verney family, superbly set in a tree-studded park. Sir William Dugdale, the antiquary, was a friend of the Verneys, and in their library was a copy of the first edition of his book, evidence of the pains he took with their arms and monuments. He illustrates the old manor house, built by the family in the reign of Henry VI but rebuilt in the 18th century. Smooth-stone west front, 1714, is in the style of Hawksmoor, with giant Tuscan pilasters and

round-arched windows boasting severe, elongated keystones. South and east fronts were extended in 1760, by Robert Adam, who added a giant Corinthian portico. Pillared *Hall* was decorated with Roman scenes by Andrea Zuchi, who painted scenes for Adam at Osterley; *Saloon* is a typical Adam room, with pairs of columns screening apses. Stables are by Gibbs. Doric *Orangery* was begun in 1769 when 'Capability' Brown was preparing plans for the transformation of the formal garden into the 'natural' landscape of today, dominated by a large lake which necessitated the construction of two new bridges. Following the desertion of the original village, the mediaeval parish church of Compton became the Verney private chapel but, to improve the view, was swept away in 1772, leaving some gravestones by the lake. New *Chapel*, 1776, is plain, with Verney monuments and armorial glass, transferred from the old chapel, and a three-decker pulpit. All that can be seen of the original village is its pitted site to the east of the house, covered with nettles.

Compton Wynyates [14] The most romantic of all English country houses, perfectly sited amid low hills, once terraced for growing grapes. Villagers were expelled in the early 16th century, when the park was made. Built by Sir William Compton in the early 16th century, around an earlier structure of the 1480s and 90s, the house has an informal exterior with mellow brick towers, lichened stone roofs and variously decorated chimneys. Bricks were probably made in situ, for the remains of open brick kilns were found, near the long pond, together with traces of rows of steps, on which the bricks would have been dried. Hardly two bricks are the same colour: they run from pale rose through all shades of orange, crimson and blood red to a bluish brown and an umber black, the darkest bricks being used for diapering. Serene northern arm of the moat is broken by water lilies and skimming swifts; the best garden is a parterre studded with clipped yew. Entrance is off-centre and the welcoming projecting porch bears the royal arms of England and a royal crown, inscribed 'Dom Rex Henricus Octav', for Sir William was page to that unpredictable and dangerous monarch, from whom he received the custody of the ruined Fulbroke Castle, near Warwick, which he used for the enlargement of Compton Wynyates. Henry stayed here on several occasions, probably with Catherine of Aragon, whose arms, which include the castle of Castile, the pomegranate of Granada and her mother's sheaf of arrows, are in a spandrel of the entrance arch. Across the courtyard, a door leads into the screens passage of the *Big Hall*; the screens date from the time of Henry VIII though some of the panels are older. Central panel, c. 1512, is supposed to represent French and English knights at the Battle of Tournai, where Sir William earned his knighthood. Ceiling and bay window, on to the courtyard, are from Fulbroke; a 16th-century tapestry, of cupids picking grapes, was probably designed by Giulio Romano and woven at Mantua. *Dining Room and Ante-Chapel* have an old glazed-tile floor, divided when the Chapel was built in 1512. *Main Staircase*, c. 1860, is by Sir Matthew Digby Wyatt. *Drawing Room* has an Elizabethan plaster ceiling, a sumptuous Elizabethan chimneypiece and panelling from Canonbury House. Windows of *Henry VIII's Room* display the stained-glass arms of Henry and Catherine, and the ceiling includes monograms of Henry, Elizabeth, James and Charles, all of whom may have slept in this room during their known visits to the house. *Council Chamber*, notable for having six doors, from which originally

three staircases ascended and three descended. Sheldon tapestry, made in the neighbouring village of Barcheston. *Priest's Room*, probably the last of the additions of Sir William Compton. *Barracks*, originally one long garret which contained sufficient arms to equip the family retinue. Fireplace in *Cavalier's Room* was part of the original 15th-century house. *Porch Room*, from which the drawbridge must have been operated. *Chapel* retains original glass, damaged during the Civil Wars, and two panels in the screen are curiously carved on each side with seven kings, the devil, Christ bearing his cross and the Coronation of the Virgin. In the grounds, the golden-stone *chapel*, covered in silver lichen, was rebuilt, c. 1665, after its destruction in the Civil War, with unusual twin naves. Earlier west tower, curious 17th-century frieze and Perpendicular windows, between strange pilasters with strapwork capitals. Plastered interior has arched ceilings, once painted with the sun and clouds, to represent day, and the moon and stars, to represent night; sun and moon are now mounted on the west wall. Dark-hardwood pulpit stands above the box pews, its ogee tester, topped by an urn, splendidly silhouetted against light plaster. Recumbent effigies of the family, mutilated by the Roundheads and recovered from the moat, and a colourful set of seventeen hatchments. Stone *spire* was probably one of a network of beacons to give warning of invasion at the time of the Armada. Stone *tower mill* still has sails.

Coombe Fields [8] Formerly known as Smite. 12th-century church (St. Peter) is now a farmhouse, *Peter Hall*, and the old village centre has disappeared. *Coombe Abbey* founded in 1150 by Cistercian monks and, during the 13th century, became the richest monastic house in the country. Coventry owes much to the monks whose

sheep enabled it to develop as a centre of the wool trade. At the Dissolution in 1539, most of the original buildings were demolished and a new house was built around the cloisters, facing across the moat to an avenue of limes. South-west wing, with its picturesque ogee gables, was built during the 17th century and during the 18th century was matched by a similar south east wing, on top of Norman work, later rebuilt by Eden Nesfield, and since demolished. In 1680–91 William Winde added a classical west front and a grand saloon with a splendid ceiling by E. Gouge. Grounds were landscaped by Capability Brown, who dammed Smite Brook to form a pool, near which are the remains of the monastic fish ponds. 19th-century formal gardens.

Copston Magna [6] Mellow brick houses around a triangular green above the crossing of the Roman Watling Street and Fosse Way. Purple-stone *church* (St. John), a simple, early 14th-century-style building crowned by a bellcote, was built in 1849 by the sisters of the seventh Earl of Denbigh, who decided that, after his conversion to the Catholic faith, they could not worship in the same building.

Corley [8] Well wooded and on some of the highest ground in the county. Prehistoric man built, above the natural precipice of *Corley Rocks*, a fort which was later enlarged by the Romans. Sandstone-rubble *church* has Norman nave with stout piers and scalloped capitals; south doorway has shafts with incised volute capitals and a patterned tympanum. Neo-Norman windows were probably added when the nave was extended in smooth ashlar; there is a wooden belfry containing five bells, the oldest of which is said to date from c. 1350. Early 14th-century chancel. Timber-framed *Corley Hall Farm*, described by George Eliot in 'Adam Bede' as the Poysers'

Compton Wynyates:
the chapel and
the beacon

farmhouse, contains some early
16th-century Renaissance panelling, with heads in medallions.
Wild, open *Corley Manor* has a
derelict *tower mill*.

Coughton [10] On the Roman Icknield Street and the skirts of the old
Forest of Arden, part of which survives around the River Arrow. In
a brick-walled churchyard by the
river stands the cream-coloured
church (St. Peter); there is a Tuscan
sundial on the base of the churchyard cross. Behind an ancient yew,
the tower, a perch for noisy pigeons,

has small belfry openings, which contrast with the generously glazed clerestory. Porch is 18th-century Gothick with a decisive ogee arch terminating in a thick, leafy finial. Light, plastered interior has sturdy four-centred arcades which spring from a stone-flagged floor and lead towards a rich orange-and-blue heraldic east window. Dark tower space has glowing figures against lush swirling greenery, 1890. Chancel opens into side chapels through tall twin arches, above which are dark hatchments, and there are many tomb chests to the Throckmorton family, that of Sir George, son of Robert who died on a pilgrimage in 1518, with three-foot-long brasses; tomb of Sir John, d. 1580, with a high alabaster attic, dominates the sanctuary. Sir George built the majestic gatehouse to *Coughton Court*, which is now part of the west front. Family's tenacious allegiance to Roman Catholicism resulted in recurrent penalties and, in 1643–4, the house was occupied by Parliamentary forces, bombarded by Royalist troops and left sacked and burning. When James II left the country, it was pillaged by a Protestant mob, who destroyed the east wing. Turreted gatehouse, so admired by Horace Walpole, is appropriately flanked by pink-orange stucco wings, with pretty late 18th-century ogee windows. Fan-vaulted gateway is now *Entrance Hall*, and on the east side is an open court, enclosed on the north and south by gabled, timber-framed wings. Impressive *Drawing Room* above, where Lady Digby is said to have awaited the outcome of the Gunpowder Plot, has large oriels to east and west. Winding stair, in one of the corner turrets, leads to *Tower Room*, once used as a chapel, and in another turret is a rope ladder to below where, in 1870, a palliasse bed, three altar stones and a folding leather altar were found. *Dining Room* and

Coughton Court

adjoining *Tribune* are splendidly panelled. R.C. *Church of St. Peter, St. Paul and St. Elizabeth* was built in 1857, by Hansom; nearby is a river ford.

Coventry [8]* An ancient settlement where the Kenilworth–Nuneaton road crosses the River Sherbourne. Saxon nunnery was destroyed by Canute, about 1016, but was converted into a Benedictine priory, in 1043, by Leofric, Earl of Chester, and Countess Godiva. During the 14th century Coventry became the fourth city in England and the Midland centre of the cloth trade, with the Merchant Guild, granted in 1340, followed by others. During the 17th century trade declined, but was revived in the 18th by ribbon and watch making. Daimler's car factory of 1896 was the start of the industry which, since it was given over to armaments during the Second World War, resulted in numerous air raids, devastating the city centre. Rebuilt on a bold plan by the City Architect, Donald Gibson, and clearly defined by an elevated ring road, the new heart is the most uncompromising post-war city centre in the country. Broadgate, a central square, with equestrian *statue* of Lady Godiva by Reid Dick, is focused on the old cathedral spire, and to the west is a wide shopping precinct, closed by a white stratified tower carrying the city's coat of arms. Transverse precinct has the fanciful Frank Lloyd Wright-influenced *Hillman House*, answered by the precariously perched *Coventry Point*, 1975, by The John Madin Design Group. *Cathedral of St. Michael*, by Sir Basil Spence, was built in 1951–62, to replace the burnt-out Cathedral Church of St. Michael, the sandstone ruins of which have been

* The named districts of outer Coventry are to be found in alphabetical order immediately following this entry (page 90).

retained as a forecourt to the new building, set at right angles. Oldest surviving part is the late 13th-century south porch, and below the north transept is a rib-vaulted crypt of about 1300. Of the soaring steeple, 1371–1430s, the earliest example of the Perpendicular style in the county, Ruskin wrote: 'The sand of Coventry binds itself into stone which can be built half way to the sky.' Chancel has an unusual polygonal apse. Down steps, under a lofty vault, covering the ancient St. Michael's Avenue, the new cathedral is entered through a fully glazed screen engraved with cocoon-like saints and angels by John Hutton, and has side walls of angled 'cliff-like slabs of stone', rising sheer as at Albi, linked by full-height windows throwing colourful light towards the altar. Against the steps is a St. Michael and Lucifer by Sir Jacob Epstein and, even before entering, the interior can be seen to be dominated by Graham Sutherland's vast tapestry, 'Christ in Majesty', lit by the side windows of the Lady Chapel. At night the illuminated interior, seen from the dark ruins, is an unforgettable experience. Compelling seated figure of Christ, with His hands raised, is surrounded by a frame of golden yellow, extended to frame the symbols of the four Evangelists in reds, purples and browns against a dominant, full, rich-green background. Vertical proportions of the Lady Chapel are carried through the nave by slender downward-tapering columns, supporting a freestanding concrete rib vault infilled with pyramids of timber slats. Side walls, which are roughcast and have large low-level inscription tablets by Ralph Beyer, are divided by windows in a sequence of hues only visible from the altar. Polished marble floor steps up to the font, a large, rough boulder from Bethlehem, set within an enormous bowed window, even bigger than the great east window at Gloucester and with luminous abstract glass,

by John Piper and Patrick Reyntiens, culminating in a burst of golden light. Dark, star-shaped Chapel of Unity has strips of golden glass by Margaret Traherne, reflected in an inlaid marble floor given by the people of Sweden. Circular, clear-glazed Guild Chapel, with panoramic view of the city, is centred on a suspended crown of thorns by Geoffrey Clarke, who also designed the high altar cross, and the lectern is a powerfully modelled bronze eagle by Elizabeth Frink. Old and new cathedrals enclose a green, facing which the early 18th-century *11 Priory Row* has giant fluted Ionic pilasters and features in common with the west range of Stoneleigh Abbey by Francis Smith of Warwick. Tile-hung *Kennedy House*, 1965, by Sir Basil Spence, is a youth centre with each dormitory expressed by a tiled pyramid roof; *7 Priory Row*, the house of John Golson, who gave a library to Coventry, has a robust rusticated doorway. Priory Row is the site of the Benedictine Priory, founded 1043, of which the cruciform *Priory Church* (St. Mary), commenced 1140, stretched from the bases of the towers of the west front, discovered near the Blue Coat School in 1856, to a north-east turret and two radiating chapels at the east end, found during excavations for the new cathedral. Remains of two of the rooms adjoin the cloister. Leofric and Godiva are reputed to have been buried in the church. *Blue Coat School* for girls was opened in 1714 and rebuilt in 1856, partly on the remains of the priory. On mediaeval cellars, the early 16th-century *3 and 4 Priory Row* were part of a large group of timber-framed buildings, demolished for the construction of Trinity Street in 1937. Large, cruciform *Church of the Holy Trinity* was built by the monks of the priory, as a parish church for the lay tenants of the monastic lands. In the Perpendicular style and with a tall spire, it retains some

The Cathedral and the ruins of St Michael's, **Coventry**

13th-century features, notably the rib-vaulted north porch. East end was rebuilt, in fashionable Bath stone, in 1786 and, though Rickman used local red sandstone for recasting the tower in 1826, his partner Hussey rebuilt the west front and recased most of the north side in Bath stone during the 1840s. Interior soars upwards towards a heavenly dusty-blue 15th-century roof ablaze with gold stars, and the crossing has a painted wood star vault, 1854, by George G. Scott, who removed the bells and ringing floor to reveal the lantern. High up on a tower pier is a fine Perpendicular pulpit, and the brass eagle lectern is 15th century. Long chancel, 1391, has closely spaced clerestory windows and various carved misericords from Whitefriars; east window is by Sir Ninian Comper,

who also fitted up the Chapel of Remembrance in the south transept. Richly panelled and painted Perpendicular font stands on steps, thought to be the base of an old market cross; and by the vicar's vestry is a fine 1930s window, by Geoffrey Webb. Philemon Holland, the great classical scholar and master of Coventry Free School, was buried in the church in 1636, and Sarah Siddons, the actress, was married here in 1773. Tuscan *County Hall* was built in 1784 by Samuel Eglinton; and the timber-framed *Golden Cross* stands on the site traditionally known to be that of a royal mint in the reign of Edward IV. *22 Bayley Lane*, c. 1500, has a fine traceried angle post, supporting a jettied first floor, and the red-sandstone *St. Mary's Hall*, built in 1342 for the Merchant Guild,

was enlarged about 1400 for the Trinity Guild, the most powerful guild in Coventry. Approached through a star-vaulted carriage-way, with a central boss depicting the Coronation of the Virgin, the main hall has a famous arras tapestry, illustrating the Assumption of the Virgin, probably installed for the visit of Henry VII in 1500. Above a minstrels' gallery, the splendid panelled roof, burnt during the war but carefully restored, has heraldic bosses and angels making music. *Old Council Chamber* was used as early as 1441, and the heavily carved *Guild Chair* dates from the mid-15th century. *Caesar's Tower*, possibly a tower of the castle of the Earls of Chester on the site of Broadgate, contains the rib-vaulted old treasury and the room where Mary Queen of Scots is said to have been imprisoned. *Undercroft*, once a tavern, has a Perpendicular chimneypiece from the City Arms Hotel. Ionic *Drapers' Hall*, 1832, by Rickman and Hutchinson, though spoilt by a later bay window, shows the influence of Soane; *Lanchester College*, 1957–64, is a reasonable grouping of Miesian forms. *New Central Library*, 1965–7, successfully harmonises with both the old cathedral and the disappointingly arid *Herbert Art Gallery*, 1960. *Civic Offices Tower*, Much Park Street, 1974, has a white 'wall veil' backed by escape balconies; nearby a deep-red-sandstone ruin, with the remains of a vaulted undercroft, may have been a 13th-century merchant's house. Cream-painted *Greyhound* retains its 18th-century character; *Whitefriars Gateway*, 1352, the outer gateway to the friary, is now a toy museum. Multistorey *College of Art and Design*, Cox Street, 1966–7, has a windowless top floor; *Gosford Street* has a number of run-down mediaeval houses. *The Whitefriars*, a Carmelite settlement founded in 1342, had a cruciform church with a central tower. 1506 east range of the intricately-vaulted cloister survives together with the vaulted chapter house and a first-floor dormitory. After the Dissolution the range was converted into a house, by John Hales, who entertained Queen Elizabeth here, and it is now the local history museum. Dilapidated mid-18th-century *Kirby House*, Little Park Street, in the style of Francis Smith of Warwick, is divided by giant Ionic pilasters of c. 1775; *7 Little Park Street* is of similar date. Dull First-World-War *Council House* has over-large figures of Leofric, Godiva and Justice, and *High Street* has some bold Victorian palazzi. Imperial *Lloyds Bank*, 1932, by Buckland and Heywood, has splendid metal doors, and the earlier *National Provincial*, by F. C. R. Palmer, a large Palladian portico. Small-scale timber-framed *Ford's Hospital*,

Greyfriars Lane, c. 1529, enclosing a narrow central courtyard, is enriched by exceptionally well carved gables, and *Greyfriars Steeple*, c. 1350, all that remains of the house established in 1234, was originally at the crossing of a cruciform church, quarried away after the Reformation. For centuries it stood alone in the fields until, in 1830–2, Rickman and Hutchinson added a thin Gothic body, bombed in the war. Greyfriars Green, enclosed by the brick Georgian terrace houses of *Warwick Row* and the stucco mid-19th-century *Quadrant*, is dominated by the oval Italianate *United Reformed church*, 1889–91, by Steane, its twin domed towers adding a decidedly Continental character. *Nantglyn*, the last house against the ring road, is where George Eliot attended Miss Franklin's school. Italian-style concourse of the early 1960s *railway station* has views on to a disappointing square and the plain brick 1880s *Drill Hall*, in Queen Victoria Road, was built when the road was cut. The Butts, once the weavers' and watch makers' quarter, has an impressive Cubist classical *Technical College*. *Spon Bridge*, built in 1771, partly of stones taken from Spon Gate, retains the remnants of some stylish obelisks. Ruined red-sandstone *Chapel of St. James and St. Christopher*, an equally forlorn sight, would be far better used as a dwelling, as during the last century. *Spon Street*, now cut in two by the ring road, has some fine examples of the timber tradition, to which have been added others moved to the site as a result of redevelopment elsewhere. 15th-century *7 Much Park Street*, moved 1970–71, has a workshop, a hall and a solar; the jettied *8–10 Much Park Street*, c. 1500, is out of scale with its indigenous neighbours. Row of weavers' cottages has wide-arched, small-paned windows; the Georgian *190 Spon Street* incorporates a piece of town wall. Crumbling red-sandstone *Church of St. John the*

Baptist, built by Queen Isabella, mother of Edward III, was the church of the Guild of St. John the Baptist. Following the suppression of the guilds, the present 15th-century building, stripped of its treasures, fell into decay and became a textile manufacturer's 'stretch yard'. Restored in 1877 by George G. Scott, who considered it one of the most beautiful churches in England, it has a central tower, spoilt by early 19th-century turrets but delicately vaulted inside to form a most attractive lantern. Rich south aisle window, c. 1896, by Kempe, and gilded south chapel reredos and aumbry, 1932, by Ninian Comper. *Bablake School* and *Bond's Hospital* are around a courtyard, enclosed on the south side by the church to which they originally belonged. Oldest range, c. 1500, is Bablake School, with a timber-framed upper storey and galleries facing the courtyard. Crowning glory of Bond's Hospital, founded in 1506 to house ten almsmen, is an exquisite series of carved gables. West end was mostly rebuilt in 1832, when the other end was linked to the school by a Bath-stone entrance arch, by Rickman and Hutchinson, with crisp cast-iron tracery. Hill Street has a *Georgian terrace* with wide workshop windows; the urbane 1950s *Belgrade Theatre* is the first full-scale professional theatre built in Britain after the war. Large areas of glass against a square, with trees and a gushing fountain. Eroded red-sandstone *Chapel of the Hospital of St. John the Baptist*, Hales Street, is 14th century with a large, lumpy late 18th-century window. At the Dissolution it was converted into a free grammar school, where, later, William Dugdale, the great antiquary and historian, was a pupil and Dr. Philemon Holland, the distinguished translator, was master. *Burges* retains some modest 18th-century houses converted into shops; and, against the Coventry Canal, *Leicester Row* has some

88

impressive 1830s warehouses with lunette openings. Now with shops on the front garden, Ionic *Bird Grove*, Foleshill Road, is where George Eliot came to live in 1841. *Church of St. Mark*, Bird Street, has a vibrant orange-and-blue Resurrection by Hans Feibusch, painted over the entire east wall. *Wheatley Street* has an arcaded brick granary with ventilated hipped roofs and *Priory or Swanswell Gate* is one of the two surviving original twelve gates to the mediaeval fortified city. *Lady Herbert's garden* incorporates remains of the city wall, and though *Cook Street Gate* lacks much original detail, the portcullis slides are still visible. Another length of wall stands where the ring road sweeps past the fully glazed *Swimming Baths*, a contrast characteristic of the reconstructed city.

Alderman's Green—Coventry
Down a rough drive towards the River Sowe, the orange-brick *Foleshill Mill* is 18th century, with a tall 19th-century weaving shop; and the *Mill House*, which contains some Jacobean carving, has a pretty Gothic exterior. Nearer the road, more weaving shops were provided with power from the mill by an overhead shaft, the corn being ground at night. Pale-brick Gothic *Ebenezer Free Methodist church* has delicately traceried iron windows and next to this, behind a forecourt with a Grecian war memorial, is an Italianate chapel. Co-operative Street looks like a co-operative venture but is actually named after the society, which had a shop on the corner. It leads to the attractive *Infants' School*, 1954, by Arcon, sited in fields descending to a lake, the result of mining subsidence.

Allesley—Coventry In 1966 a bypass made the village street shorter but brought peace to the pictur-

No 7, Little Park Street, **Coventry**

esque centre, with gabled, timber-framed and straight brick houses from the 16th to 18th centuries, set backwards and forwards on each side. To ease the gradient the road is cut into the hill, leaving the footpaths at high level, one leading past an orange-brick *gatehouse*, at the foot of the walled rectory garden. Slate headstones and yew trees in the well kept churchyard. *Church* (All Saints) of orange-pink sandstone with a west spire, has tall aisles giving the effect of a hall church. South arcade is partly Norman, and north arcade Early English. Mainly Victorian south aisle has a vibrant east window of the 1840s, and the tower a similar one depicting the four Evangelists. Chunky pitch-pine pews and font with marble colonnettes on an encaustic tile step. Of the *castle*, ruined in the 16th century, only an earthwork remains. *Paybody Hospital*, a group of buildings around a timber-framed cottage, has a large 17th-century house against the road, and the adjoining staircase hall, on the axis of the church spire, leads to an enclosed garden with a corner gazebo. *The Stone House*, 1557, with a two-storey porch and mullioned windows; and, behind a raised garden, brick-pilastered *The Lodge*, 1720. *Rainbow Inn*, 1680, and *62 and 64*, originally built, in 1500, as one house for John Marston, are timber-framed.

Bell Green—Coventry A development area with the *church* (St. Chad) designed by Sir Basil Spence. Concrete-framed campanile has various panels, and the nave and chancel form an aisleless hall which has sheer, rough-textured side walls and fully glazed end walls, reminiscent of the architect's cathedral. Wall behind the altar faces north, so there is never glare from the sun, which is allowed to pierce the side walls through small, square clerestory windows for morning and evening services, and to illuminate the whole interior

at midday. Semicircular nave of the R.C. *Church of St. Patrick* has a fan of aluminium-sheathed roofs, divided at the west end by a glazed spire. *Bell Green District Centre*, marked by a tower block of flats, contains an L-shaped pedestrian precinct; and slate-hung housing in Woodway Lane, by F. Lloyd Roche, is imaginatively grouped around courtyards and play areas. Against the River Sowe, *Manor Farm Estate*, on the Radburn principle, has a landscaped area around a tower block of flats, and gentle changes in level combined with the refined simplicity of the houses give an air of inevitability. In a lavish plantation of trees to the south of Hermes Crescent, bold four-storey flats have black windows and white balconies.

Binley—Coventry A Saxon settlement in a wood which, as part of the Craven family's Coombe Abbey Estate, remained feudal throughout the 17th and 18th centuries. Binley Colliery, founded in 1907, brought new life to the area, with a special village built to accommodate the miners, but closed in 1963. The cupola and varying projections of the *church* (St. Bartholomew), rebuilt by Lord Craven in 1771–3, have 'the rise and fall, the advance and recess' of the quality of 'movement' defined by Robert Adam, to whom the design has been attributed. Approached through an arched recess, containing a Tuscan doorway, the gracefully vaulted nave is divided from the apse by marble columns with Adam-ish capitals; to either side are shallow niches. Walls have white stucco decoration, with delicate medallions, ribbons and garlands, and there is a lavish alabaster screen, with Ionic columns, separating the Craven Chapel. Communion rails are decorated with honeysuckle in wrought iron; the east window of the Holy Family, 1776, is typical of the enamelled glass of the period.

Bleak expanse of ground, between the spoil tips of the Binley Colliery and the pastures of the River Sowe, has been covered by the large *Ernsford Grange Housing Estate*, where the contrast between architect-designed and speculatively built houses is marked, and highlights the high design standards of the Corporation. *Binley Park Comprehensive School*, Brandon Lane, 1958–62, by the C.A.'s Dept., is also bleak, with large areas of car park.

Canley—Coventry Some of its smartest housing is around the Kenilworth Road, some of its dreariest north of Charter Avenue. In between, Warwick University. *112–14 Kenilworth Road*, 1959, *9 Gibbet Hill Road*, 1963, and *South Winds* Cryfield Grange Road, 1965–6, all by Yorke, Harper and Harvey, show the influence of Frank Lloyd Wright's prairie houses. *The Spinney*, 1967–8, by Roy Geden, is a related group of individual houses; and *Mistral*, 1968, by the same architect, also shows Wright influence. *University of Warwick* was granted its charter in 1968, following the first development plan, prepared by Arthur Ling and Alan Goodman. Gently sloping northwest parts of the site are for the teaching areas; the higher, more steeply sloping ground to the south and east is for residential buildings. First buildings on the east site are by Alan Goodman, but those on the main site are by Yorke, Rosenberg and Mardell. Goodman's buildings include the two-storey *Multi-purpose Building*, 1964–5, planned around two interconnecting courts and clad with dark-brown and white tiles. Rosenberg's taller buildings are also clad with white tiles, which emphasise their good proportions, but too harshly for the Warwickshire countryside. Austere *Rootes Hall Social Building*, 1965–6, has an insistent grid and a light, attractive interior, with many brightly coloured modern paintings; *Rootes Hall* itself has staggered rectangular blocks. *Benefactors' Building*, for U.S. exchange students and international conferences, contains a central double-height reading room, and the classic *University Library*, 1964–6, a fine Miesian-style staircase. Yellow-brick *Second Hall of Residence*, 1967–9, is a welcome change from white tile, and the *housing* for visiting mathematicians, 1968–9, by Howell, Killick, Partridge and Amis, has rounded corners, suggested by the need to provide a continuous blackboard in the studies. *Church of St. John Baptist*, Westwood Heath, built in 1842–5, by Scott and Moffatt, is an early work by George Gilbert Scott.

Cheylesmore—Coventry An inner suburb, with *Cheylesmore Manor* actually within the ring road. During the 14th century it was often occupied by Queen Isabel and the Black Prince, but later became a ruin, a major part of which was demolished as late as 1956. What is left has been restored with much new timber framing to form a new Register Office. Large brick tower of the ungainly 1950s *Christchurch*, Frankpledge Road, rises above cosy semis; dark-framed blocks of *Whitley Abbey Comprehensive School* are impressively grouped around a large lake, once belonging to an Elizabethan house altered by Soane. *Cemetery*, London Road, laid out by Joseph Paxton, 1843–7, has an Italianate lodge and Grecian and Norman chapels. After the Great Exhibition of 1851, Paxton was M.P. for Coventry, and there is a spiky Gothic monument to his memory, by Joseph Goddard. Richard II laid the foundation stone of *Charterhouse*, in 1385, and what was probably the refectory still retains an Elizabethan partition and a wall painting of the Crucifixion.

Coundon—Coventry 1920s terrace housing around the large Coundon Green, which is good farmland and very rural despite the nearby Jaguar car works. Angular brick *church* (St. George) was built in 1939, by N. F. Cachemaille-Day. Entered through a large, square baptistry, the nave, which has a north aisle only, is given movement by diagonal concrete ribs supporting a conventional pitched roof.

Earlsdon—Coventry An older residential area with substantial terraces and extensive parks. Chapel Fields consisted of watch-makers' houses, with most of the masters' houses, terraced and with bay windows, facing Allesley Old Road; the workshops, in two-storied wings built onto the back gardens, increasing in length as trade prospered. Smaller watch-makers' houses in Duke, Lord and Mount Streets. Brick *church* (St. Barbara) Rochester Road, built in 1930–1, by Austin and Paley, is in the Decorated style and has a polygonal apse, lined with ashlar. Large pulpit with a bulbous base, 1661. Most attractive housing estate is the *Whoberley Estate*, 1967–8, by the C.A.'s Dept., of red-brick single-storey terrace houses with gardens enclosed by concrete-block walls.

Foleshill—Coventry Originally heathland with scattered hamlets, the earliest probably at Hall Green and Little Heath. Since Elizabethan times, private speculators have prospected for coal and, as the Stoney Stanton and Foleshill Roads were turnpiked to carry this, the hamlets did not develop in the usual way. Trade received a further boost with the cutting of the Coventry Canal in 1769. *Church* (St. Laurence) which has a Perpendicular west tower and roof, was partly rebuilt in brick in Georgian times, with gaunt cast-iron pillars. Victorian chancel and Norman font. Cachemaille-Day's 1939 *Church of St. Luke*, influenced by a church in St. Denis, has diagonal square brick piers and a zigzag brick cornice.

Hawkesbury—Coventry A canal-side hamlet at the junction of the Coventry Canal, 1769, and the later Oxford Canal, both engineered by James Brindley. North Warwickshire coalfields were among the first areas in the country to benefit from Brindley's new canals, which had a considerable effect on the infant industrial life of the Midlands. Brindley's original junction at Longford, abandoned for almost a century and a half, survives as little more than a bramble-choked ditch. Tucked away, almost forgotten, behind the huge concrete cooling towers of Longford Power Station, the later junction, known as Sutton Stop after the original tollkeeper, has changed so little that it is now almost a living industrial museum and one of the most fascinating places in the whole English canal system. Narrow, bumpy dirt track, once the route of an older canal, dips beneath the rotting beams of a timber-framed railway bridge and opens out into a spacious waterside courtyard. Graceful tow-path *bridge*, cast in the Britannia Foundry, Derby, in 1837. Gaunt, tall shell of the old *pump house*, which has a polygonal chimney stack, housed a Newcomen-type atmospheric beam engine, now in Dartmouth Borough Museum. Installed in 1821 to top up the Coventry Canal from an artesian well, it had already worked for almost a century pumping out the workings of the nearby Griff colliery. A tiny lock, unusual for its shallow fall of only seven inches, connects the Oxford Canal to the lower Coventry Canal. *The Greyhound* was once the coal office; nearby is a *Salvation Army chapel*.

Keresley—Coventry Surprisingly rural, and retaining the older part of the village at Keresley Green. Ribbon development has spread from Coventry along the Tamworth Road, turnpiked in 1762 with a tollgate just south of the village. On a lawn surrounded by giant firs, almost hiding the tower, the red-sandstone *church* (St. Thomas) an early work of Benjamin Ferry, is characteristically unassuming. Shallow chancel, oversized mouldings and spidery roof add a naïve charm. Bright, white-painted nave is alive with a forest of quaint poppy heads; wide chancel arch frames a wheel window and three lancets. West gallery with simple organ. 17th-century *Akon House* is probably the oldest building in the district; *Royal Court Hotel* was Keresley Hall. *The Shepherd and Shepherdess* was opened in the early 1800s, and the *National School* in 1852. Coventry housing arrived after the opening, in 1911, of the *Coventry Colliery*, at the south end of the Warwickshire coalfield.

Longford—Coventry 19th-century mining and weaving. Brick *church* (St. Thomas the Apostle), built in 1874, by John Cotton, has large stone pinnacles around an octagonal bell stage and a short cream-brick spire banded with red. *1–7 Hurst Road* were weavers' cottages, with large workshop windows on the top floor. *The Yews*, 198 Longford Road, is graced by a cast-iron Regency porch with bas-relief capitals; *Foxford School*, built in 1964, has a frieze of awkward figures. Pedimented *Salem Baptist church*, 1839, boasts giant pilasters and, across the Coventry Canal, the stucco *Union Place Baptist church*, built by breakaway Salem Baptists in 1827, modestly conceals an unspoilt galleried interior. *Weavers' shop*, 8 Woodshires Road, has large cast-iron-framed windows.

Radford—Coventry On Radford Brook, the village lost its separate identity during the last century. Evidence of quarrying, sand pits and a kiln, and of old field names in the naming of modern streets, e.g. Bateman's Acre, Campers Field, Thistley Field and Steeplefield. By 1838 two-thirds of the population were engaged in weav-

ing, but industry really arrived with the pre-First World War Daimler factory. In the form of an aircraft hangar, the 1950s *church* (St. Nicholas) has a slab tower; against the Coventry Canal are *Cash's Hundred Houses*, built in 1857, by Joseph Cash, to enable men weaving in their own homes to have the benefit of power-driven looms. Overhead shafting runs the length of the top workshops, lit by tall Gothic windows. Cash's ornate Venetian Gothic chimney enriches the industrial skyline, enlivened by wooden cooling towers and Courtaulds' 360-foot fume stack.

Stivichall—Coventry Red-brick Victorian terraces, pre-war semis and post-war prefabs at the confluence of the Rivers Sherbourne and Sowe, on which there were mediaeval mills. Castellated Regency *church* (St. James), which replaced a Norman building, is now the chancel to a 1950s nave. Mullioned *Stivichall Grange*, really in Stoneleigh, dates from the 14th century, but is mainly mid-17th-century; on a gently sloping site, *Grange Farm Primary School*, built in 1966, by the C.A.'s Dept., has long, framed blocks.

Stoke—Coventry By the River Sowe and on clay, which in mediaeval times was made into tiles. Kilns have been found near Harefield Road; and pipe and brickworks were active until the 19th century. *Church* (St. Michael) has a cream-coloured Perpendicular tower and a red-sandstone south aisle. Nave and chancel were built, in 1861, by James Murray, who designed the former Coventry School of Art. Perpendicular font; and, in the west window, fragments of small kneeling figures in blue robes. The undulating sward of Barras Heath leads up to the seventeen-storey *Alpha House*, a distinguished block of flats, built in 1962–3, by the C.A.'s Dept. White-brick cottages and a small hall define an

open forecourt. Richly modelled brick-and-tile *flats* in Aldermoor Lane were built in 1967–8, by Yorke, Harper and Harvey. *Health Clinic* is overglazed, and *Pinley Estate* large and anonymous.

Tile Hill—Coventry The most successful of the development areas, perhaps because it is the most rural and village-like, though the early housing is rather dreary. Tile Hill Wood provides a good background and a fine setting for the comprehensive school. *Church* (St. Oswald), built in 1957–8, is the best of three local churches designed by Sir Basil Spence and has the same elements as the other two, St. John's Willenhall, and St. Chad's, Bell Green, but arranged differently to suit the site. Though inescapably of its time, it has something of the feeling of a country church, perhaps because the church and hall enclose a generous green on which is placed the campanile, a rectangular, open concrete frame. The sanctuary is side-lit and backed by an appliqué-work hanging of two saints, by Gerald Holtom, anticipating the similarly placed cathedral tapestry. West wall, with slit windows at the sides and top, carries a Crucifixion, without a cross, by Carroll Sims. Centre does not hold together, partly because the main buildings differ in style. 1960s *Tile Hill Social Club* has a well modelled concrete staircase, but the *Shopping Centre* consists of four soulless parallel blocks with mean glazing. Eastern part is mainly inter-war, with the Godiva Cinema. *397–429 Tile Lane* are striking prefabs with white plastic panels and stained boarding; the *station* is neat and attractive; and *Cromwell Cottage*, Cromwell Lane, part stone, part timber-framed with early brick infilling. Seventeen-storey *Massey-Ferguson Office Tower*, built in 1965, by John H. D. Madin and Partners, on the fringe of the country, is the tallest building in the area.

Walsgrave-on-Sowe—Coventry

Traces of neolithic man have been found. Coal mining was carried out from the late 16th century, the growing need for coal being met by the opening of the Coventry Canal in 1769. Silk ribbon weaving came in the 17th century. Amid dark yews, the grey Perpendicular *church* (St. Mary) has an earlier red-sandstone chancel and an arcaded Norman font. Huge 1960s *Walsgrave General Hospital* looks 1950s. Light-tinted-brick *Oslo Gardens*, Nordic Drift, a group of terrace houses built, in 1962–5, by John Thorne Barton and Associates, has steep asymmetrical roofs and varnished-timber window frames; the same architects' sculptural cream-brick *Living Units*, 1968–9, provide a variety of accommodation for hospital staff, and are arranged on two levels off a series of narrow pedestrian walks.

Willenhall—Coventry

On high ground and engulfed by much corporation housing. 1950s *church* (St. John the Divine) the first of three designed by Sir Basil Spence, has the same elements as St. Chad's, Bell Green and St. Oswald's, Tile Hill, but arranged differently to suit the site. Campanile, a rectangular, open concrete frame, serves as an entrance and is linked to the church by a light covered way. Tall, aisleless hall with small low-level windows; nave is lit mainly from the fully glazed west wall, which is braced by a slender steel cross seen in silhouette. Sanctuary side-lighting accentuates the conglomerate texture of the concrete east wall and the altar, a substantial slab of timber, is enhanced by slender candlesticks and a cross. *Shopping precinct* has views past blocks of flats to the city centre; Radburn *Willenhall Wood Housing Estate*, built in 1959–65, by the C.A.'s Department, incorporates mature trees and hedgerows. 1960s *youth club* provides a lively incident in rather dreary surroundings, shunned by the timber-clad *Willenhall C. of E. Primary School*, which looks inwards onto courtyards.

Wyken—Coventry

Norman *church* (St. Mary) is by the River Sowe and has a Victorian timber belfry. Tub-shaped font, with blank arcading, is also Norman; 15th-century mural painting of St. Christopher shows a wooden windmill in a riverside landscape. 1960s *Church of the Risen Christ* was built because the Norman church had become too small. *Lyng Hall Comprehensive School* consists of a number of blocks around Green Farm pond and, successfully housing the art-room studios, a U-shaped group of barns, enclosing a small garden. *St. Austell Road Estate* has inhuman ten- and fifteen-storey blocks of flats overlooking the river, and *Caludon Castle Comprehensive School*, 1954, does not deserve its magnificent sloping site. All that remains of the castle, the only permanent nobleman's residence in the neighbourhood of Coventry, is a moated mid-14th-century grey-sandstone wall with two large windows. Red-brick *Belgrave Estate*, 1959–62, an attractive series of semi-enclosed courts, shows a sensitive appreciation of small-scale townscape.

Cubbington [8]

Long brick-and-tile terraces, riding over hills above the River Leam, and some black-and-white cottages. Nearby are the drovers' Welsh Road and New Cubbington, a dull post-war suburb of Leamington Spa. On an eminence and approached through cast-iron gates, worthy of Rickman, the red-sandstone *church* (St. Mary) has a Norman west tower, accompanied by a solitary Scots pine. Dark, unplastered interior has a massive Norman south arcade with round piers and scalloped capitals, and the font is also Norman. Benches and pulpit, 1852, are by Butterfield, who was also responsible for the chancel floor tiling and the elaborate iron-and-brass communion rail. Richly carved royal arms and an oval wooden tablet, 1702, with a boat supported by a sailor and Neptune. *West Hill* has an Italianate tower and Grecian rainwater gutters; the *Manor* is half stone, half brick. Georgian white-painted *King's Head* and Perpendicular-style school, straight from an Early Victorian pattern book. Mullioned *Old Manor House* is 17th century; and *Ledbroke Hall* has tall, round-arched windows from the days when it served as a chapel.

Curdworth [4]

Probably named after Crida, first king of the Mercians (583), and reputed to be both the oldest settlement of the English in the Midlands and the exact centre of England. Coventry–Lichfield road over the Tame is a very old highway and, when the river is low, remains of an ancient bridge can be seen. Traces of a moat and old masonry in Farthing Lane are probably the remains of the fortified manor house. Neglected brick cottages and post-war housing. On high ground, the red-sandstone *church* (St. Nicholas), has a massive Perpendicular tower. Eastern part of the nave and the chancel are the Norman rebuilding of an earlier Saxon church, and have deep window splays decorated with ancient wall paintings and inscriptions. Norman font bowl, square on top and round at base, carved with the Lamb and Flag (symbol for Christ), two pairs of standing men (the four Evangelists) and a winged monster. Round chancel arch, with zigzag decoration, is narrow, so openings have been made at the sides. 18th-century organ above was transferred from the tower arch, and has an elaborate Gothic Revival loft in the darkness of the roof space. Light, almost domestic, chancel is simply furnished and has Grecian memorials by Hollins. Inscription to Cornelius and Ann Ford, who during the 17th century lived at *Dunton Hall*, now a plain Georgian house surrounded by chestnuts.

New hexagonal *church hall* is well sited by the lych gate and the gabled 18th-century *Rectory*, replaced by a neat brick box, now awaits demolition, with the timber-framed tithe barn and *Red Lion Cottages*. In a field nearby occurred the first skirmish of the Civil War.

Darlingscott [14] A fine row of 16th- and 17th-century houses, with yellow Cotswold-stone fronts and local lias bodies. In a yew-planted churchyard surrounded by fields, the light *church* (St. George), 1873–4, has vigorous chancel arch capitals with pea pods, ferns and figs—a perpetual harvest festival. Nave corbels with hollyhocks and ivy, and more leaves on the font.

Dordon [5] On one of the highest hills in the district, between the River Anker and Watling Street. At the turn of the century the village became well known for coal mining and brick making, though 'digging' started as far back as the 14th century. Many long brick terraces, leading to distant views of fields and spoil tips and solid new houses and flats. *Church* (St. Leonard), 1867–8, by G. E. Street, is brick, inside and out, with a stone bell turret, but, since 1901, has been used as the north aisle and vestry of a larger church, by W. H. Bidlake. North door spoilt by the addition of an ordinary porch. Bidlake's exciting arcade is without capitals or bases and ends in half arches. Dark sanctuary with a stained-glass Crucifixion against foliage. Gothic *Sunday school*, 1884, and *Congregational church*, 1908. Classical *United Methodist Free Church*, 1882, has blue-brick arches. On high ground, with fine views, *Dordon Hall*, known locally as 'The Jawbones', is all that remains of the moated house built by Bishop Neulend. Partly timber-framed and with stepped end gables, it has a Georgian stone front with a cyclopean doorway. 18th-century *Hall End Farm*, formerly Holt Hall, has

small-paned windows and a cloak of ivy.

Dorridge [7] Known as 'Derrech' in 1400, and a mere hamlet until 1878, when the station was built and G. F. Muntz laid out two estates with substantial brick villas. Simple brick *church* (St. Philip), 1878, by E. J. Payne, is dwarfed by a stone chancel, built in 1886, by J. A. Chatwin. Light, whitewashed nave has a quaint painted-glass west window, and the darker chancel an alabaster reredos beneath a rich 'Light of the World', after Holman Hunt. Arts and Crafts *vicarage*, 1928, by W. H. Bidlake, has simple round arches. Opposite the station, the Victorian *Forest Hotel* has picturesque half timbering and pierced gables, and the shops are similar, though more stern. Handsome *456 Station Road* is Queen Anne Revival and the pretty *school*, Widney Road, Gothic Revival with buff-brick dressings. Four Ashes Road has large houses set in their own grounds, notably the Arts and Crafts *The Grange*, which has an impressive central hall.

Dorsington [13] Small, with timber-framed and brick cottages and farmhouses scattered around a green, and a simple 18th-century *church* (St. Peter). Of light-red brick, on a blue-lias base, probably the foundations of an earlier building, it has a slim west tower with a straight parapet sprouting pinnacles. Gothic windows and Cotswold-stone roof. Handsome octagonal font on panelled mid-17th-century pedestal, and Jacobean pulpit. Georgian *New House Farm* has small-paned windows within wide-arched openings; blue-and-yellow-stone *Moat House Farm*, once the retreat of the Bishop of Gloucester, stands against a large timber-framed barn and isolated, timber-framed *Baggington* was also moated.

Dunchurch [9] A large, partly thatched village which grew

around the old coach road from London to Holyhead, served by the stucco-faced *Dun Cow* and the *Bell*, which once stabled forty pairs of post horses. The Square, which has trees, leads to the weathered red-standstone *church*, (St. Peter), mainly the work of the monks of the Cistercian Abbey at Pipewell in Northamptonshire, who incorporated Norman arcade bases and chancel walling. Haughty Perpendicular tower has a large window lighting a tall plaster-vaulted baptistry, created after the removal of the west galleries in the early 19th century. By the end of the 15th century the church was famed for its richly carved furnishings, including canopied choir stalls, a rood screen and bench ends, but of the latter only three survived a late Georgian bonfire to make way for 'fine new deal pews . . . to gratify the growing taste for comfort and seclusion'. East window by Kempe has a superb Crucifixion, against a golden hanging above a blue mediaeval town, and the organ is an excellent modern design with polished pipes in tall oak boxes. Triptych to Thomas Newcombe, printer to Charles II, James II and William III, who, in 1693, founded the nearby *almshouses*, rebuilt in 1818. Timber-framed *Guy Fawkes House*, formerly the Lion Inn, is where the Gunpowder Plot conspirators met to arrange their plans and the mutilated yet dignified *school house*, 1707, was designed and built by Smith of Warwick at the expense of Francis Boughton. *Statue* of Lord John Scott, by J. Durham, erected by his tenantry in 1867, has contemporary dress. *Market cross*, an obelisk erected in 1813, is inscribed with mileages. A short distance along the Rugby Road is a small group of timber-framed houses, and one of puddled clay with thick walls and small windows; and further west are the *stocks* and *Working Men's Club*, rebuilt in a modern Georgian style after war damage. Southam Road has some thatched whitewashed terraces and, replacing a cosy Early Georgian house, the Ionic stucco-faced *Dunchurch-Winton Hall*, built c. 1840, has an elegant staircase. Handsome *Toft Manor House*, Toft Hill, overlooks the new Draycote Reservoir and the orange-brick Caroline-style *Dunchurch Industrial Staff College* was built in 1906, by Gilbert Fraser for John Lancaster, owner of the Rugby Gas Company. In magnificent gardens, laid out by T. H. Mawson, it has a convincingly Edwardian dining room built in the early 1960s. Every effort was made to match the main building, including opening up the local brickworks and employing the original apprentices. Middle Court, originally the stables, has a stern central tower. Cubist *Methodist church*, 1935. Brick *Bilton Grange*, 1841–6, by A. W. Pugin, is entered through a porte-cochère tower supporting an open belfry. *Entrance Hall* has an unusual heraldic floor, and the *Long Gallery* a bold canopied fireplace, complete with fire dogs. *Staircase Hall*, the most interesting space in the house, ascends to a painted wood ceiling and the cantilevered timber staircase has carved animals holding scrolls. Galleried *Hall*, with an elaborate fireplace and fine glass. One *Lodge* is of the gatehouse type, and another is of yellow brick patterned with red.

Earlsdon *see* Coventry.

Earlswood [8] Timber-framed barns and Georgian cottages and farms in undulating country, with lakes draining into the River Blythe. At Salter Street, the Stratford-on-Avon Canal is spanned by a blue-brick bridge, and nearby is the *school*. *Church* (St. Patrick) stands behind the cast-iron railings of the Early Victorian building, the formal plan of which obviously influenced the present brick structure. A landmark for miles around, the gabled west tower, built in 1860, by G. T. Robinson,

for Thomas Burman of Warings Green, has roguish details which fail to give it life. Wide, gabled portal borders on the vulgar, and the vigorously vaulted porch houses a dark, spiky Ten Commandments which must be the original reredos. Light, wide body, 1899, by W. H. Bidlake, paid for by the will of Miss Elizabeth Burman, is very different, with deeply splayed buff-brick wall piers, predating the arcades of St. Agatha's, Sparkbrook, and simple arches which divide a Bodley-esque stencilled ceiling. Pulpit is of the refectory type; and, up steps beyond an elaborate screen, flanked by statues of St. Chad and St. Patrick, the east window is set above a richly vaulted sanctuary, framed by carved angels swinging gilded censers. Vault is painted and, against a background of pink angels, an intricately carved reredos has a painting of the Last Supper by F. W. Davis. West gallery, on clustered shafts and dainty font, enclosed by a parclose. Chancel, being longer than the earlier one, is on arches over graves and a timber cycle rack. In the churchyard are descendants of Thomas Burman of Shottery, a member of Stratford-upon-Avon Corporation in the late 17th century.

Easenhall [9] An estate village to the south of Newbold Revel (see Stretton-under-Fosse) which has a green bounded by a long barn and a brick *chapel*, 1873, with a quatrefoil in the gable. Two thatched cottages have pretty bargeboards; and four pairs of Victorian semis, with blue-brick arches and pierced timber gables, are obviously by the architect of the lodge to Newbold Revel, which has a more elaborate gable towards the drive. Road to Brinklow has three more lodges, but Italianate and single-storey.

Eathorpe [8] Just south of where the Roman Fosse Way crosses the River Leam. Past a fantastic Jacobethan lodge, late-17th-century

Eathorpe Hall, once the seat of the Vyners, has a long-nine-bay classical front. Strangely tiled, windowless room is said to have been for falcons. Victorian *stables* overhung by trees, and extensive views to the south over the valley of the River Itchen.

Edgbaston *see* Birmingham.

Elmdon [7] Torn apart by the busy Birmingham–Coventry road and Birmingham Airport. *Lodge* to the demolished Elmdon Hall is a miniature Doric Temple, and the park is well wooded. Garden walling, a sinister pool, overhung by yew trees and a fine lake, now bordered by the Rover car factory and a housing complex. Surprisingly, the smooth-stone *church* (St. Nicholas), built in 1780–1 for Abraham Spooner, when he was over ninety years of age, is Gothic with simply branched tracery. West gallery, a pretty plaster-vaulted apse and elegant monuments to the Spooners. Early in this century the gaunt 18th-century *rectory* was occupied by Canon Hayter, who lived there in some state, boasting a shining equipage with a top-hatted coachman. In later years he was aghast and bewildered when two cooling towers appeared on his horizon, replacing Lord Norton's noble Hams Hall.

Ettington [14] Greystone, speckled brick and stucco on high ground near the Roman Fosse Way. Crumbling 18th-century Gothic *tower* of the old *church* (St. Thomas à Becket) by Thomas Johnson, is gaunt and ivy-clad, though still housing the Lord's Prayer, Commandments and Creed. Late 17th-century pulpit and classical monuments are at the *new church* (Holy Trinity), built in 1902–3, by Ford Whitcomb. Brick *school*, 1871, has pierced bargeboards and a pyramid-roofed clock tower. By the sedge-choked River Stour the dove-grey château roofs of *Ettington Park* pierce the English sky. The most impressive High Vic-

Ettington Park
and detail of screen

torian house in the county—the 1858–62 remodelling of the 1641 house, which Evelyn Philip Shirley found considerably out of repair. The architects, John Prichard and Seddon, completely encased the earlier building in ochre and brown stone, with thin bands of lias, Ruskinian Venetian Gothic detail, and many narrative reliefs, by H. H. Armstead, illustrating events in the history of the Shirley family. Groined porte cochère, plainer than the original design, is linked to the side wings by an arcaded glass-roofed porch with plants, which must have provided a most exotic reception. *Entrance Hall*, with a rich

Elizabethan-style fireplace by Willcox, is divided from a top-lit *Staircase Hall* by a small-scale arcade and to the right, on the site of the original entrance hall, the Regency Gothic *Library*, admired by Rickman, enjoys a fine view of the church, that belonged to the destroyed old village, set against dark trees. Pinnacled doorway has a traceried ogee arch with mirror glass, as at Strawberry Hill, and the chimneypiece, said to have been copied from Windsor, is below a window with kings in bright glass. Traceried bookcases and, to the classical-style *Ballroom*, a door faced with false book spines—Cook's 'Voyages', Bruce's 'Travels', etc. Through a Tudor-style doorway, the *Dining Room* has inlaid panelling; and the small, polygonal-ended *Chapel* has elaborate murals lit by worn stained glass. Twin-arched late 17th-century *loggia*, from Coleshill Park, topped by

large pineapples and flanked by sagging glasshouses. On undulating lawns above the river, the ruined grey-stone *church* (Holy Trinity) has the air of an 18th-century folly. Spiky picturesque pinnacles crown its massive Norman tower. This was the church of Ettington Inferior, now covered by the deer park of the Shirleys. The nave arcades are continued east as a dark avenue of trees; and the south transept, converted into the Shirley mortuary chapel in 1875, is rich with splendid treasures, including two windows by Evie Hone, 1948–9. Panelled plaster ceiling, 1825, is by Rickman and, on a black-and-white-marble floor, his stately pews have delicate cast-iron tracery and finials, concealed by light-oak graining. Impressive monuments, the most striking, 1775, by J. F. Moore, with standing figures of Earl and Countess Ferrers and a draped figure of their son, reclining on a sarco-

phagus. Tower has two rooms, the first with heavy beams, grim animal faces and a Tudor-style fireplace and the other, at belfry level, like an 18th-century Gothic library with arcaded walls, traceried casement windows and, over the fireplace, a fine terracotta, 1725, by Agostino Corlini. In a window, a dead bat, a reminder that the house was a setting for the film 'The Haunting'.

Exhall [8] (near Coventry) Coalmining community in an area of mines worked since the beginning of the 17th century, though the shaft at Exhall Colliery was not sunk till 1863. Approached along an avenue of standard roses, the dignified tower of the *church* (St. Giles) is still recognisably Perpendicular, but the body has lost much through 'restoration'. Chancel is Early English with lancet windows; and the north aisle, 1609, serves as

Farnborough Park & (*opposite*) the oval pavilion

Farnborough Park: Entrance Hall

a mausoleum for the Hales family of Newland Hall, whose arms are on the east gable. South aisle, 1842, and Grecian monument to Anne Brooks, 1839, by W. Morgan of Exhall. *Newland Hall* has traces of 14th-century work, mullioned 17th-century windows and part of a moat.

Exhall [10] (near Stratford-upon-Avon) By the Roman Icknield Street, which skirts a hill crowned by *Oversley Castle* and *Oversley Wood*. Known as 'Dodging Exhall', from its inaccessibility before the 18th century, its timber-framed cottages have since been joined by brick cottages and bungalows. Made light

by a large south window, inserted in the 14th century, the Norman *church* (St. Giles) is entered through a Victorian porch with trellis tracery on the door, a decisive motif repeated in a north window and on the pulpit. Long chancel has a rich Annunciation in the style of Kempe. An early 18th-century rector, Dr. William Thomas, revised and augmented Dugdale's 'Antiquities of Warwickshire' (1656).

Farnborough [15] Mullioned ochre houses. Along a stone-walled lane, the simple *church* (St. Botolph) has a long, stone-roofed body and inadequate belfry and spire by George G. Scott. Unusual Norman

doorway, with bold Celtic-style door furniture. Clear-glazed north aisle lights the nave through a dull arcade, built in 1875, by Scott, under the leadership of Archdeacon Holbech. This was the last of a series of alterations and additions which obscured the development of the mediaeval plan and the position of the chapel of the Visitation of Our Lady. Tie beams of the north aisle roof are said to have come from the nave, which is only slightly wider, and the Decorated chancel arch has a reused Norman lozenge chain. Reticulated east window, by Wailes, 1857–8, has bright, acid colours; and two other windows have heraldic glass, one

100

with the shields of the patrons and vicars of the Holbech family. Inscription to Mrs. Wagstaffe, d.1667, has a pretty surround with vines and roses in pots. Stucco Regency *Old Vicarage* is entered through a garden wall, linked to the house by a quadrant veranda, housing a large niche. Holbech Hill has modern pale-brick houses with white boarding. *Reading room* and *school* were provided by Archdeacon Holbech, as was a new road to Avon Dassett through walled Farnborough Park. This superb landscape has large clumps of trees and a stream, dammed to form a series of lakes, including the Lady Lake, on which a woman in white is said to appear. The manor was sold in 1684, to Ambrose Holbech, who must have commissioned the rich brown-ironstone and grey Warwickshire-sandstone west front. Magnificent cedar-of-Lebanon, and a fine view over Warmington to the Edge Hills. Spectacular terrace walk has a simple Ionic *temple*, and an 18th-century domed oval pavilion with Tuscan columns and a rococo interior. Sanderson Miller, who lived at Radway Manor, only a few miles away, possibly supervised some of the architectural and landscape work. Etruscan-red *Entrance Hall* has busts of emperors, and a gorgeous chimneypiece with a vigorous leaf frieze. Oblong *Staircase Hall* crowned by a richly garlanded late 17th-century dome. Perhaps the finest room in the house is the *Dining Room*, with its perfectly balanced rococo detail and fine white-marble chimneypiece, the overmantel framing a view of the Capitol at Rome, after the original by Panini, around which the room was designed.

Fenny Compton [11] Originally a number of clearings in the forest by a stream at the foot of Mill Hill. Yellow-stone houses and barns are grouped around greens, linked by twisting roads, and later brick

Fillongley stained glass

buildings bind the original centres into one open-textured village. On high ground, away from the roads, the *church* (St. Peter and St. Clare) has a stumpy tower crowned by a short, fat spire carrying a green weathercock. Porch, dated 1673, is still Gothic; domestic-scale interior has dainty arcades, the one on the south copied from the Decorated north arcade when the Victorian south aisle was built. Light, stone-flagged tower space. Chancel has a small arch, a darkly glazed east window and large, closely spaced south windows. Wainscot reveals the height of the Georgian box pews, incorporated into lower ones, and the pulpit, c. 1700, also has fielded panels. Around the churchyard, tall terrace houses have large windows; brick *Red House*, 1707, built as the rectory, has Jacobean plasterwork. *Woad House*, Bridge Street, has a Decorated window, and opposite is the *Old Bakehouse*. Hornton-stone *The Orchard*, Dog Lane, built in the 1960s, by D. H. Robotham, has a single-storey wing partly enclosing a courtyard.

101

Fillongley [5] Agricultural, though divided by the Coventry–Tamworth road, and many of the inhabitants work in Coventry. At one time it had two churches and two castles, but of the castles, said to have been demolished by Oliver Cromwell, only some ruins and a moat survive, at *Castle Farm*. Around a stream, and with houses set backwards and forwards along the winding main street. *Church* (St. Mary and All Saints) dates from Norman times, though the west tower is basically Early English. Wide, hall-like nave with colourful fragments of Decorated glass. Painted and gilded stone reredos is the gift of Thomas Garner, who restored the church in 1887, and the gilded Majestas in the chancel arch is one of Sir Ninian Comper's last works. Curious 17th-century table tombs and, beneath a yew, the tomb of George Eliot's uncle, Isaac Pearson, a rich farmer. *School*, 1877, and *Methodist church*, 1892. Approached along a secluded drive, Grecian *Fillongley Hall*, built in 1840, by J. L. Akroyd of Coventry, for the Rev. George Bowyer Adderley, has smooth stone walls, plain window openings and large Ionic columns. Stone-paved *Entrance Hall*, top-lit by a circular lantern, has giant red-scagliola columns, with white Ionic capitals, and an archaic pink-granite fireplace, with unfluted Doric columns rising above a central slab. Top-lit *Staircase* and *Library* have ochre-scagliola columns. Garden front, shaded by a long cast-iron veranda, has three linked *reception rooms*, one oval and with vases in niches. Original decorations and furniture in the style of Thomas Hope.

Foleshill *see* Coventry

Four Oaks [4] Prosperous Arts and Crafts suburb, against Sutton Park in the grounds of the demolished Four Oaks Hall, a 17th-century mansion by Sir William Wilson. Well sited on a bend in the Lich-field Road, the cruciform *Methodist church*, built in 1907–8, by Crouch and Butler, with a bold central tower, forms an attractive group with the *church hall*, *parsonage* and *caretaker's house*. Arts and Crafts Perpendicular, with an austere interior. Of the houses the best of all, Lethaby's The Hurst, has been demolished, but Ernest Newton's tile-hung *The Leasowes*, 107 Lichfield Road, built in 1893, survives, with ample bay windows looking out onto a sequence of enclosed gardens, by C. E. Bateman. Rural *Wythens*, 17 Barker Road, 1898–9, by W. H. Bidlake, Birmingham's most sensitive Arts and Crafts architect, has a double-storey porch, and his tile-hung *The Dene*, 2 Bracebridge Road, a straight, barn-like roof. Wooded gardens of Bidlake's *Saint Winnow*, 22 Lady-wood Road, 1902, have what is reputed to be one of the original four oaks. Steeply gabled *12 Brace-bridge Road*, built in 1906, by Hay-wood Farmer for his own occupation, has a pretty stable block, crowned by a cupola. Suave *Bryn Teg*, 35 Bracebridge Road, 1904, by C. E. Bateman, a master of the pastiche, is Cotswold-stone-hung; and his classical *Maes-y-Lledr* (formerly Hawkesford), 14 Brace-bridge Road, built for his architect father, is of reused bricks under a Cotswold-stone roof. Coach house reminiscent of a dovecote. Grand, classical *Carhampton House*, 11 Lut-trell Road, on the site of Four Oaks Hall and built out of its materials, in 1901–4, by C. E. Bateman, has deep, coved eaves. Brick *Redlands*, 1 Hartopp Road, again by Bateman, was for Richard Parkes, who demolished his house in Northumberland and brought the bricks with him. Stables enclose a fore-court. Garden front has unusually tall bay windows, crowned by shaped gables. Pretty octagonal dovecote. Unassuming *Woodgate*, 37 Hartopp Road, was built in 1897, by W. H. Bidlake for himself, with a low sweeping roof against a staircase tower. Part-half-timbered *Rohedin*, 7 Richmond Road, built by the architect, artist and medal-list William Charles Midgley for himself, has a large, gilded grass-hopper weather vane and an attic studio overlooking Sutton Park. Midgley wrote 'A Short History of the Town and Chase of Sutton Coldfield', and was co-author of books on 'Plant Form and Design' and a history of the Royal Birmingham Society of Artists.

Frankton [8] Brick cottages and houses, and lias-and-red-sandstone *church* (St. Nicholas). Heavily buttressed, squat west tower has a pyramid-roofed Perpendicular belfry and the body, mostly 1872, by George Gilbert Scott, has small clerestory windows and a timber-framed porch. Henry Holyoake, 1657–1731, the first important headmaster of Rugby School, was rector here from 1712. Georgian *Old Rectory*, with a massive Doric porch. *Manor house* is also Georgian, and has a staircase said to have come from the Priory, Warwick.

Freasley [5] (near Dordon) Named after Freiga, a Saxon mother earth goddess, and approached through fields, past the spoil tip of Hall End Colliery, shaped like an ancient stepped pyramid. Picturesque timber-framed cottages, Georgian farms and a long pool. Timber-framed *church* (St. Mary) was built, in 1894, under the same roof as an adjoining cottage. On the site of the original manor house, the foursquare brick *Freasley Hall*, 1723, has a golden-stone plinth, a high-pitched roof and two substantial chimneys.

Gaydon [11] Flat clay on a bed of limestone, suitable for Gaydon Air-port, though with an abundance of clear springs. Early Georgian houses, some of which are thatched, are of local lias bonded with ochre stone but later ones are of pale speckled brick. New houses, against the main road, have fancy facing

Detail in the Pompeian Gallery, Packington Hall, **Great Packington**

bricks. On a bend, the neat ochre *church* (St. Giles), rebuilt in 1852, by D. G. Squirhill of Leamington, has a rich Crucifixion in the east window. Rustic-work *village hall*, built in 1886, was originally thatched.

Grandborough [12] On the River Leam and to the north of a puzzling grid of roads and field lanes against the Roman Fosse Way. Huddled around the grey Perpendicular steeple of the *church* (St. Peter). Red-sandstone Decorated body has a light, whitewashed interior with red-sandstone arcades and a wide chancel. 18th-century communion rail and gabled Caen-stone reredos,

introduced in 1849 when the 18th-century ceiling was removed to reveal an unusual mediaeval roof. Small clerestory windows were inserted in 1862–3. To the Gilks family, two rows of Gothic headstones, hung with shields, face the east end of the church and Church Road has simple slate-roofed terraces. *Shoulder of Mutton* has timber framing, and the elegant 1840 *school* wide-arched windows. Jacobean-style *vicarage*, 1844, and lias-and-brick *barn*, once timber-framed. In the fields to the north, *Birchen Fold* and its shored-up neighbour are also timber-framed, with stone stacks.

Great Alne [10] Picturesque early 19th-century houses by the River Alne, on which, in Domesday times, there was a mill. Footpath leads past an old farmhouse, with Regency Gothic windows, to the white stone *church* (St. Mary Magdalene) which has a rendered bell turret, orange-lichen-touched roof and galleries. White Regency Gothic *The Lodge* has delicate tracery and a fret porch; and the robust Italianate *Alne House* is of local pale brick. Upright Italianate station, spoilt by standard windows and paint, stands against a railless, grassed way. Georgian *The Mother Huff Cap* holds its own against rows of post-

103

Great Packington church
by Joseph Bonomi, 1790

war semis. Huff Cap is a term for
strong ale. Long, low *National
School*, 1840, is Italianate, with
dainty round-arched windows; the
new flat-roofed school enjoys extensive views across the river valley. At
New End Farm a road to Shelfield
is possibly part of the salt way from
Droitwich to Warwick.

Great Packington [8] With a
pedimented, tower-like porch, *Old
Hall*, built in 1679, incorporates
parts of the original house, built by
John Fisher when the Dissolution

104

closed the priory, and has a robust staircase leading to a large, garlanded room. *Packington Hall* originally built in 1693, by Sir Clement Fisher, who adorned the park with statues, canals and 'vistos', doomed to vanish without trace beneath Capability Brown's mirrors of still water, vast green expanses and encircling belt of woodland, softened by outlying clumps. Brown's plans for the park, dated 1751, are early work of exceptional interest, and have notes by the third Earl of Aylesford such as 'take this away' scrawled across whole woods. The Earl's next project, in 1762–6, was the rebuilding of the *stables* by William and David Hiorn, with pyramid-roofed corner towers, and in 1762 he approached Matthew Brettingham the Elder to remodel the house. His surveyor, Henry Couchman, described the extent of the alterations as 'no less than adding a wing to each end of the house, filling up the niche or half H, which was in the west front, and making a storey under the old house, and then building another storey over the whole building'. This work, completed in 1772, resulted in the restrained, well proportioned exterior of today, only with an open first-floor loggia on the garden front, eventually filled in, in 1828, to make a library. During his stay in Italy, the fourth Earl of Aylesford developed an admiration for Piranesi, who greatly influenced his drawings. His architectural tutor was Joseph Bonomi, who produced drawings for Packington as early as 1782, and decorated the house room by room over a period of about twenty years. *Entrance Hall* owes its T shape and columns to Brettingham, though his wall niches have been replaced by panels with Pompeian motifs, probably by Bonomi. Walls of the *Music Room*, by Bonomi, are now concealed by hangings, and the ceiling has medallions of musical instruments. Lofty *Main Staircase* is basically by Brettingham, but in detail it belongs to Bonomi's period. Walls are pure white below, but deepen in tone as they ascend towards a glazed circular lantern, to give an even brightness; details are in blue, grey and gold. *Pompeian Gallery*, probably dating from the first decade of the 19th century, and inspired by the fourth Earl's collection of Etruscan vases, is the largest and finest Pompeian scheme in England. Dado is of scagliola, in imitation of Siena marble and porphyry, following the format of rooms excavated at Pompeii, and the dazzling walls and ceiling are divided into panels, with figures and scenes of animals painted on a black ground, almost certainly by J. F. Rigard, an Italian portrait and history painter. Fireplace by Bonomi is the only executed part of his Roman design for the room, which determined its division into three parts by a screen of columns at each end. Curtains were originally of broad red-and-black-satin stripes, and the gilt Grecian chairs are in the style of Thomas Hope. *Dining Room* has a ceiling by Bonomi, painted by Rigard, and a magnificent sideboard by William Kent. *Library*, also with a Bonomi ceiling, is lined with elegant neo-classical bookcases, 1828, by Henry Hakewell, who also laid out the terraces around the house. Important *church* (St. James) built by Bonomi for the fourth Earl in 1789–90, as a thank-offering for the return to sanity of George III, is the most important late 18th-century church in England, in advance of anything similar by Soane, and one of the first truly international neo-classical buildings in the world. Built of brick, probably as a result of the fourth Earl's admiration of Roman ruins, and with tripartite lunette windows, similar to those shown on his drawing of Diocletian's Baths in Rome, it has four corner towers with lead domes and finials. The fourth Earl's drawing also shows a cross vault, resting on free-standing columns against the walls, and tunnel-vaulted spaces, pierced by low, round-arched openings, all of which must have influenced the square, cross-vaulted nave, with similarly pierced tunnel-vaulted arms. Red-sandstone columns, supporting the cross vault, are copied from the primitive Doric Temple of Neptune at Paestum; and the plaster walls and vault are painted in imitation of ashlar. Pedimented altarpiece has a painting by Rigard; the organ, c. 1750, was inherited from Lord Aylesford's first cousin, Charles Jennens of Gopsal, Handel's patron, together with all Handel's manuscripts.

Great Wolford [14] Stone estate cottages and farms to the west of the sharply steepled early 19th-century *church* (St. Michael), enclosed by farm buildings and an ancient earthwork. Broad, aisleless nave. Short chancel houses 18th-century Ingram family monuments, rescued from an earlier building destroyed by fire. Bellcoted *school* and timber-framed *Fox and Hounds*.

Grendon [5] In open, undulating country against the Leicestershire border. Narrow mediaeval bridge, which before 1825 carried the road across the River Anker, is now surrounded by sheep. Long, low *church* (All Saints) has a noble west tower, by R. C. Hussey, surprisingly Georgian for 1845. Rendered porch, 1820, and light interior with patches of bright glass, much rich woodwork and many dark hatchments. Panelled plaster ceilings, probably by Hussey. Late 17th-century Chetwynd pew, crowned by an achievement, trumpeting angels and flaming urns, has an impressive silhouette; beyond is a unique, delicately coloured window, 1800–20, by Joseph Hale Miller, who was largely responsible for the revival of stained glass. Dark 13th-century chancel with large 16th-century window blocked by 18th-century niche, housing a life-size mourning woman and an urn, by Sir Robert Taylor. Rich 17th-century communion rail with cherubs' heads, and elaborate Jacobean pulpit. Mayor's pew, 1618, from St. Mary's, Stafford, and carved royal arms, from the chancel screen. 18th-century reredos is now in a local farm building. Well cut mid 15th-century alabaster of a lady, probably from Ingestre, and several 18th-century tablets. Early Victorian Tudor-style *Rectory* incorporates part of the 18th-century building. Stucco Jacobean-style *Grendon Hall*, the seat of the Chetwynd family, was demolished in 1933, leaving a corner with octagonal pinnacles, a handsome early 18th-century *outbuilding* and prettily gabled *North Lodge*, 1878. A mill existed in 1086, and pedimented *Croft House* was built in 1781, above the old mill race. At Bradley Green, the modest *Rectory Cottages*, built for George Chetwynd in 1829, were formerly the Goat's Head Inn, frequented by navigators on the adjoining Coventry Canal. Poor Gothic *school*, 1871, also for the Chetwynds, and *Swan Farm*, Watling Street, 1853, with the Chetwynd goat's head. *Blue-brick houses* are evidence of the local brickworks. *Methodist church*, Grendon Common, extended in 1885, has round-headed cast-iron windows.

Guy's Cliffe

Guy's Cliffe—Warwick [11]

Ruined mansion on a rock above the River Avon, one of the most picturesque sights in the county, and with the romance of ancient legend. In Saxon times Guy showed remarkable heroism in coping with dragons and other wild and wonderful beasts that beset fair damsels in those days, before marrying Rohand, daughter of the first true Earl of Warwick. Later he succeeded to the title and, after subsequent adventures, left Warwick on a pilgrimage to the Holy Land, slaying the cruel giant Amarant on the way. He kept his return to Warwick a secret, even

from his wife, living as a hermit in a cave at Guy's Cliffe almost until his dying days. In the cave in which he is supposed to have lived is an indecipherable inscription. In the early 19th century, the symmetrical 18th-century house was made romantic by Gothic extensions, rising sheer from the rocks against the river and closing an avenue of tall trees from the Warwick–Kenilworth Road. Through a fanciful gateway, original 18th-century entrance faces across a gravelled forecourt to a row of rock-hewn chambers linked to the house by an underground pass-

age. Ahead, the court enters a cavernous subterranean stable overlooking the river, and, against its high-arched entrance, the mid-15th-century *chapel* tower is crowned by tall, picturesque pinnacles. Late 18th-century Gothic façade and 1422 partly rock-hewn double nave, with later plaster vault. Carved from the living rock, powerful 15th-century figure of Guy is appropriately larger than life.

Halford [14] Above a weir, on the winding River Stour, divided by the Roman Fosse Way, and served by

The river at Guy's Cliffe

the Georgian *Bell Inn*. Against the new river bridge is the mediaeval one, and below this the lias Norman *church* (St. Mary) has a 13th-century tower with lancets. Lively tympanum, depicting an angel holding a scroll, is certainly the most imaginative piece of Norman figure sculpture in the county. Well-lit coursed-rubble interior has white marble monuments. Norman chancel arch flanked by unusual Norman niches, one with a defaced figure in flowing robes, possibly St. John, with traces of turquoise, red and black. Robust neo-Norman pulpit. South aisle, rebuilt in 1862,

has a Baroque altarpiece. Fire hooks for pulling down burning thatch. Picturesque part-timber-framed *manor house* and sparsely sash-windowed *Old Vicarage*. A Regency house has a jagged iron-fret balcony; Gothic *Folly Lodge* and the taller *folly*, overlooking the river valley, are also Regency.

Hall Green *see* Birmingham.

Hampton-in-Arden [8] Timber-framed and brick cottages of local forest oak and clay. Through a wide lych gate, the predominantly cream-stone *church* (St. Mary and St. Bartholomew) has a red Nor-

man chancel and an embattled Perpendicular tower. Well-lit tower space and sturdy Norman north arcade. Vigorous aisle window, 1968, by John Hayward, of Christ bringing light to the souls of the departed. Bright narrow chancel has two deeply splayed Norman windows, the remains of a Norman door, and an unusual heart tomb. East window, given by the Rt. Hon. Sir Frederick Peel (son of the Victorian statesman), in memory of his first wife, niece of Shelley, has portraits of Chaucer, Shakespeare, Milton etc. In 1878 Eden Nesfield thought the 'fabric dreadfully disfigured' and subsequently rebuilt much of the chancel, the stones being numbered and used again, and a Tudor chantry 'of barbarous design and execution—built in haste'. Remains of the mid-15th-century cross, originally over twenty feet high. Black-and-white *Moat House* is on the site of the old manor house. *White Lion* conceals its timber framing, and overlooking a valley to the south, Doric *Fentham Club* has a 1913 hall with an unusual Greek doorway. Gothic *girls' school*, 1849. To the north of the church, the road plunges downhill between estate cottages, including pretty *Bank Row*, 1852, and a *terrace* by Nesfield, 1868, its pargetted upper floor overhanging the pavement. Gothic *Providence Chapel*, 1838, *schoolhouse*, 1782, and round-arched *school*, erected by the charity of George Fentham, a mercer of Birmingham. Disappointing *Hampton Manor House* was built in the early 1870s, by Nesfield for Sir Frederick Peel, and has a tall, slate-roofed clock tower with carved signs of the zodiac. Pretty tile-hung *lodge*, mullioned *Manor Cottage*, originally two cottages and stables, and, behind a topiary yew hedge, decaying glasshouses. Peel was a railway commissioner, and London–Birmingham trains, which originally stopped here for him, still stop, even after inter-city electrification.

Hampton Lucy [11] In the valley of the River Avon, and with the majestic west tower of the Georgian Gothic *church* (St. Peter) soaring above all. Surely the most splendid of Rickman and Hutchinson's churches, it was built in 1822–6 by the Rev. John Lucy, to replace a modest Early English structure. Reminiscent of Rickman's slightly earlier Church of St. George, Birmingham, the body is also divided into seven bays and has identical cast-iron aisle windows. Light, spacious nave and aisles, divided by elegant arcades, are cross-vaulted in plaster. In 1856 the flat east end was replaced by a splendid apsidal chancel intricately vaulted in stone. The architect was George Gilbert Scott, who also added the two-storeyed north porch and removed many of the earlier imitation materials. West doors, probably panelled in cast iron and oak-grained, were replaced by genuine hardwood with wrought metal-work, the porch ceiling gave way to a stone vault and the tower arch was filled with a trumeau and an ogee-foiled roundel, below a stone-traceried circular window, probably the result of the removal of a west gallery with an organ. All but two of the original pews, with cast-iron poppy heads, were replaced by ones fashioned from the elm of Charlecote Park, and the pulpit is vaguely Byzantine, with metalwork by Skidmore of Coventry. Choir stalls, which have delicately carved canopies on thin shafts, are said to be similar to those in the Lady Chapel at Ely and the brilliant orange, blue and purple east window is by Thomas Willement, F.S.A., heraldic artist to King George IV. Executed in 1837 for the original east window, it was illustrated by Willement as the frontispiece to his list of works, published in 1840. In the vestry is a monument to Hutchinson, who

Hampton-in-Arden:
The clock tower

died at Leamington Priors in 1831, and is buried on the north side of the churchyard. Pretty Tudor-style *school. Avonside,* originally the old grammar school, has lost its symmetrical arrangement of windows. Behind Gothic cast-iron gates, the serene orange-brick *Hampton Lucy House* (formerly the rectory) overlooks the lush Avon valley. Triangular village green has modern houses facing a brick terrace; beyond the white *Boar's Head* are timber-framed and thatched cottages. *The Langlands,* a sympathetic group of houses, built in 1975, by The Architects Design Group (Nottingham), has brick barn-like forms; and the Gothic river *bridge* has cast-iron tracery.

Hampton-on-the-Hill [11] Brick cottages and modest houses around the entrance to the extensive *Grove Park,* part wooded and part dotted with sheep. Decaying stucco-faced house, built in the Tudor style in the reign of William IV, is on the site of an Elizabethan house reputed to have replaced Lord Leicester's hunting lodge. Elaborate early 17th-century chimney pieces, including one from Kenilworth, and magnificent views over Warwick. Small trees grow in the plaster-vaulted porch, and a large terracotta fountain is half hidden by long grass. The Dormer family has rebuilt its house in mellow red brick on an even better site with views across the Roman Fosse Way to Edge Hill and the Cotswolds. Designed by Francis Pollen, the new house is one of England's few really modern country houses and, as it is all on one floor, has pyramid-roofed corner pavilions to give emphasis. Glazed internal courtyard and, lined with family portraits, a large drawing room with full-height sliding windows against a terrace. Regency Gothic R.C. *church* (St. Charles) was built in two stages, first the dark transepts, then the light nave. Richly decorated niche houses the altar.

Handsworth *see* Birmingham.

Harborne *see* Birmingham.

Harborough Magna [9] Brick farms and cottages. *Church* (All Saints) with Perpendicular tower 13th–14th-century body and unsympathetic Victorian south aisle, possibly the recasing of a Georgian reconstruction. Dark chancel has a striking east window with tense elongated figures in pale blues and pinks ascending into a Prussian-blue sky. Welcoming hand of God the Father (see Brinklow). Early Victorian *Old Vicarage* and Georgian *Home Farm,* with wide casement windows.

Harbury [11] A fascinating network of streets on high ground between Roman Fosse Way and some cement workings, from which the fossilised remains of an icthyosaurus were transported to the National History Museum, South Kensington. Lias 16th- and 17th-century cottages with steep roofs, indicating that they were thatched, and contrasting brick terraces. Large *church* (All Saints), though much restored, has a leaning 13th-century tower supported by massive lias buttresses. Brick Georgian belfry, with Gothic openings, and a fine weathervane. Tower space has an unusual tapering pillar as the font, and plain nave is lit mainly from the aisles. Dark, scraped 13th-century chancel with canopied stone reredos, 1879, and jolly Gothic tiling. Lias *Wissett Lodge* has white-painted windows and the mullioned *Wagstaffe School,* founded in 1611, is now a house. Cruck cottages and part-timber-framed *Shakespeare Inn* and *Stone House.* Stone-and-brick *Tower Mill* has lost the sails which killed the original miller, but his ghost is said still to appear. *Chapel Street* has an upright lias chapel with a lantern in the fanlight, and *Deppers* is elegantly Italianate.

Hartshill [5] On a ridge, above the River Anker and with distant views of Derbyshire. Stone quarries, including *Blue Hole.* Probably a Roman station against the Watling Street, as Roman pottery has been discovered. The site was found suitable for a *castle,* little of which remains. Michael Drayton, poet, was born here in 1563. East Warwickshire coalfield has wrought great changes, and the sandstone neo-Norman *church* (Holy Trinity), built in 1843–8, by T. L. Walker, boasts a magnificent west portal in local blue brick made of clay from the mine workings. Brindled brick *library,* 1852, intended as a church school. Behind a large beech against the green, the *Old Meeting House* is now a private house. On a volcanic hill against a deep quarry, the timber-framed *Hartshill Grange* has a big brick-and-stone ingle, and a later plastered wing. Before the Dissolution it belonged to Merevale Abbey and later to the Earl of Essex, the friend of Elizabeth I, but was forfeited when he was beheaded as a traitor. George Fox and Nathaniel Newton stayed here, after a Quaker meeting in the adjoining barn, and Benjamin Bartlet is said to have written his 'History and Antiquities of Mancetter' in the now ruined 18th-century gazebo. *British Waterways Maintenance Yard* has a workshop and a cottage, both on arches over an arm of the Coventry Canal, and nearby is an elegant Regency porch.

Haseley [8] (near Halton) In broad, undulating fields above Inchford Brook, which flows past the site of the recently demolished Old Manor House to the south of the original village. Small, heavily buttressed *church* (St. Mary) is domestic in character. Norman doorway and white-stone Perpendicular tower. Reminiscent of the rural hamlet of the 18th-century, part-plastered interior has a ceiled wagon roof, a dark pulpit and box

Hampton Lucy church

pews. Stone *Manor House*, built in 1875, with steep roofs and a tower, stands against trees.

Haselor [10] On a tributary of the River Alne, which powers a late Georgian *water mill* complete with machinery. High on a hill, enjoying magnificent views of low wooded hills, the battlemented *church* (St. Mary and All Saints) has a small Norman tower with narrow bell openings. Whitewashed, stone-flagged interior has a mausoleum to the vicar Cornelius Griffin, with brightly coloured glass, 1854, by Holland of Warwick. Blocked chancel arcade with primitive capitals and, above the altar, a fine stained-glass Crucifixion in the style of Kempe. At the foot of the hill an upright Victorian house has a blue-and-purple slate roof, and the polychromatic brick *school* quaint plate tracery.

Hatton [11] On the Birmingham–Warwick road and the Grand Union Canal, the latter descending into the Avon Valley by a series of locks. Delicately carved lych gate leads to the *church* (Holy Trinity), which has a white Perpendicular tower, housing German 16th-century glass from a Tree of Jesse. Body was rebuilt with a rock face for the Hewletts of Haseley, and 18th-century monuments recall the earlier structure. Tombstone to Mrs Maynard by Eric Gill. Picturesque *school* is overpowered by the brick *village hall*, 1924. By an old barn and shrouded in trees, the elegant *Old Rectory* was built in 1749–57, with local bricks from Rowington and Horton. In 1785 it was enlarged by Dr. Parr, a former master at Harrow, who, after writing a solemn protest in the Parish Prayer Book against the omission of the name of Queen Caroline from the liturgy, was appointed her chaplain. He lived on very friendly terms with the villagers, to whom he gave a dinner to celebrate May Day. *Hatton House* was improved in 1912, by T. H. Mawson.

Hawkesbury *see* Coventry

Henley-in-Arden [10] Once densely wooded, Henley sprang up under the protection of the de Mont-forts' great castle of Beaudesert, across the River Alne, and became an important market town. Market-place, with the remains of the market cross, opens off the timber-framed and brick High Street, over three-quarters of a mile long, and bent around the 15th-century *church* (St. John Baptist), the tower of which catches the eye in each direction. Essentially as originally built, but without its original furnishings. These included the rood screen, an important feature of Perpendicular churches, especially in the absence of a chancel arch as here, and the blaze of 'coates' in the south windows, now filled with dull Victorian glass from the restoration of 1856. White-stone, shallow-arched north arcade with tall octagonal pillars. Door into the adjoining 15th-century *Guildhall*, a close-studded timber-framed building with an arch-braced roof. Revived ancient Court Leet and Court Baron are held here. *Lloyds Bank*, facing the market cross, was drastically restored in 1916, but a timber-framed gable survives similar to those on the *White Swan*, a well known late 16th-century coaching inn, refronted a century later with double-storey bay windows. Here, Boswell thought, Shenstone wrote his famous lines about 'the warmest welcome at an inn'— the poem is entitled 'Written in an Inn at Henley'. Timber-framed *Blue Bell* has a tall gateway and, just south of the almshouses, a private house was originally the Cross Keys, an ancient sign representing the arms of the Papal See. Two *houses* on the corner of Bear Lane were the Bear and Ragged Staff; and, facing the market place, timber-framed *George House* was the Old George. The great coaching age, which did not begin until the latter part of the 18th century, helped to bring Henley into touch with the outer world, and in 1788 the town was served by a mail coach and four post coaches daily. Tall, classical *Stone House* has tri-partite lunettes and, immediately south of the church, the rectory has oval windows. Behind iron railings, the romantic *Yew Tree House* is part plastered; in New Road, the rough-cast *Brook End*, built, in 1909, by C. F. A. Voysey for the Misses Knight, of the Knights of Barrells Hall, Ullenhall, has an octagonal dining room as well as an octagonal library.

Hillborough [10] (near Welford-on-Avon) Once larger and, though given to the monks of Evesham, wrested from them in Saxon times. In the 15th and 16th centuries the village suffered both the plague and enclosures and *Hillborough Manor*, which includes the remains of an early timber-framed manor house, has part of a stone wing probably built from the materials of the deserted village, including those of the church (St. Mary Magdalene). Several ghosts include the White Lady, thought to be Anne Whateley, who pined away when Shakespeare married the other Anne; the Screaming Man, a shepherd who was stoned to death by peasants, whose enclosure rights had been taken; Polly, a wronged Victorian maid; and a ghost rider or ghostly coach, which crosses the fields near the house. Recently a guest sleeping in the Ghost Room felt hands on her forehead, and another heard whispering and footsteps above. Beneath the roof, the *Long Gallery* runs the length of the Elizabethan wing. Tree of Heaven and circular 14th-century *dovecote*. 18th-century *crop barn*, probably built from the timbers of the original manor, has a threshing floor and a winnowing door. Now a modern house, it has an impressive, partly full-height interior, by Michael Reardon for himself.

Detail of 16th-century Throckmorton brass, **Haseley**

Honiley

at its crossing over the Stratford-on-Avon Canal, bright with houseboats. During the 19th century the village supported a number of trades, including brick and rake making: in one year alone, one timber works produced 2,000 dozen rakes. Restless red-brick *church* (St. Thomas), by John Cotton, has a yellow-brick pyramid spire. Built in 1879, largely through the generosity of Thomas Burman, it is the Established Church's answer to the soaring stone *Baptist church*, built in 1877, by George Ingall at the expense of G. F. Muntz. *Royal Oak*, 1937, by F. W. B. Yorke, has a large expanse of tiled roof and twin white gables.

Honiley [8] (near Wroxall) Near a disused airfield and the old creeper-clad *Honiley Boot*. Wide forecourt, flanked by the 17th-century service wings of the former hall, is centred on wrought-iron churchyard gates. Dark-green yews and white Baroque steeple of the *church*. Dedication to St. John the Baptist is derived from the ancient well of that name in a field to the north-east, reputed to have had healing powers and to have been used for the baptism of early converts. Designs for the present church, built in 1723, the year of Sir Christopher Wren's death, are said to have been drawn by the master himself, on a tablecloth, whilst dining with the patron, J. Saunders of Honiley Hall. Unusually confident west tower has a short English spire, supported by eight luxuriant consoles. Light, white-plastered nave retains its fixtures and fittings. West gallery is supported on grey-pink-marble columns, and the small apse has marble pilasters. Bulgy-balustered communion rail.

Honington [14] In the park-like countryside of the Stour Valley. Approached from the main road between pineapple-topped gate piers and over a classical bridge. Stone cottages and barns cluster

Hillmorton [9] A suburb of Rugby in a loop of the Oxford Canal against which the red sandstone *church* (St. John Baptist), mostly of c. 1300, is said to have been built by Thomas Astley, who died fighting at the Battle of Evesham. Long nave has a 16th-century clerestory and a tie-beam-and-arched-brace roof. West gallery and 18th-century box pews and

pulpit. In one of the pews is a trapdoor, under which is an early 15th-century brass. 14th-century canopied lady, and defaced knight and priest. James Petiver (1663–1718), botanist and entomologist, was born here.

Hockley Heath [7] Shops and houses but few trees, strung along the Birmingham–Stratford road

Honington church

around a long space closed at one
end by timber-framed *Magpie
House*. Stone-walled drive, overhung with thick yews, leads to the
walled churchyard, carpeted with
buttercups and encircled by trees.
Grey, lichen-covered classical
church (All Saints), 1680, has a 13th-
century west tower and a steep,
mediaeval-looking roof behind an
urn-topped parapet. Light, spacious interior is divided by Tuscan
arcades. Box pews, cut down by the
Victorians, and richly carved
pulpit and stalls reminiscent of

Honington Hall

Wren's City church furnishings. Dark hatchments. Wide apse, painted with the Lord's Prayer, Creed and Ten Commandments. Splendid marble figures of Sir Henry Parker, a London merchant, and his son Hugh, 1713; a macabre Rococo tablet to Joseph Townsend, 1763, and a mourning male figure by an urn, by R. Westmacott, similar to those at Ilmington and Preston-on-Stour. In 1685 Sir Henry Parker built nearby *Honington Hall*, a comfortable brick house, studded with busts of emperors. Sumptuous plasterwork and, in the style of Kent, a domed octagonal saloon with putti reclining on the pedimented doorways.

Hunningham [11] Thatched timber-framed and brick cottages and barns in broad, undulating country below the Roman Fosse Way. Massive arched bridge over the River Leam is probably mediaeval, but was partly rebuilt

during the 17th century. Irish-yew walk leads to the humble *church* (St. Margaret), virtually untouched by the Victorians. Red-sandstone walls have grey ashlar buttresses; and the lichen-covered tile roof is crowned by a weatherboarded bell turret, boasting a confident copper cock. Self-consciously simple mid-Victorian north aisle has a reset Norman doorway. Economical plaster-and-lath chancel arch.

Hurley [5] Georgian houses on a hill to the south of Baxterley church. Quaint prefabricated Gothic *church* (The Resurrection) was built in 1861, with cast-iron uprights, boarded walls and a simple flèche. *School*, extended in 1892 in the Jacobean style, has a perverse *house*, built in 1887, with awkward blue-brick arches. Late 17th-century *Atherstone House* is of brick with stone-mullioned windows; and, at the top of Knowle Hill, the plain 18th-century *Hurley House* has lost

its outbuildings to make way for neo-Georgian houses. Sombre *Hurley Hall*, at right angles to the road to Baxterley, is said to have been rebuilt in 1612, but from all appearances is Early Georgian. The home of Wildive Willington, one of Oliver Cromwell's henchmen, the house was used during the Commonwealth for local marriages.

Idlicote Around a pool and on top of a small hill which merges into the taller, well wooded Idlicote Hill. Buried in undergrowth, off the drive to the big house, the humble lias *church* (St. James) has a moss-covered roof and a shingled bell turret shrouded in trees. Norman doorway with Georgian door. Jane Austen interior, divided by broad arches springing from a conglomeration of box pews, is lit by two lancets with Georgian leading. West gallery, ogee-shaped font cover and three-decker pulpit, complete with tester. Incomplete

Jacobean screen is decorated by pretty pendants; and the late 13th-century chancel leads to an early classical south chapel through a Tuscan arcade. Stolid, grey *Idlicote House* has white-framed windows and an octagonal 18th-century *dovecote*, for over 1,000 birds, ogee arches and battlements.

Ilmington [14] Spacious and surrounded by hills, with several quarries in the high ground of Ilmington Downs. Buildings and boundary walls are of orange-brown stone, with the exception of a few red-brick Georgian and modern houses, which add interest. *Church* (St. Mary) stands in a walled churchyard, studded with well cut headstones, the base of a cross and an elaborate Georgian Gothic monument. Massive Norman tower, with slit windows, earlier nave and Early English chancel with lancets. Doorway, with zigzag decoration, is interrupted by a later niche (for a statue of the Virgin?). Wide interior has a large Norman tower arch dwarfing the earlier chancel arch; chancel has an arched plaster ceiling, probably influenced by that at Preston-on-Stour, where there is an earlier version of the standing mourner, to Francis Canning and his wife, also by Westmacott. Early Victorian Gothic *Old School House*, and later R.C. *Church of St. Philip*, with a bell turret. Mullioned *Hobdays*, 1709, and *Crab Mill*, 1711, and picturesque manor house. By ridge-and-furrow fields, evidence of the extensive open-field arable of the mediaeval village, pedimented, early 18th-century *Foxcote* has giant columns and Soane-ish stables. Modern whitewashed *house* with deep overhanging eaves shows the influence of Frank Lloyd Wright. To the north-west of the church, a *chalybeate spring*, found in 1684, enjoyed a considerable vogue for some years.

Kenilworth Castle

Kenilworth [8] Majestic ruined sandstone castle, founded by the Clintons, inspired Sir Walter Scott to write his famous novel. Later abbey manor was granted to the Augustine Canons in 1122. Finham Brook flows through both the abbey and castle enclosures, which physically control the town's road pattern. New Street is 14th-century; in 1545 Henry VIII's surveyors reported that there were 'many fair houses', some of which survive in Castle Green and High Street. The growing importance of the market, established by 1267, resulted in the construction of timber-framed houses along the Warwick Road, few of which have survived 20th-century commerce; and a drove road through the town from Balsall Common to Southam encouraged the opening of public houses. In a landscape setting against Abbey Fields, the rich-red-sandstone *church* (St. Nicholas) has an octagonal belfry and a spire, which contribute much to the High Street. Gorgeous Norman doorway, possibly from the priory, Perpendicular nave arcades of slightly differing dates, and heraldic transept window, 1832, by David Evans. Monument to John Bird, d.1772, is by Nollekens, and a fine white-marble figure of Mrs. Caroline Gresley on a bed, watched by her husband and child, is by Westmacott. Architectural fragments and tiles are from the *priory*, the remains of which include a vaulted gatehouse giving access to High Street. Castle was often in royal hands: John acquired it, and Henry III gave it to his sister Eleanor and her husband Simon de Montfort, Earl of Leicester. In the Baron's Wars it became Earl Simon's chief fortress, but it returned to the King, who gave it to his son Edmund, Earl of Lancaster. By succession it came to John of Gaunt, who made large additions; and in 1563 Elizabeth granted it to Robert Dudley, Earl of Leicester, who received her here

119

Kineton

to straight-roofed brick houses, which wind up Castle Hill opposite a cluster of thatched timber-framed cottages known as *Little Virginia*. High Street has elegant 18th- and 19th-century town houses, overlooking Abbey Fields; and further east, beyond a magnificent oak, the street narrows, before widening out to meet Fieldgate Lane and Bridge Street, both with Georgian houses providing an impressive visual stop. Fieldgate Lane has a neo-Georgian house, by H. M. Fletcher, and New Street leads to the timber-framed *Manor House* and a converted water tower. Across *Townpool Bridge*, Georgian and Victorian houses on Abbey Hill enjoy magnificent rural views.

Keresley *see* Coventry

Kineton [11] Grey-and-brownstone houses above the River Dene, against which there is a motte-and-bailey castle. In the 13th century Stephen de Segrave had a Tuesday market, but this had died out by 1840, when the market house was pulled down and a school built on the site. It was here that King Charles I met Henrietta Maria. Surrounded by robust 17th-century headstones, carved with cherubs, garlands, books and skulls, the ochre-coloured *church* (St. Peter) was partly rebuilt in 1755, by Sanderson Miller, and remodelled by one of his descendants, the Revd. Frank Miller, Vicar of Kineton 1834–89, who removed Sanderson's ogee-headed windows and Gothicised the old chancel. Thickset tower has a deeply moulded Early English doorway, a Perpendicular belfry, and a Gothic parapet. Stone-vaulted tower passage is by Sanderson Miller. Light nave and aisles are divided by delicate arcades. Rich sanctuary with Edwardian glass and furnishings, including the free classical reredos, organ case and rood screen, by John Belcher. Ingenuous marbled-wood old reredos, painted with a dove,

four times. Ruins, entered through *Mortimer's Tower*, are enclosed by a 13th-century curtain wall, against which Leicester built a long, timber-framed *barn*. Nearby are the foundations of the *Chapel*, built by John of Gaunt, and to the west is the massive 12th-century *Keep*, built by Henry II, which, with the 14th-century *Great Hall* and *Leicester's Buildings*, partly encloses the inner court. Outer court runs all round this group, and on the west side a doorway leads to the *Great Mere*, once a large lake, part of the extensive water defences. Leicester's turreted *Gatehouse* faces across gently banked Castle Green cherubs and the Commandments, is now at the west end, next to a large royal arms, and the classical wall monuments, one by Whitehead of Southam, have been banished to the north transept. Timber-framed and lias marketplace spoilt by a central, chapel-like *library*. Mullioned *Swan Hotel* was built in 1668 and, by the road to Banbury, an Arts and Crafts *war memorial* is surrounded by thatched brick and stone cottages. Lias-and-brown-stone *manor house* and, in *Bridge Street*, many stone Georgian houses.

Kingsbury [5] Here, high above the River Tame, the Kings of Mercia are said to have had their palace. Old centre is now surrounded by spec. houses. *Church* (St. Peter and St. Paul) is on an exposed western ridge; and, in the river valley below, vast gravel pits are gradually being filled with ash from Hams Hall Power Station. Impressive tower, c. 1300, multi-coloured Norman body, with some Georgian brickwork, and sturdy 15th-century porch roof. Norman piers and Gothic arches support plain plastered walls and an 18th-century ceiling. Norman chancel arch was removed in 1887, and the scraped chancel has a plaster ceiling, divided by a dark timber truss. Lofty, whitewashed Bracebridge Chapel, built c. 1300, is now a vestry. Mutilated mediaeval effigies and Georgian benefactors' board. Beyond a ravine, curtain-walled *Kingsbury Hall*, is now a farmhouse. Victorian *vicarage* has pierced bargeboards. Plum-coloured *school house*, built c. 1667, has a stone sundial; *Board School*, built in 1884, has later extensions. *Hemlingford Bridge* is 18th-century; *Kingsbury Mill*, successor to one mentioned in Domesday, made gun barrels for the Napoleonic Wars.

Dovecote at **Kinwarton**. The lower photograph shows the revolving inspection ladder

Kings Heath *see* Birmingham.

Kings Newnham [9] Brick Georgian houses behind well mown grass verges where the Roman Fosse Way crosses the River Avon Of the *church* (St. Lawrence) only the tower remains—a desolate creeper-clad landmark with a Norman window and a pyramid roof.

Kings Norton *see* Birmingham.

Kinwarton [10] (near Alcester) Down a lane, against the River Alne, the elegant late 18th-century *rectory* stands between a black-and-white farm and the small, grey *church* (St. Mary). Simple weather-boarded bell turret and porch date from Butterfield's restoration of 1847. Aisleless cream-washed interior, which has an elaborate 18th-century chandelier, is given character by the woodwork and glass of the 1840s rather than by earlier work. Rood cross stands on an ogee arch above a frieze of quatrefoils; the east window, by O'Connor, has a moving Crucifixion, with rich figures against a sad grey ground. Also by Butterfield are the tiling, benches, pulpit, organ case and corona. Circular 14th-century *dovecote*.

Knightcote [11] A long terrace of thatched brown-stone cottages and a superb chequered-brick house in the valley of the River Itchen. Round-arched *Wesleyan chapel*, 1837, is also chequered; but Gothic Revival *Old School House* is spoilt by new windows and roughcast.

Knowle [7] A timber-framed and brick village which has become a dormitory for Birmingham and Coventry. High Street has old buildings, between shops, in both Stockbroker's Tudor and Banker's Georgian. Perpendicular *church* (St. John Baptist, St. Lawrence and St. Anne) consecrated in 1402, is of white Arden sandstone, with a chancel extension in red Kenil-worth sandstone. Stately embattled west tower. Impressive interior, well lit by a later clerestory, is fortunately without a chancel arch. Roof beams were once decorated in a design of red and white. Arch on the north side of the nave opens into a shallow transept, which has a timber ceiling studded with bosses. In 1921, a lavishly carved stone screen was erected to define The Soldiers' Chapel, richly decorated and furnished, by W. H. Bidlake, with carving by the Chipping Campden school. Door to the left formerly gave access to the rood screen which, during the restoration of 1860, was left in the churchyard while a controversy raged about its retention. Intricately vaulted in dark wood, it was eventually refixed further east. At one time there was a processional way beneath the sanctuary; but, since this was abandoned in the 18th century, the chancel floor has been levelled, leaving the sedilia and piscina at high level. Misericords are carved with foliage and animals; and the pulpit, by Alexander Millard of Chipping Campden, has an old hourglass, made by the local carpenter in 1673, which runs for twenty minutes. Timber-framed *Guild House*, built in 1412, served as a shop before its restoration in 1912, by W. H. Bidlake, who also designed the Hollington-stone churchyard cross. Pretty polychromatic village *school* and cottages. Small-scale *cottage homes* were built in 1886. Half-timbered *Milverton House* is linked to a rendered Jacobean-style *terrace*, built c. 1840. Timber-framed *Chester House*, built in the 15th century, is now the library. Further north, picturesque *Grimshaw Hall* has decorative framing, bracketed bay windows, fine Tudor chimneys and a charming porch.

Ladbroke [11] Where the Coventry–Banbury road crosses a tributary of the River Itchen. *Church* (All Saints) is a mixture of cream and ochre stone, the tall 14th-century tower with alternate bands, small openings and a recessed grey spire. Aisle windows are square-headed; porch has large former roof corbels, with animated faces, from the demolished Radbourne church. Tall, dark nave. South-east window incorporates parts of original figures, St. Cuthbert with St. Oswald's head, under Gothic painted-glass canopies; and a well drawn white-and-gold north aisle window, 1911, by Webb, displays the arms of the Durham and Townshend families. 13th-century chancel with a Hardman-style east window and stodgy north windows by Kempe and Tower. Effigy of a priest, said to be of Roger de Paveley, the second rector of Paveley, 1298–1303, was found under the floor during the restoration of 1876, by Sir George Gilbert Scott, who copied the original floor tiles, designed the font and removed memorials. Brick cottage has painted timber framing and deep thatch; beyond a large cedar, the stucco-faced *Old Vicarage* is elegantly sash-windowed. Lias *Ladbroke Hall* is 17th-century.

Ladywood *see* Birmingham.

Langley [10] A hamlet on a brook by a small bellcoted *church* and several modern bungalows. Black-and-white cottages and luxurious houses.

Lapworth [7] Impressive white-stone *church* (St. Mary) and cream-washed, timbered and brick cottages, on a wooded hill skirted by the Stratford-on-Avon Canal. Almost free-standing tower has a later, darker spire. Road winds round a 15th-century chantry chapel, raised above a vaulted churchyard underpass, to allow processions, and from which it is reached by two spiral staircases. Powdery-white-stone nave has 13th-century arcades and a large clear-glazed clerestory beneath a fine Perpendicular roof. Above one of the arcades is part of a Norman window. West window is bright with Georgian heraldic glass, including the arms of a rector. Dark north chapel has a tender Madonna and child by Eric Gill, surrounded by 13th-century painted roses. Classical mural monument on an apologetic Gothic slate is to James Way, rector, d.1816, and a colourful royal arms, 1819, is by Isaac Brown of Rowington. New buff-brick *rectory* retains red-brick outbuildings, with a timber-traceried window. Downhill, past timber-framed *Lapworth Grange*, Tudor-style *Lapworth Court* is a complete early 19th-century piece; and, over a humpbacked canal bridge, stands Georgian Revival *Lapworth Hall*.

Lea Marston [5] Agricultural and with two separate hamlets, Lea and Marston. Built by Charles Bowyer Adderley in the 18th century, stone-faced *Hams Hall*, with an entrance hall frieze by Thorwaldsen, was dismantled to make way for the present power station and the upper floors re-erected, in 1919–21, at Coates in Gloucestershire. Of his stay in 1895, Gladstone wrote: 'The visit to Hams fills—shall I say?—a fragrant place in my recollection'; and it was here that the rich, philanthropic first Lord Norton, 1814–1905, pioneered self-government for parts of the British Empire and formulated the New Zealand Constitution. Now thirteen giant cooling towers dominate the surrounding countryside. Adderleys lie in a peaceful churchyard, guarded by a heavily cusped cross. Nave of the *church* (St. John the Baptist), built c. 1300, is down steps; and the chancel, rebuilt in 1876–7, has a black-and-white-stone floor, giving the effect of a private chapel. Coade-stone wall monument to Lettice Adderley, 1784, and white-marble ones by Hollins. Brick *Woodhouse Farm*, once seen from the park, has full-height pilasters. Of the 18th-century farmhouses,

around a green with a large cedar, *Oakwood* was made Tudor, c. 1840. *Old School* and *Bridge Cottage* are also in the Tudor style of the 1840s. Over the river, derelict, part-timber-framed *Coton Hall* is secluded and mysterious.

Leamington Hastings [12] A delightful village by the River Leam; several timber-framed cottages. Large *church* (All Saints) has a red Perpendicular tower, weathered to a grey green, the west doorway graced by an ogee gable and slender attached pinnacles, to welcome the squire from the neighbouring manor house. Spacious part-Early English nave has a boarded ceiling and yellow-to-rust heraldic glass. Small north aisle window indicates the position of a former transept. Late Gothic Revival woodwork serves as a chancel arch; and, though scraped, the chancel, which has 17th-century square-headed windows and a moulded cornice, is reminiscent of a grand drawing room. Communion rail is a simple arcade of lancets. Bust of Sir Thomas Trevor, 1656, one of Charles I's Barons of the Exchequer, has a leathery cartouche supported by a wide-eyed angel. *Manor house* has a massive chimneystack, an early 19th-century wing and a Victorian south front, facing across the valley. Lias cottage with Tudor doorway, and round-arched brick stables. Mullioned *almshouses*, 1633, *post office*, with corrugated iron over thatch, and patterned-brick *smithy*.

Leamington Spa *see* Royal Leamington Spa.

Leek Wootton [8] On a hill and with magnificent views over the Avon valley. New houses replace thatched timber-framed and stone cottages. On a pre-Christian site, high above the road, the elegant 18th-century Gothic *church* (All Saints) so offended the Victorians that, besides adding the inevitable

deep chancel, they removed all plaster, inserted intricate window tracery and reconstructed the roof with public-school hammerbeams. Mediaeval vestry with fine reticulated window. Timber-framed *The Rock*, behind a mutilated wych elm, and derelict stone *post office*, *bakery* and *village store*. Amid trees by the river, orange-brick *Hill Wootton Mill* has a tall, creeper-clad chimney; and, caught by a shaft of light, the white-painted Georgian *mill house* has Jacobethan embellishments.

Lighthorne [11] In a coomb, and approached from above the rooftops. Steeply roofed stone houses face each other across greens; and, above the road, a Victorian wellhead has Jacobean details. Dull rock-faced *church* (St. Lawrence) is John Gibson's 1875–6 rebuilding of a smaller structure, of which only the pretty Georgian Gothic tower survives. Dark interior is saved by unusual glass: a bald St. Lawrence on a grating above licking flames, a heavily punctured St. Sebastian with flowing golden locks and a fine collection of 17th-century painted arms in reds and golds. Pond was a fish stew.

Lillington [11] (near Cubbington) Mediaeval church and roughcast First World War houses between large areas of housing, near Royal Leamington Spa. Keuper sandstone and marls are concealed by glacial deposits, in which have been found the remains of elephant and rhinoceros. Chancel of the darkened cream-stone *church* was extended in pink stone in the 14th century, and the ponderous nave has arcade piers copied from an unusual respond of similar date. Proximity of Leamington has resulted in luxurious embellishments, such as a black-and-white-marble floor, a richly carved reredos, windows by Kempe and a Burne-Jones-style tapestry. Gaunt 18th-century house, and an earlier building of stone, with dainty Arts and Crafts railings. Marked by a slender copper spire, the centrally planned R.C. *Church of Our Lady* is bright with chunky glass.

Little Compton [17] In a valley between steep hills at the extreme southern tip of the county, and, in 1555, known as Compton 'in the flowers'. Buff-ragstone terraces, with walled gardens. Ivy-clad *Little Compton Manor* partly encloses the walled churchyard, its gables rising above the church. Part pre-Reformation, it was remodelled, in 1620, by Archbishop Juxon, who balanced the south elevation, now centred on massive ball-topped gate piers. South side of the *church* (St. Denis) has a squat, saddle-back-roofed tower, supported by massive clasping buttresses. Heavy, fractured font. Wide, plastered body, an 1863–4 rebuilding by E. A. Bruton, has a short, stout arcade and a light south chapel. Italianate *Baptist chapel*, 1870s.

Little Packington [8] Scattered and divided by a link road to the M6, a disused railway cutting and the meandering River Blythe, skirting Packington Park. Picturesque Georgian Gothic *Park Farm* with pinnacled stepped gables, dainty glazing and a weathered ogee-panelled sundial. Disused 13th-century *church* (St. Bartholomew) has a timber-framed belfry; an 18th-century headstone depicts the Good Samaritan. Sandy-rendered *Church Farm* stands against a timber-framed barn; and, beyond the railway bridge, is a river ford surrounded by willows and oaks. Flaking *Old School* has sash windows and a Gothic vent.

Little Wolford [14] (near Great Wolford) High drystone wall, housing a dribbling lion's-head fountain, is broken by the wrought-iron entrance gates of the *manor*, a modest part-timber-framed building with extensive views across

Nethercote Brook. With an elaborate chimneypiece, the hall is collegiate in character and has 16th-century heraldic glass. Brick *estate cottages*, with pretty bargeboards and tiling, are dated 1858; council houses are pebbledashed.

Long Compton [14] Stone cottages around a twisting valley road. Farmland stretches up the steep hillsides in long strips. Standing Neolithic or Early Bronze Age monolith, known as the *King Stone*, and high up, across the county boundary, a jagged circle of the same date, known as the *Rollright Stones*. St. Augustine chastised the local lord for not paying his tithes and, because he did not relent, excommunicated him. When, from the altar, the saint commanded that 'no excommunicated person be present at Masse', a dead man arose out of his grave and went into the churchyard. After the service he was found to be patron in the time of the Britons who, though warned, never paid his tithes and died excommunicated. St. Augustine therefore summoned from his grave the dead man's priest, who forgave his companion in death and the live lord repented. Though the *church* (St. Peter and St. Paul) was founded at an early date, the earliest recognisable part is the light, spacious early 13th-century nave. Late 13th-century chancel, heavily restored by Woodyer, who must have designed the sharply gabled stone reredos and the aggressively traceried wood screen. Pretty ogee-arched pulpit, probably part of the Perpendicular font; new font has flowing tracery around a shaped bowl. Cavernous Gothic porch, 1620, with stone seats and a defaced early 14th-century effigy, leads out into a stone-walled churchyard, with clipped yews and a thatched two-storeyed *lych gate*, possibly originally a cottage. Thatched houses and, beyond a stream, a long Gothic house beneath a slate roof. Pedimented 18th-century *vicarage*, originally covered

in Long Compton slates, is overpowered by Victorian extensions. Base of *village cross* has been converted into a water supply. *Primitive Methodist chapel*, 1881. *Friends' Meeting House*, 1670, and classical *Wesleyan* and *Congregational chapels*. The first R.C. chapel was that of the Sheldon family at Elizabethan Weston Park. When the mansion was pulled down, its windows were built into *Manor Farm House*. Blore's Jacobean-style Weston House, built in 1827–32, was demolished in the 1930s.

Long Itchington [11] Many-gabled black-and-white *Tudor House* and later brick houses around pond beneath trees. St. Wulfstan, Bishop of Worcester, was born here; he gave loyalty to William the Conqueror as monarch, but was never in favour of Lanfranc, the Norman Archbishop of Canterbury. On being asked by Lanfranc to surrender his staff, he drove it into the tomb of Edward the Confessor, from which it could not be removed until the Archbishop begged St. Wulfstan to reassume office. On the river bank, *church* (Holy Trinity) has a grey west tower, accentuated by red buttresses and crowned by the stump of a spire, blown down in 1762. Earliest part is the south aisle, which has a 12th-century doorway, lancet windows and two fine tomb recesses, probably for the priest John de Odingsels and his aunt. Tall nave, 14th-century rood screen and bright chancel, c. 1300. Elaborate hatchment is to Lady Anne Holbourne, granddaughter of Dudley, Earl of Leicester, who entertained Queen Elizabeth I here. Churchyard is enclosed by a house and barns. Georgian *Manor Farm* contains the remains of the 15th-century hall; Gothic *school* is unmistakably Victorian.

Long Lawford [9] In undulating countryside and a loop in the River Avon. Many modern houses and, beyond a humpbacked railway

Lower Shuckburgh

bridge, the humble *Railway Inn*, the sub-Arts and Crafts *Caldecott Arms* and a roughcast cottage *post office*. Italianate *chapel* with cream-brick pilasters. Against the grounds of Holbrook Grange, the 1839 buff-brick *church* (St. John) has lancet windows, a fishscale-slate roof and a pinnacle at each corner. Light, plastered nave is divided from the shallow chancel and identical west end by tall, plastered arches. One of the most complete interiors of its date in the county: its grained furnishings include a two-decker desk and a pulpit; and there is rich glass, by W. Holland of Warwick, studded with swirling gold bosses.

Long Marston [13] Once known as Marston Sicca, as it is badly drained and has no springs. Partly rendered lias *church* (St. James) is stone-roofed and has an unusual timber-framed west tower on four great oak posts, standing inside the walling of the lower stages. Belfry stage and hipped roof were added in the late 19th century, when stucco and sham battlements were removed. Stone-flagged cream-washed interior is spanned by a wide chancel arch beneath a painted royal arms. Chancel has a queenpost roof, a Perpendicular window with fragments of old glass, and a Norman pillar piscina. Wall

monuments to the Tomes family include one to Mary d.1751, with downward-tapering pilasters, which adds much to the exterior; and the churchyard has a number of robust table tombs wreathed in ivy and brambles. Lias Tudor-style *Old School*, also with a stone roof, and timber-framed *Orchard Cottages*. Mullioned *The Goodwins* is late 16th-century; and *King's Lodge*, where Charles II came in disguise, retains the original meat jack which he was made to wind, and in so doing was struck by the cook for his clumsiness. Also of interest are *Sicca Lodge*, *Hopkins*, *Long Marston Grounds* and the *post office*.

Lower and Upper Shuckburgh [12] In a valley, where the road to Southam crosses the Oxford Canal and decides to cross back again. Near the *vicarage*, built by Croft, is clearly defined ridge and furrow. Lively *church*, Croft's 1864 rebuilding of a 17th-century structure, has decidedly eastern details, which show the influence of George Shuckburgh, following his return from the Crimea. Of yellow stone banded with lias, and with a hexagonal steeple. Fantastic scalloped gable, Saracenic arches, gristly window tracery and purple-gravel mosaic. Nave has serrated red-brick arches and an awkward timber roof. Varnished pitchpine pews with eastern finials. Restrained by a number of later iron ties, the brick vault over the chancel has tile infilling; and the tower space is similarly vaulted, above a tub-shaped 13th-century font. Towards Upper Shuckburgh, timbered *estate cottages*, 1895, stand around the pyramid-roofed *school*. At first sight, secluded *Shuckburgh Hall* is Early Victorian, but the weathered stucco entrance front, built in 1844, by Kendall, hides an older timber-framed house backing into a hill. Wooded park has a herd of deer, and peacocks strut along the terrace. From Cannon Bank there are marvellous views as far as the Black Mountains. Shuckburghs have been here since the beginning of the 12th century. Richard Shuckburgh met Charles I while hunting on Beacon Hill and, after fighting for him at Edge Hill, was defeated on Shuckburgh Hill and carried away to Kenilworth Castle, where he was forced to purchase his liberty. In consideration of his father's sufferings and his own zeal, his eldest son John was made a baronet by Charles II. *Entrance Hall* has an elaborate Jacobean-style fireplace; *Staircase Hall* is lit by a stained-glass window, illustrating the story of Richard and John Shuckburgh, and a circular roof opening reminiscent of the Pantheon. Charles II *Saloon* has an oval ceiling painting and English Mortlake tapestries, illustrating the four seasons; *Dining Room* has a Victorian Jacobean-style ceiling with pendants, and a large painting, by Melchior, of the mad King of Bavaria's game larder. To the south, the ground rises sharply to a golden *yew-hedge fort*, a copy, by George Shuckburgh, of the one at Redan in the Crimea. Above sweeping lawns, the Hornton-stone *church* (St. John Baptist) is the 1660s rebuilding of the part-12th-century structure, ruined by Cromwell and in which he stabled his horses. Victorian belfry, nave roof, chancel and chapels, the latter with small white-stone coffin lids built into the outer walls. 16th-century glass, and many white-marble memorials to the Shuckburghs, perhaps the most interesting of them to Sir George Shuckburgh-Evelyn, 1804, by Flaxman, with a globe and an astrolabe, for he was an astronomer and gave his name to a crater on the moon. Lady Shuckburgh-Evelyn, 1797, shown on a Grecian couch, is also by Flaxman. Pew ends, not unlike those at Lower Shuckburgh, wood pulpit, with twisted columns and carved heads, and lectern with angels and lions. By the altar, hands emerge from curtained Gothic niches to point to the Lord's Prayer, Creed and Ten Commandments in open books. A monument to Catherine Shuckburgh, 1683, boasts a bare breast; and the south chapel has recumbent effigies to John Shuckburgh, 1631, and his wife. Grand, arcaded brick *home farm and stables*, reminiscent of Soane, and a pyramid-roofed *dovecote*.

Loxley [11] At the foot of Long Hill. *Church* (St. Nicholas) stands upon one of the oldest foundations in the county, the site having been given by Offa, King of Mercia, to the Cathedral Church of Worcester in A.D. 760. Saxon herringbone chancel wall. Orange-sandstone tower has a 13th-century cream belfry; Georgian body has parts of a table tomb built into the vestry. White plastered nave is full of light which reflects on to the ceiling, defined by a simple cornice. Darker tower space houses the old stocks. Georgian pulpit, wall-mounted so that it can be seen from the box pews, and Norman pillar piscina. White-marble tablet to a vicar, the Rev. George Huddesford, d.1809, by Richard Westmacott and a remarkable chancel window, 1740, of St. Nicholas holding lilies, below a star and a woman's face. St. Nicholas also appears on the lectern drop, by Anthony Green, where he is shown wearing pyjamas and bedroom slippers. Casualties in the battle of Edge Hill, 1642, are said to be buried in the churchyard, which every spring is carpeted with wild violets, forget-me-nots and blue anemones. Late Georgian *Loxley Hall*, which has polychromatic brick additions, may have been a grange of the Priors of Kenilworth. An elegant chimneypiece from Stivichall Hall, Coventry, by the Bulkington-born sculptor Richard Hayward. White-painted *Fox Inn* matches the surrounding houses; and the Tudor-style *school* has a precariously perched bellcote.

Luddington [10] Thatched and tiled timber-framed houses around a green. In fields by the River Avon, the quaint lias *church*, 1871–2, by John Cotton, but not one of his best, replaces the ancient chapel-of-ease to Stratford in which Anne Hathaway and William Shakespeare are said to have been married. Destroyed by fire, its foundations can still be traced, near the blacksmith's shop; and the original font, which has a quatrefoil frieze, is now in the new church. Busy spirelet, yellow-brick dressings and pretty timbered porch. Simple, dark interior has an inbuilt stone pulpit and a geometric font.

Maxstoke Castle

Mancetter [5] (near Witherley) Originally the Roman Manduessedum, a posting station astride the Watling Street, marked by a rectangular earthwork enclosing an area of six acres. Possibly settled as early as A.D. 60, the site may be that of the defeat of Queen Boadicea and the Britons. Pottery kilns and evidence of glass working. Mediaeval centre is around the Green where the variegated-sandstone *church* (St. Peter), dating from the early 13th century, is probably on the site of a wooden church, built as early as A.D. 930. Short, tall nave has a large, deeply splayed west lancet against an ochre-coloured Perpendicular tower. Wide chancel arch and Decorated chancel. Simple Victorian east window glazed with rich early 14th-century figures from the Merevale Tree of Jesse. Plastered walls have two boards, 1833, to the Marian martyrs of Mancetter, Robert Glover and Joyce Lewis, burned at Coventry and Lichfield in the 1550s; a stodgy bust of Edward Hutton in a wig, 1690; and several monuments to the Bracebridge family, reputed to have lived in Warwickshire since the 12th century, and buried in a vault against the east end of the north aisle. Round-arched brick south porch carries a sundial and a plaque with vigorous strapwork. Whitewashed *almshouses*, 1728 and 1822, the

latter fronted by a delicate Gothic veranda. Behind a forecourt, with a gazebo in each corner, the timbered early 14th-century *Manor House* has a central hall and projecting wings, the hall trusses on posts forming aisles. 18th-century *Manor House Farm* with timber-framed barn; early 19th-century stucco *Vicarage*. Arts and Crafts *1–3 The Green*, built in 1908, incorporate some old timbers. Functional-tradition *coal depot* boasts a bell turret; the sash-windowed *Plough Inn* is part 16th century.

Mappleborough Green [10] Below steep Gorcott Hill, on which the timbered *Gorcott Hall* enjoys extensive views over the Arrow Valley. Above the village, the modest *church* (Holy Ascension), built in 1888, by J. A. Chatwin for Sir William Jaffray, is approached past a delicious pair of Georgian Gothick cottages, their orange-brick walls showing traces of the more fashionable whitewash, behind delicate fret porches. Pink-sandstone church now weathered to a light green; smooth-stone interior has small arcades and soaring tower and chancel arches, the latter framing three richly glazed lancets. Stone-vaulted chapel is divided from the chancel by a delicate iron screen.

Marton [8] Thatched black-and-white cottages, urban brick terraces and the *church* (Saint-Esprit, a unique dedication) rebuilt following a disastrous fire of the 1870s. 13th-century south doorway and Perpendicular south arcade. Victorian work, by George Purshon of Leamington Spa, is precise and cold, and the extensive tower wall is decorated with an awesome arrangement of painted-metal texts. Organ, south door and baptistry also have texts. Octagonal font was given by the builder, James Marriott of Coventry. Gothic *school*, 1859, with the schoolmaster's house under the same roof; part-Elizabethan *manor house*; and red-brick Victorian *chapel* with lan-

Maxstoke Priory and church

cets. *Marton House* has fine cast-iron porch brackets; in the fields beyond the stone river bridge, a timber-framed farmhouse hides behind a Georgian front.

Maxstoke [5] Eastwards from Coleshill's noble steeple rise the towers of moated *Maxstoke Castle*, over a mile to the north of the village, a sprinkling of cottages and farms around a priory and

a church. Compact rectangular fortress with a massive turreted gatehouse and, at each corner, an octagonal tower, in one of which stayed Richard III, shortly before Bosworth. Built by William de Clinton in the 1340s, it was partly remodelled a century later by Humphrey Stafford and, in 1524, was granted by Henry VIII to Sir William Compton of Compton Wynyates. Later Sir Thomas

Dilke fitted it up, and most of the interior features are of his time. Vaulted gateway leads to cobbled inner court. Timber-framed north range houses oak *Drawing Room*, which has a massive carved-wood chimneypiece bearing the arms of Sir Thomas Dilke and his wife, and a handsome pillared lobby said to have come from Kenilworth Castle. Great Hall and Chapel were on the west side, and the kitchens on the south. *Banqueting Hall* has a kingpost roof, Elizabethan windows and a Gothic Revival fireplace; *north-west tower* has an original tile floor supported on a rib vault. Ancient deer park, which has a lake, is now a golf course. Across rolling unspoilt country, ruined red-sandstone *priory* stands gaunt against the sky. Founded in 1336, for Augustinian Canons, by the same William de Clinton, it is dominated by a tall slice of the central tower of the large aisleless church. In a long, high wall against the road, a vaulted outer gatehouse leads to an inner one, now converted into a farmhouse, and the adjoining brick farm buildings are alive with animals and the everyday workings of the farm. By the wide moat stands the Victorian *Old Rectory*; and, just outside the priory wall, aisleless Decorated *church* (St. Michael) lent itself admirably to a Georgian remodelling, the elliptical plaster ceiling just catching the apex of the free-flowing east window. Box pews, pulpit with light inlay, dark hatchments, and painted royal arms, 1774, by Allport of Birmingham. A copy of Raphael's painting of St. Michael in a landscape, originally in the altarpiece, has been banished to the gallery. *Woodbine Cottage*, Dukes End, exposes its crucks.

Merevale [5] Magnificent hilly country with belts of mature trees and panoramic views across Leicestershire. In a hollow, the remains of the Cistercian *Merevale Abbey*, founded in 1148, are now a farm.

Buttressed walls of the refectory have a reading pulpit; and the cloister can be identified. Red-sandstone *church* (Our Lady), originally a capella-ante-portas of the Abbey, is approached through Clutton's Gothic gatehouse to Merevale Hall, linked to the 13th-century west front. Down steps, the brick-paved porch, furnished with old coffins, is enclosed by a fine Perpendicular screen. Short 13th-century nave has blocked arcades, as the north aisle is ruined; south aisle has Georgian vestries. West light emphasises the wall monuments and the informally arranged 13th- and 14th-century effigies. Long, delicately arcaded chancel, c. 1500, has a large east window richly glazed with an early 14th-century Tree of Jesse, probably from the Abbey. Decorated south aisle. High-quality brasses to Robert, Earl Ferrers, 1412, and his wife; small organ, used by Handel and window in memory of the Victorian architect, Robert Jenninns. Sensationally sited on a precipitous hill, turreted Jacobean-style *Merevale Hall*, the seat of the Dugdales, rises above the trees to dominate the surrounding landscape. An 1840 rebuilding of a long Georgian house, it was designed by Edward Blore, who helped Walter Scott with Abbotsford, and supervised by Jenninns. Finely jointed stone, well distributed shaped gables and numerous skimpy towers. Strapwork staircase leads to an arcaded landing with Venetian windows. Many precise plasterwork ceilings. Entrance was moved to the end of the house, in 1842, to increase privacy. Garden terrace leads to further terraces, and a long walk by W. A. Nestfield. Near Atherstone, two stone lodges have central chimneys and pediments on all sides.

Meriden [8] Along a wide green which has an old sandstone cross, reputed to be at the centre of England. The church marks the original village, which moved to the main

road to provide inns and alehouses for passengers. The 1958 by-pass left the quietened village a prey to spec. builders whose unsympathetic housing has engulfed the old cottages. *Pool*, once one of the village's most attractive features, became so dry that it was made into a garden; the orange-brick *Manor House*, built in 1814, has an exact replica as an extension. On a hill outside the village, *church* (St. Lawrence) has a stolid Perpendicular tower and a part-Norman chancel and the nave, which has mediaeval arcades, is lit from the aisles by tall early 19th-century Perpendicular windows. Timber-framed *Moat House*; and, secluded beyond a belt of trees, pedimented stone *Meriden Hall*. Georgian *Darlaston Hall*, the original Bull's Head, was known as the 'handsomest inn in England' when Princess Victoria stayed here in 1832. *Obelisk*, in memory of the motorcyclists who died in the two World Wars, attracts cyclists from all over the Continent. Though Meriden is traditionally known as the centre of the local motorcycle industry, embracing B.S.A. (Birmingham Small Arms) and Coventry Eagle, only Norton and Triumph have been manufactured here since the Second World War, during which they were used by despatch riders. Round-arched brick *Forest Hall*, built in 1788, by Joseph Bonomi for the Woodmen of Arden, the oldest archery club in the country, has a horn reputed to have belonged to Robin Hood, and a vigorous bust of Wriothesley Digby, by Nollekens. Timber-framed *Walsh Hall*, with carved brackets and a massive chimney-stack. On Meriden Heath, in 1745, the Duke of Cumberland set up his headquarters during his attempt to block the Young Pretender's advance to London.

Middleton [4] Well wooded and with modest 18th- to 20th-century houses around the *church* (St. John Baptist), its handsome Perpendicular tower rising above all. South doorway, sheltered by an 18th-century brick porch, is Norman, with zigzag decoration; lofty, plastered nave has a generous Perpendicular clerestory. Delicately traceried Perpendicular screen and a fine late-15th-century brass to Richard Bingham, Justice of the King's Bench. Large white monument, which necessitated the blocking up of a window, is to Francis Willoughby, d.1675, who carried out the scientific classification of insects and fish, and a south aisle window is by Kempe. Polychromatic brick *school*, c. 1870, has unusual Venetian windows. Secluded and crumbling, stucco-faced *Middleton Hall*, once the seat of the Willoughbys since the 15th century, is now deserted. In the 16th century the intrepid Hugh took command of an expedition to the White Sea, and opened up, for the first time, a trade between England and Russia. Unfortunately he later sailed to the coast of Lapland, and perished miserably. Francis Willoughby was knighted by Queen Elizabeth I, who kept court here for a week, consuming '69 beeves, 128 sheep and more than 2,000 chickens, with other provisions in proportion'. Francis Willoughby, the celebrated ornithologist and man of letters, was born in a panelled room, once shown with pride; and John Ray, a fellow naturalist, filled the gardens and neighbouring woods with curious plants, many of which survived into this century. In recognition of Francis's attainments, his son had the odd distinction of being created a baron in infancy, but, as he died young, the title passed to his brother who, as the first Baron Middleton, undoubtedly built the *Dining Room*, *Drawing Room* and *Library*, and created the present *Hall*, a theatrical space entered from a half landing. Deer park has given way to flooded gravel workings, which reflect the ochre-coloured west front, divided by giant fluted

pilasters; courtyard has earlier buildings, one with a Norman window. Handsome timber-framed building has later brick infill and, seen through a carriageway, two sandstone chimneystacks.

Milcote [10] (near Clifford Chambers)

In the fields near the River Avon, the once moated *Milcote Manor* has a stone chimneystack dated 1564, and a long, timber-framed barn. Against a graveyard orchard, *Milcote Hall Farm* was the home of the Adkins family, whose Greek Revival monuments can be seen in Weston-on-Avon church. Gabled and pebbledashed around a massive brick chimney, it has a pedimented Georgian front with a Regency veranda and, on the underside of a splendid full-height staircase, a large, painted sundial.

Monks Kirby [9]

Timber-framed and brick houses in rich, undulating country. Magnificent *church* (St. Edith) was once part of a Benedictine priory, founded in 1077. Massive tower has a soaring red-sandstone base supporting a comfortable beige belfry with shaped gables and pinnacles, obviously built after the fall of the spire in 1701. Impressive porch, covered by a star vault. Exceptionally fine Perpendicular nave arcades must have been positioned by the walls of the Early English chancel, with which they enclose one undivided space. Exquisite mediaeval canopy; Hardman New Testament scenes in the east window; sentimental Lady Augusta Fielding and the seventh Earl of Denbigh and his Countess, 1881. Timber-framed house, facing The Trees, is said to be the old vicarage; the present, pretty 1843 *vicarage* has diaper brickwork and a patterned tile roof. *Manor house* is similar. *St. Edith's Close*, 1974, by Kendrick Findlay and Partners has split ridges and weatherboarding. Of Newnham Paddox, the seat of the Fieldings, nothing remains except the splen-

did iron gates decorated with cockatoos, dragons and bearded faces..

Moreton Morrell [11]

Thatched, timber-framed and Georgian houses and, in a spacious churchyard, the humble *church* (Holy Cross). Simple stone tower, with a reset Norman window, and Georgian brick buttresses. Cream-washed plaster interior, virtually untouched since Georgian times, has rude timber trusses and clear-glazed Georgian Gothic windows. Painted royal arms and, dominating the chancel, a large alabaster monument, 1635, with bold, kneeling Richard Murden and wife surrounded by cherubs, skulls, etc. Thatched 17th-century cottage is believed to be the former home of the Randolph family. William Randolph, b.1650, emigrated to Virginia in 1672, and his grand-daughter Jane married Peter Jefferson, father of the more famous Thomas, who drew up the Declaration of Independence and became third President of the U.S.A. Manor House surrounded by yew hedges. Curved avenue of Wellingtonias leads to the severely classical stone *Agricultural College* (originally Moreton Hall), built c. 1906, by W. H. Romaine-Walker, for C. T. Garland, an American citizen who later served in the British Army during the First World War. His *real-tennis court*, outside the wrought-iron entrance gates, is Edwardian Queen Anne, revelling in pediments and parapets; spacious, well proportioned dining room and clubroom, known as the dedans, have marble fireplaces and faded photographs of eminent players, which contribute to an air of bygone opulence. Dressing rooms tell a similar story, with mammoth baths and shower bath, along with the buttonhooks and shoehorns which grace the ornate table and the stags' heads which peer down the passage walls. The huge volume of the court, black-plastered by Joseph Bickley, who died with his secret, is surrounded at high level by a garlanded frieze, and has the usual lean-to galleries.

Morton Bagot [10] In undulating country with groups of large trees in the hedgerows. On a high hill, a pair of tall wellingtonias stands against the timbered bell turret of the *church* (Holy Trinity), a modest white-stone structure with an orange-tile roof. Simple cream-washed nave has an octagonal font and, on the pew ends, branched candleholders. Scraped chancel is enriched by a Hardman east window and a magnificent prayer desk, from the Catholic chapel on the Profumo Estate at Avon Dassett. Black and white *Church Farm* with a long, timber-framed barn.

Moseley & Balsall Heath *see* Birmingham.

Napton-on-the-Hill [12] Originally thatched ochre-stone terraces and slated, speckled-brick houses around a chestnut on a green. Walled churchyard with splendid views. Long, red-roofed *church* (St. Lawrence) has a classical tower, similar to that at Priors Marston, late 13th-century transepts with stepped lancets, and a Norman chancel with a sundial. South doorway, c. 1200, with early stiff-leaf capitals. White plastered nave, Norman carving on the chancel arch, and Perpendicular east window. Stone *tower mill* has been restored; and, at the foot of the hill, against the Oxford Canal, is an old brickworks.

Nether Whitacre [5] Scattered around the modest rubble *church* (St. Giles), set in fields. Simple sandstone tower, covered with light-green lichen, is studded with carved faces, possibly from an earlier structure; and the rock-faced south wall and angular windows are the result of a ruthless restoration of c.1870. Dim interior has harsh geometric glass, cement-rendered walls, an encaustic-tile floor and pitchpine pews. Stained-

17th-century Murden monument, **Moreton Morrell**

glass, early 14th-century kneeling angel holds a censer. Vestry, originally the Jennens Chapel, retains Richard Hayward's mourning woman, sarcophagus and collapsing pyramid, to Charles Jennens, who selected passages from the Bible for Handel's 'Messiah' and endowed the village school. Robust 18th-century headstones, and a very elegant early 19th-century headstone, with a draped urn in bas-relief. Plum-coloured *Old Rectory* was built in 1872, by R. F. Jennings of Atherstone; and timber-framed *Church House*, where the priest lived prior to 1872, has a central porch with twisted

columns. Moated and walled *Whitacre Hall*, the home of the Jennens family, early ironmasters of Birmingham, has a Jacobean gatehouse with Civil War bullet holes. Georgian farmhouse has a prettily gabled stucco wing. At *Hoggrills End* is a timber-framed house with a carved fleur-de-lis.

Newbold-on-Avon [9] Decaying cottages and new houses, above the *church* (St. Botolph) by the River Avon. Perpendicular west tower and wide north porch with rows of canopied niches. South porch, either Gothic Survival or Revival, has a shell niche. Clear-glazed Early

Victorian chancel, in the Perpendicular style, is dominated by John Hunt's standing monument to Sir William Boughton and his wife of Little Lawford Hall, originally protected by the wrought-iron tower screen. A member of Queen Anne's parliament, he wears high-heeled shoes and a wig falling over his cravat. White relief to Sir Egerton Leigh of Brownsover Hall, 1818, shows him on a couch with an angel pointing upwards. He was the second husband of Theodosia Boughton, following the execution of her first husband for poisoning her brother with laurel water. Georgian *vicarage* has unusual surface-mounted window frames, with rounded top panes. Gothic red-and-cream-brick *Methodist church*, 1879. All that survives of *Little Lawford Hall* is the stable block, 1604, now made habitable. The hall was pulled down about 1790 as 'a thing accursed', possibly following a ride of the Elizabethan 'One-Handed Boughton', whose coach, drawn by a team of six phantom horses, was believed to ride about the countryside.

Newbold-on-Stour [14] Grey-lias and pale-brick cottages, and a tall Georgian house in chequered brick. Large village green with a cob coachhouse. Early English-style *church* (St. David) built in 1833, stands against a fine tower, once with a spire. *Methodist chapel*, 1910. Impressive *lodge* to Ettington Park has an ample bay window rising to steep grey-slate roofs; beyond a large oak, the *White Hart* dates from 1560.

Newbold Pacey [11] Down a secluded gravel drive, in the valley of Thelsford Brook. By the lush park of the hall, the Early English-style *church* (St. George the Martyr) is the 1881–2 rebuilding, by J. L. Pearson, of a humble rustic pile with a timber bellcote. Distinctive saddle-back-roofed tower, and two re-used Norman doorways. Sumptuous late Gothic Revival reredos has St. George slaying the dragon; care-

14th-century angel, **Nether Whitacre**

fully grouped at the west end, the old classical monuments include a very sensitive demi-figure of Edward Carew, 1668, and his baby daughter, beneath a splendid coloured cresting. In the chancel lies Thomas Castle Southey, a nephew of the poet, and vicar here when the chuch was rebuilt. Behind a walled garden, the small-scale Queen Anne *rectory* has a panelled interior and a richly balustraded staircase. Timber-framed house, Victorian *estate cottages*, and stark stucco *hall*, with handsome *stables*.

Newton [9] (near Clifton-upon-Dunsmore) Comfortable Georgian

farms, Edwardian *Newton Chapel*, following the lines of the adjoining house, and the 1920s Gothic mission *church* (The Good Shepherd) with a bright, creamwashed interior.

Newton Regis [2] Thatched timber-framed cottages and Georgian brick farmhouses around a duck pond, with weeping willows. Cream-grey *church* (St. Mary) has occasional pieces of red sandstone, a 13th-century west tower, with a later spire, and a squint for the local leper. Both nave and chancel have Perpendicular clerestories; north chancel window is filled with thin

133

Newbold Pacey

red bricks, as in Cotman's day. Curious, almost round-headed arches, which look as if they were made ogee as an afterthought, also occur at Seckington, where Charles I fought after praying in this church. Early 19th-century *Newton House* has consciously elegant stone elevations and the timber-framed *post office* an elliptically arched orange-brick front added in the late 17th century.

No-Man's-Heath [2] (near Newton Regis) Once at the junction of four counties: Stafford, Leicester, Derby and Warwick; and, during the 18th century, an open common, ideal for squatters, who gradually enclosed it. Notorious for its prize-fights. Parochial annals record that

repairs to the weathercock were necessary when it had been riddled by shots from a gun. Small High Victorian Gothic *church* (St. Mary), built in 1863, is an essay in brick. Heavy arch at the west end supports the bell turret, and the poly-chromatic chancel arch has black-mastic-filled decoration. Circular plate-traceried east window glazed with a Morris-style Annunciation.

Northend [11] Thatched and tiled cottages around a small green on the northern slopes of the Bour-ton Dassett Hills. Towerless *church* is Early English Revival, with three stepped lancets in the chancel, now used as a vestry. Symmetrical, gabled *manor house*, and mid-17th-century *Green Farm House* in deep-

ochre stone. East end of a 14th-century *chapel* has a 17th-century priest's house; perched above the green, the orange-brick *Wesley Chapel* was built in 1831.

Northfield & Longbridge *see* Birmingham.

Norton Lindsey [11] Derelict windmill, timbered cottages and, on an eminence, 13th-century *church* (Holy Trinity), crowned by a bell-cote. Sympathetic north aisle was built by Ewan Christian, in 1874–5, and the dark interior resounds to the heavy tick of a clock in memory of Queen Victoria's Jubilee. Primi-tive Norman font bowl, and oak pulpit incorporating Jacobean panels. Chancel, too small for the choir stalls, has delicately painted

Victorian glass in rectangles. Massive yew tree, and humble Italianate *Sunday school*.

Nuneaton [5] A Saxon settlement on the River Anker, once at the edge of the great Forest of Arden but now in open country. 'Nun' was added in 1290, following the establishment of the Benedictine nunnery. 13th-century Prioress held a weekly market and an annual May Fair. Coal mining, which began as early as 1300, became profitable by 1700 and, by the late 19th century, an extensive industry exploring the deeper seams. Excavated clay was made into bricks and tiles. Severely damaged during the war, the town centre was rebuilt to a plan by Gibberd. Pinnacled *church* (St. Nicholas) has an impressive white-washed nave with elegant Late Gothic arcades and continuous clerestory windows. Timber nave and aisle ceilings, c. 1500. Chancel was lengthened during the 19th century, when Ewan Christian constructed the chancel arch to follow the arched chancel roof. Leeke Chapel, built c. 1350, is named after John Leeke who, in 1507, altered and endowed it as a chantry. Carved head of a king supporting the aumbry is said to be that of Edward III, and the combined piscina and credence is also 14th century. Alabaster effigy of Sir Marmaduke Constable, who received from Henry VIII the gift of Nuneaton Priory. Gothick south doorway decorated with ballflower on a wandering stalk; 1840s Grecian and Gothic tombs. Miniature *Old School*, which received its charter from Edward VI, was rebuilt in 1696, and has a delicate hexagonal cupola. Early pupil was Robert Burton, the author of 'The Anatomy of Melancholy'. Large *vicarage*, which has shaped gables, is 'Milby Vicarage' in George Eliot's 'Scenes of Clerical Life'. Hard Tudor-style *church schools*, 1848. *King Edward VI College*, built in 1880, by Clapton Crabb Rolf,

shows Butterfield influence; and an 1897 extension has half timbering and tile hanging. Distinctive *Public Library*, built in 1966, by Sir Frederick Gibberd, is pierced by lunettes reminiscent of Ledoux, and houses the George Eliot, Michael Drayton and Robert Burton collections. 1890s *Barclays Bank* has elaborate buff-terracotta balconies, and the later Belgian-influenced *11 Market Place* is probably by Birmingham's greatest exponents of the material, Essex Goodman and Nicol. Stone *10 Market Place*, built in 1894, is vaguely Jacobean; the *Leeds Permanent Building Society* has a spire; and, closing the vista along the market place, 1909 *National Westminster Bank* is disarmingly Queen Anne. Splendid Arts and Crafts *Nuneaton Conservative Club* has an arcaded balcony; and, catching the eye on a curve in the road, Austrian-inspired *3 Abbey Street* has elaborate timbers and a dome. *Abbey Church of St. Mary the Virgin* is a daughter house of the Order of Fontevrault, which was regarded with such special favour by the Angevin royal family that Henry II, Eleanor his wife, and their son Richard Lionheart were all buried at Fontevrault. Building started in the 1150s, but about 1230 the central tower collapsed, destroying the presbytery and part of the transepts. King Henry III granted twenty-five oaks for restoration. After the Dissolution, the buildings were converted into a considerable manor house for Sir Marmaduke Constable, but by 1763 had become a picturesque ruin. In 1877 part of the nave was rebuilt; and, beyond the massive mutilated crossing piers, the chancel, reconstructed on the original foundations, has mediaeval tiles representing the Wheel of Life. North transept was reconstructed in 1931. Cloister was to the south of the nave, with the chapter house on the east side. Font is from Godstow Priory, and the pulpit was once part of the three-

decker in the parish church. Stone Arts and Crafts *vicarage* has tall clustered chimneys and long ranges of mullioned windows, blocked here and there as if adapted over the centuries.

Offchurch [11] Thatched cottages, brick farms and post-war bungalows on a hill where Offa, King of Mercia, is said to have built a hunting lodge and a church. Heavily buttressed *church* (St. Gregory) has an impressive north doorway and a crisp Perpendicular tower, pock-marked by Cromwell's soldiers. Two carved stones, now built into the north wall, may be part of the lid of Offa's coffin. Wide Early English porch leads to a scraped, aisleless nave, made gloomy by poor Victorian glass; beyond a distorted Norman arch, the chancel, lengthened in the late 13th century, has Norman windows. Memorial to Lady Aylesford, 1914, is by Goodhart-Rendel. To the north and west are magnificent views over the river valley and, below the church, the mellow 18th-century *vicarage* has a brick triglyph frieze. In 1815 Field observes that 'the Parsonage House is surrounded by delightful pleasure grounds conspicuously touched in every part by the hand of taste and elegance. The lover of picturesque objects will admire the cottage school house. ....'. In extensive grounds past a pretty brick lodge, Gothic *Offchurch Bury*, built in 1829, incorporates a 17th-century porch. Pedimented *stables*, a lake backed by trees, and pillars reputed to resemble those at S. Sophia and to have come from Offa's house.

Oldberrow [10] Though Ullenhall seems to have been the church to which the Knights of Barrells regard themselves as parishioners, Oldberrow, of which a view could be obtained from Lady Luxborough's gardens by one of the 'vistas', was much nearer to Barrells Hall (see Henley-in-Arden and Ullenhall). On a hill, the small sandstone *church* (St. Mary), mainly rebuilt in 1875, does not seem to have ever had a proper tower, much as Lady Luxborough and her poetic circle must have wished for one. Single-cell body, lit by an assortment of small, old windows, is divided by a prettily traceried screen. Rich east window, with well drawn white figures beneath elaborate gold canopies, is in memory of the Revd. Samuel D'Oyley Peshall, d.1859, whose family were rectors for 150 years. One rebuilt the church and then, also in the Gothic style, but in cream brick, the rectory, now known as *Oldberrow House* and hiding behind a magnificent cedar-of-Lebanon. Backing onto Barrells Park, gabled, timber-framed *Oldberrow Court* also hides, but behind a cluster of old red-brick farm buildings.

Oldbury [5] On very much higher ground than the surrounding countryside, and with extensive views from the site of a small Iron Age hill fort, removed in 1954 to make way for a covered reservoir. *Oldbury Hall*, owned by the Phillips family, was burnt down in the 1940s, leaving some 18th-century walling, a few outbuildings and a pyramid-roofed apple boffy. Pebbledashed *cottages*, 1861.

Old Milverton [11] Small and on a low hill, encircled by the River Avon. Distinctive *church* (St. James) was built in 1879–80, by John Gibson. In the late 18th century the curate rode over from Warwick to use a crumbling stone building with a wooden tower; but, following the rapid development of the Spa of Leamington and the growth of New Milverton, a new chapel was built in 1835. In 1878 the advowson was sold to Lady Charles Bertie Percy of Guy's Cliffe, who decided to 'restore' the building in which she and her tenants worshipped. 'Restore' is the word used on her mural monument, but nothing is left of the old fabric except the foundations and the lower part of the tower, now

carrying a pyramid-roofed wooden belfry. 1880s chancel windows have finely drawn figures against golden hangings, and a nave window is in memory of Dr. Henry Jephson, the celebrated Leamington physician. Long, timber-framed barn and Gothic, Tudor and plain *estate cottages*.

Olton [7] Once part of the manor of Ulverley, a name which declined as nearby Solihull grew, leaving Ulverley, the Old Town, ultimately Olton. Substantial late Victorian villas. Timber-gabled shops and a 1930s classical bank face across the busy Warwick Road to the towerless red-sandstone *church* (St. Margaret). Its two building periods are distinguished by the texture of the stone: smooth ashlar for the chancel, built in 1879, and a rock face for the robust nave and aisles, built in 1895–6, by Ben. Corser, who lived nearby and also designed Dudley School of Art and Free Library. Brick *Capuchin Friary* was built in 1873, by Dunn and Hansom. Picturesque reservoir, and a small park.

Over Whitacre [15] Scattered and with the small sandstone *church* (St. Leonard), built on a hill in 1766, now commanding views over Hams Hall cooling towers. Soaring Baroque steeple has large, round-headed belfry openings, with chunky Gibbs surrounds, and the spire, of 1850, replaces an ogival dome. Well lit nave has a west gallery, small-scale monuments and an inlaid octagonal pulpit; elliptical chancel arch frames a Venetian east window. Georgian Gothic house is of stone, and classical *Monwoode Farmhouse* of brick. Gothic *Monwoode Stone Cottage*, built c. 1800, has an ogee gable; and, in a field, a tall chimneystack is probably Tudor. Against the 16th-century bridge, across the River Bourne, part-sandstone *Furnace End Mill* has a 19th-century front, hiding timber-framed cottages, and the sash-windowed *Bull* is now closed on account of subsidence. Against trees, glistening black-and-white *Botts Green House*, built in 1593, has no rival other than the church and, with its well maintained herringbone strutting, sandstone porch and peaceful gardens, exudes an air of quiet prosperity.

Oxhill [14] Pronounced locally as 'Ocshull'. A cluster of brown-stone and red-brick houses against a tributary of the River Stour, in the Vale of the Red Horse (see Tysoe). By Whatcote the blue-lias subsoil was worked for road metal. In 1183 Robert de Stafford granted the monks of Bordesley twelve acres of land 'on the torrent of Oxhill where my oxherds dwell'. Mostly Norman *church* (St. Laurence) has a Perpendicular tower, around which white pigeons flutter. Cavernous Gothic porch leads down to the white-painted, aisleless nave. Tub-shaped Norman font, with Adam and Eve naked and ashamed; rich Perpendicular rood screen, across the tall tower arch; and traceried 15th-century bench ends, now copied throughout the nave. Tall, light

above and opposite, **Over Whitacre** church

Oxhill

chancel. Outside are the remains of
the preaching cross; and avenue of
larches; and, to the south-east, the
grave of a negro slave girl, d. 1705,
to Thomas Beauchamp, gent. of
Nevis. He is believed to have been
a sugar planter and to have married
one of the rector's twin daughters.
Long, low *Peacock Inn* is 17th-cen-
tury; and, derelict stone *Oxhill House*
was built by James Ward in 1706.

Packwood [7] (near Hockley
Heath) *Packwood House* is approached through a walled close and a
forecourt, to the left of which is
the enclosed *Carolean Garden* with its
four gazebos. Splendid wrought-

iron gate opens onto John Fetherston's unique *Yew Garden*, meant to
symbolise the Sermon on the
Mount. 'Multitude Walk', a long
procession of conical yews, leads to
a raised walk bordered by twelve
great yews—the Apostles—culminating in the centre in four still
greater trees—the Evangelists.
Mount is ascended by a spiral walk
between low box hedges; and at the
top, looming above all, is a single
giant yew. Many-gabled, timber-
framed house is mid-16th-century
and, since the late 18th century, has
been covered with a sandy render-
ing which emphasises its varied
form. *Hall* has a rich oak floor,

Elizabethan glass and Flemish
tapestries; panelled *Dining Room*,
looking onto the Carolean Garden,
has 17th-century Flemish glass.
Drawing Room, which is also
panelled, houses a small panel of
Elizabethan tapestry, from the
Sheldon factory at Barcheston,
depicting Judith with the head of
Holofernes. *Staircase* and *Passage*,
built in 1931–2, have an oil portrait
on plaster of King Charles II, said
to have been removed from the ceiling of the Ball Room at Windsor
Castle by Sir Jeffrey Wyattville.
Ireton Room, named after Cromwell's
general, who slept here before the
battle of Edge Hill in 1642, boasts

The Yew Garden, **Packwood** House

an elaborately carved Jacobean overmantel. *Great Hall*, used as a cow byre and barn prior to being linked to the house by a 1930s long gallery, incorporates a stone fireplace and plaster overmantel, taken from an old wine shop in Stratford-upon-Avon. Substantial mid-17th-century *stables* have brick pilasters and cornices. Approached past an old moated grange, with two red-brick bridges for access, the simply roofed *church* (St. Giles) has an embattled Perpendicular tower, said to have been built by Nicholas Brome, in atonement for his murder of the priest, found 'chokking' his wife under the chin. Above the chancel arch are the remains of an early 14th-century painting, representing the three living kings met by the three dead; chancel is glazed with mediaeval fragments and an impressive Arts and Crafts window, c. 1913, by R. Stubington, who first studied under G. F. Watts. Brick north transept, built as a family pew in 1704, has Victorian Gothic tracery, and an early 14th-century stained-glass Crucifixion. Here in 1706, when his father was fifty years old, Samuel Johnson's parents were married.

Pailton [9] Brick houses and neat prefabs scattered around a road junction with a granite war memorial. Sturdy brick *church* (dedicated to St. Denis in recognition of the ties between the local Benedictine priory—Monks Kirby—and France) was built in 1894, by W. Chick, in an appropriate Norman style with an arcaded apse and an apsidal vestry. Stucco *Lady Mary's Home* is basically timber-framed, and has a bold porch in the local carpenter's interpretation of the Tuscan order.

Perry Barr & Kingstanding *see* Birmingham.

Pillerton Hersey [14] Pale-lias cottages and mottled-brick terraces in undulating country near the Roman Fosse Way. *Church* (St. Mary) has a brown, roughly coursed Perpendicular belfry and a fine mid-13th-century chancel with a delicately shafted priest's doorway, and a naïve plate-traceried east window. Interior, well lit from clear-glazed cast-iron frames, is small-scale, with a carved Perpendicular roof and a tall tower porch, with white cartouche monuments. Remodelling of the Georgian-character north aisle, in 1845, introduced an Early English-style window, copied from Wicken, Bucks.; a Jacobean-style roof; and pews of pitchpine, direct from Russia. Perpendicular south aisle has a flamboyant royal arms. Once round, distorted chancel arch; rare green Georgian glass, in the east window; and Early Georgian panelling, in the priest's vestry. Lias Georgian *vicarage* has a red-brick face.

Pillerton Priors [14] Tall, shallow Georgian house faces a row of new bungalows across the busy Stratford-upon-Avon–Banbury road. Church was burnt to the ground in 1666; and, though the village is mostly new, lias barns survive beneath rusting corrugated iron, presumably replacing thatch. By the road to Ettington, a small plantation is known as 'Moll's grave', after a gypsy buried at the nearby crossroads. She drowned herself, and her screams are said to have been heard at night.

Pinley Abbey [11] The remains of a remarkably early Cistercian nunnery, founded in the 11th century, set in a green valley. Some church walling has a small Perpendicular doorway; a timber-framed *house*, c. 1500, possibly that of the abbot.

Polesworth [5] A mining community in a valley within a bend in the River Anker. Until recently, open-cast mining ran right up to the vicarage, and even the river was diverted to obtain coal; but Abbey Green is now green again, and the river back where it was. Part-timber-framed main street has been spoilt by demolition and new building lines; against the railway, there is nothing but suburban sprawl. Timbered 15th-century *abbey gate-house* leads to the secluded Norman *church* (St. Editha), all that remains of the abbey, founded c. A.D. 827 by Saint Modwena, with King Egbert's daughter Editha as abbess, and which once extended eastwards to the mound in the churchyard. Massive, stumpy tower, rebuilt in the 14th century by Sir Richard Herthill of Pooley Hall, has an 18th-century parapet. Originally entered from a south cloister by a Norman doorway, now much weathered, the spacious interior is almost equally divided into nave and north aisle by eight Norman arches on massive cylindrical piers. South windows are 14th-century and, high up to avoid the cloister roof, the simple three-light windows date from a thoughtful restoration by G. E. Street, who added high-pitched roofs, influenced by the one over the gatehouse. He roofed the aisle above the Norman nave clerestory; and, within the walls of the nunnery church, added a new chancel, specifying that the mix for the foundations be thrown into place from the scaffold! Floor tiles are reproductions of reject tiles from a house in Potters' Lane. Tomb of Sir Richard Herthill has an exceptional effigy of a croziered abbess, c. 1200, and there is a splendid alabaster of his daughter. Mellow brick Arts and Crafts *vicarage*, built in 1868, incorporates some braced timber arches and a large fireplace from the Elizabethan manor house, built by Sir Henry Goodere. 17th-century wing was once a school where Michael Drayton is said to have been taught. Long, timber-framed *tithe barn*, and an early 18th-century dovecote. Round-arched brick *Congregational church*, was built in 1828, as the Independent chapel; *Nethercote School*, founded in 1638, now occupies an 1818 Tudor-style building of quadrangular form. Romantically sited on a wooded hill above the Coventry Canal, battlemented brick *Pooley Hall*, said to have been built in 1509, by Sir Thomas Cokayne, has a miniature private chapel (St. Mary), built by the authority of Pope Urban IV. *Bramcote Hall*, the home of the Burdetts of Foremark since the Norman conquest, is Early Georgian. *Obelisk*, erected by Sir George Chetwynd, marks the site of the old chapel (St. Leonard) at Hoo, founded during the reign of Henry I; *Alvecote Priory* is now only a few pieces of ruined wall.

Preston Bagot [10] (near Beaudesert) Scattered around a steep hill, crowned by the church. River Alne is followed by the Stratford-on-Avon Canal, constructed in 1816. Mellow timbered *manor house*, built in 1570–80, and orange-brick outbuildings are set against trees. Norman *church* (All Saints) has a shingled bell turret and a long doorway and three deeply splayed windows. Broad Neo-Norman chancel arch, on stumpy columns, and short chancel were built in

1870, by J. A. Chatwin. Burne-Jones-style east windows, for Mary Ryland.

Preston-on-Stour [14] Around a large green, above the river weir. Through iron gates and along an avenue of giant yews, pinnacled *church* (St. Mary) was remodelled in 1752–64, by Edward Woodward of Chipping Campden, to suit the Gothic taste of James West, of Alscot Park. Mediaeval tower and nave have remarkably correct 18th-century Gothic windows; rebuilt chancel, resembling the Rococo Gothic of Alscot Park, has a segmental arch, a segmental ceiling, and gilded ogee-arched panelling framing the classical monuments to the West family. Spiky ogival screen, in red and gold, was made in 1755, by Phillips. East window has a collection of small 17th-century scenes, concerned with death, given by James West in 1754. A Grecian sarcophagus in front of a portrait medallion of Thomas Steavens, hung on an obelisk, was designed by James 'Athenian' Stuart and executed, in 1781, by Thomas Scheemakers; and a standing mourner, by an urn, to James West, 1797, is an early work by Sir Richard Westmacott. Plain tablet to Harriet West, 1815, is also by Westmacott; and over-large Hope and Faith to James Roberts West, 1838, are by Richard Westmacott jnr. Georgian *house* is divided by plain pilasters; large, timber-framed *vicarage* has decorative gables; and *Old Manor House*, 1659, is similar. Brick *school*, 1848, has a white-painted bell turret; Tudor-style *estate housing*, 1852–5, is in two rows of semis with fishscale-tile roofs and free-standing outhouses. *Alscot Park* was bought in 1749 by James West, a lawyer, who lived in the Piazza, Covent Garden, and collected so many old books and manuscripts that at his death they took twenty-four days to sell; some went to the Bodleian and the British Museum.

With the help of Edward Woodward, he remodelled an existing house near to the river; and, between 1762 and 1764, added a higher north wing at right angles, all in the Gothick style. Battlemented and turreted south elevation with a porch, 1825, by Thomas Hopper. *Entrance Hall* has ogee-arched plaster-panelled walls, and *Drawing Room* an intricate fan-vault patterned ceiling. Beyond the hall, top-lit *Main Staircase* has Gothick panelling; and the adjoining taller north wing contains *Study* and *Library*.

Princethorpe [8] Tudor-style yellow-brick *cottage*, surely straight from a pattern book, faces the Roman Fosse Way; and in fields, *Princethorpe College* (St. Mary's Priory), built for French Benedictine nuns from Montargis, dominates the landscape. Earliest buildings, by Craven, are of pale brick: *old church*, 1837, with thin tracery and a square turret, and *Guest House*, 1840, with a turreted centrepiece and wild Rococo Gothic glazing. *Nuns' cemetery*, 1838, is a circular cloister; and Norman-style *mortuary chapel*, 1843, by J. A. Hansom, is vaulted. Large fluorescent-red-brick *new church*, built in 1897–1901, by Peter Paul Pugin, has a sea-green-slate roof and a soaring, self-confident tower; commanding the interior from behind a gilded iron screen is a sumptuous ciborium.

Priors Hardwick [12] At the foot of Berryhill, between the Welsh Road and the Oxford Canal. Yellow-stone houses and barns cluster around the green below the Hornton-stone *church* (St. Mary). Gaunt, grey-lichened tower is part 13th-century, and has a weathervane of a drover in a smock. Tall, aisleless nave and 13th-century chancel, well lit by large, finely traceried windows, the east with a delicate lattice of lead holding diamonds of old white glass. Spacious sedilia and piscina, and dark-balustered communion rail, c. 1700. By a thick

belt of trees stands the stone *Butcher's Arms*.

Priors Marston [12] Mullioned yellow-stone houses around a steep hill, against the old Welsh Road, along which sheep were driven from Wales. In a flat churchyard, dark, stately cedars stand guard over the *church* (St. Leonard), its grey-lichened tower with Early Georgian Tuscan pilasters and elementary tracery. Chancel was rebuilt in the 1860s by Spragg and Jones, who were probably responsible for the south porch, harsh plate-traceried south windows and hard plaster lining. Thatched ochre-stone house and buff-brick council semis. Above a fall in the road, *Westfield Farm House* has a bracketed shell porch; and upright *High House* hides behind cut yews. Grey-stone Georgian *house* has a Gothic *folly*, enhanced by a weeping ash; and heavily restored *Falcon Inn* is in the Cotswold tradition. Pale-red-brick *Wesley Chapel*, 1858, and corrugated-iron *Co-op*.

Quinton [13] A mediaeval village with new housing for the army garrison. *Church* (St. Swithin), all that a village church should be, has Norman arcades, a Perpendicular clerestory and, above the chancel arch, a powdery Elizabethan royal arms, painted over a part-visible doom. Light Early English chancel has lancets and a Victorian east window complete with bright glass. North aisle east window frames a golden 15th-century crucifixion against a rich red ground; two excellent heraldic windows by Christopher Webb have lilies, birds and butterflies. Effigy of Sir William Clopton, who fought at Agincourt; and fine brass of Lady Clopton, c. 1430, who on the death of her husband took a vow of widowhood and lived as an anchorite in a nearby cell. Around the church, some timber-framed cottages have thatched roofs, and the 17th-century *Old Vicarage* a stone roof. Slightly earlier *College Arms*, facing the green, displays the lilies and ermine lozenges of Magdalen College, Oxford, large landowners in the neighbourhood. Victorian Gothic *school* has deep bands of golden stone and *Quinton Grange*, built in 1879, is Arts and Crafts with tile hanging.

Quinton *see* Birmingham.

Radford *see* Coventry

Radford Semele [11] Semele preserves the memory of the manorial family seated here in the reign of Henry I. In the fields behind a tall 1889 lych gate, the basically Norman *church* (St. Nicholas) has a rubble-walled nave with an original window and a Perpendicular tower, its belfry tracery long since gone. Victorian Perpendicular-style chancel with an excellent east window by Kempe. Extensive view across the River Leam towards Coventry. *The Glebe House* (formerly the vicarage) built c. 1850, is entered through a Tuscan doorway; but the present 1960s *vicarage* is a disaster. Jacobean *Radford Hall* has gabled wings, with squat, unconvincing Gothick finials; and nearby two Gothick *houses* are reminiscent of the work of Sanderson Miller.

Radway [14] Long brown-stone terraces around a green enjoying the shelter of the treed Edge Hill escarpment. Many steep roofs, some of which are still thatched. Broach-spired *church*, built in 1866, by C. E. Buckeridge of Oxford, replaces a humble brick building at the other end of the village, in which pioneer Gothic Revival architect Sanderson Miller of Radway Grange provided a 'magnificent and handsome pew' with a coved ceiling, presumably for his own family. Dark body and light tower space with white-marble monuments to Sanderson Miller and his family, and an excellent semi-reclining figure of Royalist Captain Kingswell, who fell at the battle of Edge Hill in

1642, fought mainly along the old road from Radway to Kineton. Predominantly orange-and-yellow Renaissance window, given to Sanderson Miller for his Edge Hill Tower, represents the parable of the unjust steward throttling his debtor and Jacob bringing pottage to Isaac, while Esau is still hunting in the background. Norman piscina and Butterfield-inspired pink-veined-marble reredos. Gate to *Radway Grange* is by a thatched stone cottage, and the drive hugs a high stone wall against which a statue of Caractacus enchained stands over a small, fern-filled pool. Also intended for the Edge Hill Tower, he was found to be too large for his niche. Urn on a plinth is inscribed IMORTAM and, through a stone gateway, entrance courtyard has classical stables topped by a cupola. Steeply gabled Elizabethan house was built out of the stones of a convalescent home for the monks of Stoneleigh, and has an arched grotto with still water. It was bought by Sanderson Miller's father; the son began his Gothick improvements about four years before Horace Walpole started Strawberry Hill. South front, facing Edge Hill, has two-storey bay windows, decorated with strawberries, and a heavily framed doorway with a lacy cresting. Panelled east front has cusped ogee-arched windows which enjoy views of a chunky yew garden. In the dining room, Fielding, the novelist, read 'Tom Jones' in manuscript to the Earl of Chatham, Sir George Lyttleton and Sanderson Miller for their approval before it was printed; in the park is a clump of trees planted by Chatham. Pond was the fish stew of the monastic cell, now marked by broken ground. *St. Thomas's Well* and *obelisk*, 1854. On the escarpment, octagonal *Edge Hill Tower*, built in 1746–1750, by Sanderson Miller as a place to entertain his friends, marks the spot where the King's standard stood on 23 October 1642

before the King descended the hill to give battle to the army under Lord Essex. Obviously based on Guy's Tower at Warwick, its tall, wafer-thin battlements are precariously perched on big brackets, and there is an embattled gateway, to which it was connected by means of a drawbridge. Centre of the roof was embellished with the royal arms, and below were those of the kingdoms of the Saxon Heptarchy. Adjoining inn is Victorian; nearby *cottage*, 1744, also by Sanderson Miller, was originally thatched.

Ratley [14] Dark-ochre houses of local Hornton stone, stepped down the precipitous Edge Hills to a small enclosed green. Light, grey-lichened *church* (St. Peter and Vincula), remarkable for its unadorned masses, has elegant ogee-arched windows, which must have influenced Sanderson Miller's work, especially at Lacock, and an unusually simple south arcade which would have delighted the early Gothic Revivalists. Five steps down, the tall, narrow nave is ceiled in plain plaster, enhancing the Georgian Gothick character. Pier to the right of the chancel arch receives four arches, which give a vaulted effect. Octagonal 13th-century font, and Georgian pulpit with amusing Victorian panels. Canopied Decorated piscina, richly tiled sanctuary floor, and large stone-and-marble Victorian reredos. Churchyard cross retains its crucifix; former *vicarage* was refronted c. 1840. Allotments were given by Lady Lucy Pusey, on the advice of her son, Dr. Pusey.

Rowington [8] An early clearing in the Forest of Arden, and a parish in late Saxon times. From Foxbrook, where a black-and-white cottage faces a timber-framed barn, the Hatton–Rowington road winds uphill to the battlemented *church* (St. Lawrence) perched high on the crest against trees. Spared the fate of Claverdon by Birmingham's

Details in **Royal Leamington Spa**

green belt, Rowington seems untouched by the 20th century. Church plan is unusual: the tower was built, c. 1300, inside the eastern end of the nave, leaving a short western part which has a Norman north wall and a large, clear-glazed Perpendicular west window. High nave arcades, of powdery light-grey stone, were introduced c. 1400; and a fine arched Perpendicular ceiling is decorated with bosses. Dark tower space has a lush window by Kempe in memory of Peter Bellinger Brodie, vicar for 45 years and a prime mover of the extensive 1871 restoration by G. F. Bodley, who rescued the church from ruin and left the interior rich with colour and with an organ gallery, unfortunately removed in 1903. One of the joys of the beautiful Decorated chancel is its fine timber roof adorned with gilded suns and stars; and there is a glowing white, gold and blue east window with eight figures of saints. Victorian *vicarage* has pretty shaped gables and a fine view east across the valley, no doubt enjoyed by Charles Gore, the first Bishop of Birmingham, when he came to stay; smooth-stone Regency *Rowington Hall* has a hillside pool surrounded by trees. In a deep cutting, the Grand Union Canal passes through a tunnel under the road, to which it is linked by access tunnels for horses. *Shakespeare Hall* was the home of Thomas Shakespeare, whose son was apprenticed to William Jaggard, 'a well-known pirate publisher', who published 'The Passionate Pilgrim'. John Fetherston, F.S.A. believed William Shakespeare to have been related to the Shakespeares of Rowington, to have visited them here, to have worshipped at neighbouring Baddesley Clinton, and to have meditated on 'As You Like It' in Hay Wood before writing his play at Shakespeare Hall.

Royal Leamington Spa [11]
An elegant Regency watering place, with tall stucco terraces along broad straight roads leading to the banks of the picturesque River Leam. River winds its way through a series of open spaces against the Grecian pump room and the Gothic church. Mineral springs were known as early as the Elizabethan period and, according to Dugdale, by the mid-17th century were used for preserving meat. Not till over 100 years later were they applied to 'seasoning the human frame': it was in the 1780s, following the discovery of a new spring not far from the original well first remarked by Camden, that the real development of the spa began. One well, until recent years covered by a stone building, is outside the *church* (All Saints), a tall Continental Gothic structure, begun in 1843, which boasts a proud, pinnacled tower, added by Blomfield when he extended the nave in the 1890s. Dark, cathedral-like interior has colourful rose windows in the transepts, said to be modelled on Rouen, and a glowing apse. In 1841, A. B. Granville wrote: 'Every road leading into Leamington has been seized upon and flanked with buildings.' Long *Victoria Terrace*, 1836–8, is divided by giant Corinthian columns; further south, the railway, 1844, charges across the rooftops of High Street at the centre of the old town, with the *Crown Hotel*, built as a vicarage, and the stucco *police station* as the town hall, in 1831. Across balustraded *Victoria Bridge*, built in 1808–9, by H. Couchman jnr., severely Doric *Royal Pump Room*, 1813–14, is by C. S. Smith, a pupil of Sir Jeffrey Wyattville of Windsor Castle fame. In 1841, Granville reported that 'At Leamington, unquestionably, no dross of society, or even ambiguous characters, will be found among those who assemble at the Pumproom for their health and the waters.' Jephson Gardens, laid out in 1834, and typical of their date, have a spiky fountain and a statue of Dr. Jephson, who was largely responsible for establishing the town's reputation as a spa. Facing the Greek Doric portico of Euston Place, a curved terrace heralds the *Parade*, 1808, the grandest street in the town, 'the rendezvous of the beaux and belles—pedestrians as well as equestrians'. Today the tall terraces, punctuated by giant coupled pilasters, house fashionable shops and stores, and *Regent Hotel*, built in 1818–19, by C. S. Smith, is a three-star. In September 1819 the Prince Regent visited Leamington and granted the new hotel the right to use his name and coat of arms. Against the river, Clutton's red-brick R.C. *Church of St. Peter* is still impressive, though without its spire; incongruous red-brick *Town Hall*, which intruded into the Parade in 1885, is by J. Cundall, who was responsible for at least three of the town's churches. In the 1820s Edward Willes commissioned John Nash, architect to the Prince Regent, to draw up an ambitious scheme, of which the impressive *Newbold Terrace* and some nearby villas may be a remnant. *Lansdowne Crescent* and *Lansdowne Circus* were designed by William Thomas, 1800–1860, who emigrated to Canada at the age of 43 with a wife and ten children, and then designed St. Michael's Cathedral and St. Lawrence Hall, Toronto. Faced with stucco, the Crescent is graced by a delicately fretted iron veranda; and the equally attractive Circus is a ring of paired classical houses, also with fine ironwork. At *10* lived Nathaniel Hawthorne, the author. *Warwick Street* has two exceptionally dignified terraces, and *Clarendon Place* the elegant pavilions of an intended crescent, one of many incomplete speculations. *Clarendon Square*, 1825, is enclosed by tall terraces with Greek Doric porches; gabled stucco villa with Perpendicular windows is typical of the town's peculiar contribution to the urban scene. *6* was the home of Napoleon III after the collapse of the Second Empire. As Prince

Louis Napoleon, he was a familiar and sought-after figure in the winter of 1838–9, staying briefly at the Regent Hotel. Lytton Strachey attended the impressive Tudor-style *Leamington College*, built in 1847, by D. G. Squirhill, and the same architect was also responsible for the *cemetery*, Brunswick Street, 1852. *Church of St. Mark*, Rugby Road, was built in 1879, by George Gilbert Scott the younger, and has glass by Kempe.

Rugby [9] A market town known for the famous Rugby School, founded in 1567, which faces down High Street towards the Market Place. Little more than a village in the early years of the 19th century, Rugby expanded slowly following the arrival of the railway, which encircles its northern fringe with a majestic, elliptically arched viaduct striding across the countryside. In 1899 Willans and Robinson constructed their electrical engineering works, and others followed. Shops now occupy the front rooms of the Georgian-tradition terrace houses; and the appropriately curved Regent Street is overpowered by a robust steeple by Butterfield, added to the mediaeval parish *church* (St. Andrew), in 1895–6. Butterfield also added a porch, and in 1877–85 a loftier nave with banded piers and a high faceted ceiling richly painted with geometric patterns. Nave and chancel are a continuous space, given mystery by a flying stone arch, which springs from vigorously carved wall capitals to support a large stone cross immediately beneath the apex of the ceiling. High reredos is assertive, but has been compromised by the substitution of mock-mediaeval paintings for Butterfield's barbaric inlaid marble cross, now banished to the vestry. Stone *Lloyds Bank* stands on the site of the moat to the castle, built by Sir Henry de Rokeby during the reign of Stephen and demolished during the reign of Henry II.

Against the churchyard, Church Walk also bounds the extensive, well planted churchyard of the now closed *Holy Trinity*, a large, well proportioned church, built in 1852–4, by George Gilbert Scott. *5 Hillmorton Road* is the birthplace of Rupert Brooke; Lawrence Sheriff Street has the main entrance to *Rugby School*, and is named after its founder. Formerly opposite the parish church, where the Lawrence Sheriff Almshouses stood till the summer of 1961, the school was moved to its present site in the middle of the 18th century. Earliest surviving buildings, 1809–42, by Henry Hakewell, are in the Tudor style and of yellow brick; these include arched entrance tower and *Arnold Library*. Paved *Old Quad*, also by Hakewell, has a clock turret and an arcade leading to larger *New Quad*, for which Butterfield was appointed architect in 1867. To the street, *New Schools* are totally asymmetrical, their ponderous bulk, mainly of yellow brick in deference to the earlier buildings, relieved by red and black brick, bands of moulded brick diaper work, numerous arcades and a broad, corbelled chimney. To the quad, glazed arcades catch the sun over the top of the *Chapel*, built in 1872, by Butterfield, with a large octagonal central tower terminating in a steep pyramid roof. The effect of the interior is one of great space, emphasised by the broad transepts divided from the nave by slender arcades with banded piers. Beneath the painted ceiling of the apse, the 16th-century stained-glass Adoration of the Magi is from Aerschot, near Louvain, and other windows are by Hardman, Kempe and Morris, the west in the style of Burne-Jones. Marble monument by Chantrey has bas-relief busts of Homer and Virgil and, besides recumbent effigies of Dr. Arnold and Arthur Stanley, there are monuments to Matthew Arnold, Lewis Carroll, Walter Savage Landor and Rupert Brooke. Noble

Close has some splendid trees, including a few elms known to be 300 years old. Red-brick *School Field*, Barby Road, a large house, built in 1852, by George Gilbert Scott, makes an interesting comparison with turreted stone *Bradley House*, possibly by Hakewell, and *Kilbracken*, by Butterfield. Striking *Temple Reading Room and Museum*, built in 1878, by Butterfield, has a banded stone interior. *Statue* on the front lawn of the author of 'Tom Brown's Schooldays' (Judge Thomas Hughes) is by Brock. *Temple Speech Room*, built in 1908–9, by Sir T. G. Jackson is a mixed bag of styles, and *New Big School*, again by Butterfield, surprisingly indecisive. *High Street* has post-war stores; and beside Georgian *Windmill Inn*, a red-and-cream-brick palazzo, built in the 1860s, for the Local Board of Health, retains a grand central board room. Red-brick *Methodist church* presents a provocative juxtaposition of forms. Late Georgian *Horse Shoes Hotel* is the birthplace of the astronomer Sir Norman Lockyer. Tudor-style *Percival Guildhouse*, built c. 1840 as a private house by the antiquary Matthew Bloxham, is approached through a walled garden enclosed on one side by Hussey's gabled *Church of St. Matthew the Evangelist*, built in 1841. *Warwick Street* has cream-brick houses with Doric porches; Pugin's R. C. *Church of St. Marie* has a spectacular slender steeple by Bernard Whelan; and white *116 Dunchurch Road*, built in 1934, by Serge Chermayeff, belongs to the early Modern Movement.

Ryton-on-Dunsmore [8] Divided by the busy Coventry–M1 link road as it crosses the heathland to the south of the River Avon. New brick houses and shops face across the road to the old centre, where the tall cream-coloured Perpendicular tower of the *church* (St. Leonard) contrasts with its red Early Norman body, which has north and south

Rugby School Chapel (Butterfield)

The parish church, **Rugby**: Butterfield's nave and chancel arch

doorways and a number of blocked windows. Brick south porch and clear-glazed lunette above it, which date from c. 1800, are classical, but brick north chapel, of the same date, is Gothick. Plastered nave has north gallery, box pews, finely carved Jacobean pulpit, traceried stalls and 17th-century communion rail. Domestic-scale *church hall*, built in 1975, and extensive views over the Avon valley.

Salford Priors & Abbots Salford [10] In the gently undulating fruit-growing country of the Avon valley. Given by Kenred, King of Mercia to the Abbey of Evesham in 708; by Edward the Confessor's time the parish had passed to the Countess Godiva. Timber-framed cottages and barns against the twisting Stratford-upon-Avon–Evesham road are still thatched. Local blue lias was used by the Normans for their *church* (St. Matthew), of which all that survives are the base of the tower and a busy doorway with bold zigzag decoration, the latter of yellow oolite stone, as blue lias is not suitable for carving. Tall, narrow nave, of great length in relation to its width, is linked to a wider south aisle by three rather primitive late 12th-century arches. North wall has tall lancets, but white-painted interior is mainly lit from an adjacent large, clear-glazed window with exceptional surging tracery. Darker chancel has three stepped lancets; large tablet, 1631, to the Clarkes, is ablaze with eighteen coats of arms. Sir Simon Clarke increased the height of the tower, on the pinnacles of which he also carved his arms. His second wife Lady Dorothy was the daughter of Thomas Hobson of

149

Sherbourne

Cambridge, a famous carrier, who is reputed to have allowed the hire of his horses only in strict rotation; hence the expression 'Hobson's Choice'. The memorial to Sir Simon is a stone coffin lid by the south door. The screens at the west end probably date from the restoration of 1873–4, and contain stained glass figures rescued from demolished Emscote church, War-

wick. Also from Emscote is the statue of St. Dubricius, the only Bishop of Warwick, which fits a niche in the stair turret against the south wall, probably originally used by beacon lighters to guide travellers across the nearby ford. Neat Georgian house, with deep, simply coved eaves and an elegant staircase, once housed the parish room; and a short terrace almost

hugs the pavement. Lias *Slatter's Mill*, sensitively converted by Walter A. Thomson, has an exterior staircase; in the fields, tall Elizabethan *Salford Hall* is topped by many ogee gables. Approached through a long stone and timber-framed structure with a finely drawn sundial, the present hall is said to be the rebuilding of a moated house further east. Part-timber-framed service wing has sash windows, and a more formal wing bold full-height projections, fully mullioned at first-floor level. At the top of the house is a beautiful gallery, seventy-five feet long, which allows good views of the Avon valley and the verdant Cleeve Hill. At *Rushford* lived Perkins, the Victorian photographer; Victorian *Old Granary*, imaginatively converted by Walter A. Thomson, has a raised, slatted walk leading to a garden gazebo. Bomford and Evershed Ltd., local farm-equipment manufacturers, produced the first reversible plough and a mechanical dredger which saved many country-house lakes.

Saltley and Ward End
see Birmingham

Sawbridge [12] (near Grand-borough) A scattered hamlet by the River Leam. Rendered-lias *Manor Farm*, built in 1654, by a yeoman, Thomas Childs, has a ruined Gothic Revival wing. In 1689, several Roman urns 'of grey earth curiously polished' were discovered just inside the entrance gate, where there is a small mediaeval fish pond. Timber-framed *Red Roofed Farm* has thatch covered with red-painted corrugated iron, and a nearby house is similar.

Seckington [2] Set on a rock; it was here that the Saxon nobles murdered King Ethelbald in 757. Beyond a rock-hewn cutting, the cream-grey *church* (All Saints) raises an impressive 13th-century tower with a slender spire. Aisleless, hall-like nave has curious ogee arches, as at Newton Regis; marks on the jambs of the chancel opening show that there was once a rood screen, of which the existing low screen may be part. Jolly alabaster monument to Robert Burdett, d.1603, with many kneeling figures and two elegant late 18th-century wall tablets to the Dobbs family, of black slate painted cream. Engraved slate headstones. Georgian *Old Rectory*

has later mullioned windows and a sharp Gothic wing; *Old Hall* large cross windows and elegant *Church Farm* a flight of steps. Extensive *motte-and-bailey castle* still stands about thirty feet high.

Selly Oak *see* Birmingham

Sheldon *see* Birmingham.

Sherbourne [11] A pretty pale-brick estate village, in wooded country against Sherbourne Brook. Well cut yew hedges lead to an upright, timbered *school*, built in 1881, by John Cundall, architect of Leamington Town Hall, and a pretty ochre-washed *cottage*, built as the vicarage by Yeoville Thomason. Louisa Anne Ryland, daughter of Samuel Ryland, the Birmingham wire manufacturer, who bought the estate in 1837, was a fervent patron of the arts: really splendid *church* (All Saints), rebuilt for her in 1862–4, by George Gilbert Scott, stands beyond an old timber-framed house, and has a soaring slender steeple reflected in a lake. The strike of the clock resounds across the surrounding country. Richly glazed, vaulted tower space leads to dignified Decorated-style interior, which shows Scott at his best. Moulded nave arcades have shafts of pink Ipplepen and verde-antico marble; baptistry, defined by a high, flying arch across the nave, has an impressive white-marble font inlaid with a mosaic of polished stones. Gorgeous un-varnished choir stalls with fine naturalistic foliage. Samuel Ryland added to the earlier church a chapel in which was placed a tomb chest, 1843, by Pugin, recording John and Martha Ryland, buried in Edgbaston, their son Samuel Ryland 'formerly of Edgbaston late of Sherbourne', his wife Anne and their daughter Louisa Anne Ryland, d.1889, who rebuilt the chapel around the tomb and added the consciously quaint Hardman glass. Most of the glass is by Clayton and Bell, and below their large east

window is an elaborate alabaster reredos. Arcaded pink-alabaster dado with spandrels filled by delicately carved foliage by F. W. Pomeroy, who actually worked on site, from real flowers and leaves. Beyond a high orange-brick wall is the substantial early 18th-century *Sherbourne Park*, the home of the Smith-Rylands, who still own the village.

Shilton [8] Terrace houses and barns along the busy Coventry–Hinckley road, above which the cream-and-red Perpendicular *church* (St. Andrew) stands against a rendered-brick lych-gate. Exceptionally finely cut 18th-century headstones. Powdery cream-stone nave arcade and, separated from the nave by a low timber screen, incorporating some lively mediaeval tracery; dark, stencilled chancel. Long 18th-century barn hides Tudor-style *Shilton House Farm*. The original *Church of England First School*, founded by the Revd. J. Million in 1725, was demolished to make way for the London North Western Railway and rebuilt in 1849. *Baptist chapel*, 1867, and three cut-down *weavers' cottages*.

Shipston-on-Stour [14] Thriving market town at the centre of the rich, pastoral Feldon, and once one of the greatest sheep markets in the kingdom. A network of narrow streets with modest terrace houses, it remained feudal until the beginning of regular long-distance stage-coach traffic, which brought handsome coaching inns, such as the *George Hotel* and the *White Bear* in High Street, really the market place. *Church* (St. Edmund) retains its 15th-century west tower, but its Norman and 17th-century body was rebuilt, by Street, as early as 1855, the year he moved to London. Spacious interior is divided by youthful arcades, and well lit by clear glazed windows, no two alike. Backing onto fields, mottled light-brick Georgian houses face a petrol filling station and a clump of trees.

White Horse Hotel leads to long, two-storeyed Sheep Street, lined with a mixture of stone, brick and stucco, and one of the most attractive small-scale streets in the county. Many of the early 18th-century houses are of grey lias, but the more ambitious early Georgian *Manor House*, which has battlemented Victorian stables, is of deep-ochre-coloured stone. Brick Georgian *Bell Inn*, with a segmental-arched coachway. *Council Offices*, formerly the rectory, have a French Renaissance extension, and the sashed stucco face of *3 High Street* hides a timber frame. Heady *Sheldon Wine Merchants*, built, in 1892, with a pyramid roof balancing an oval-windowed gable, has 18th-century cellars; further south are the rock-faced *Wesley Chapel* and a pretty ogee Gothick *hall*, possibly an earlier chapel. Narrow Old Road, now free from busy traffic, has small houses, two of which are also Gothick.

Shirley [7] A mile of unprepossessing ribbon development, with a busy shopping centre, on Birmingham–Stratford road, surrounded by post-war housing within walking distance of the open country. Small mediaeval hamlet developed rapidly in the mid-19th century, owing to the proximity of Birmingham; and, though it still retains the open areas of Shirley Park, Palmer's Rough Recreation Ground and Bill's Wood, is built up with undistinguished houses and a large industrial estate. Early English-style *church* (St. James), built in 1831, has a weathered stucco tower, surprisingly at the east end; and, as is usual with churches of this date, original shallow sanctuary has been replaced by a deep High Victorian chancel. *Plume of Feathers* was once well known for cockfighting; Erno Goldfinger's handsome concrete *Carrs Paper Ltd.*, Cranmore Boulevard, built in 1954–6, strides across a fully-glazed entrance hall.

Shottery [10] Famous for comfortably thatched *Anne Hathaway's Cottage*, the farmhouse home of Shakespeare's wife, around which have been woven countless romantic stories of the poet's youthful courtship. A long, timber-framed building at right angles to the road, the oldest part dates from the 15th century, and the furniture is that used by successive generations of the family. Old-fashioned cottage garden and an orchard. Village has been spoilt by an extensive car park against cream-painted *Bell Inn*. Opposite black-and-white cottages, pink-brick *church*, built in 1879, by Joseph Lattimore, boasts a remarkable wood pulpit, with vigorous clumps of foliage; mediaeval *manor house*, now a school, has a hammerbeam roof and a square dovecote.

Shotteswell [14] Rich-ochre houses on the steep Edge Hills above a tributary of the River Cherwell, marking the county boundary against Oxfordshire with its neat patchwork of fields. Steeply sloping churchyard, crammed with memorials, is bounded by long houses, the lower window sills almost level with the eaves of the Hornton-stone *church* (St. Lawrence). Well dug into the ground, the 13th-century west tower is sparsely windowed and carries a short, broad spire accompanied by a weatherbeaten spruce. Light, small-scale nave has a Norman north arcade with broad round arches. Norman font. Rich woodwork includes a part-14th-century parclose, bench ends, pulpit and tower screen with traceried Perpendicular panels, and a late 17th-century communion rail. Early 17th-century Flemish reredos depicts Justice, the Fall, the Annunciation, the Nativity with shepherds, God the Father, the Three Kings, the Crucifixion, the Resurrection, Fortitude and Hope. *Flying Fox Inn* is built around a courtyard; the Georgian *Wesleyan church* has a Victorian porch.

Shuckburgh see Lower Shuckburgh

Shustoke [5] Agriculture and reservoirs. Sir William Dugdale (1605–86), the famous Warwickshire historian, who became Garter King of Arms, was born here. *Church* (St. Cuthbert) has a soaring early 14th-century tower and spire of beautiful variegated sandstone, with touches of lichen. Massive body is covered by a plain high-pitched roof reaching up to the belfry openings. Early 18th-century headstones with cherubs' heads. Wide interior is spanned by round timber arches of the late 19th century, a restoration after much damage had been done by lightning. Norman fragments, including a window in the vestry and a capital in one porch, have been built in. In the chancel is a double piscina with trefoiled arches, and Dugdale's tomb and wall monument with the inscription on a black panel under a shield-charged pediment. Six stone *almshouses* and a school, built by Thomas Huntback in the late 17th century, are tiled and have small dormers. In Shawbury Lane is the white-painted *Old Vicarage*, of c. 1820, and a timber-framed barn, part of *Church Farm* beyond, a romantic stone-and-brick building of the 17th and 18th centuries. Brick buildings around the farmyard with stone-dressed lunette windows, and a dovecote for quite some 400 birds. Timbered *Priory Farmhouse* has a brick front with similar lunettes; and timber-framed *Old Rectory*, once divided but recently made into one home again, has an open-tread staircase, plenty of notched beams and wall-to-wall carpeting. *Blyth Hall*, where historian Dugdale lived most of his life, has shaped gables and a chimneystack dated 1629. It was refronted in the early 18th century. Moated *Shustoke Hall*, a fine Caroline mansion, was at one time the home of Thomas Huntback. High-

Shipston-on-Stour

pitched roofs of the soaring Venetian Gothic *Whitacre Waterworks* are visible from afar. One of Martin and Chamberlain's few surviving buildings for the Birmingham Corporation Water Committee, it stands proudly against the reservoir behind an avenue of firs. Cathedral-like pump houses originally housed James Watt beam engines, which pumped water to Birmingham from the rivers Blythe and Bourne, but now, since the opening of the Elan Valley scheme in 1904, electric pumps supply water to Coventry and Nuneaton. Long filter house, spanned by pierced cast-iron arches, against a covered carriageway with seven gables. Chimney has been demolished. Circular pure-water well with a conical roof. *Superintendent's house and office* have Gothic relieving arches, as Philip Webb's Red House, and a circular corner tower with a spire.

Shuttington [2] A hamlet on a hill overlooking a network of subsidence lakes around the River Anker, a magnificent landscape with sheets of silver water and large clumps of dark trees. A few 18th-century farmhouses, some early 20th-century terraces and a recent sprinkling of detached houses lead to the grey-and-orange Norman *church* (St. Matthew), which has a fine Norman doorway, said to have been moved from Alvecote Priory,

153

No 936 Warwick Road, **Solihull** by Soane

and a copper-capped, weather-boarded bellcote. Plastered interior is very Georgian in character, as the neo-Norman windows look classical and there is an 18th-century pulpit.

Small Heath, Sparkbrook & Sparkhill *see* Birmingham.

Snitterfield [11]   Originally neolithic and with an ancient road, the Marroway, along which the men of Mercia marched to attack the warriors of Wessex. Roman burial urn, discovered near the church, is a reminder that the Romans were also active in these

parts. Richard Shakespeare, grandfather of William, farmed land here and rented a house, probably near the Marroway–Warwick road junction. He is almost certainly buried in the churchyard; and his son John, the father of the dramatist, is thought to have been baptised in the church. In Queen Elizabeth's time much of the land was unenclosed, but an attempt at enclosure was made towards the end of William's life. Today the village, in the form of a square, consists of many pretty Early Victorian houses in the Tudor style, Georgian farms and a few thatched timber-framed cottages. Above the road, the long

church (St. James) has a rich-cream-coloured tower pierced by twin belfry openings. Ample tower arch frames a massive Decorated font beneath fine hatchments; nave is 14th-century with a Perpendicular clerestory. Early 18th-century pulpit with oval panels. Finely painted glass; St Matthew and St. James Major, c. 1877, by F. Holt and Co. of Warwick. Rough rag-stone chancel, c. 1300, has cold glass by Frampton, in memory of the Smith family. Richly tiled floor, superb 16th-century stall ends, and Jacobean communion rail. In the churchyard, canopied slab to the memory of the family of Robert

Middleton Atty of Ingon Grange, which is now a pile of rubble in a field. All that survives of Snitterfield Manor, the house of the Hales family and then the Earls of Coventry, is a high wall and *Park House Cottages*. Built c. 1700, under a long tile roof ending against a Dutch gable, they have cross windows looking south over a fish pond. Victorian estate cottages include the *saddler's cottage*, which has a stone oriel and tall stacks; next to this is a timber-framed *barn*, said to have belonged to Shakespeare. Georgian *Yew Tree Cottage* and *Pool View* were originally Clyde Higgs Farm; Georgian Gothic *Park View* has prettily traceried windows behind a picturesque weeping ash. *Park House* stands behind a large coachhouse, topped by an ogival dome; across the brook, on the site of the old gasworks, are the clear-cut, whitewashed brick forms of a house, built, 1966-73, by D. H. Robotham for himself. *Methodist church* has twin lancet windows and a spired bellcote; beyond a pretty street of red-brick cottages, some robust timber-framed and brick barns are touched with orange lichen.

Solihull [7] A forest settlement on an unsound, miry hill topped by the church, the spire of which has been rebuilt three times. Market started in 1242; in 1417 Henry V claimed the manor as his own. The chief occupations were farming and the manufacture of hunting weapons and agricultural implements, which led to the clearing of the woodlands and the construction of timber-framed 'halls' and houses. Between the wars, *High Street*, which was partly cobbled, still had private houses; and, in spacious grounds around the village, stood the big Victorian and Edwardian houses of the Birmingham industrialists. Today High Street is a smart shopping street, with a mixture of old and new; further out is a deep belt of well kept suburban

homes. On the site of a Norman building, a remnant of which survives, the large red-sandstone *church* is dedicated to St. Alphege, Archbishop of Canterbury 1006–1012, who was martyred by the Danes. 13th-century central tower has a 14th-century belfry and a spire, which close the vista along High Street. West front dates from the lengthening of the nave in 1535, when the south aisle and possibly the soaring nave arcades were added. Perpendicular stone reredos, and a classical one, c. 1700, with a painting of the Crucifixion, by de Craeyer, a pupil of Rubens. Chancel and Chantry Chapel of St. Alphege are late 13th century, the latter with a rib-vaulted undercroft known as the Chantry of Holy Well. Communion rail, 1670, is surely one of the most splendid of its period, with groups of twisted balusters between square geometric panels and pierced acanthus foliage. Lively east window, by Wailes, west Jesse window, by Kempe, and 1956 north chapel window, by Lawrence Lee, depicting the murder of Thomas à Becket. Comfortable neo-Georgian *rectory*. Timber-framed and Georgian The Square has a First World War *memorial*, by W. H. Bidlake, in the form of a mediaeval cross. Pretty stucco Gothic *134 High Street* is timber-framed, as is the gabled post-Reformation *manor house*, really the house of the Greswold family, Thomas having been appointed custodian of the manor by Henry VI. Tudor-style R.C. *Church of St. Augustine*, built in 1839, by A. W. Pugin, has a scored-plaster nave dominated by tall figures of saints under even taller canopies, reaching almost to the ceiling; lavishly stencilled and gilded chancel has a richly painted stone altar. Majestic Venetian Gothic *Old Council House* is by J. A. Chatwin, who also designed the Tudor-style *Lloyds Bank* and the Italian Gothic *grammar school*, sporting its slender battlemented tower.

18th-century *grammar* school, Park Road, is where the young Samuel Johnson was refused the post of headmaster. Here William Shenstone and Richard Jago were pupils. Malvern Park has a magnificent *bronze rearing horse*, 1875, by J. E. Boehm, which is full of movement. Behind imposing gate piers, early 18th-century *Malvern Hall*, built by the Greswolds, was altered by Soane, as early as the 1780s, and painted by Constable, in 1822, for Henry Greswolde Louis. Constable's painting shows a three-storey building with four bay wings added by Soane, but in the early 19th century the top floor was removed and the wings were truncated. Soane's wide segmental porch has monolithic Ionic columns which support a frieze of delicately garlanded ox heads, and his chaste entrance hall has an arcade of typically Soane-ish arches, in front of a fine iron balustraded staircase. Soane also built a most impressive '*barn à la Paestum*' against the Warwick Road, a bold brick building with coupled Doric columns and a central arched carriageway. Embattled 16th-century *Hillfield Hall* stands on the site of a 14th-century building, and of the large timbered 'halls' the 14th-century *Solihull Hall*, Streetsbrook Road, retains its original roof trusses; the gabled 16th-century *Malvern Park Farm*, Widney Manor Road, is delightfully unrestored; and *Berry Hall* and *Ravenshaw*, both in Ravenshaw Lane, are also 16th-century. Long, L-shaped *Lovelace Hill*, 123 Widney Manor Road, was built in 1908, by C. E. Bateman, for Brigadier Ludlow, on his return from the South African War. Dutch in character and of the architect's usual reused bricks, its extensive tile roof is crowned by a most attractive glazed cupola.

Southam [11] A small market town, on a rise to the east of a lias-limestone escarpment and the river Itchen, a tributary of which flows

Southam churchyard

past the church and supplies a holy well. In 1227 Henry III granted a charter to the market, which flourished up to the early 20th century, with cattle in Coventry Street, pigs by the Bull Inn and a general market on Market Hill. The market accounts for the extraordinary number of inns and public houses. The Welsh Road, a part of the old Welsh drover's road towards London, was the principal road in earlier days. Wide Market Hill has brick terrace houses, above a raised pavement, and opposite are the stucco-faced *Craven Arms*, a posting stage with a filled-in gallery in the courtyard, and the splendid Elizabethan *manor house* with carved gables. Cast-iron Gothick gates lead to the silver-lias *church* (St. James), which has an unusually pinnacled red-sandstone spire on a heavily buttressed lias tower, built high above the river. Sunny, spacious interior retains a fine old roof decorated with carved angels, flowers and Tudor roses. Lettering on the tower wall is all that is left of the Tudor painting of the Creed, Commandments and Lord's Prayer; comparatively rare royal arms of Charles I was made for the chapel of the Tailors' Guild, St. Ewan, Bristol. 1854 chancel has copies of the original windows, with fine free-flowing tracery; north side of the churchyard, an avenue of limes commemorating the victory of Waterloo. Downhill, part-Georgian *The Abbey*, on land once owned by the abbey, has later shaped gables, and stands behind a magnificent cedar-of-Lebanon which must date from the 18th century. Feathery false acacia and weeping elm add a Chinoiserie touch to the Gothic *Stoneythorpe Hotel*, part of the kingdom's first Provident Dispensary, established here in 1823. Lower end of Market Hill is closed by Georgian terrace houses following the curved road to Banbury. Grecian *Old Court House* has a Soane-ish porch; *Bull*, a later carriage arch; and the humble *Crown*, Regency bows. Gabled *Old Mint*, once the Horse and Jockey and possibly where the Southam tokens were minted, is of lias. Gothic *National School*, built in 1816, is hidden by a later patterned-brick front and the *Congregational church* allows playful cast-iron tracery. Outside the village is the pebble-dashed-concrete *model village* of the Rugby Portland Cement Company.

Spernall [10] Scattered orange-brick farms in the valley of the River Arrow, enclosed by tree-studded hills. Early 19th-century Tudor-style cottages and a stucco-faced Georgian *vicarage*. Modest, ivy-clad stone-and-brick *church* (St. Leonard) stands derelict on a hill from which there is a wide view south along the river valley. Plastered interior, littered with paraffin stoves, has a narrow chancel arch, and the small early Victorian chancel is neo-Norman with an overlarge wheel window. White-marble monuments to the Chambers family by Allen of Birmingham. Among the 17th-century rectors was Henry Teonge, the diarist, whose work, published in 1825, paints a vivid picture of life in the navy.

Stivichall *see* Coventry.

Stockingford [5] Built up during the 19th century, when the main industries were coal mining, brick, tile and drainpipe making and the manufacture of ribbons. United to Nuneaton in 1639, and now a suburb with little separate identity. Austere Italianate *church* (St. Paul), built in 1822–3, by J. Russell, is of noble proportions. Large, round-arched windows with Florentine tracery are shaded by the deep eaves of a low-pitched roof, reminiscent of St. Paul's, Covent Garden. West tower; mean Gothic Revival chancel; panelled plaster ceiling; west gallery; 1922 east window, by R. Anning Bell. Second vicar, the Revd. J. E. Jones, commemorated by a white-marble tablet, is immortalised in George Eliot's 'Scenes of Clerical Life'.

Stockton [12] A cement workers' village on the blue lias used for the manufacture of lime and cement. By 1850 workings were 'very extensive', and Stockton cement has been used for many large structures, including the Victoria Embankment, London. Set against fields and the *manor house*, church (St. Michael) has an old red-sandstone tower, and a local-lias body, built in 1863–73, by W. Slater, incorporating sandstone Perpendicular chancel arch and Decorated chancel windows. East window by W. Holland of Warwick. Archdeacon Coley was so popular here that, after his death, he was carried round the church in a glass-topped coffin. Long, cream-painted *Barley Mow* faces across the village green to *butcher's cottage* and its free-standing shop. Tudor-style *school* has an Arts and Crafts extension; pale-brick Italianate *school house* dates from 1843. Cream-brick cottages, some banded with red brick. In a tiny building, once used by the Co-op, Neville Neal and his son Lawrence specialise in making graceful rush-seated cottage chairs, as made in the last century by Philip Clissett, of Bosbury near Ledbury, who gave lessons to the eager Ernest Gimson. Just as Gimson apprenticed himself to Clissett, so one Edward Gardner learnt the trade from Gimson himself and later taught Neville Neal at his Priors Marston workshop. Rushes are collected in the autumn from the upper River Leam in sufficient quantity to last the winter through, and hung from rafters to dry.

Stoke *see* Coventry.

Stoneleigh [8] Once a number of hamlets, the names of which now represent manor houses or small farms. Timber-framed and rich-red-brick cottages around a sloping green, with a horse chestnut. 1851 *smithy* is still in operation, for this is riding country. A trade that was much practised here was that of fuller, the name given to those

who finished newly woven cloth, and there were six fulling mills. Thatched *cruck cottages*, red-sandstone *old almshouses*, built in 1594, and prettily gabled *estate cottages*. By the River Sowe, the *church* (St. Mary), of red sandstone from the top of Motslow Hill, is essentially Norman. Two linked dragons, over the north doorway, biting their own tails. Massive Norman west tower supports a minimal Perpendicular belfry; light, plastered interior has Norman arches to both tower and chancel, the latter with zigzag decoration. Evenly spaced Decorated-style windows. Norman font is from Maxstoke; early 19th-century fixtures and fittings include box pews, pulpit, and, on the west gallery, fine cast-iron royal arms, between gold-lettered benefactions. Norman chancel was meant to have been vaulted, and has ugly restored wall arcading, again decorated with zigzag. Vaulted recess houses an alabaster tomb to Chandos, Baron Leigh, d.1850; and up steps over the Leigh vault is a plaster-vaulted Georgian Gothic chapel with colourful heraldic glass. A Civil War battle was fought on the hill to the south-west, and the Roundheads are said to have fired through the church windows at the vicar in his pulpit. Elegant, gabled *parsonage* has new bow windows with bottle glass. Against the abandoned river ford is a cluster of timber-framed cottages; substantial cross-windowed *school* was once the court house. Tudor-style *New Almshouses* and impressive timber-framed *Manor Farmhouse*. Red-brick and dark-tile *Walker's Orchard*, which incorporates an old barn, follows Lord Leigh's commendable specification for new building on his estate, following the ignorant development of Stoneleigh Close; and an early 18th-century house has a Victorian Tudor-style front, applied to make it more suitable as a vicarage. Early 19th-century *Sowe Bridge* is by Rennie, and *Stare Bridge* is late mediaeval.

157

Against the river, beyond the 14th-century *Gatehouse and Hospitium*, 12th-century Cistercian *Stoneleigh Abbey* has been incorporated into the grandest Georgian mansion in the county, with its mediaeval cloister as the inner courtyard. *Chapter House*, with a central column, and vaulted *Dormitory Undercroft*. Mighty Baroque *West Range*, built in 1714–26, by Francis Smith of Warwick, is certainly his best work. Giant Ionic pilasters spring from a massive rusticated basement, which outcrops from the gently sloping river bank. Ends of *Saloon* are divided by tall yellow-scagliola columns; and the chimneypieces have caryatids and Atlases. Here Queen Victoria dined in state when she visited Warwickshire in the almost tropical heat of June 1857. *Staircase* was decorated in the 1760s by John Bastard and William Hiorn, who inserted a Venetian window; *Chapel*, which faces south, retains its original fittings. The old Leighs would not go to Stoneleigh church, where they would have had to pray for the Hanoverians; and there is a legend that Prince Charles Edward was secretly at the Abbey. Chapel had black draperies, in memory of Miss Mary Leigh, when a senior line of the family inherited the estate in 1806. Their arrival brought Jane Austen, whose mother was a Leigh; though it is to Mrs. Austen, not Jane, that we owe a delightful account of life here at the time. On the second floor is a Louis XVI-style white-and-gold suite, created for Victoria and Albert, which incorporates genuine Chippendale furniture and rich French wallpapers. North range *porch*, *Long Gallery* and *Stables* are by C. S. Smith, a pupil of Sir Jeffrey Wyattville. River Avon, once widened to enhance the view, has now been reduced to its original width. In the grounds are the buildings of the National Agricultural Centre, scene of the internationally renowned Royal Show.

Stratford-upon-Avon [11] Compact mediaeval market town, the birthplace of William Shakespeare. Smooth-flowing River Avon divided the extensive Forest of Arden, to the north, from the pastoral Feldon, to the south, rich in corn and green grass; and the town sprang up by the river crossing. Wooden bridge was replaced by Sir Hugh Clopton's late 15th-century structure, once known as 'the causeway' because of its extensive approaches across the swampy meads. The flood plain is now gardens, around the Royal Shakespeare Theatre, which stretch as far south as the parish church. Across the water are fields; and the town, a mixture of black-and-white mediaeval and red-brick Georgian, rises uphill towards the Rother (horned cattle) Market, where William Shakespeare's father John, the glover, must have bought skins to take back to his house nearby. Set amid tall limes, the large cruciform *church* (Holy Trinity) has a central tower with rose windows and a spire by William Hiorn of Warwick. Handsome vaulted porch leads to a spacious nave, which has generous Decorated arcades, a large Perpendicular clerestory and an enormous, darkly glazed west window. Vista east is punctuated by the dark space beneath the tower, above which is a sumptuous Gothic organ case by Bodley, probably inspired by the reredos in the Beauchamp Chapel, Warwick. Bodley's excessively enthusiastic restoration, 1888–98, so annoyed William Morris that he protested against his earliest patron. Nave roof, 1825, by Harvey Eginton of Worcester. Chancel, built of limestone from Shirley in the 15th century, has large windows, the one over the altar flanked by tall niches for images. Original hammerbeam roof is adorned by elaborately carved, shield-bearing seraphs. 16th-century misericords depict a variety of subjects; and there is an altar tomb to Dean Bal-

shall, 1491, who built the chancel. Monument to William Shakespeare, with a stolid painted bust, within a column-flanked niche, was made by Gerard Jansseni, the son of a Dutch tomb maker, whose yard was close to the Globe Theatre. Bust is said to have been copied from a death mask taken by Dr. John Hall who, with his wife Susannah, Shakespeare's eldest daughter, supervised the erection of the monument. Both the Shakespeares and the Halls are buried beneath the chancel. Clopton Chapel has effigies of William and Anne Clopton, and other monuments are by Rysbrack and Westmacott. Broken bowl of the font, in which Shakespeare was baptised, was found in 1823. *Avonfield* is alleged to have been built with stones from the Charnel House; *Library and Art Gallery*, built in 1881, indicates the craftsmanship of Dodgshun and Unsworth's fantastic Gothic theatre, burnt out in a fire of 1926. Based on the fashionable notion of Shakespeare's Globe, the curved southern end, which once supported a half-timbered storey, can still be seen incorporated into the Cubist brick building, a competition-winning design of Elizabeth Scott in the late 1920s. Of the opening ceremony Maxwell Fry wrote: 'The vast crowd moved through the streets, gay with paper flowers, maypoles and English Morris dancing and a vision sustained it. The air was heavy with associations, Shakespeare, England, merry springtime, daffy-down-dilly.—As it came in sight the vision paled and faltered. No doubt timber-framing was expected, and the new brick was very red.' Today it has weathered, and the bold masses which rise from the river are reminiscent of an ancient castle. Timber-framed *Alveston Manor Hotel*, c. 1500, is now separated from its early 18th-century gazebo by the road; and the recently rural bank of the Avon has been sacrificed to the new Stratford Hilton

Stoneleigh Abbey ▷

Stratford-upon-Avon: William Shakespeare in the church and on the town hall

and a new public baths. From the bridge, an exceptionally wide street, once divided by timbered houses, runs uphill to a domed Regency *Market House*, originally open on the ground floor. *Red Horse*, which has a Doric porch on the site of its original carriageway, is where Washington Irving wrote his account of Stratford in his famous 'Sketch Book'. Timber-framed *Shakespeare's Birthplace* has been so altered and restored that little of the original fabric remains. Living room has a large fireplace and a stone floor, broken by ill treatment when the house was used as a butcher's shop, and immediately

above is the poet's birthroom, lit by the famous window inscribed by Sir Walter Scott, Thomas Carlyle and Isaac Watts. Another bedroom is spanned by original queen-post roof trusses. Garden contains the trees, shrubs, herbs and flowers mentioned in the poet's works. 1960s *Shakespeare Centre*, by Laurence Williams, has engraved glass doors by John Hutton of Coventry Cathedral fame; Disney-land *Jubilee Memorial Fountain*, the gift of George Washington Childs of Philadelphia, was dedicated by Irving, in memory of Shakespeare, in 1887. Long, timber-framed *Mason's Court*, Rother Market,

retains its original hall plan; *White Swan Hotel* has three richly painted scenes from the Apocryphal Book of Tobit. Timber-framed High Street was brought to light by the removal of brick and stucco at the turn of the century. *The Cage*, on the corner of Bridge Street, was originally the town prison, and later the house of Thomas Quiney, vintner, who married Shakespeare's daughter Judith. Dark, vaulted chamber

Stratford-upon-Avon: ▷
p162 Church Street and Mason's Court
p163 The town hall and Clopton Bridge

◁ **18th-century gazebo by Clopton Bridge, Stratford-upon-Avon**

behind the vintner's cellar is probably a cell. *Harvard House* was built in 1596, following the disastrous fire of 1594 and, with its jettied floors, oriels on brackets and rich gables, is the most elaborately carved building in the town. Home of Katherine Rogers, mother of John Harvard, founder of the American University, it was bought for America by Edward Morris. *Garrick Inn* has decorative curved struts forming star-shaped panels; *Tudor House*, on the corner of Ely Street, was revealed at the instigation of Marie Corelli. Ely Street has an 18th-century Gothic house; hot-red-brick and terracotta *Midland Bank*, 1883, by Harris, Martin and Harris, incorporates scenes from Shakespeare's plays, by Barfield of Leicester. Vista along High Street is closed by golden-stone *Town Hall*, built in 1767, by Robert Newman, and with a lead statue of Shakespeare by John Cheere, presented by Garrick. Ground floor was originally open, and painted along the Chapel Street elevation is a bold Georgian 'GOD SAVE THE KING'. Many-gabled black-and-white *Shakespeare Hotel*, of both the 16th and 17th centuries, and *New Place Museum*, the house of Thomas Nash, who married Shakespeare's granddaughter, have also lost classical masks. Of New Place, where Shakespeare spent his last five years, only the foundations remain. It was bought in 1753 by the Revd. Francis Gastrell of Lichfield, who cut down the mulberry tree planted by the poet, to save himself the trouble of showing it to visitors, and peevishly demolished the house to avoid paying rates. At the end of the garden, a relief, by Banks, shows Shakespeare between the dramatic muse and the genius of fine art. *Knott Garden*, a replica of an Elizabethan garden, has an intricate interlaced pattern made up of box interspersed with savory, hyssop, lavender cotton, thyme and other herbs. Chapel Street is terminated by the battlemented tower of

the *Guild Chapel*, originally built in 1269, by Robert de Stratford, for the Guild of the Holy Cross, the ruling body in the town up to the Dissolution. Nave was rebuilt in 1496–7, by Sir Hugh Clopton, with large windows and a Doom painting with Christ in Majesty. Long 15th-century *grammar school*, originally the Guildhall, has a jettied first floor supporting the Over Hall, where Shakespeare is believed to have studied; and, in an intimate court behind, the *Pedagogue's House* is probably the original school house. 15th-century *almshouses* and Georgian Gothic house. Georgian *Mason's Croft* was the home of Marie Corelli, and gabled, timber-framed *Hall's Croft* that of Shakespeare's son-in-law, Dr. John Hall. At right angles to the road to Birmingham, a terrace of brick-and-stone cottages, with a monopitch roof, was built in 1939, by F. R. S. Yorke and his father.

Stretton-on-Dunsmore [8] A very pretty village around a stream, which flows through the green enclosed by timber-framed and brick cottages. Though shorn of its pinnacles and parapet, the majestic ogee-arched tower of Rickman's *church* (All Saints), 1835–7, rises from a hill. Little mediaeval church can still be traced in the churchyard, and much of its masonry is in the wall between the old vicarage and the Manor House. Built of cream-grey stone from Attleborough, the William IV building has a tall tower porch with cast-iron-traceried doors and a gallery from which can be viewed a large, white benefactors' board. Spacious, plaster-vaulted interior is divided by delicate Perpendicular-style arcades, and the west gallery retains the original organ case. Castellated reconstructed-stone pulpit and ambo. Short chancel has 17th-century glass, portraying Christ at Emmaus, which was given to the old church by the Revd. H. H. Norris, Rector of Hackney. Part-

16th-century *Manor House* is not the original manor; Georgian *Old Vicarage* is of chequered brick.

Stretton-on-Fosse [14] A figure-of-eight village above the Roman Fosse Way. Guided into the village by a yellow-stone wall, the road plunges downhill beneath trees to the *church* (St. Peter), rebuilt and enlarged in 1841, with a spired, octagonal belfry. Jacobean-style west gallery frames a neat, plastered interior decorated with poppy heads. Hammerbeam roof and bright geometric east window.

Stretton-under-Fosse [9] Once part of Fenny Newbold, which became known as Newbold Revel, and to which Sir Thomas Malory, the author of 'Morte d'Arthur', succeeded in 1433. Timber-framed and brick hamlet pales at the grandeur of *Newbold Revel*, built for Sir Fulwar Skipwith in 1716, on the site of the old manor house 'bedecked with the armorial bearings of the Revels and Malorys. Engraved in Colin Campbell's 'Vitruvius Britannicus', it is attributed to Francis Smith of Warwick. Gravel forecourt, extensive gardens and a lake. Main fronts were filled in at ground-floor level by Edgar Wood, c. 1900, who also added the 'Cricketers' Wing', to accommodate the county teams, and created a double-height saloon. Rich inlaid staircase, fine plasterwork and elegant marble chimney-pieces. Ogival-domed *Stables*, round-arched *Chapel*, by Harrison and Cox, and corner-windowed *Assembly Hall*, by Weightman and Bullen.

Studley [10] Where the Birmingham–Alcester road crosses the River Arrow; it became more than a village as it expanded with the growth of the needle industry, which was mentioned as early as 1695. James Pardow, the first to apply steam power to needle making, established a mill here in 1800, and the population doubled in the next fifty years. In the reign of Henry II, a man named Peter either founded the priory or transferred it from the House of Austin canons he had already founded at Wicton in Worcestershire; what remains of his building is embedded in the 16th-century *Priory Farm*, which has a tall chimneystack and an 18th-century porch. Timbered and rough-cast *Old Barley Mow* was no doubt a granary and salt store for the monks, who converted it in 1534 to cater for travellers. In the fields across the river, the variegated *church* (Nativity of the Virgin) has a robust Perpendicular tower, Norman herringbone masonry and a rich-orange-sandstone chancel with a red-tile roof. Norman north window with 13th-century tendrils painted on the reveals, and a large 13th-century coffin lid, from the priory, with a vigorous foliated cross. In the churchyard, a stepped pyramid covers the family vault of Francis Lyttleton Holyoake Goodricke, Bart.; in a field to the north, the orange-brick *Old Castle* has many gables. High Street branches off the busy main road to climb uphill between late Georgian houses, now converted into shops, and early 19th-century villas. *Glenthorne House* has a Greek Doric porch. Main road has been spared conversion and, opposite a pretty Greek Revival terrace, the mellow balustraded late-17th-century *manor house* stands behind a high brick wall, broken by a fine pair of wrought-iron gates. In the fields, fort-like *Studley Castle*, built in 1834, by Beazley, has a big central keep.

Sutton Coldfield [4] A 'Royal Town', by charters of Henry VIII and Charles II, which, since the extension of the North-Western Railway, has become a residential suburb of Birmingham. Crowning a hill, sandstone mediaeval church was once hemmed in by Georgian houses, some of which survive. High Street runs along a prominent ridge of sandstone above the moor-

land country of Sutton Park, which came with the charter of 1528, obtained by Bishop Vesey, a close friend of Cardinal Wolsey. Born as John Harman in the old stone farmhouse at Moor Hall, Vesey won favour at court and, as Bishop of Exeter, turned a decayed village into a relatively prosperous town. He built fifty-one stone houses for the poor, a few of which survive. *Church* (Holy Trinity) has a squat mediaeval tower. Tall, round-arched nave is the 1760 rebuilding of a partially collapsed mediaeval structure. Norman font, with unusual projecting heads, is from Over Whitacre; and fine 18th-century pulpit has a tester supported on two thin columns, part of a consignment of rich early 17th-century woodwork thrown out of Worcester Cathedral in the 1870s. More of this makes up the choir stalls, side screens and sanctuary panelling, and it is now the chief glory of the church. Colourful arched chancel ceiling, decorated in 1914, by C. E. Bateman, with Tudor roses and angels. Chancel aisles were built in 1533, for Bishop Vesey, and the one on the north, which houses his effigy, was recreated as the Vesey Chapel, in 1929, by C. E. Bateman. He added an elaborate Renaissance screen and richly decorated the ceiling with the Beatitudes, and the squirrels, owls and oak leaves of Sutton Park. Iron gate to the porch was formerly part of the railing to the Vesey tomb, and a south aisle window has a compelling Supper at Emmaus, 1907, by M. Lowndes. High Street is mainly Georgian and of brick, with the exception of the stucco-faced *Three Tuns Hotel*, a coaching inn with a carriageway through to the back and its name in bold Egyptian letters. Uphill the street scene gives way to the modish early 18th-century *Moat House*, by Sir William Wilson, who was responsible for the rebuilding of St. Mary's, Warwick—his design being preferred to that of Sir

Christopher Wren! Cool 1960 *Petty Sessional Courthouse*; miniature early 19th-century Gothic *R.C. church*; and 1900s Queen Anne-style *School of Art*, with swags of fruit and a columned cupola. Behind trees, the *grammar school*, originally endowed and built by Bishop Vesey, now occupies an early 18th-century house, and lining the way to Four Oaks are many Victorian Gothic houses. Pebbledashed *5* and *7 Anchorage Road*, are by C. E. Bateman, 7 for his own occupation; and, behind a cut yew hedge, *62* and *64*, c. 1902, may also be his work. On the edge of the escarpment overlooking the railway, the Gothic *town hall* was originally an hotel for rail travellers; and, shorn of its tower, George Bidlake's Venetian Gothic *Old Town Hall*, Mill Street, is ablaze with bands of brick and tile. *The Parade*, a long green with trees, was once known as The Dam, from the bed of the old mill pool, and, beyond the well-mannered brick-and-faïence *Odeon*, some old timber-framed cottages and a *smithy* face across the Birmingham Road to the *Old Stone House*, an exceptionally large Vesey cottage. Picturesque *Seven Gables*, Digby Road, built in 1898, by Joseph Crouch for his own occupation, has copper-canopied fireplaces, stained glass by Mary Newell and, in the galleried hall, a mural, by F. W. Davis. Of peasant archers returning from the butts, it illustrates Morris's 'A Dream of John Ball'. *Top o' the Hill*, c. 1899, by E. Butler for himself, is less attractive, and *Wyndhurst*, by the same architects, has an elegantly canopied porch. Down a long drive overhung with trees, moated *New Hall* retains a grey-stone range from the original house, built c. 1200, but is mainly 16th-century. Battlemented brick 18th-century tower, and a red-sandstone Victorian wing. Oak-panelled great hall. Plants Brook drains Sutton Park into the River Tame, past the Vesey *New Hall Mill*.

Tanworth-in-Arden

Sutton under Brailes [14] Widely spaced around a long green which has large trees, an obelisk war memorial and an elegant Regency house. Overgrown churchyard hides vigorous 17th-century headstones and the *church* (St. Thomas à Becket) has a welcoming south tower. Tower porch houses many cross-cornered benefactors' boards, banished by the Victorians, who scraped the walls, patterned the floor and furnished in pitchpine. Narrow Norman doorway, 13th-century chancel and a most attractive Perpendicular bay window, waiting to be drawn by Prout. *School*, 1852.

Tanworth-in-Arden [7] On high ground and originally a clearing in the Forest of Arden, of which an old oak at Beaumonts is a remnant. Many of the houses are

timber-framed and, with others of Georgian brick, face a long green. Old spreading chestnut stands in front of the one remaining pub; handsome tower of the 14th-century *church* (St. Mary Magdalene) carries a broad broach spire. Grey Umberslade-sandstone body is 14th-century. North arcade was demolished in 1790, when the nave was covered by a single-span roof ceiled with plaster. The vicar at this time was Philip Wren, a great-grandson of Sir Christopher, and there are reasons to believe that he did not approve of these changes. Though the arcade was rebuilt in 1880, the nave is spacious and leads through a wide arch to a remarkably out-of-line chancel with a large east window. At the sides of the altar, two stone brackets on slender shafts would have supported figures of the Blessed Virgin

and St. Catherine. When the Archer vault under the sanctuary was cut down, in 1948, it was found to contain twelve lead coffins with inscriptions. Thomas Archer probably designed the large standing monument to his parents and grandparents, which has a dark, broad obelisk rising from a white-marble slab, on which sit two weeping putti and two skulls. Smaller monument to the last of the family, was designed by John Hickey who, besides executing chimney-pieces for Soane, exhibited a bust of Mrs. Siddons as Cassandra at the Royal Academy. Mellow brick *Doctor's House* has side wings and arched sash windows, and the Victorian *school house* attractive cast-iron railings. Stark stone *Umberslade Park*, built by Francis Smith of Warwick for Thomas Archer's eldest brother Andrew, was later extended, by

W. H. Bidlake and Phené Spiers, for G. F. Muntz. Tall *obelisk* erected by Andrew Archer's son, when he was created Baron Archer of Umberslade in 1747.

Temple Balsall—Solihull [8]

Temple Balsall takes its name from the Knights Templar, a military-religious order, founded to protect pilgrims to the Holy Land from attack by the Saracens. Land at Balsall was given to them about 1150 and, before their downfall in 1312, had become an important centre. On a rise above a tributary of the River Blythe, the soaring orange-sandstone *chapel* was built either by the Templars or their successors the Knights Hospitallers, dissolved in 1540. Other buildings were grouped around a large court with the hall and main lodgings on the north side, part of which survive, and a large barn on the south, still standing in 1721. Decay was halted in 1662 when Lady Anne Holbourne reroofed the chapel; in 1849, George Gilbert Scott sorted out the tracery to the best of his ability, increased the walls to their original height and crowned them with a steeply pitched roof. Scott's trivial detail, particularly disturbing on the exterior, is less obtrusive in the cavernous interior, dominated by pre-Scott, brightly coloured saints, which account for the exceptionally simple tracery of the west window. In a dell, a picturesque terrace of cottages conceals the mediaeval *hall*; and the brook is spanned by a simple wooden bridge. Yew-lined walk from the road is between the Bailiff's Georgian *Temple House* and Hurlbutt's late 17th-century *Hospital*, founded by Lady Anne's surviving sister Lady Katherine Leveson. Original pedimented buildings face each other across a quadrangle; and the twin Tudor-style towers at the far end belong to the 1836 *vicarage*, approached along a winding drive. Dainty *school*, 1676, with stone cross windows and a cupola. Road to

Balsall has both timber-framed and modern houses; soft-orange-brick *Church of St. Peter*, built in 1871, has a bold Arts and Crafts window, by R. Stubington, depicting Charity, in blue and pink, surrounded by bottle glass.

Temple Grafton [10]

Granted by Ceolred, King of Mercia, to the Abbey of Evesham in 710. By mistake the title was granted to the Abbot himself, a prelate of very dubious character, and, in an endeavour to right this error, the authorities forged a complete new set of title deeds, which still exist. In 1179, the manor was granted to Henry de Grafton, to act as a buffer state between the Earl of Warwick and the equally militant Earl of Beauchamp. Subsequently, the estate was granted to the Knights Templars, who built the original church and fortified manor house. In 1862 the manor came into the hands of James William Carlisle, who pulled down the old church and erected the present one; demolished the manor house and built Temple Grafton Court; and also built the vicarage, the school and most of the older cottages in the village. He died in 1892. Yellow-and-brown-stone *church* (St. Andrew), built in 1875, by F. Preedy, has a timber-framed belfry and a gloomy interior with too much stained glass. Gabled *Old Vicarage*, 1867, with flush mullions; Gothic *C. of E. Primary School*, 1874, with plate tracery. Georgian *Church House* has a timber-framed barn, and the Tudor style *estate cottages* date from 1855. Arts and Crafts *Temple Grafton Court*, built in 1876–9, is timber-framed and tile-hung.

Thurlaston [9]

In the 14th century monks built a chapel dedicated to St. Edmund, King and Martyr. Present brick *church*, built, in 1849, on land given by the Duke of Buccleuch, was designed, by William Butterfield, to double as a school. Steeply roofed tower serves as the

schoolmaster's house; and the body is spanned by timber arches, which spring so vigorously from the tops of the walls that they are restrained by iron ties.

Tiddington [11]

Roadside community linked to Stratford-upon-Avon by large, well-to-do houses, some of which back onto the river. Chequered brick Georgian and plain Victorian terraces face each other across the busy road; and the jolly, polychromatic-brick school, unbelievably as late as 1896, commemorates the 60th year of the reign of 'our gracious Sovereign Lady Queen Victoria'.

Tidmington [14]

In the valley of the River Stour where it is crossed by the busy Oxford–Stratford-upon-Avon road. *Bridge* is probably 18th-century with an early 17th-century arch; and across Knee Brook is a narrow *packhorse bridge*. *Church* is one of the smallest in the diocese of Coventry; pyramid-roofed 13th-century tower has twin bell openings and an original corbel table carved with faces. Doorways are c. 1300, the chancel is 16th-century and the rest mostly 1874–5. Font, carved with a triumphant Christ, may be late Saxon. Panelled Perpendicular bench end, and an arms of George III. Gabled *Tidmington House*, c. 1600, has sash windows, an 18th-century veranda and low, pilastered pavilions.

Tile Hill, *see* Coventry.

Tredington [14]

At the crossing of the Roman Fosse Way and the busy Oxford–Stratford-upon-Avon road, which separates the spec. houses from the old village centre encircled by the river. In a self-consciously picturesque setting, *church* (St. Gregory), has a most impressive 14th-century tower crowned by a sharp 15th-century spire. Cream nave and aisles, and a rich-ochre chancel. Norman south doorway was enriched with zigzag carving by the Victorians; two-storeyed Perpendicular porch has many attractive textures. Heavy oak door yields to reveal a spacious interior with majestic Norman piers. Above the arcades are the remains of Anglo-Danish windows and doorways, said to date from 961, which must have opened on to a deep west gallery. A superb set of benches has buttressed and traceried ends; raised tower space is divided from the nave by a low, balustraded rail, probably the 17th-century communion rail. Richly carved Jacobean pulpit and painted royal arms. Scraped chancel has elaborate east window tracery by E. Gibbs, filled with glass by William Holland of Warwick; lower panels of the Perpendicular screen have been incorporated into a replacement by Sir Arthur Blomfield. *Brick mill* similar to the one at Clifford Chambers. *Rectory*, once larger than most country houses, and rebuilt on a smaller scale in the early 1840s with some mediaeval windows, has been abandoned for an even smaller house. *School* is trying not to look Victorian, now that it is a dwelling; *wheelwright's cottage and outbuildings* have eroded daub and deep thatch.

Tysoe & its hamlets [14]

In Vale of the Red Horse, so named from a figure of a horse cut into a red hill above the church. Original figure, reputed to have been some hundred yards long and seventy yards high, was dedicated to the Saxon horse god Tui, from which the village takes its name. Along the foot of the Edge Hill escarpment, Church or Middle Tysoe, in which the church stands, was the largest of the three Tysoes, but was overtaken in the last century by Upper Tysoe, leaving Lower Tysoe as a loosely knit hamlet. Large, pinnacled *church* (The Assumption) has a Norman south doorway beneath a carved Lamb and Cross. Scraped interior reveals the arches of two 11th-cen-

tury upper nave windows above the south arcade, which has robust 12th-century pillars with scalloped capitals and pointed 13th-century arches. Octagonal Perpendicular font, with crudely carved but tender figures below a later, prettily pinnacled cover. East window is glazed with small, soulful scenes linked by vine trails, 1876; and the oldest glass depicts St. Nicolas of Tolentino, an Augustinian associated with both the Canons of Stone, who held this church, and the Knights Templar, who held land in Lower Tysoe. Churchyard cross retains part of a crucifix; bellcoted, brownstone *school*, 1856, by George Gilbert Scott, incorporates a house. Slated Georgian farmhouse with Venetian windows, and a long stone barn. Upper Tysoe also has stone barns but mixed with thatched and pantiled cottages. Mediaeval *manor house*, with 17th- and 20th-century additions; *Peacock Inn* has a fine painted sign.

Ufton [11]

On a promontory between the River Itchen and the Grand Union Canal. In the 1860s nearly all the land belonged to Balliol College. Vista along the lias and red-brick street is closed by the *church* (St. Michael), separated from the village by the busy A425. Multi-coloured Perpendicular tower stands uneasily on the edge of a deep cutting containing the road; above the churchyard entrance, 14th-century preaching cross retains its original pinnacled top, framing a Crucifixion. 13th-century south doorway opens into a tall, scraped interior of character, made dark by hard Victorian glass. West tower window has large-scale figures of St. John and St. Jacob, with flamboyant draperies; larger north window is Pre-Raphaelite-inspired. Victorian chancel arch springs from the side walls; light, plastered 13th-century chancel is lit by low-level lancets. Across the cutting behind a tall

pine, a derelict Georgian house commands a magnificent view over the Roman Fosse Way to Royal Leamington Spa. Small-scale lias *school*. Gabled *Old Rectory* stands in a garden abounding in large specimen trees, beneath which is a crumbling traceried window, surely from the church.

Ullenhall [10]

Timber-framed and red-brick cottages around a rough granite cross in a densely treed valley. Above the village Seddon built, in 1875, a yellow-stone *church* (St. Mary), which is nearer than the *old church*, only the chancel of which survives, furnished with Jacobean panelling, a wrought-iron communion rail and cast-iron Commandments. Though Early English in detail, the interior of the Victorian building has a Romanesque character, strengthened by a stencilled wagon roof, a round apse and, beneath the altar, a circular mosaic pavement with rings of crosses, crowns, leaves, fish and water. In a wooded park, plain but dignified *Barrells Hall* appears to have grown from an early 17th-century farmhouse, which later in the century was called the manor house. By 1730, when it was purchased by Robert Knight, afterwards Lord Luxborough and Earl of Catherlough, the house had become a small country residence, to which was added a lofty Corinthian portico, designed by Bonomi. The Earl's natural son, Robert Knight, not being on good terms with his own son, the Revd. Henry Charles Knight, and never acknowledging his paternity, did all he could to depreciate the estate, leaving it neglected. When the son eventually inherited, it was sold, in 1856, to William Newton, a Birmingham merchant, who removed the portico and built a lofty hall with a glazed cupola. East wing was added in 1883. Robert Knight was the son of the cashier of the South Sea Company, who after the collapse of the 'Bubble', fled to the Con-

Upton House

tinent with a reward of £2,000 on his head. The son's wife, Henrietta, is described by Horace Walpole as 'high coloured' and 'lusty', with a 'great black bush of hair' in which at first she wore the portrait of her husband, from whom she soon 'was parted—upon a gallantry she had with Dalton, the reviver of Comus and a divine', and 'retired to a hermitage on Parnassus'—by which is meant Barrells, which she made the centre of a well known 18th-century literary coterie, including the poets Shenstone, Somervile, Jago and Richard Graves. Her interest in her garden was fostered by Shenstone, whose

prose and verse she tried to imitate. First buried in the chapel at Wootton, her body was later removed to a mausoleum in the park; but, when this was demolished in 1830, was again removed, with other members of the family, to a new vault under the chancel of the old church. Avenue of trees from Barrells to a point on the Ullenhall road, nearest to Henley, still remains, and it is said that the Knights had intended to continue it into the town (see Henley-in-Arden and Oldberrow). Modernised *Crowleys*, in Ullenhall village, stands on a moated site; at timber-framed *Hall End Farm* the notorious

forger William Booth was born in 1776.

Upton House [14] (near Ratley) Brown-stone classical house, set in fine grounds high up on Edge Hill, the site of a village depopulated in 1499. Parts date from the 15th century; the two main fronts from 1695; and Sanderson Miller is said to have carried out alterations during the 1730s. In 1757, the house was bought by Child the banker, who ran away with the daughter of the Earl of Westmorland and married her at Gretna Green. Interior is mostly 20th-century and has a magnificent collection of

169

pictures. Down a hill, against the county boundary, are the *Temple Pool*, and a Tuscan *temple* by Sanderson Miller.

Walsgrave on Sowe *see* Coventry.

Walton [11] (near Wellesbourne) Deep in woods on the brow of a hill, large Decorated-style *Walton Hall*, built of stone in 1852–62, by George Gilbert Scott, has a tower on the entrance front and a long colonnade to the garden. Lofty *Entrance Hall* with a similar colonnade; *Staircase* has tall windows containing armorial glass. Bell-coted Georgian *Chapel of St. James* has a Tuscan porch and a square chancel with a Venetian window; but far more exciting is the recently ruined Cyclopean *Bath House*, almost certainly by Sanderson Miller. Domed plaster ceiling with a border of broken stalactites and shellwork by Mrs. Delany (see Wellesbourne). An uneven field to the south is the site of Walton Deivil, destroyed in 1509, after forty people had been expelled; Dene Brook, originally the Wellesbourne, has been dammed to form a lake.

Wappenbury [8] (near Eathorpe) In the rural Leam valley to the south of Wappenbury Wood. Behind a giant Celtic cross and a tall wellingtonia, the red-sandstone *church* (St. John Baptist) has a smooth south-west tower housing white-marble monuments, banished from the nave during the ruthless restoration of 1886, when the south arcade was rebuilt. Victorian arch frames an Early English chancel with three stepped lancets. Early Georgian *farmhouse* has a pedimented doorway; and, down a lane, beyond a thatched cottage, secluded R.C. *chapel* is on the river bank. The earliest Benedictine foundation in the country, the house was given to the church by the Clifford family, in 1734; and the adjoining brick chapel, said to be

by A. W. N. Pugin, has simple lancet windows. Giant cypress acts as a spire. Ball-topped gate piers against the road herald Cotswold-tradition *Wappenbury Hall*.

Warmington [14] In rich cornland at the foot of Edge Hill, where the main road cuts through the steep escarpment to give an even gradient up to the ridge. Well sited against the cutting, the brown-Horton-stone *church* (St. Michael) has a steeply sloping churchyard, with large early 18th-century table tombs sheltered by pines. Plain-parapeted west tower, and large expanse of tile roof. Small-scale interior is lit from the aisles. New riven-slate floor, impressive Norman arcades and cut-down screen. Chancel, which is inclined to the north, has a very pretty Decorated sedilia with gabled nodding arches. East window contains good Victorian glass with sharply drawn figures; small south window is Pre-Raphaelite-inspired. Below the church, the brown-Horton-stone village is clustered around a large, sloping green which has a pond and a sheep dip. The two gables of the *manor house*, built c. 1600, represent the solar and service rooms; further east, 17th-century *Grove Farm House* retains its cross windows. Early Georgian *Old Rectory* has moulded stone window surrounds, giant angle pilasters and well designed interiors.

Warton [12] A linear village formerly two hamlets, one on the brow of a hill. Economical *church* (Holy Trinity) was built in 1841, by Thomas Johnson, and, though in the Early English style, is classical in form. Tuscan *14 Austrey Road*, built in 1775, is one of the few survivors among the Georgian houses, which are rapidly being replaced by mundane spec. developments.

Warwick [11] An historic town with an ancient castle high above the meandering River Avon, channelled into its rocky base. In the centre,

on the highest ground, the majestic tower of the parish *church* (St. Mary) rises above the huddled houses set in the rich green fields of Warwickshire. Of the collegiate church, established in 1123, only the crypt survives. Mediaeval tower, nave and aisles were consumed in the 1694 Fire of Warwick and rebuilt, by Sir William Wilson of Sutton Coldfield, in the then unfashionable Gothic style, presumably to blend with the surviving chancel. A spacious hall, ceiled by a plaster vault, nave and aisles are well lit by large, clear-glazed windows with curious Continental tracery. Darker chancel, finished in 1392, has a stone vault supported on a spider's web of flying ribs. Reredos, by William Butterfield, is below an original window, considerably restored in 1870, and the north and south windows are by Kempe in his usual greens and yellows. In the middle of the chancel, recumbent alabaster effigies of Thomas Beauchamp, Earl of Warwick, and his wife hold each other's hands. The part-polygonal chapter house has a similar vault. Richly decorated Beauchamp Chapel, built in 1443–64, in accordance with the will of Richard Beauchamp, Earl of Warwick, who died in Rouen in 1439, is perhaps the finest chantry chapel in the country, and encloses a superb central monument to the Earl. Gilded-brass effigy, mounted on a Purbeck-marble tomb chest enriched with gilded-brass 'weepers', shows him in plate armour, with a muzzled bear and a griffin at his feet, and his hands raised in prayer. Chapel is elaborately vaulted and, in a panel over the altar, there is a figure of the Blessed Virgin as Queen of Heaven. Reredos, a splendid Gothic piece, with a relief of the Annunciation beneath a stalactite-encrusted canopy, replaces the original, destroyed by the Parliamentarians in 1632; framework of the east window, filling the entire east wall above, is decorated with richly coloured bands of canopied saints and angels which are among the best mid-15th-century sculpture in the country. Stained glass, 1441, has many figures, including St. Thomas à Becket, St. Alban, St. Winifred and St. John of Bridlington, in their original positions in the upper parts of the side lights. Alabaster tomb of Ambrose Dudley, Earl of Warwick, d.1589, and that of Robert Dudley, Earl of Leicester, the favourite of Queen Elizabeth, who died in 1588. Between this chapel and the choir is a miniature chapel with delicate pendant fan vaulting. Early 18th-century portal to the Beauchamp Chapel is a surprisingly convincing Gothic piece for its date. South transept has a fine early 15th-century brass to Thomas II Beauchamp and his wife; and a tablet with an urn is to William Hiorn, the architect and builder, d.1776. William and Mary tower, built on arches over the pavement, effectively closes the vista up Church Street, lined with red-brick Georgian houses, enclosing a delicate war memorial cross by C. E. Bateman; on three corners of High Street and Jury Street, in a straight line between the East and West Gates, ambitious town houses, probably built as patterns for the rebuilding of the town after the fire, have elaborate cornices. Rusticated *Court House*, c.1725–8, by Francis Smith, contains a splendid ballroom with an elegant musicians' gallery; Jury Street, untouched by the fire, retains timber-framed buildings and the part-Jacobean *Lord Leycester Hotel*, originally the town house of the Archers of Umberslade. Castle Street, closed by Warwick Castle's stately Guy's Tower, has the timber-framed house of Thomas Oaken, perhaps the richest man in 16th-century Warwick. Once leading to a mediaeval bridge below the castle walls, it was cut short, in 1790, by extensions to the castle

grounds. Red-brick and stucco High Street has an Egyptian-influenced late 18th-century doorway, which once led to a Masonic Lodge, and the handsome, smooth-stone *Warwick Arms Hotel*, c.1790, by Eborall, with tripartite windows. Past the sympathetic *National Provincial Bank*, 1924, by F. C. R. Palmer, the street dives down to the *West Gate*, with walls of living rock, between Tudor gabled, timber-framed houses, saved from the fire by south-west winds. Above the street, timber-framed *Lord Leycester's Hospital* and the battlemented *St. James's Chapel*, perched over the West Gate, make a superb group. Founded by the Earl of Leicester, in 1571, who took over the premises of the combined guilds of Holy Trinity and St. George, the hospital is arranged around a courtyard. Guild hall, and a larger hall where Fulk Greville entertained James I. Tall, pedimented *Congregational church*, 1825. View along Swan Street, which has an impressive timber-framed house, c.1630, is closed by William Hurlbutt's classical *town hall*, built only forty years later. Originally on open arches, the first floor is now used as a museum. Market has a splendid stone-faced house, 1714, probably by Francis Smith, and is closed by the 1960s *county offices* by Eric Davies. Down steps and across Theatre Street, tall early 17th-century *Marble House* is shrouded in trees. Panelling probably came from Norbrook; it was here that Francis Smith had his office. Following the opening of the Grand Union Canal, in 1792, Saltisford acquired several industrial buildings; Wallace Street has a massive 18th-century *worsted spinning manufactory* which, like the stone-backed *Eagle Engineering Works*, has an elegant Georgian house, presumably for the master. Elegant stucco-faced octagonal *gasholders* date from as early as 1822; neglected light-brown *chapel* of the *Leper Hospital*, stands in front of the

timber-framed *priest's house*, which is even more derelict. View of the town from the north-west is now spoilt by the harsh lines of the latest extension to the county offices; and little remains of the nearby *Warwick Priory*, founded in 1124. Warm brick William and Mary *Northgate House* has Georgian sash windows facing up Northgate Street, the finest street in the county, to the tower of St. Mary's Church. Primitive Doric *county gaol*, built in 1777–83, by Thomas Johnson, must have looked even more forbidding before the insertion of modern metal windows; and in 1776 a description, by John Howard, of the underground prison helped the way to prison reform. Ionic *Judge's lodgings*, 1814. Red-sandstone *Shire Hall*, built in 1753–8, by Sanderson Miller, has a full-length stone-lined room and two octagonal courtrooms. Painted-stucco and red-brick Georgian houses complete the scene. The precincts of St. Mary's originally stretched from what is now Old Square to the Butts, where there is a mediaeval wall. 15th-century *East Gate* carries the spindly *St. Peter's Church*; and, just outside, Roger Hurlbutt's richly corniced *Landour House*, built in 1692, heralded the post-fire classical revolution. Behind splendid wrought-iron gates, long, golden-stone *St. John's House* was built in 1626–66, on the site of a 12th-century hospital for travellers; beyond a row of neglected timber-framed houses, neat 18th-century Gothic *St. Nicholas's Church*, by Thomas Johnson, is probably on mediaeval foundations. Timber-framed Mill Street is overpowered by the cliff-like walls of *Warwick Castle*, the best view of which is from the magnificent single-span *Castle Bridge*, built across the River Avon in 1793, to carry the diverted London Road around the extended castle grounds. Impregnable south front and rounded Caesar's Tower rise sheer from the rock above the ruins of the 14th-century *Great Bridge*, and are reflected in a sheet of water overhung with trees. Present approach, by the gatehouse at the top of Mill Street and the drive cut through the rock, dates from 1797. According to legend, the first defence works of importance were erected by Ethelfleda, daughter of Alfred the Great, in 916, and the steep mound at the southern end of the courtyard is still known as *Ethelfleda's Mound*; though this is mainly Norman for it supported a Norman motte-and-bailey castle. During the next two centuries the large courtyard was enclosed, but its walls were razed to the ground in 1264, by the forces of Simon de Montfort, who imprisoned the Earl and Countess at Kenilworth. Most of the existing fortifications were built by the Beauchamp family. In the mid-14th century, Thomas Beauchamp the elder constructed the pink-sandstone *Clock Tower* (gatehouse), *Caesar's Tower* and the connecting curtain wall; and nearly fifty years later his son balanced Caesar's Tower, about the gatehouse, by the twelve-sided

Warwick Castle from the bridge

St. Mary's **Warwick** ▷

Guy's Tower. A splendid group, these towers make a memorable entrance to the courtyard, from which they were clearly recorded by Canaletto. In 1461 Richard Neville, Earl of Warwick, Shakespeare's 'proud setter up and puller down of Kings', placed his young cousin Edward IV on the throne and became virtual ruler of England. His daughter married the Duke of Clarence, after whose death the castle went to Richard III, who began a big tower, of which the polygonal *Bear and Clarence Towers* are the original turrets. *Conservatory* was erected to house the magnificent white-marble 4th-century *Warwick Vase.* Procured by Sir William Hamilton, it was found, in 1770, at the bottom of a lake close to Hadrian's villa near Tivoli. Living quarters are in the south range, over a vaulted early 14th-century semi-basement. Overlooking the river, the consciously mediaeval stone-lined *Great Hall* has a Victorian hammerbeam roof and is furnished with a display of gleaming armour around a portrait of Elizabeth I in her coronation robes. Elaborate sideboard, by Wilcox, exhibited at the Great Exhibition of 1851. Gilded, white-painted *State Dining Room*, 1764–6, by Timothy Lightoler, is dominated by the Van Dyck portrait of Charles I on horseback—though throughout the Civil War the castle was an important Parliamentary stronghold. Tall, narrow 18th-century Gothic *chapel.* Along the river front, a late 17th-century suite includes the *Red Drawing Room*, with gilded, red-lacquered panelling, outstanding buhl furniture and a wealth of fine pictures by Raphael, Rubens and Van Dyck; and the magnificent *Cedar Drawing Room*, richly panelled in Lebanese cedarwood, in 1681, by William and Roger Hurlbutt, and hung with a number of Van Dyck portraits. *Green Drawing Room* has a portrait of the Fifth Duke of Albuquerque by Moroni; *Queen Anne's*

Bedroom, which takes its name from the bed used by the Queen at Windsor, has a swirling late 17th-century ceiling and, below a portrait of Queen Anne by Kneller, an elegant chimneypiece by Westmacott. The walls are hung with the celebrated Brussels tapestry, 1604, by Franciscus Spiringius. *Blue Boudoir*, dominated by Holbein's uncompromising portrait of Henry VIII and with several paintings by Rubens, has extensive views over the river.

Wasperton [11] Red-brick farms and cottages and some modern houses in the wide valley of the meandering River Avon. Enclosed by evergreens, *church* (St. John Baptist) is a red-sandstone box of 1736, with 1843 Gothic windows, south aisle and chancel by George Gilbert Scott. Vaguely Austrian timbered bell turret and porch are also by Scott. Pulpit has Flemish carved scenes; and, beyond a heavy timber screen by Scott, the east window has bright glass, by Hardman to a design by Pugin. Rich encaustic-tile altar and parcel-gilt communion rail, with sharp-beaked birds holding mistletoe. Coffin-shaped slab, with a moss-covered cross, is to Thomas Garner, the well known architect, d.1880, and his wife Louise, d.1881, of Wasperton Hill, a long, red-brick farmhouse enjoying a magnificent view over the Thelsford Brook valley. Pale-brick *Cedar House*, c. 1840, has prettily cusped gables; and orange *Manor Farm* contains an early 14th-century aisled hall, and has a massive clustered chimneystack.

Water Orton [4] Road to Sutton Coldfield crosses the River Tame by a round-arched bridge, said to have been built by Bishop Vesey with stone from the old manor house of Sutton Coldfield. In Old Church Road, timber-framed and Regency houses cluster around the old churchyard, which has a broken 15th-century cross and a massive

pink granite sarcophagus, overshadowed by tall trees.

Church, rebuilt on a new site in 1879, by Bateman and Corser, is in their usual gawky Gothic, with rock-faced stone walls and a poor steeple. Aisleless south wall is pierced by two tiers of windows and both chancel arch and ceiling have bold Morris green stencilling. Victorian Gothic houses are of red brick banded with yellow; Arts and Crafts *23 New Road*, built in 1899, faces inter-war semis. Decidedly Edwardian *station* has a stumpy curvilinear tower; Gothic *Wesley Chapel*, 1868, is of polychromatic brick; *Digby* pub, possibly Early Victorian, but trying to look Queen Anne, is painted pink! By a large chestnut, Georgian *Overton House* rises above a timber-framed wing; and the tile-hung Arts and Crafts *school* faces a large green playground.

Weddington [5] Cluster of modern houses in the fields bounded by the River Anker and the Watling Street, from which it probably derives its name. Original hamlet was destroyed when the Marquess of Dorset enclosed the whole manor, turning it to pasture, in 1491. Delicious thin-orange-brick *church* (St. James) is probably the structure erected by Gilbert Adderley, at his own expense, possibly on the sandstone foundations of the previous building, said to have been destroyed by fire and of which only the 14th-century north transept survives. 18th-century windows were made Gothic in 1875, for Henry Cunliffe Shawe of Weddington Hall; and the change in style was completed by Blomfield's restoration of 1881, for S. Fox of Achenson. Brick pyramid spire, Norman font, pulpit, from a three-decker, and cut-down box pews. Elaborate monument to Humphrey Adderley, a Gentleman of the Wardrobe to Henry VIII, Edward VI, Mary and Elizabeth I. Weddington Hall or Castle, a

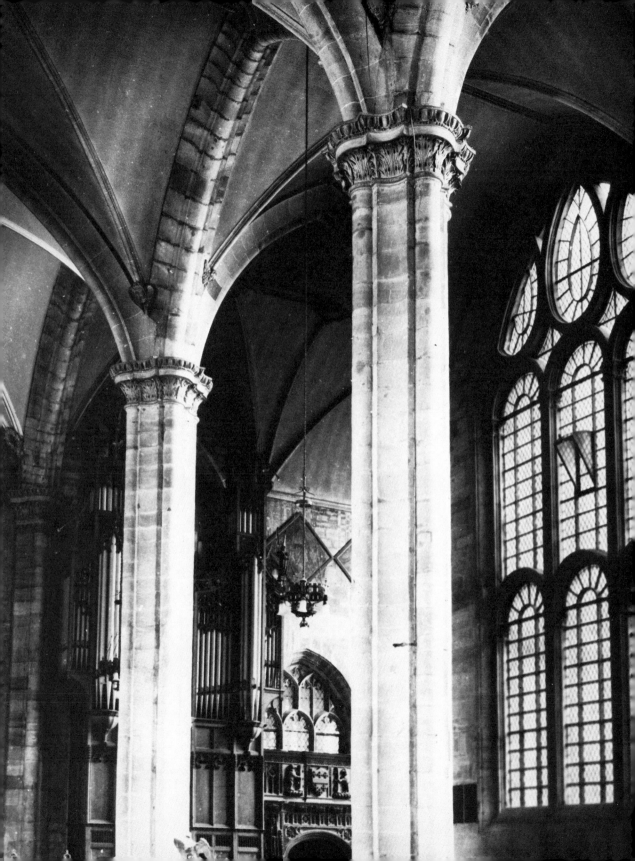

picturesque fort, was demolished between the wars.

Weethley [10] Exposed hamlet against the Worcestershire border. On the far side of an old red-brick farm and a derelict timber-framed house, the village pond is surrounded by uprooted trees and a twisted barn, unfortunate witnesses to the exposure of the site. Tall, bellcoted Victorian *church* (St. James), by E. Haycock of Shrewsbury, stands high above a rich valley, its steep, storm-damaged roof cutting into the sky, as if to defy the elements.

Welcombe [11] *Welcombe Hotel*, the largest mid-Victorian Elizabethan house in the county, is the 1867 rebuilding, by Henry Clutton, of a Regency Gothic structure. Owner was Mark Philips, M.P. for Manchester, said to have been the model for the archetypal Victorian industrialist, Mr. Millbank, in Disraeli's 'Coningsby'. Unlike the earlier, more romantic Merevale Hall, this stolid brick mansion is content to nestle in a fold in the Warwickshire landscape, where William Shakespeare is known to have owned many acres of arable land. Main hall, in the centre of the entrance front, is fully panelled and has a large black-and-white fireplace; staircase, positioned as at Aston Hall, has a similar pierced-strapwork balustrade. *Obelisk*, erected in 1876, by Robert Needham Philips, in memory of his elder brother Mark. *The Dingles*, a series of irregular Y-shaped trenches, in places some forty feet deep and through which runs the main drive, may be early British entrenchments, but are more probably the result of water in a

In the Beauchamp Chapel,
St. Mary's, **Warwick**
above Robert Dudley and his wife with Ambrose Dudley in the foreground
left The Richard Beauchamp effigy and *opposite* figures on his tomb chest

Lord Leycester's Hospital, **Warwick**

geological fault through the heavy red-marl subsoil. Anglo-Saxon weapons were discovered in the tumulus beneath the 18th-century summerhouse.

Welford-on-Avon [10] Timber-framed and brick cottages around a green, with a tall maypole, in the market garden of the Avon valley. The manor was given by Selwyn, Earl of Gloucester, to the Saxon priory of Deerhurst, near Tewkesbury, a cell of the Abbey of St. Denis, Paris. Norman *church* (St. Peter) stands on the site of a smaller one, built by the monks, of which the font bowl is the only recognisable remnant. Rendered blue-lias walls and a south doorway with zig-

zag decoration. Nave and aisles are divided by pairs of large round arches; square-headed Perpendicular aisle windows have carved heads of Henry VI and Margaret of Anjou. Decorated chancel, much restored by George Gilbert Scott, who replaced the arch by a wider one, retains some original glass; east window has a 1920s version of a Jesse window, by Christopher Webb. Timber-framed *lych gate* was 14th-century but has recently been renewed; around the church are several black-and-white cottages. Georgian *rectory* is pebble-dashed; handsome *Cleavers*, built in 1713, tolerates a flamboyant period porch added in the 1950s. Against the weir, *Welford Mill*, now a house, retains two undershot wheels.

Wellesbourne [11] Once Wellesbourne Hastings and Wellesbourne Mountford, and now large and straggling around the crossing of the Warwick–Oxford road over the River Dene, which joins the Avon in Charlecote Park. In the late 1960s, the river reverted to its original course and thundered through the village, rising at one point to five feet. Virginia-creeper-clad *church* (St. Peter), also used by the Roman Catholic community, was mostly refaced in 1847–8, by J. P. Harrison. Spacious interior has the Norman chancel arch reset so well into the north wall of the chancel as to seem untouched, and the effect is similar to that of the Norman chancel arcade at Walsoken, calmly captured by the pale washes

178

of J. S. Cotman's watercolour. Around the sanctuary is a veined-marble arcade inlaid with gold mosaic. East window with yellow-canopied scenes of the Annunciation, Crucifixion and Nativity against blue grounds; west window, by Holland of Warwick, with figures of Samuel, Moses and Isaiah. Glass by Willement shows Jesus raising Jairus's daughter and the widow's son at Nain, and a window of the Twelve Apostles came from the London Exhibition of 1857. In the churchyard, a fantastic table tomb, boasting a shield-charged pediment, is decorated with a skull and bones; mellow-red-brick *vicarage*, 1698–9, has lost most of its cross windows. *Footbridge* has pretty Gothic brackets; thatched cottages follow the curve of the road to Chestnut Square, enclosed by black-and-white *King's Head*, cross-windowed *Little House*, 1699, and pedimented *Red House. Wellesbourne Hall*, built in 1697–1700 and the former home of the Granville family, has an interesting connection with King George III. After a difficult early life, Mary Granville, born in 1700, married, as her second husband, a Revd. Delany. Then, being widowed and of straitened means, she started making magnificent pictures of flowers out of hundreds upon hundreds of minute pieces of paper. After completing a thousand, her eyesight failed and she retired to Windsor, where George III gave her a house and a pension of £300 a year. She was a favourite of George III and his family, who often visited her, and much of her work is now in the British Museum. Here two of the fireplaces are of her greatly admired shellwork. *Welles-borough House* was built by William Lowe in imitation of his mansion on his American plantations; gabled *manor house* has been faced

Warwick:
above Northgate House,
right The old gas works

with brick; *Coopers*, once a butcher's shop, has patterned glazing and pierced bargeboards. Small-scale Chapel Street is enclosed by speckled-brick *Old House*, a bow-windowed *shop* and the cross-windowed *Old School House*. Polychromatic-brick *8–12* have pretty porches; the timber-framed bakery has a brick front; and, on a bend in the road, a pedimented *chapel* is now houses.

Weston-in-Arden—Nuneaton [5]

In 1313 the manor passed to William la Zouche; mullioned and gabled *Hall*, set against a bank of tall trees, was built about the time of the eleventh Baron, who was the sole dissenter at the trial and death sentence of Mary, Queen of Scots. Behind a large gravelled forecourt, symmetrical south front has a plain doorway, through which the sculptor, Richard Hayward, who lived here during the late 18th century, must have brought his antique fragments of classical art. Extension of 1892–3 is enriched by a jolly Jacobean doorway, carved with the initials of F. A. Newdigate; stable block, built in 1920, was considered a showpiece at that time. Since becoming an hotel, the hall has been extended further; interior retains some interesting panelling of the 16th century and later. Red-brick R.C. *Church of Our Lady of the Sacred Heart* was built in 1899, by Gualbert Saunders, in the Early English style.

Weston-on-Avon [10] (near Luddington)

Thatched cottages by the broad River Avon. Squat, late 15th-century church (All Saints) is battlemented, except where a south chapel has been removed, leaving the arcade exposed as window, and where the bright-red-tile chancel roof shelters the walls. 18th-century porch, remarkable continuous row of north windows, and elliptical chancel arch. Roundel of mediaeval floor tiles is formed by as many as sixteen tiles; there are mid-16th-century brasses

to Sir John and Sir Edward Grevill. Greek Revival monuments, mainly to the Adkins of Milcote, are by Davis of Bidford. Base of the churchyard cross remains. On a bend in the road at Weston Sands, some pretty Victorian brick cottages are open to the four winds.

Weston-under-Wetherley [8]

Scattered along a road below the red-sandstone *church* (St. Michael), which has small belfry openings and an unusually complete 13th-century aisle. Chancel is Norman, with traces of the original windows, and on the north side is a Perpendicular chapel. *Hall* is set against Cubbington Wood; beyond a cluster of timber-framed and brick houses, *hospital* was originally built, c. 1840, as a reformatory for boys, in 100 acres of farmland against the River Leam.

Whatcote [14]

Farms and cottages around the *church* (St. Peter), from which there is a fine view over the Stour valley. Part-brown-stone Perpendicular tower contrasts with slate-roofed body, which has traces of whitewash, presumably applied to conceal its patchy appearance. Norman doorway and windows, and several Gothic openings at different levels. Nave has lost its Georgian ceiling, but retains its uneven wall plaster. Tub-shaped font, three richly carved Perpendicular benches, an 18th-century pulpit and a cast-iron stove, with a trailing flue. Small, crimson-curtained Gothic arch leads to the room-like chancel, furnished with a balustraded communion rail. Mosaic tablet is to William Sanderson Miller, d.1909, of Radway Grange, some time rector of Whatcote and the last member of the family to be squire of Radway. Fragment of Burne-Jones-inspired glass, 1911, by James Powell and Sons, is a reminder that the south porch and part of the nave wall were destroyed by bombs during the Second World War. Mediaeval churchyard cross is topped by an

18th-century sundial; ruined stone cottage adjoins a handsome row of barns, their thatch long since replaced by corrugated iron.

Whateley [5]

A hamlet on a hill, over subsiding mine workings, necessitating iron ties. Attractive black-and-white cottages; golden-stone *Whateley Farm* spoilt by new windows. *Whateley Hall Farm* has a massive chimneystack and the remains of a 17th-century staircase; by the drive, an impressive timber-framed barn stands high above the road. In the fields, stone *Holt Hall Farm*, part rebuilt in brick, consists of three parallel ranges, the middle shorter than the others to allow a court, and containing a surprisingly magnificent staircase of c. 1640, finely carved with birds and animals.

Whichford [14]

Many modern houses around a spacious green in magnificent undulating country, studded with trees *Church* (St. Michael) is remarkable for its delicately traceried Perpendicular clerestory, which contrasts with the simple bell openings of the plain, early 14th-century tower. Brown-stone sundial. Dark void of the south porch is emphasised by the continuation of the south aisle roof; south doorway, which has lethargic zigzag decoration, belongs to the Norman church, possibly built by the de Mohuns. Wide, white-painted nave has a 13th-century north arcade with fat piers. Grained Gothic pews, which have doors, date from the restoration of 1845, by Thomas Johnson, and the pulpit, which is of the refectory type, is entered from the south chapel. John (IV) de Mohun died on an expedition to Scotland, c. 1323; and in the south wall recess, a coffin lid, decorated with an engrailed cross, is thought to be his. John (V) de Mohun, d.1376, was enrolled as one of the original Knights of the Garter, but died without an heir. Engrailed crosses also appear in north aisle windows, where three attached golden roses represent a special gift from the Pope, and in each of the chancel windows. Simply arcaded communion rail may also be by Johnson. Golden-stone tomb chest has a brass on a black lid; several classical monuments are to the Watkins family and others. Incomplete early 18th-century *rectory* of brown stone with cream dressings; *school* of eccentric dry walling.

Whitchurch & Wimpstone [14] (near Alderminster) Timber-framed 17th-century houses and a few farms in the fields between Humber Brook and the River Stour, described by anglers as a 'winter river'. Amid trees on the river bank and approached by a field path from a gated road, the ochre-and-grey *church* (St. Mary) has a silver-shingled bell turret. Of the Anglo-Saxon hamlet nothing survives, and of the later buildings only a red-brick tithe barn and a cottage. Original church, probably built of wood and thatch by monks from Deerhurst, is said to have been rebuilt in stone about 1020, when the herringbone masonry on the north wall could have been constructed. Wider western part of the nave, cut short in 1670, may have been the original nave and the narrower part the chancel. Chunky Norman south doorway is probably from the west end, and two large posts support the bell turret. 13th-century chancel, well lit by old yellow-and-white glass, has a Perpendicular east window flanked by two mutilated niches. White-stone tomb chest, incised with a cross, chalice, Bible and black-mastic-filled lettering to the 15th-century rector, William Smyth. Facing the church across the fields, pale-brick *rectory* has Doric columns in antis, and elliptically arched stables. Timber-framed *Old Forge* and *farmhouse*; and pale-brick estate cottages, 1857, as at Alderminster and Preston-on-Stour. At Crimscote is a 17th-century pigeon house.

Whitnash [11] A strange mixture of timber-framed houses and brick bungalows, with the eighteen-hole golf course of Leamington and County Golf Club. Above a sloping green, the smooth Perpendicular tower of the *church* (St. Margaret) is accompanied by a large spruce. Heavily restored by George Gilbert Scott in 1855, chancel retains a mediaeval lancet; nave, rebuilt in 1880, has a short south aisle by Scott, 1867. Porch is richly paved; capitals throughout have lush naturalistic carving, which around the altar was executed by Miss Agnes Bonham. East window by Holland. Brass to Benedict Medley and his wife, who bought the manor in the time of Henry VII, to whom he was Clerk of the Signet; another, to Richard Bennett, rector 1492–1531, shows him in an alb, stole and chasuble and holding the chalice with the Host. Scattered timber-framed houses and an Early Victorian *school* are now engulfed by suburbia.

Wibtoft [6] Pretty timber-framed village near the crossing of the Fosse Way and Watling Street, the site of the 1st- to 2nd-century Roman settlement of Venonae, of which nothing is now visible. *High Cross*, 1712, records that 'Claudius, a certain Commander of a Cohort, seems to have had a camp towards the street, and towards the Fosse a tomb.' Aisleless *church* (St. Mary) has a mediaeval wall with bands of rounded purple stones; and the other walls, of brick with timber-traceried Gothic windows, stand on stone lower courses, which may also be mediaeval. Late 19th-century bell turret.

Willenhall *see* Coventry.

Willey [9] A small village with a slim *church* (St. Leonard), the body of which hides behind the slender Perpendicular tower. Early English south doorway. Dark, long nave leads to an even darker chancel.

Old circular font; an unusual 14th-century sepulchral slab, with an effigy partly revealed through quatrefoil openings; and a Gothic Revival monument to Robert Beresford Podmore, rector for 40 years. Opposite the church, some brick cottages have timber framing; white-painted *Sarah Mansfield*, formerly The Plough, now has flock wallpaper.

Willington [14] (near Shipston-on-Stour) Informal mixture of old and new around a loop road, against the River Stour. Some cottages are still thatched; a stone house has a ranch-house extension larger than itself.

Willoughby [12] Regency farms, later terraces and many modern houses, those in Brooks Close on the site of the manor house, from which a balustraded 17th-century porch, now at *Vale House*, is said to have been rescued. In the fields, *church* (St. Nicholas) has impressive Perpendicular arcades and windows, a George III arms, painted on canvas by S. Cox of Daventry, and a delicate stained-glass Crucifixion. Elegant yellow-brick Regency *vicarage* with arcaded red-brick stables, 1836.

Wilmcote [10] Whitewashed and speckled-brick cottages in undulating, well treed country. Stratford-on-Avon Canal is followed by the railway, which has a pretty pinnacled bridge. Lias from the quarries was used for the repair of St. Mary's, Warwick, after the fire of 1694, and early in the last century, four stone terraces were built to house new workers. Near Gipsy Hill Farm are the remains of a lime and cement works. Silver-timbered *Mary Arden's House* was the childhood home of Shakespeare's mother and the lias farm buildings now house a collection of old Warwickshire farming implements and rural bygones. Straight-roofed blue-lias *church* (St. Andrew), built, in 1841, by Butterfield, has his characteristic bellcote. In the Middle Ages there was a small guild chapel, vested in the Guild of the Holy Cross at Stratford-upon-Avon, who provided a priest; the priest's house has only recently been demolished to make way for the new bungalows at Swan Fold. Of the chapel, closed when the guilds were suppressed at the Reformation, no traces remain, though the top of the processional cross is a fine mediaeval pewter crucifix dug up on site. Present church site was chosen by the parents of E. B. Knottesford Fortescue, the Lords of the Manor at Alveston, and in the following year their son was ordained to the tiny living. From the first a centre in which the principles of the early Tractarians found adequate ceremonial expression, the church claims to be the earliest in which full Catholic teaching and practice were restored within the Church of England after the centuries-long lapse. It was here that eucharistic vestments were worn for the first time after the Reformation, and the splendid set in the vestry includes festal Spanish and French purple Latin-shape examples, both of the 18th century. Early Tractarian fathers such as Newman, Manning, Pusey and Keble were constant visitors to the parish, and for years there was in use a green chasuble that belonged to Newman. Through an upright west doorway flanked by tall lancets, the dark, small-scale nave is richly stencilled, and has finely drawn Biblical scenes and texts on zinc wall plates, executed by a former incumbent. Uninterrupted side walls accentuate the length, though they support a chancel arch; originally there was a rood screen. West gallery and Celtic-style font, a copy of that at St. Martin's, Canterbury, said to be the oldest in England. Pulpit has Biblical scenes; above the stone altar is a rich stained-glass Crucifixion. Men sat on the south side, where there are racks for top hats. It was

to this church that Butterfield added his first secular buildings, a stone *school*, 1844, and a most attractive stone *guest house*, 1845; and it was here that the first retreat was held in the Church of England, attended by some forty priests, including both Manning and Newman, who each planted a yew. Original idea of the house, which is now a vicarage, was that it should be a guest house for the retreatants, who, for sleeping purposes, overflowed into the adjoining school, now spoilt by later flat-roofed extensions.

Winderton [14] (near Brailes) A cluster of houses and barns on the crest of a steep hill crowned by a gem of a Victorian *church* (St. Peter and St. Paul). Some of the houses are still thatched; and there are magnificent views across the lush Feldon towards Brailes. Designed by William Bassett, this complete replica of a 13th-century shrine was erected in 1878, at the expense of Canon E. Thoyts, in memory of his parents, and possibly occupies the site of a chantry chapel mentioned as early as the beginning of the 13th century.   Brown-Hornton-stone exterior has a bold pyramid-roofed tower, in the base of which is a high-vaulted porch protected by rusty gates.   Dusty-red-and-white-stone interior has shafted lancets ablaze with rich glass. Lush foliated capitals, veined-pink-marble reredos; challenging white cross, reminiscent of Butterfield, and green brass fittings, for the congregation has dwindled away.

Winson Green & Hockley *see* Birmingham.

Wishaw [5] (near Over Green) Loosely knit hamlets in rolling countryside. In the fields, small *church* (St. Chad) has a calm 18th-century Gothic tower divided into stages by classical cornices. 13th- and 14th-century arcades support a later clerestory; low-level chancel

arch leads to a rubble-walled chancel supported around the exterior by heavy, raking buttresses. Simple 19th-century vestry is probably by A. B. Phipson of Harborne, who 'repaired and restored' the church. Large 18th-century wall monuments are out of scale with the building; a smaller oval one to Thomas Lander, d.1809, is by Studholme Sutton. Inscription to Thomas Bayles, 1696–1744, the local schoolmaster, records that he gave towards education, new seating and a weathercock upon the steeple, so the previous tower probably had a spire. At Over Green, Regency stucco *Old Rectory* stands by a timber-framed *tithe barn*; and *Moxhull Park* boasts both classical and Gothic lodges. All that remains of the big house is a pedimented stable block, now the *Belfry Hotel*. Grove Lane has a pretty Gothic cottage; and *The Grove*, though spoilt by modern casements, contains splendid cruck trusses.

Withybrook [9] Red-brick farms and houses where a twisting road descends to cross a tributary of the River Sowe. Approached across the fast-flowing brook, *church* (All Saints) is of cream-orange stone with patches of red sandstone, and has a stumpy north-west tower, which adds interest to the interior. Thick ogee-panelled door opens on to a light, spacious south aisle, with large low-level windows containing jolly fragments of old glass. Lofty Perpendicular nave, well lit from the west, darker chancel, of the same period and mutilated Easter Sepulchre with a tomb chest, soldiers and an angel, the recess delicately painted with powdery pink and blue leaves. Site of the village of Hopsford, depopulated before Dugdale's time, can be seen on the ground within the angle of a road bend, to the west and north of Old Hall Farm, and the ford, with its street leading down to it, is quite clear.

Wixford [10] Black-and-white cottages and brick barns in a Keuper-Red-Marl hollow by the River Arrow. On a remote rise, Norman *church* (St. Milburga) is topped by a Victorian timber-framed bell turret. Churchyard has stepped base of the old cross; and the porch is reached under the low branches of an ancient yew. Norman south doorway. Long, narrow body shows traces of Early English origin; ambitious Perpendicular south chapel, d. 1411, and his wife, are two including whole small figures. Large, canopied brasses, to Thomas de Cruwe, the founder of the chapel, d.1411, and his wife are two of the finest in the county. He was legal adviser to Margaret Beauchamp, Countess of Warwick.

Wolfhampcote [12] Original village ruined by an enclosure of 1501, was in the fields to the north of the large *church* (St. Peter), now abandoned and derelict. Squat 13th-century tower has primitive lancets; low-pitched aisle roofs give a strong horizontal emphasis. At the east end is a large 18th-century Gothic mausoleum. Bricked-up south porch, ancient font, 14th-century screen and late 17th-century communion rail. From 1395 to the Dissolution, the rectory was in the hands of the collegiate church of St. Mary, Warwick.

Wolston [8] Pale-brick Regency houses, many roughcast semis and some dark-brick modern houses lead to the part-timber-framed village street, enlivened by a tributary of the River Avon. In the fields, cream-limestone-rubble *church* (St. Margaret) is basically Norman, with a reused south doorway and an original crossing below a squat central tower. Much damage was done in 1759 when the steeple collapsed into the chancel, but the rebuilding, entrusted to Job Collins of Warwick, was completed by the end of 1760. The width of the Norman nave is indicated by the arcades, which are 14th-century; late 15th-century clerestory supports a 17th-century roof with dark, moulded beams. Chancel, c. 1300, has been carefully restored, and the roof is decorated with shields and foliage ornament. East window tracery dates from 1866; 17th-century communion rails are from Rowington. South transept incorporates two large, cusped tomb recesses with effigies, c. 1300. Manor house was demolished around the First World War, when some parts went to America, and beyond The Plantation are the ruins of an old *water mill*. Wolston Priory has a redsandstone front; and inside, the screens passage is clearly visible. Here the Puritan 'Marprelate Tracts' were printed, attacking the Established Church after the Spanish Armada. Round-arched *Baptist church* is cream painted; and the Flemish Loyal Equity Lodge No. 2565 M.U. Oddfellows Hall, built in 1890, is now the *village hall*. Against the railway embankment, a long, speckled-brick terrace has a Regency-style porch; near the stone-faced *railway bridge*, 1837, are the earthworks of the early 13th-century *Brandon Castle*. Once with a rectangular keep, it was destroyed as early as 1266, probably by Simon de Montfort during a raid from Kenilworth.

Wolverton [11] On the side of a hill with the 13th-century *church* (St. Mary) near the crown, gained by a winding mossy footpath between banks of snowdrops. Cosy building with a comfortable bell turret. Pink-washed interior has deeply splayed lancet windows, one with an amusing conglomeration of old glass and a group with old white and deep yellow. Nave roof is round-arched and boarded; and, as there is no chancel arch, the delicately traceried wood screen is full height. Chancel is almost as broad as it is high; east window allows a view of a stately old tree. Light, slightly worn Morris window, in memory of Mrs. Margaret Mayhew, is of Elizabeth and John the Baptist, and Mary and Jesus. Long creamwashed *rectory*, basically an old timber-framed cottage, has pretty Early Victorian bay windows and gables, and a larger-scale stucco wing. Many red-brick barns. Romantic *Wolverton Court* consists of a long, low timber-framed building linked to a tall 18th-century house by a handsome piece of Queen Anne Revival, by Clough Williams-Ellis, and reminiscent of his work at Portmeirion.

Wolvey [6] On a knoll above the River Anker which was once the habitation of Ulve (the Wolf). On the site of a Saxon building, the warm-cream-coloured *church* (St. John Baptist) has a west tower, the lower part of which is probably 12th century, and a Norman south doorway with zigzag decoration, as well as an unusual fleur-de-lis motif. During the 14th century the south aisle was reconstructed, by Alice de Astley, as a memorial chantry to her husband Giles, killed at the battle of Bannockburn in 1314; and the nave was widened, throwing the tower off-centre. At the same time the north aisle was added; but, after the roof fell, in 1620, the outer wall was rebuilt to fit the shortened old timbers. Delicate cast-iron glazing bars are probably early 19th century. Among the non-resident vicars, the Revd. Hugh Hughes was George Eliot's Mr. Crew of 'Scenes of Clerical Life'. Effigies of Thomas de Wolvey, d.1305, and Alice (Clinton) his wife were originally under a canopy, in the eastern bay of the north aisle, part of which survives. *Wolvey Hall*, originally built by Thomas in 1250, was rebuilt by Thomas Astley in 1677, following the destruction of the earlier building during the Civil War. Orange-brick centre bays are of this date, and side projections of 1887. Italianate *Baptist chapel* has a later chancel; modest *school* has a quaint blue-brick bellcote.

◁ **Winderton** Church

Wootton Hall, **Wootton Wawen**

Wood End [5] (near Tamworth) A mining community with a mixture of Edwardian houses, inter-war semis, post-war prefabs and recent spec. housing. *Edge Hill Methodist Free Church*, 1900.

Wootton Wawen [10] Timber framing and whitewashed brick where Birmingham–Stratford-upon-Avon road crosses the River Alne. When the district was more thickly wooded the river would have been larger and, until the turnpike improvements and the building of the first bridge, travellers through Wootton were likely to encounter some hazard if the lively Alne, which supported some five mills, was running high. Sweeping bend of the road was clearly as prominent in Tudor times; but road improvements in the 18th century turned the bend more sharply to the north, on to higher ground above flood level, leaving the old route still visible in a field. In the mid-1960s the bend was further modified by the removal of the Priory Pool. Between the years 723 and 737 Aethelbald, King of Mercia, gave twenty hides of land to a monastery, which may have come to an end in the Danish wars, and on the site of which was built an Anglo-Danish church. After the

Conquest the church and land were given to the Benedictine Abbey of St. Peter of Castellion of Conches, who established a small alien priory here, which in 1443 was bestowed by Henry VI on his new foundation, King's College, Cambridge. Above sloping Church Field, white-stone *church* (St. Peter) has an attractively battlemented nave, a central tower and a steeply roofed early 14th-century south chapel, covered with rich-orange tiles. Church, which exhibits almost every style of architecture, was described by George Gilbert Scott as 'an epitome in stone of the history of the Church of England'. Of the 11th-century Anglo-Danish building, by Wagen (or Wahen), who gave the village its name, more than half the height of the primitive central tower remains, with long-and-short work and a round archway on each side, suggesting a cruciform plan. Best example of its period in the county, the dark tower space, now used as the chancel, is lit by splendid blue-green abstract glass, by Margaret Traherne, in memory of F. W. B. Yorke, architect father of F. R. S. Yorke of Modern Movement fame. Highest arch is to the west, where the 11th-century nave was replaced in the 12th century by a wider one, the north wall of which survives, with some herringbone masonry, traces of a Norman doorway and a window. Present nave was made light in the Perpendicular period by a fine clerestory and a large west window, beneath which is a small doorway, thought to have led to the priory. West tower arch is concealed by a graceful ogee arch linking two delicately traceried parclose screens; above the south door is a painted Georgian royal arms. Large, brick-paved south chapel has a barn-like roof and a large east window of five stepped lights, c. 1330. Fragments of 14th-century wall painting with small red flowers; and many wall monuments, which cover a blocked win-

Wootton Wawen

dow. Francis Smith, d.1606, lies uncomfortably on his side, beneath his coat of arms, and the place of the altar has been usurped by a presumptuous urn to Henry Knight, cashier of the South Sea Company, who fled the country with a considerable price on his head when the 'Bubble' burst in 1720. Wide, lofty chancel with a large Perpendicular east window glazed with old white glass. Pedimented 17th-cen-

tury *Wootton Hall* was the childhood home of Mrs. Fitzherbert, who lived here even after her marriage to the Prince Regent. Former R.C. *chapel*, 1813, has a most remarkable Greek Doric interior. Ornamental lake, known as the *Serpentine*, is fed by the Alne; and there is a high-level pond, to drive the wheels of a large corn and paper *mill*, built in the late 18th century. Road is spanned by an aqueduct of the

Manor Farm, Wootton Wawen

Stratford-on-Avon Canal, constructed in 1813, by W. Whitmore, engineer, on tapering brick piers. Italianate *school* is now a house; timber-framed and creamwashed-brick *Manor Farm* has a splendid apsed door hood, decorated with a basket of lively grapes, gourds and flowers.

Wormleighton [12] Thatched and tiled cottages below the rich Horn-ton-stone *church* (St. Peter), built in the 13th century. Squat west tower is enhanced by a large copper beech. Ochre slatted porch gate opens onto a whitewashed interior with massive golden-stone arches and, high up over the small tower arch, a painted royal arms. Delicate Perpendicular rood screen and loft were brought from Southam, during the Civil War. Chancel, too narrow for stalls, has Jacobean panelling beneath a stylised east window. Members of George Washington's family appear in the registers as early as 1595, and Robert Washington was married here. Down in the fields to the west are the extensive earthworks of the mediaeval village, depopulated in 1498. A spring once fed a reservoir and a series of stew ponds for Friday fish; and the moated manor stood where boats now ply along the

Oxford Canal. Moved uphill, *manor house* has a surviving brick part and, against dark majestic firs, a magnificent stone gatehouse, dated 1613, emblazoned with the Spencer arms. Here Prince Rupert rested on the eve of the Battle of Edge Hill in 1642. Stone *school and mistress's house*, 1839; and *estate cottages*, 1848.

Wroxall [8] The estate of the first Earl of Warwick, after the Conquest, and held of him by Richard, whose son Hugh de Hatton was a prisoner in the Holy Land for seven years. After praying to St. Leonard he was released, upon a vow to build a Benedictine nunnery, and transported in chains to Wroxall, where his wife did not recognise him until he showed her part of a ring broken between them. Of *Wroxall Abbey*, said to have been founded in 1141, only part of the church and two pieces of cloister survive, one of which, though small, is thought to be the chapter house. Broad avenue leads, between specimen trees and the white-stone ruins, to the hard Victorian mansion. North aisle of the abbey church, consecrated 1315, is now the *church*, with a battlemented

brick tower, 1663–4, within the west end. Dark interior has 'one of the most complete assemblies of mediaeval glass in the county'. Nave and chancel are defined by a gawky Victorian screen; and the walls have a number of classical monuments to the family of Sir Christopher Wren, who bought the estate in 1713, at the age of eighty-two. Though it is doubtful whether he ever visited Wroxall, he is reputed to have designed the *curved wall* in the Wren Garden. In 1812, the Fifth Christopher Wren repaired the church and, with the help of Bateman, 'effectually ruined' the Elizabethan house. In 1861, the abbey was bought by James Dugdale of Liverpool, whose ancestors came from Clitheroe, as did those of the famous Warwickshire historian. *Farmhouses, blacksmith's house, cottages* and *gas house* were soon rebuilt in polychromatic brick and the blue-brick *school*, with its red and yellow bands, is certainly the most lively piece of structural polychromy in the county. Not content with the mellow old house next to the church, Dugdale rebuilt further west, again in brick. A hard Gothic pile, with fierce gables and relentless plate glass, it

has a stained-glass staircase window, by T. Drury, depicting the legend of Hugh de Hatton, and said to have been exhibited at the Paris Exhibition. Formal gardens give way to an informal park descending to a brook.

Wylde Green [4] Cosy suburban houses, in bosky gardens, around the wide Birmingham–Sutton road, lined with neo-Georgian shops and an arid grey-brick shopping centre. Village shop is still a post office. Massive brindled-brick *church* (Emmanuel), built, in 1909–16, by W. H. Bidlake, has tall clerestory windows, a gabled polygonal apse, added in 1926, and a curved north chapel, by G. H. While. Entered through a low-vaulted baptistry, with a small Burne-Jones-style window, the nave soars upwards between tall wall arcades, enclosing clerestory windows, and a chancel arch of cathedral proportions. Tall, brick-lined choir, windowless except for a small, richly glazed roundel, high up under the vault, leads to a brilliantly lit sanctuary, a lantern of delicately tinted glass.

Index

(B) or (C) after a place-name indicates that it will be found following the main Birmingham or Coventry entry in the Gazetteer

Abbots Salford *see* Salford Priors
Adderley, Charles Bowyer *see* Saltley (B)
Adderley family *see* Lea Marston; Fillongley
Adkins family *see* Milcote; Weston-on-Avon
Alne, River *see* Alcester; Beaudesert; Great Alne; Kinwarton; Preston Bagot; Wootton Wawen
Alscot Park *see* Preston-on-Stour
Anker, River *see* Atherstone; Attleborough; Hartshill; Nuneaton; Polesworth; Shuttington; Weddington; Wolvey
Annesley family *see* Clifford Chambers
aqueducts *see* Aston Cantlow; Wootton Wawen
Arbury Hall *see* Arbury; Astley *and* p. 18
Archer family *see* Tanworth-in-Arden; Warwick
Arden, Forest of *see* Arbury; Berkswell; Coughton; Nuneaton; Ratley; Stratford-upon-Avon; Tanworth-in-Arden *and* p. 15
Arden, Mary *see* Aston Cantlow; Wilmcote
Arlescote *see* Avon Dassett
Arnold, Dr. *see* Rugby
Arnold, Matthew *see* Rugby
Arrow, River *see* Alcester; Arrow; Coughton; Studley; Wixford
Astley Lodge *see* Arbury
Aston Hall, 17
Austin Friars *see* Atherstone
Avon, River *see* Ashow; Barford; Bidford-on-Avon; Bretford; Charlecote; Church Lawford; Guy's Cliffe; Kings Newnham; Long Lawford; Luddington; Milcote; Newbold-on-Avon; Old Milverton; Stoneleigh; Stratford-upon-Avon; Tiddington; Warwick; Weston-on-Avon *and* p. 15
Aylesford family *see* Great Packington; Nuneaton *and* p. 18

Balliol College, Oxford *see* Ufton
Balsall Common *see* Kenilworth
Balsall Heath *see* Moseley (B)
Barras Heath *see* Stoke (C)
Barrells Hall *see* Oldberrow; Ullenhall
Barton *see* Bidford-on-Avon
Bateman, C. E. *see* Castle Bromwich; Four Oaks; Kings Heath (B); Northfield (B); Solihull; Sutton Coldfield; Warwick; Wroxall
beacons *see* Burton Dassett; Compton Wynyates
Beauchamp Chapel *see* Warwick *and* pp. 17, 18
Beauchamp family *see* Warwick
Beighton, Henry *see* Chilvers Coton
Bennett's Hill *see* Birmingham; Saltley (B)
Biddulph family *see* Birdingbury
Bidlake, W. H. *see* Dordon; Dorridge; Earlswood; Edgbaston (B); Four Oaks; Handsworth (B); Knowle; Moseley (B); Small Heath (B); Solihull; Tanworth-in-Arden; Wylde Green *and* p. 18
Bilton Grange *see* Dunchurch *and* p. 18
Birmingham & Fazeley Canal *see* Birmingham; Erdington (B)
Birmingham Canal *see* Birmingham; Ladywood (B) *and* p. 15
Blakesley Hall *see* Yardley (B) *and* p. 17

Blomfield, Sir Arthur *see* Royal Leamington Spa; Tredington; Weddington
Bloxam family *see* Brinklow
Bloxham, Matthew *see* Rugby
Blue Coat School *see* Coventry
Blue Hole *see* Hartshill
Blythe, River *see* Barston; Earlswood; Little Packington; Shustoke
Bodley, G. F. *see* Bilton; Clifton upon Dunsmore; Northfield (B); Rowington; Stratford-upon-Avon
Bonomi, Joseph *see* Great Packington; Meriden; Ullenhall *and* p. 17
Booth, William *see* Handsworth (B); Ullenhall
Bordesley *see* Oxhill *and* pp. 17, 18
Botanical Gardens *see* Edgbaston (B)
Boulton, Matthew *see* Birmingham; Handsworth (B); Small Heath (B); Winson Green (B)
Bourne, River *see* Over Whitacre; Shustoke
Bracebridge family *see* Mancetter
Bradley Green *see* Grendon
Brandon Castle *see* Wolston
brasses *see* Baginton; Coleshill; Coughton; Hillmorton; Merevale; Middleton; Quinton; Selly Oak (B); Weston-on-Avon; Whitnash; Wixford
Brindley, James *see* Birmingham; Hawkesbury (C); Winson Green (B) *and* p. 15
Bromford Bridge *see* Erdington (B)
Bromley family *see* Baginton
Bronze Age settlement *see* Baginton
Brooke, Rupert *see* Rugby
Brown, Capability *see* Arrow; Charlcote; Compton Verney; Coombe Fields; Great Packington *and* p. 15
Burdett family *see* Polesworth
Burman family *see* Earlswood
Burne-Jones, Sir Edward *see* Birmingham; Acocks Green (B); Winson Green (B)
Butterfield, William *see* Aston Cantlow; Cubbington; Kinwarton; Rugby; Selly Oak (B); Thurlaston; Warwick; Wilmcote

Cadbury, George *see* Bournville (B); Northfield (B); Selly Oak (B)
Cadbury, J. *see* Moseley (B)
Cadbury, Richard *see* Bournville (B)
Camden *see* Royal Leamington Spa
Canonbury House *see* Compton Wynyates
Capuchin friary *see* Olton
Carlisle, James William *see* Temple Grafton
Carolean garden *see* Packwood
Cash's Hundred Houses *see* Radford (C)
castles *see* Astley; Beaudesert; Castle Bromwich; Fillongley; Hartshill; Kenilworth; Maxstoke; Studley; Warwick; Wolston; Wyken (C) *and* p. 16
Chad Brook *see* Edgbaston (B)
chalybeate spring *see* Ilmington
Chamberlain, J. H. *see* Birmingham; Edgbaston (B); Harborne (B); Ladywood (B); Moseley (B)
Chamberlain, Joseph *see* Birmingham; Winson Green (B)
Chambers family *see* Spernall

Chantrey, Sir Francis *see* Alcester; Handsworth (B); Rugby
Charlecote *see* Hampton Lucy *and* pp. 17, 18
Chatwin, J. A. *see* Acocks Green (B); Aston (B); Birmingham; Bordesley (B); Catherine de Barnes Heath; Dorridge; Edgbaston (B); Handsworth (B); Mappleborough Green; Moseley (B); Preston Bagot; Solihull; Winson Green (B)
Chetwynd family *see* Grendon; Polesworth
Clarke, Sir Simon *see* Salford Priors
Clifford family *see* Wappenbury
Clinton family *see* Kenilworth
Clopton family *see* Clopton House; Stratford-upon-Avon
Clutton, Sir Henry *see* Baddesley Ensor; Edgbaston (B); Merevale; Royal Leamington Spa; Welcombe
Cole, River *see* Acocks Green (B); Chelmsley Wood; Coleshill; Hall Green (B); Small Heath (B)
Coombe Abbey *see* Binley (C); Churchover; Coombe Fields;
Corser, Ben. *see* Olton
Court Baron *see* Henley-in-Arden
Court Leet *see* Alcester; Henley-in-Arden
Coventry Canal *see* Atherstone; Coventry; Foleshill (C); Grendon; Hartshill; Hawkesbury (C); Longford (C); Polesworth; Radford (C); Walsgrave on Sowe (C) *and* p. 15
Craven family *see* Binley
Cundall, J. *see* Royal Leamington Spa; Sherbourne

Davis, J. S. *see* Birmingham; Charlecote
d'Ednesoure, Thomas *see* Baddesley Ensor
Deerhurst Priory *see* Wellford-on-Avon; Whitchurch
de Mohun family *see* Whichford
de Montfort family *see* Henley-in-Arden
de Montfort, Simon *see* Kenilworth; Warwick; Wolston
de Montfort, Thurstan *see* Beaudesert
Dene, River *see* Combrook; Kineton; Wellesbourne
Digby family *see* Coleshill
Dobbs family *see* Seckington
Dormer family *see* Hampton-on-the-Hill
Draycote Water *see* Bourton-on-Dunsmore
Drayton, Michael *see* Clifford Chambers; Hartshill; Nuneaton; Polesworth
Dudley, Robert earl of Leicester *see* Kenilworth; Long Itchington; Warwick
Dudley Canal *see* Selly Oak (B)
Dugdale family *see* Baddesley Ensor; Merevale
Durham family *see* Ladbroke

earthworks *see* Allesley (C); Brinklow; Burton Dassett; Chesterton; Great Wolford; Mancetter; Welcombe
Eborall *see* Warwick
Edge, Charles *see* Birmingham; Edgbaston (B); Handsworth (B); Winson Green (B)
Edge Hills *see* pp. 11, 15, 16
Edge Hill Tower *see* Radway
Edge Lane *see* Beaudesert

Eliot, George *see* Arbury; Astley; Chilvers Coton; Corley; Coventry; Fillongley; Nuneaton; Stockingford; Wolvey

Feldon *see* Shipston-on-Stour; Stratford-upon-Avon; Winderton *and* p. 15
Feldon 'Cathedral of' *see* Brailes
Fenny Newbold *see* Stretton-under-Fosse
Ferrers family *see* Baddesley Clinton; Ettington
Ferrers, Henry *see* Baddesley Clinton
Ferrers, Robert *see* Merevale
Fetherston, John *see* Packwood; Rowington *and* p. 15
Finham Brook *see* Kenilworth
Foleshill Mill *see* Alderman's Green (C)
follies *see* Baxterley; Halford; Priors Marston
Fonthill Abbey *see* Charlecote
Fosse Way *see* Armscote; Blackwell; Brailes; Brinklow; Church Lawford; Compton Verney; Copston Magna; Eathorpe; Ettington; Grandborough; Halford; Hampton-on-the-Hill; Harbury; Hunningham; Kings Newnham; Pillerton Hersey; Princethorpe; Stretton-under-Fosse; Tredington; Ufton; Wibtoft
Foxbrook *see* Rowington
Fulbroke Castle *see* Compton Wynyates

Galton family *see* Claverdon
gardens *see* Admington Hall; Arbury Hall; Arrow; Compton Verney; Compton Wynyates; Coombe Fields; Dunchurch; Handsworth (B); Packwood; Stratford-upon-Avon; Stretton-under-Fosse; Wroxall
Garland, C. T. *see* Moreton Morrell
Garner family *see* Beaudesert; Bishops Tachbrook; Fillongley; Wasperton
Goodwin, Francis *see* Birmingham; Bordesley (B) *and* p. 18
Gorcott Hall *see* Mappleborough Green
Gough Calthorpe family *see* Edgbaston (B)
Gough family *see* Perry Barr (B)
Grand Union Canal *see* Catherine de Barne Heath; Hatton; Rowington; Warwick
Granville family *see* Wellesbourne
Gravelly Hill *see* Erdington (B)
Gresley family *see* Kenilworth
Greswolde family *see* Solihull (B); Yardley (B)
Grevill family *see* Weston-on-Avon
Greville, Sir Fulke *see* Alcester; Warwick
Grevis family *see* Moseley (B); Kings Norton (B)
Grey family *see* Astley
Griff Colliery *see* Hawkesbury (C)
Griff House *see* Chilvers Coton
Grimshaw Hall *see* Knowle *and* p. 17
Grove House *see* Hampton-on-the-Hill *and* p. 18
Guy's Cliffe *see also* Old Milverton *and* pp. 15, 18

Hakewell, Henry *see* Great Packington; Rugby
Hales family *see* Exhall; Snitterfield
Hall Green *see* Foleshill (C)
Hams Hall *see* Lea Marston
Hardwick, Philip *see* Birmingham *and* p. 16
Harman, John *see* Sutton Coldfield
Hathaway, Anne *see* Luddington; Shottery
Hay family *see* Acocks Green (B); Yardley (B)
Hay Hall *see* Acocks Green (B)
Hay Mills *see* Acocks Green (B)
Hayward, Richard *see* Arbury Hall; Bulkington; Loxley; Nether Whitacre; Weston-in-Arden
Heaton, Ralph *see* Birmingham; Kings Norton (B); Winson Green (B)

Hewlett family of Haseley *see* Hatton
hill forts *see* Beaudesert; Corley, Oldbury
Hill Wootton *see* Leek Wootton
Hobbiss, H. W. *see* Edgbaston (B); Handsworth (B); Small Heath (B)
Hobson, Thomas *see* Salford Priors
Hoggrills End *see* Nether Whitacre
Holbech family *see* Farnborough
Holte family *see* Aston (B); Erdington (B)
Hopsford *see* Withybrook
Hussey, R. C. *see* Barford; Coventry; Grendon; Rugby; Saltley (B); Winson Green (B)
Hutton, William *see* Moseley (B); Saltley (B)

Icknield Street *see* Arrow; Bidford-on-Avon; Coughton; Exhall; Ladywood; Perry Barr (B) *and* p. 15
Ingram family *see* Great Wolford
Itchen, River *see* Bishops Itchington

Jaggard, William *see* Rowington
Jago, Richard *see* Solihull; Ullenhall
Jefferson, Thomas *see* Moreton Morrell
Johnson, Samuel *see* Aston (B); Packwood; Solihull
Jones, Inigo *see* Barton-on-the-Heath, Chesterton

Kelmscott Chaucer *see* Winson Green (B)
Kempe, C. E. *see* Aston Cantlow; Atherstone; Atherstone-on-Stour; Binton; Bourton-on-Dunsmore; Charlecote; Church Lawford; Churchover; Claverdon; Clifton upon Dunsmore; Coventry; Dunchurch; Lillington; Middleton; Radford Semele; Rowington; Royal Leamington Spa; Rugby; Solihull; Warwick
Kenilworth Priory *see* Loxley
Kingshurst Brook *see* Chelmsley Wood
Kingstanding *see* Perry Barr (B)
King Stone *see* Long Compton
Knight family *see* Henley-in-Arden; Oldberrow; Ullenhall
Knights Templar *see* Temple Balsall; Temple Grafton; Tysoe
Knottesford, Revd. *see* Billesley; Wilmcote

Landor, Walter Savage *see* Bishops Tachbrook; Rugby
Lapal Tunnel *see* Selly Oak (B)
Leam, River *see* Birdingbury; Eathorpe; Grandborough; Hunningham; Leamington Hastings; Radford Semele; Royal Leamington Spa; Sawbridge; Stockton; Weston-under-Wetherley
Lines, Samuel *see* Birmingham
Little Heath *see* Foleshill (C)
locks *see* Bishopton; Kings Norton (B); Hatton; Hawkesbury (C)
Longbridge *see* Northfield (B)
Longford *see also* Hawkesbury
Lucy family *see* Charlecote
Ludford-Astley family *see* Ansley
Lunt, the *see* Baginton

Magdalen College, Oxford *see* Quinton
Mancetter *see also* Alcester
Marroway *see* Snitterfield
Martin, Frederick *see* Birmingham; Edgbaston (B); Harborne (B)
Mary Queen of Scots *see* Coventry; Weston-in-Arden
Maxstoke Priory *see also* Aston (B); Stoneleigh; Yardley (B) *and* p. 16
Merevale Abbey *see also* Hartshill; Mancetter
Middlemore family *see* Kings Norton (B)
Miller, Sanderson *see* Arbury Hall; Farnborough; Kineton; Radway; Ratley;

Upton House; Walton; Warwick *and* pp. 15, 18
Mills family *see* Barford; Billesley
mineral springs *see* Ilmington; Royal Leamington Spa
Moll's grave *see* Pillerton Priors
Morris, William *see* Birmingham; Bishops Tachbrook (B); Rugby; Stratford-upon-Avon; Winson Green (B); Wolverton
motte-and-bailey castles *see* Beaudesert; Brailes; Brinklow; Kineton; Seckington; Warwick
Mowbray family *see* Brinklow

Newbold Revel *see* Stretton-under-Fosse
Newcombe, Thomas *see* Dunchurch
Newdigate family *see* Arbury; Chilvers Coton; Weston-in-Arden
Norton, 1st Baron *see* Adderley

Oscott College *see* Perry Barr (B)
Over Green *see* Wishaw
Oversley Castle *see* Arrow; Exhall. — Wood *see* Exhall
Oxford Canal *see* Brinklow; Brownsover; Hawkesbury (C); Hillmorton; Lower Shuckburgh; Napton-on-the-Hill; Priors Hardwick; Wormleighton *and* p. 15

Parr, Dr. *see* Hatton
Petiver, James *see* Hillmorton
Peyto family *see* Chesterton
Phillips family *see* Oldbury
Phipson, A. B. *see* Harborne (B); Wishaw
Pollen, Francis *see* Hampton-on-the-Hill *and* p. 18
Preedy, F. *see* Alderminster; Binton; Kings Heath (B); Moseley (B); Temple Grafton
Prichard, John *see* Ettington *and* p. 18
priest's hole *see* Armscote; — chamber *see* Barcheston; Compton Wynyates; Coughton
Pugin, A. W. N. *see* Aston (B); Birmingham; Coleshill; Dunchurch; Erdington (B); Handsworth (B); Rugby; Sherbourne; Solihull; Wappenbury; Wasperton *and* p. 18
Purefey family *see* Caldecote
Pusey, Dr. *see* Ratley; Wilmcote

Queen's College *see* Birmingham

Radburn *see* Willenhall (C)
Ragley Hall *see* Arrow & Ragley
Randolph family *see* Moreton Morrell
Raynsford family *see* Clifford Chambers
Rea, River *see* Birmingham; Bordesley (B)
Repton, Humphry *see* Moseley (B) *and* p. 15
Rickman, Thomas *see* Birmingham; Castle Bromwich; Coventry; Erdington (B); Ettington; Handsworth (B); Moseley (B); Stretton-on-Dunsmore; Winson Green (B)
Rollright Stones *see* Long Compton
Roman roads *see* Fosse Way; Icknield Street; Watling Street
Rowbotham, D. H. *see* Fenny Compton; Snitterfield *and* p. 18
Rugby School *see* Brinklow; Brownsover; Frankton; Rugby
Rupert, Prince *see* Wormleighton
Ryland family *see* Sherbourne

Salem Baptists *see* Longford (C)
Salisbury family *see* Brandon
salt road *see* Butlers Marston; Great Alne; Perry Barr (B)

Sarehole Mill *see* Small Heath (B)

Scott, George Gilbert the younger *see* Royal Leamington Spa

Scott, Sir George Gilbert *see* Ansty; Bilton; Brownsover; Coventry; Canley (C); Farnborough; Frankton; Hampton Lucy; Ladbroke; Rugby; Sherbourne; Temple Balsall; Tysoe; Walton; Wasperton; Welford-on-Avon; Whitnash; Wootton Wawen *and* p. 18

Scott, Sir Walter *see* Kenilworth; Merevale; Stratford-upon-Avon

Seckington *see also* Newton Regis

Serbian Orthodox Church *see* Selly Oak (B)

Seymour-Conway family *see* Arrow

Shakespeare Hall *see* Rowington

Shakespeare, John *see* Clifford Chambers; Snitterfield; Stratford-upon-Avon

Shakespeare, Richard *see* Snitterfield

Shakespeare, Thomas *see* Rowington

Shakespeare, William *see* Aston Cantlow; Bidford-on-Avon; Charlecote; Clifford Chambers; Hillborough; Luddington; Rowington; Shottery; Snitterfield; Stratford-upon-Avon; Warwick; Welcombe *and* pp. 15, 18

Sheldon family *see* Long Compton

Shenstone, William *see* Henley-in-Arden; Solihull; Ullenhall

Sheriff, Lawrence *see* Brownsover

Shirley family *see* Ettington

Shuckburgh family *see* Bourton-on-Dunsmore; Lower Shuckburgh

Smite Brook *see* Coombe Fields

Smith, Francis *see* Coventry; Stoneleigh; Stretton-under-Fosse; Tanworth-in-Arden; Warwick

Smith-Rylands family *see* Sherbourne

Soane, Sir John *see* Cheylesmore (C); Solihull; Tanworth-in-Arden *and* p. 17

Soane Museum *see* Aston (B)

Soho Clock Factory *see* Winson Green (B)

Soho Manufactory *see* Handsworth (B)

Sole End Farm *see* Astley

Sowe River, *see* Alderman's Green (C); Baginton; Bell Green (C); Stivichall (C); Stoke (C); Stoneleigh; Wyken (C)

Sparkbrook *see* Small Heath (B)

Spence, Sir Basil *see* Coventry; Bell Green (C); Tile Hill (C); Willenhall (C) *and* p. 18

Spencer family *see* Wormleighton

Squirhill, D. G. (of Leamington) *see* Gaydon; Royal Leamington Spa

Stanley, Arthur *see* Rugby

stocks *see* Berkswell, Coleshill; Dunchurch; Loxley

Stone, Nicholas *see* Charlecote

Stour, River *see* Atherstone-on-Stour; Cherington; Ettington; Halford; Preston-on-Stour; Whitchurch

Stratford Canal *see* Aston Cantlow; Bishopton; Earlswood; Hockley Heath; Kings Heath (B); Kings Norton (B); Lapworth; Preston Bagot; Wilmcote; Wootton Wawen

Sutton Stop *see* Hawkesbury

Swift, River *see* Churchover

Tachbrook Malory *see* Bishops Tachbrook

Tame, River *see* Aston (B); Birmingham; Castle Bromwich; Curdworth; Edgbaston (B); Kingsbury; Perry Barr (B); Water Orton

Telford, Thomas *see* Atherstone-on-Stour; Ladywood (B); Winson Green (B)

Teonge, Henry *see* Spernall

Teulon, S. S. *see* Edgbaston (B); Ladywood (B); Perry Barr (B)

Thomas, Dr. William *see* Exhall; Royal Leamington Spa

Thornley family *see* Bickenhall

Throckmorton family *see* Coughton

Toft Hill *see* Dunchurch

Townshend family *see* Ladbroke

toy museum *see* Coventry

tunnels *see* Kings Heath (B); Kings Norton (B); Selly Oak (B); Rowington

turnpike roads *see* Foleshill (C); Keresley (C); Perry Barr (B); Wootton Wawen

Ulverley *see* Olton

Umberslade Park *see* Birmingham; Tanworth-in-Arden

Vale of the Red Horse *see* Oxhill; Tysoe *and* p. 16

Verney family *see* Combrook; Compton Verney

Vesey, Bishop *see* Sutton Coldfield; Water Orton

viaduct *see* Bordesley (B); Rugby *and* p. 16

Voysey, C. F. A. *see* Bishops Itchington; Henley-in-Arden *and* p. 18

Vyner family *see* Eathorpe

Walker, T. L. *see* Attleborough; Bedworth; Hartshill

Walpole, Horace *see* Arrow; Coughton; Radway; Ullenhall

Ward End *see* Saltley (B)

Warwick and Birmingham Canal *see* Acocks Green (B); Bordesley (B); Small Heath (B)

Warwick Vase *see* Aston (B); Warwick

Wasthill Tunnel *see* Kings Norton (B)

watermills *see* Arbury; Baginton; Brailes; Haselor; Leek Wootton; Small Heath (B); Welford-on-Avon; Wolston; Wootton Wawen

Watkins family *see* Whichford

Watling Street *see* Atherstone; Copston Magna; Dordon; Grendon; Hartshill; Wibtoft

Watt, James *see* Birmingham; Handsworth (B); Shustoke

Welsh Road *see* Cubbington; Priors Hardwick; Priors Marston; Southam

Weoley Castle *see* Selly Oak (B)

West family *see* Preston-on-Stour

Westmacott, Richard *see* Aston (B); Berkswell; Honington; Ilmington; Kenilworth; Loxley; Preston-on-Stour; Stratford-upon-Avon; Warwick

Westwood Heath *see* Canley (C)

Whitefriars *see* Coventry

Whitmore, W. *see* Wootton Wawen

Willington, Wildive *see* Hurley

Willoughby, Francis *see* Middleton

Willoughby, Hugh *see* Middleton

Wilson, Sir William *see* Arbury Hall; Castle Bromwich; Four Oaks; Hall Green (B); Sutton Coldfield; Warwick

Wimpstone *see* Whitchurch

windmills *see* Arrow; Chesterton; Compton Wynyates; Corley; Harbury; Napton-on-the-Hill; Norton Lindsey

Woolner *see* Birmingham

Worcester and Birmingham Canal *see* Edgbaston (B); Kings Norton; Selly Oak (B)

Wormersley, Peter *see* Alveston *and* p. 18

Wren, Sir Christopher *see* Arbury Hall; Honiley; Sutton Coldfield; Tanworth-in-Arden; Wroxhall

Wulfstan, St. *see* Long Itchington

Yardley, manor of *see* Sheldon (B)

Yew Garden *see* Packwood

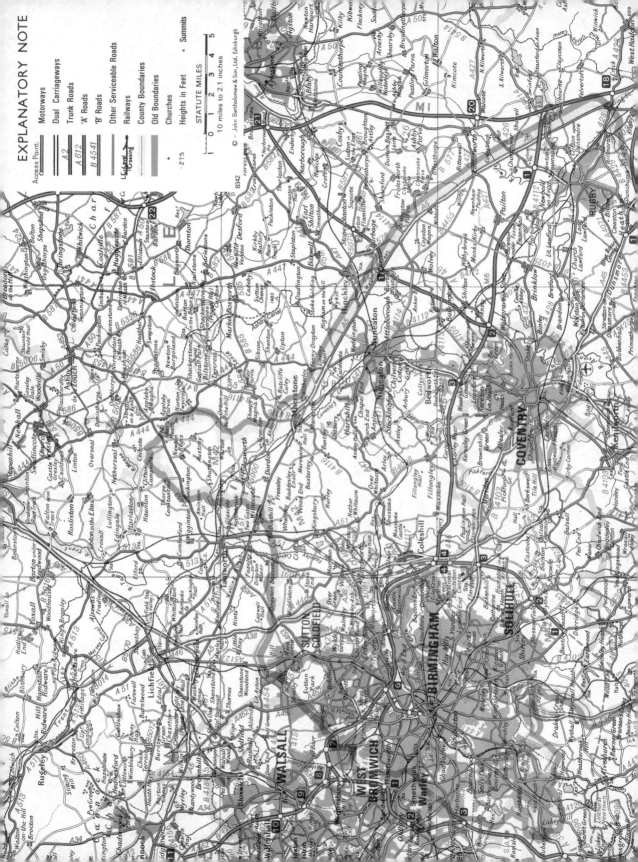

EXPLANATORY NOTE

Access Point

Motorways	
Dual Carriageways	
Trunk Roads	A2
'A' Roads	A 612
'B' Roads	B 4541
Other Serviceable Roads	
Railways	
County Boundaries	
Old Boundaries	
Churches	+
Heights in Feet	▲ Summits

·275

STATUTE MILES

0   1   2   3   4   5

10 miles to 2.1 inches

© – John Bartholomew & Son, Ltd. Edinburgh